Also by John Buckley
Family Politics

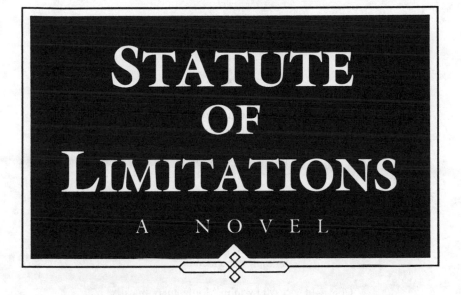

STATUTE OF LIMITATIONS

A NOVEL

John Buckley

SIMON AND SCHUSTER

New York   London   Toronto   Sydney   Tokyo   Singapore

Simon and Schuster
Simon & Schuster Building
Rockefeller Center
1230 Avenue of the Americas
New York, New York 10020

Copyright © 1990 by John Montgomery Buckley

SIMON AND SCHUSTER and colophon are registered trademarks
of Simon & Schuster Inc.

Designed by Carla Weise / Levavi & Levavi
Manufactured in the United States of America

1   3   5   7   9   10   8   6   4   2

Library of Congress Cataloging in Publication Data

Buckley, John, date.
Statute of limitations : a novel / John Buckley.
p.   cm.
I. Title.
PS3552.U343S77   1990   90-33851
813'.54—dc20   CIP

ISBN 0-671-69095-7

For Anna

"I did not think in 1969 that I would be in this room today, I'll confess . . ."

> —Senator Dan Quayle, at a news conference at the Republican National Convention, August 17, 1988

Standing at the bar of the 9:30 Club, Thomas O'Malley found himself to be the only person in the room wearing a tuxedo, just as he had been the only person to exit the inaugural ball upon the triumphal entrance of the new President.

It wasn't a protest. He was in search of recognizable fun, was all. In the room he'd left, there were hundreds of women in strapless gowns, the men all dressed as members of an order. Here there was a bartender with a shaved head and a dangling cross earring who looked at him as if he were some kind of freak, though he neutrally proceeded to serve him the vodka. A very different evening from the one O'Malley had set out on soon commenced with a lousy set by a thrash band from Baltimore, a better performance by the visiting Feelies, and a memorable panic at the coat check where he discovered that someone had successfully made off with his wallet.

It had gotten late and the friends attending different balls around town who were supposed to meet him there were nowhere to be found, so he left the coat-check girl what change there was in his pocket and managed to stagger through the crowd. There was a couple necking on the stairway and he had to squeeze by them, but there was fresh air out there somewhere and he decided to pursue it. This led him to the glaringly bright corridor he'd entered a few hours and a number of vodkas ago. The sound of the platter the DJ was spinning inside the dark nightclub followed him as he headed outside. The muffled explosions of a record by the Pixies echoed behind him when he walked out onto F Street and found it had snowed enough for drunken punks to make perfectly formed angels on the sidewalk.

It was still snowing and he imagined a thousand children's trumpets stuck to their lips: just the threat of it was enough for them to have once again canceled an inaugural parade. The nation's powers, civilian and military, had juggled the morning's festivities while the networks filled time. Anchors and correspondents had enthused over colorful history from similar events that had failed before. There were tales of canaries freezing in their cages, of presidents who'd died from the colds they'd caught, and, of course, the hapless young trumpeters who had been welded to their instruments by the arctic air at an inaugural parade sometime long ago.

Even though it was snowing, it was not much warmer now than it had been this morning when the outdoor address by the freshly sworn-in President had been 86'd within moments of his assuming the office. Network commentators were wondering aloud which justices of the Supreme Court might be done in by the weather just as the decision was made to shuffle the dignitaries indoors. O'Malley had not been among them; he'd ended up being forced to watch the speech on television, like everybody else. Which was one more reason to sneak out from the ball and go have fun on this final night of freedom.

Now he warmed his car and rubbed his hands and wondered momentarily if the exhaust that curled in the air behind him was as powerful as the alcohol fumes that seemed to freeze with each breath, as playful as ghosts.

He put the car in gear and drove down Tenth Street, turning right on Pennsylvania on what was to have been the parade route not only for the President on his way to his new home, but for the thousands of majorettes who were to have twisted and twirled along the avenue. He mourned what would have been the sight of their white calf boots slipping and sliding in the manure from the military horses who still marched at these things. He'd read in the *Post* that the horseshit was measured not in pounds but in tonnage, which would have been a fitting conclusion to the presidential campaign if the cold snap had not canceled it.

O'Malley's car slipped and slid a little as well, helped along by the snowfall and his impressionistic steering. The flags were all frozen and the stands that had been erected for the parade stood empty, a fringe of fresh snow like a cushion upon them. There were no cars to be seen gliding along the avenue. It wasn't until he was two blocks from the White House that the roadblock forced him to stop in a slight skid and the police officer matter-of-factly asked him for his license.

"Don't have it," he said with some effort. Their breaths intersected visibly through the open window. The cop, red-faced and bulbous-nosed, appeared not to want any trouble. The only reason the street was blocked off was this was the route for the President's motorcade, which only minutes before had returned him from his review of the balls in his honor.

The cop asked him where he lived and he told him. He asked him where he worked, and he told him that too.

"I don't quite believe that," the cop said, looking at the mess inside his car.

When O'Malley asked him if he was the last Irish-American to have to work a traffic detail he quickly found himself outside of his car with his face against the window, looking in. The cop was right. His immediate universe was a mess. This final fling had been a bad idea. And now he was heading to jail for the evening. It was a hell of a way to start his career at the White House.

atherine Tierney's prose matched her carriage. It was regal, overly formal, though occasionally, when events called for it, entertainingly frisky. If he had to come up with a single point of complaint it would be her Latinate constructions, her unwillingness to write in any recognizably Anglo-Saxon shade of the English language. She made you think of grand events, rococo ballrooms, the musty historicity of an elegant trunk, when more often than not what was called for was the direct conjuring of the everyday. The twist, not the waltz. Baseball with a broken-in mitt, not some partridge hunt with a 20-gauge Purdey.

O'Malley nonetheless was glad she'd been named chief speechwriter. If during his first term there was to be a constitutional convention, she could make the President sound like he was one of the Founding Fathers casting his ideas upon the sea of history. Until that time came, O'Malley found her useful because she seemed quite genuinely to appreciate his own meat-and-potatoes style.

His was different from Colin Denholm's, too. Colin's speeches were bugle blasts, aimed at lifting an audience to a cry of "Argggh!" He had nominated the President, there's no question about it, exalting him from the status of a mere Cabinet officer to an inspiring and exciting leader of the Democratic party, and he'd done it in a way Katherine never would have been able to: he'd found sneaky ways to make base desires and resentments sound folksy and noble, all at once. His was a utilitarian talent; he did the trick almost whenever it was called for, and for that reason he was often overworked, out of humor, and beaten down. He would emerge from an all-nighter with a speech that could make you hoot and holler just reading it, yet often the look on his face was as if a zombie had sucked his breath away. During the campaign, he'd been the only one in the speechwriters' shop who wrote with his jacket on and his shirtsleeves buttoned—this during the full yowling heat of a Washington summer—and he had never been spied going out with the group to drink beer and celebrate what was an almost unbroken, year-long string of political successes, culminating in the President's dramatic drubbing of his opponent.

There were other speechwriters who'd made the transition from the campaign to the offices in the southeast corner of the first floor of the Executive Office Building, but when O'Malley looked for inspiration and guidance as to how to become better, to improve his style, the two poles he alternated between were Katherine's and Colin's. He felt that if he were able to connect between those two, his writing would be charged with that special electricity that moved audiences on behalf of the nation's new chief.

He was perhaps overly sensitive. His writing was better than he thought it was. During the campaign, what speeches he'd been called to deliver to Katherine's desk had been almost universally approved. Seldom had he suffered the ignominy of having to watch a speech he'd slaved over be handed to a rival to rework. But he was a little touchy about how exactly it was he came to be a speechwriter, about the strange events that led to his becoming the wordsmith traveling with the candidate during the hectic months of the general election.

His break came in the summer before the election year, six months or more before the Iowa caucuses. With permission from his D.C. law office, he'd volunteered to do some advance work for Secretary William Hardison, who was widely known to be testing the waters for a presidential bid, and thus on a Fourth of July weekend he'd been in charge of the parade route motorcade at the annual celebration in Spirit Lake. The corn was already crawling across every visible expanse, crowds of rural families had arrived from two counties away, and O'Malley, thrilled to be there, was in full advance-man regalia: overly citified, it's true, in a pin-striped suit amidst the farmers in their overalls and caps festooned with feed-company insignia, a walkie-talkie in his hand, his mirrored sunglasses reflecting the hot Midwestern afternoon.

And then a combine ran amok and began to harvest schoolchildren on the parade route, within minutes of the five-jet fireball disaster at the local air show, and it was O'Malley who pressed upon the slack-jawed candidate the hastily scribbled words of comfort in time for the evening news. The combination of Tom O'Malley's instant, sorrowful eloquence, along with the terrific empathy expressed in Hardison's voice, made for a sound-bitten sweep on the network news and sweet satellite feeds from Davenport to Des Moines. Spirit Lake's epidemic bad luck created a president. Hardison, the Caring Cabinet Officer, was launched on a roll that just didn't stop, and he swept O'Malley up with him.

is White House pass was a ticket of admission to a place where O'Malley would have paid them to let him work. He began to enjoy his walks there each morning from his small apartment in Adams Morgan. "Yippee yi oh kiyay," he was likely to say as he skipped down Eighteenth Street. He refused to be cavalier—hoped he'd never be cavalier—about precisely where it was he hung his hat each day. Walking up the steps of the Executive Office Building was not like going to work at some bank, no matter how ornate the bank building. It certainly wasn't like going to work in the gleaming expanse of Swedish furniture and glass that had been Connerly, McSweeny and Donilon, the K Street law office in whose antiseptic environs he had previously toiled.

Only weeks before, he'd survived his arrival that first frigid morning in the same evening wear in which he'd sleeplessly paced his shriek-filled cell in the District of Columbia's stir, having lost his perfect absence of a police record among other more tangible things that night: his wallet, in advance; his suspenders to a shivering junkie whose pants were in need of them; and more than anything else, his drunken equanimity and sense of being above the law. He publicly chalked up his arrival in such a state that first day of work to nothing so much as youthful high jinks, to exuberance on behalf of Democracy's changing of the guard; but for all his unapologetic stance, before he'd gone home to shower and change his clothes, he'd scoured the Metro section for any mention of his predicament, and waited on edge for a phone call from a *Post* reporter just wondering what one of the new administration's new speechwriters had been doing arrested for DWI while the President had campaigned against intoxication of all kinds. The phone call did not come.

Once he'd realized he'd gotten away with immediate public exposure—if not the evening's pending legal consequences—those promises of modified behavior that he had made to God began to suffer from creeping qualification. He couldn't lose that sense that his bluff was about to be called, but the antennae that reported directly to his guilty conscience were of primitive discernment. Which of his sins were to come to light, he could not say. Yet doing even a partial inventory of his past, there were dozens of items that could spell hot water for him if his White House mentors found out about them. There were whole catalogues of behavior, which while normal, even innocent enough for a college student of his day, could get him bounced from his present perch as swiftly as the pounding of a judge's gavel.

Because of these imprecise feelings of impending doom, it made sense to him that on this particular cold February morning, his arrival at Room 118 was met not with the usual cheer on the face of Buffy Chapin but with something that went way beyond a frown. Buffy, the office's Must-Hire secretary whose family lines, having intersected with the First Lady's somewhere near New Canaan, had overcome, at least so far as the White House Personnel Office was concerned, her obvious and total incompetence. She usually compensated for her failings by being nauseatingly pleasant. Today, however, O'Malley was met with a form of terror on Buffy's face that would more properly have bespoken purges and pogroms, and not just a simple request that he move it, and pronto, to the Chief of Staff's office.

"Katherine's there," Buffy whispered as if the walls had ears. If her eyes had gone any wider, her skull would have split along the part in her hair. "So's Colin. And Will," she said with what obviously was to her the proof that something terrible had been set in motion, for if Will Ames, the office's gentle, talented, born-again speechwriter was in trouble along with the rest of them, then Will's predictions must be coming true: the end, truly, *was* near.

"What's this all about?" O'Malley asked her calmly as he took off his overcoat and scarf and put them on the coatrack. He couldn't help but feel that his camel-hair coat sagged there like a condemned man on the gallows.

"I don't know, but Katherine told me to tell you to get right over there."

This was certainly a great day for him to have worn a loud paisley tie with a shirt slightly frayed under his double-breasted suit. If Jesus truly held him in pampered grace, on this day of all days he would have dressed like a junior executive at ITT, which is where Chief of

Staff Harold Whitney had spent twenty-five years before, midway through the campaign, coming on as chairman.

His effect had had some salubrious consequences on their electoral chances, it had to be admitted. Whitney's arrival at the campaign had been a great cover for the axing of deadwood, which had been in the works long before he'd been called into service by his old buddy, Secretary Hardison, but Whitney was accorded full credit. As far as O'Malley was concerned, what Harold Whitney had brought in with him from his days as chairman of ITT was their dress code, a silly belief that a campaign was a rational organism, and an autocratic style that had won him few fans. Now he ran the White House—some of the belligerent columnists claimed it was only a matter of time before he, not Hardison, ran the country—and first thing this morning he had called into his office everyone O'Malley could think of who had worked on the recent inaugural address. This was more than mere bureaucratic terrorism. Normally, Whitney would not have acknowledged their existence, or at least that of anyone but Katherine, the boss of their shop. A simple phone call could suffice for expressing displeasure.

Buffy's phone rang with the muted, tasteful ding and dong of all White House phones. These gently urgent tones were, he sometimes thought, perhaps the most pleasing of rewards for having won the election, for at the campaign, loud and raucous phones rang everywhere and all the time, to the point where going to work was like entering a particularly noisy, even noisome, monkey house at the zoo. Near the end of the campaign, the sounds of phones ringing followed him everywhere: his runs along Rock Creek, through meals, in dreams.

"He'll be right over," Buffy was saying, looking at him as if his dawdling was imperiling her ability to escape the Gulag. "You better get over there," she said to him with wholly uncharacteristic forcefulness.

"Buffy, settle down." She glowered. Looking down at his tie one more time, he figured there was nothing he could do about it now, so he did as she wished.

He clumped down the steps to the basement exit, too preoccupied to notice those he passed staring at him, wondering, no doubt, how he thought he could get away with such clothes. It was a chilling hundred feet from the Old Exec to the entrance to the White House, and the fleet of cars reserved for the VIP's parked along the driveway suggested something on the level of a Cabinet meeting in progress. Uh oh. If he was being called to this, he really was in trouble. He remembered the inflexible schoolboy code: Admit Nothing, Deny Everything. Sometimes, a speedy explanation—a lie—could far outperform the truthful one.

He turned left inside the double doors, where self-important West-Wing denizens bustled with show-offy urgency, and he felt his heart beating, thought he could hear it in his ears, as he walked down the hallway and burst into the tastefully appointed lobby. Clearing his throat, he paused for a second before he strode across the lobby, opened the door on the other side of the room, and trotted down the carpeted hallway to the Chief of Staff's office as if he did this every day.

"I'm . . ."

"They're expecting you," said the perfectly coiffed receptionist. If her jaw were any harder, she could have doubled as a nutcracker. No one either under forty or the level of a GS-15 should have such self-confidence, he thought. There was an efficiency to her movements which implied that dismissing him took no more effort than flicking the switch of a garbage disposal. She was probably five years younger than he. It seemed to him that everyone in the outer office was staring as he exhaled quickly, braced himself, and opened the mahogany door.

". . . Goddamn commitments and policy," the Chief of Staff was saying to Katherine, Colin, and Will. A quick glance around the room showed Bill Tiswell, Whitney's smug and self-important deputy, slouching in one of the upholstered couches, his ever-present half-grin on his ever-tanned face, while O'Malley's three speechwriting coworkers sat at attention.

Whitney paused from his rant. He stood silver-haired and erect as the Lord as O'Malley sat down next to Katherine at the conference table. Whitney's posture suggested an admiral who'd be honored to go down with the ship. But not today. "I was telling your colleagues that policy is among the things speechwriters will not set, Mr. O'Malley," Whitney said in his harsh corporate lockjaw. "That's a hell of a tie you're wearing, mister." It was as if the tie were the proximate cause of Whitney's losing an otherwise chipper disposition.

O'Malley didn't know the Chief of Staff even knew his name. He'd never remotely acknowledged his presence on the campaign plane even though Hardison often had called him up to the forward compartment to go over a speech or a statement that was to be delivered at the next stop. Words, Whitney had been quoted during the campaign as saying, were not his domain, which had been a relief to those speechwriters who feared what effect his arrival might have. But now they were in the White House and from what he could glean from his first minute in the room, all that had changed. *Everything* was Whitney's domain, as the bulging veins on his pink forehead were not so subtly making clear.

"I've asked Katherine," he went on a bit more calmly, "and Mr. Denholm and Mr. . . ."

"Ames," squeaked Will.

"How the section in the inaugural address that stated the President would go on a trip to Nicaragua, Colombia, and Chile before the spring was out managed to be included. I've been meaning to find out since the inaugural, but. . . ." He waved his hand to indicate how busy he'd been starting up a whole new government. "Now, they've pleaded ignorance," he said, motioning to O'Malley's colleagues, "which leads me to wonder just what role you had in the crafting of it."

"Six sentences, four additional words, and a perorational reprise."

"Excuse me?"

"I, uh, had six sentences, as I'd written them, included in the speech, sir. In addition there were four words, 'perilous,' 'empowerment,' and 'heart wrenching,' that I, uh, persuaded the President to, well, substitute, sir."

Whitney's imitation of a basilisk wasn't half bad. "And the reprise?"

O'Malley smiled. "A perorational reprise is what the President calls those cadences with built-in dramatic lacunae, sir, in this case the section near the end that went, 'No more hunger in Africa . . . disease in South America . . .' "

"Arguments from Congress . . ."

"Or back talk from my wife."

No one in the room knew what had possessed either Katherine or Colin, normally the most mild-mannered staffers, to let fly with quips in such a situation, especially one that revealed the insouciance often expressed within the speechwriting shop. Bill Tiswell sat up straight, as if such unprofessionalism was beyond his ken. He looked to O'Malley like a man with an indictment, or at the very least, a contempt of Congress citation in his future. Whitney just stared at them, a little nonplussed, but Tiswell's face now colored as if they'd just poked fun at the oath of office itself.

"That is actually," O'Malley found himself saying, "a little joke we had about the, uh, perorational reprises, sir."

"Well, that's fine," growled Whitney, "but I've got a problem. Somehow the Secretary of State and I both missed the reference in drafts of the inaugural address to the trip to South America, and now reporters are asking when the President's going on his first State visit."

"You were on the routing sheet," said Katherine, referring to the covering memo that accompanied all presidential speeches as they made their way through the Cabinet and various presidential assistants for approval. Though they had not yet been in power, the transition team had handled the inaugural address according to White House S.O.P.

"Well, yes, technically that's true," began Bill Tiswell.

"But the fact of the matter," Whitney said evenly, "is that I approved the version that came across my desk at four-thirty on the afternoon of the nineteenth. I want to know which speechwriter put that commitment in there on the draft that was sent around at eight-thirty. A policy statement like that shouldn't be included on the evening before the President delivers his inaugural address. If I'd known that was going to be sprung on us, I wouldn't have gone to the inaugural gala that night." Ah hah, thought O'Malley: he's covering his ass. "Now, I'm told that the four of you were the ones who worked on it," Whitney continued. He seemed to be summoning a large breath of air for his final charge. "I want to know how that goddamn commitment got in there."

"O'Malley was the last one to work on it," blurted Colin. Thanks a lot, Colin. It was true that he'd sat down with the President-elect as he made his final changes. It had been a pleasant evening. Hardison's house in Bethesda was filled with packed boxes, and the Secret Service agents were everywhere, pressing their fingers to their ears to catch the instructions that were coming to them in mono. They'd gone over the speech one final time, line by line, as the new First Lady, on several occasions, came down in curlers to ask O'Malley his opinion of various dresses she was undecided about for particular events. He'd felt like a member of the family. Now, just a couple of weeks later, he wondered if the corporate hard-ass before him was going to have his hide for the sin of helping the President craft his own words. All eyes were on O'Malley.

"Although I'm responsible for anything that comes out of the speech-writing shop," said Katherine protectively.

"Did you put that in there?" Tiswell asked O'Malley directly, as if he would have loved the answer to be yes so they could fire him on the spot. His cruel, handsome face held the pleasure of a sadist about to pull apart the wings of a fly.

"I, uh . . ."

"Because, you know, these things get approved through channels, O'Malley," continued Tiswell. He had the faintly crazed look of someone who memorized organizational charts.

"Yes, but . . ."

"And there's no question that this was not approved either by me or by the Secretary of State," said Whitney. "How could you have taken it upon yourself to make policy like that?" He seemed genuinely curious, as if it were a mystery he needed to solve before politely having O'Malley transferred to the nether reaches of the Department of Health and Human Services. Katherine was looking down at the table.

"I didn't," said O'Malley. Katherine looked up. "The President did."

Chief of Staff Whitney looked at Tiswell. "You know, I wasn't against it. Been trying to figure out how it slipped in there, is all. It's a hell of an idea, this trip to South America."

"I thought so too, sir."

"The President's first State visit. I like it."

"Me, too," said Tiswell. They had embarked on a routine they were good at: sycophancy facing up, contempt facing down.

After a few minutes of listening to the others congratulate themselves on their statesmanship, the speechwriters let themselves out. They didn't even wait to be dismissed.

"Back to the salt mine," said Colin. They walked back across the drive to the Old Exec.

I'm telling you this out of common courtesy," his mother was saying on the phone. "You and Sputnik were like twins. Your father was gone for three days when they launched it; Ike wouldn't even give him the time to phone. So I ended up having to call a taxi to take me to Georgetown Hospital, not knowing whether at any moment the world you were being born into was going to be annihilated. I've spent every day of your life remembering that feeling. You remind me of nuclear war. So that's why we've taken that ad out in the *Times*, and that's why we're going to picket in front of the White House. I thought you should know."

His mother especially wanted him to know that his working in the White House didn't embarrass her.

Kit Bowles had a big four-poster and O'Malley's object, somehow, was to get her there. It had an elaborate canopy from which fabric draped like a parachute caught in a banyan tree. O'Malley sat nodding as she trilled along about Mr. Smith's second coming to Washington, all the while concentrating on moving her, by telepathy if possible, from where she sat on the couch to that grand playhouse that was the center, truly, of her comfortable efficiency apartment overlooking Rock Creek Park. They'd had too much wine, it was getting late, and he'd desired her since college.

Her boss was a dweeb, she was in the midst of telling him, as O'Malley hunkered down and concentrated on strategy. Kit Bowles. She looked different, but it had been a while since college. Then she'd had a big head of wild brown hair that she played with constantly, sweeping it this way and that, a chestnut tsunami. Now she'd had it cut short, and her hands danced idly in the air while she told him stories. Aside from her hair, she didn't look that different. Her face still had an architecture that proclaimed a magical intersection of good genes and fitness, that suggested a detour back there somewhere on the road toward clean living. Her eyes still had the Hyperborean mirth of a prankster.

They'd known each other for so long that he feared if he leaned over and licked her ear she might say, "That was nice," and go on talking as if it were no more than a pat on the hand. If he gradually shimmied across the couch so he was sitting really close to her, she might stare in his eyes and declare what great *friends* they were, and how glad she was they had run into each other after not having been in touch for years. Most of all, he feared if they didn't spontaneously gravitate toward that bed, and soon, they might start talking about David Nicole, Kit's former boyfriend and the person who, once upon a time, had been O'Malley's best friend.

The room reeked of him, at least of his secondhand presence. That bodhisattva by the door, the thankas on the wall: all must have come from that trip to the Teeming Subcontinent David and Kit had taken while they were still at school, before the troubles started. He briefly thought of Kit as she had been then, and as excitable as she appeared still to be, there was something she'd relinquished and he knew what it was. Back then, David Nicole and his nicotine-stained hipsterisms had been the solitary object of her interest. She had husbanded several octaves of her laugh just for him. In those days, O'Malley and his girlfriend, Tawnee, had been but appendages to the larger force of Kit and David. But everything had changed. And now he did not want to think about what had happened later when it was David and Tawnee who had connected, when Nicole's larger force, his epic irresponsibility, proved fatal to her.

He wanted only to think about Kit, whom he had last seen, it must have been ten years ago, at CBGB one Christmas week when he'd been staying in New York with his mother and John Cale had played. Memory was vague, but David must have been out on bail and for the time being they were all still friends, rocked by the arrest to be sure, but making the most of what innocence was left. Kit had been grim, it was coming back to him, scared as she should have been about what was going to happen to David, and still more than a little crisp from how nearly she'd been burned. He couldn't remember that much about the evening, only that it was the last one he spent with both of them. The next time he'd seen David, Kit had been off in Europe, modeling, he'd heard, though ostensibly she was there to go to grad school. Everyone knew she was there just to get away from David and his difficulties.

Now she was in Washington, in a position of some responsibility, in a position even of substance, and it spoke to him of the path she had taken, a parallel journey away from Nicole. They both could have stayed under his sway, but both had escaped, leaving adolescence, drugs, perhaps even a degree of selfishness behind. Now they kept their feet, Hays Commission–style, resting on the floor on a somber Tabriz. He knew that if he were to succeed in wooing Kit Bowles to bed, finally, after years of wishing to, the name David Nicole could not be spoken.

And so, after she had finished describing the comic events that led to the appointment of Senator Partridge, and the even stranger happenstance of her becoming his legislative director, O'Malley, seeking to avoid any mention of Nicole, fell upon his reliable conversation filler, the protracted separation of his mother and his father, the war between the O'Malleys.

"My dad I look in on from time to time," he said. "He's still in town, puttering. My mother's still in New York, trying to find a socially acceptable way of having him put to death. She's still involved in all these causes," he said, leaning toward her.

"Oh, poor Thomas." She knew all about his parents.

"It's not like I have to go bail her out anymore. She has a whole three-page list of instructions from her lawyer, who, frankly, I think enjoys her getting arrested. They plan it according to his vacation schedule. I don't think she pays him fees, I think she just vouches for his tax write-offs. Last year, when she was arrested in Nevada at a nuclear waste dump site, they timed it for the ski season. He flew in, made her bail, and was at Park City, Utah, in time for cocktails. A few months later, when she was arrested at the Pentagon, I swear it was timed for the cherry blossoms."

"I remember when you had to bail her out in Northampton."

"That should have been the tip-off: she couldn't just come up for Amherst's parents' weekend, she had to turn it into a protest against CIA research at UMass. Can you imagine how embarrassing it was to have to bail your mother out on parents' weekend?"

"It's not like you didn't have enough cash in those days," she said, laughing.

"No, cash wasn't a problem for Nicole or me," he said, and then instantly regretted it. He waited for the genie to climb out of the bottle.

"He's here, you know," she said. Oh, he was certain of that. The genie was there. But she meant Nicole, in the flesh, in D.C.

He looked at her aquiline nose, the slight sprinkle of freckles on her forehead, the pert bob of hair surrounding her face, and he felt his own face grow hot. "Nicole's in town?"

"Within a quarter mile of where we sit," she said matter-of-factly. "He owns a restaurant in Adams Morgan called Globe. Perhaps you've heard of it."

"I live a block from it," he murmured. What was Nicole doing here, now? He supposed he had a right to be here. Washington was his hometown as well. But if he ever had, there now was no way he could afford to be friends with David Nicole. Even if that were possible. No, there was no way he could allow himself to be friends with Nicole once again, not now that at last he'd put the centripetal spin of order on his life. Nicole was disorder, all centrifugal force, gale winds, doom. In a wan voice, he asked, "You've seen him?"

"A couple of times. Briefly."

"He's, he's doing all right?"

"Appears to be," she said primly. "Business appears to be good. Business appears to be legitimate."

He sat slumped in the couch for a moment, a little distant from Kit, no longer considering lust as an option. What he considered was that the gods were filled less with play than with spite, for while he'd known it wasn't merely fortuitousness that he'd run into Kit the night before at Restaurant Nora, he'd convinced himself it was a wholly good thing. He'd been vain enough to be thankful to Fate for that reintroduction, as if Fate bundled good news in packages. And here he was finding out that the price of once again meeting up with Kit was having contact with David Nicole, when O'Malley was, in a very real sense, most vulnerable and least prepared for any intrusion from the past. And Nicole wasn't just any intrusion. He suddenly felt Nicole's orbital tug like the moon out the window over Rock Creek Park. If he could have, he would have laughed at the notion of Nicole showing up in Washington now while he was suffering through a background check that would determine whether he would keep the new job he'd landed at the White House. He almost jumped when Kit leaned over and took his hand. "Don't think about him now," she said. He sat there for a moment with his mind fast-forwarding not to bliss but to disaster, which eventually only heightened his desire.

The apartment in which O'Malley lived had few virtues other than its view, which for Washington was spectacular. At night he could stare out over the gentle declension from Adams Morgan to the nation's Mall, bisected by the obelisk of the Washington Monument. Near its tip, two ruby red eyes pulsed in darkness that was free of the clutter of any surrounding skyscrapers. One of the things he often disliked about Washington was that, downtown at least, most of the architecture was a variation on a theme of squat, there being strict limitations as to how high buildings could rise. For some reason, long ago Congress had developed an insecurity about being looked down on. But mooning dreamily out his window facing east, O'Malley was grateful for his unimpeded view, for his illusion of space in the middle of what often was a pretty nasty neighborhood.

In the morning, as the sun climbed over the distant Mall, he thought the texture of the city he could see out his window was vaguely Mediterranean, another fortunate illusion given that the land below had been dredged from swamp. From any other section of the city, that notion may have been absurd. He'd grown up in Washington, had been to parties where there had been arguments over how strong was the parallel between the Federal Triangle, the Mall, and the Place de la Concorde, or between Embassy Row and the formerly European sections of Shanghai, but the conceit of looking down toward Dupont Circle and thinking of Italy appeared to be his alone.

That he had ended up in this dismal apartment around the time the campaign had started did not noticeably bother him. The apartment he had shared with a fellow associate from Connerly, McSweeny and Donilon on the Kalorama side of Connecticut Avenue had been far more luxurious, to be sure. But when after three months of living together, she'd boxed up his belongings and dropped them one by one into the alley out back, he'd accepted his expulsion as his due. That he'd slept through her adventure in moving didn't add to his claims of attentiveness. They'd been fighting, their incompatibility overruling whatever physical magnetism had brought them together in the first place, and the way things had been heading, he would soon have had to lock up the kitchen knives to ensure a restful sleep. With their warfare moving beyond the level of her replacing, mid-song, Clash albums on the stereo with those by Joni Mitchell, it was a relief, in a way, to get out.

He'd taken the first available apartment whose rent was reasonable and whose toilet flushed, and he'd picked up his boxes, scattered as they were from their sixth-floor bomb bay, and moved that very afternoon. The neighborhood was funky, for white Washington, though it was taking on the gentrified air of institutionalized Bohemianism, with ethnic restaurants whose prices were heading skyward, galleries that took over the leases of Laundromats, and here and there the self-conscious night spot.

This period was memorable for the sensation of packing and driving like a maniac to Dulles Airport, often at 6:30 A.M., to catch the campaign charter, only to return in the dead of night before starting out all over again. It was not memorable for any event that took place in his apartment, and certainly not for romance. He'd made a commitment to the campaign, only to find that the vow was monastic. The campaign used all his energy without providing in return any release more pleasurable than hopped-up adrenal glands. He had been surprised, a little disappointed, it's true, that there had appeared to have been more sex among his coworkers at Connerly, McSweeny than there was on the Hardison campaign. This was the first illusion he had about American politics that had crashed during the course of the long campaign.

This was one among many reasons why, on the Sunday after he'd become reacquainted with Kit Bowles, he whistled while he worked over an omelette on the gruesome gas range that had come with the apartment. It was the first night he'd slept there in four. They'd had to spend the night apart from each other; they were exhausted and their pelvic bones were tender to the touch, and if he stayed over again, he knew they could not trust themselves even if they promised in advance to forswear any more lovemaking.

So he whistled along to Lou Reed and burned his fingers on the pan. It was a sunny, frolicking morning, one of those many Washington winter days that toy with your emotions, promising spring when there are three more paralyzing snowstorms yet to come.

To his right there was a photograph of himself with his parents, taken at a time when his mother and father still spoke. The daughter of Louis Ingram, the toy manufacturer, Barbara Ingram O'Malley in the late 1940s had been a congressional aide to that notorious Red, Vito Marcantonio of New York. It was then that she'd met Robert O'Malley, a lawyer and foreign policy expert who'd married her despite the fact that merely being seen with her was a risk to his career in the State Department. While she'd been a glamorously eccentric mom, trying to inculcate into him both of the passions—Catholicism and Leftism— to which, incongruously, she'd converted, these days O'Malley found it hard to take her all that seriously.

It bothered him that she was a limousine liberal who gave to every "correct" cause, but seldom took the time even to inquire into his well-being. To O'Malley's sensibility, rather than genuinely caring for him, his mother was too intent on treating Barry Commoner like royalty, on giving Helen Caldicott just what the doctor ordered, on holding fundraisers for each of Jesse Jackson's presidential bids. Recently she'd conceived an absurd interest in aiding such certifiably crazy leftists as Peru's Sendero Luminoso, whom he considered to be the Khmer Rouge on crack. No, she was his mother, and he paid as much attention to her as he could, but she was not his friend the way his father was.

O'Malley worked at the edge of his kitchen with his back to his bookshelves, filled mostly with novels and those monsters he'd had to plow through at law school. He'd attended law school relatively late, not being accepted at UVa. until he was twenty-five, and between squeezing a diploma out of Amherst and taking his LSAT's, he'd spent a lot of time screwing around, mostly in New York, working a series of odd jobs that ranged from bartending to housepainting. At those moments when he'd felt up to taking on larger responsibilities, he'd done some advance work for candidates, most prominently parade routes and motorcades for Mondale, and it was through friends from that campaign that upon graduating from law school, he'd ended up in his hometown at Connerly, McSweeny and Donilon. While he'd always been a quick pen, always had written his papers at school with a minimum of agony, it had been quite a surprise, to him more than anyone, when Hardison, for whom he'd volunteered as an advance man, insisted he come on board his campaign not to advance events, or even as his personal coat carrier, but as a writer of the words the Democratic nominee would use to move crowds.

He'd come a very long way from almost having gone to jail with David Nicole.

He stood there by the Gauguin with his hands up in the air, praying that she wouldn't squeeze the trigger. The dogs were growling and baring their teeth, and O'Malley wondered if this time he was done for. "Easy, Carmela, put the shotgun down," he said reasonably, but she didn't budge from the doorway to his father's upstairs den.

She was shorter than O'Malley by at least a foot, but in addition to the no doubt loaded over-and-under 12-gauge, her advantages included Danny, his father's young yellow Lab, leaning on his front paws in the manner of an adept attempting the Yogic Salute to the Sun. He wasn't standing like that for exercise. There were visible drops of saliva gathering at the corners of his mouth, which bared an impressive array of nasty-looking teeth.

Zippy, the not exactly terrifying Brittany spaniel puppy, was scrunching up his nose and rhythmically flashing red gum and enamel, while old Peggy, Danny's ancient mama, still showed she had fight in her graying black frame. Though Peggy had been around since O'Malley was fourteen, though she'd gone with him on hunting trips and long wandering treks through the dark of night, she growled like she had her heart in it, and she certainly looked game, if but given the order by Carmela, to tear out the throat of her master's son.

"C'mon, Carmela, put down the gun. Where's my father?" But Carmela just stood there with the shotgun pointed about chest high.

"Is my father asleep? Is he taking a nap?" It was four in the afternoon, and O'Malley had walked here from his apartment for an unannounced visit with his father. He did this often. This time, as in times past, he let himself in with the keys he'd had since high school, and shouted hello. When there was no response, he'd walked through the dining room to the large kitchen, expecting to be overrun by the dogs, expecting to have to negotiate with the semi-mute Guatemalan with high Mayan cheekbones his father called his housekeeper. She jealously guarded any information about his father's whereabouts and would not deliver messages O'Malley left, so much so that when he rang him up, he prayed that if his father was not there, at least his machine would be on. Leaving a message with Carmela was a guaranteed waste of breath, and it wasn't just because she refused to admit she couldn't speak English.

Carmela, it was clear, was more than his father's housekeeper, though the old man had never acknowledged it. The dogs had given it away. They did so now. O'Malley knew the nature of his father's relationship with Carmela from the way the dogs responded to her. She was maybe twenty-five years old, not unattractive, and his father had returned from Guatemala with her three years ago. That she was his father's lover didn't bother him. That she held a shotgun on him did.

"Carmela, cut the crap," he commanded, but the dogs, loyal to her, proceeded to growl all the louder. The hackles on Danny's neck stuck higher in the air.

All he'd done was walk up the creaky staircase of the old house on N Street in which he'd been brought up, and finding the frame of Gauguin crooked, he'd moved to straighten it. A minor work by gallery standards, though nonetheless magnificent, his mother had bought it for his father thirty years ago, a gesture meant to commemorate their Tahitian honeymoon.

O'Malley had heard the door open downstairs and the dogs come bounding in, fighting with each other for first dibs on the toilet bowl. He hadn't paid any attention to them, he'd simply stepped back on the Persian rug, and judging the painting still to be askew despite his first try, he'd moved forward once again to straighten it.

And that's when he'd turned and found the three dogs he often played with growling at him, the tiny Indian servant who slept with his father pinning him there with the shotgun. He didn't have the slightest doubt she would blow him away. The notion of him splattered against the masterpiece was of but faint consideration to her.

"Dad!" he called, and the dogs growled louder. But in a minute he heard his father sleepily calling out from the bedroom, "What? Who's there?" With that, the dogs' alarm system somehow seemed called off. They whined, and spun around and around in the doorway.

Carmela didn't put down the gun until his father stepped into the room. He'd been sleeping off his luncheon wine and he looked quite ghastly in his bathrobe, his silvery hair, or what was left of it, matted this way and that.

"Oh, Carmela, put the goddamn gun down. It's Thomas, for Chrissake."

She did as she was told, but O'Malley got the distinct message from her parting glance that next time she'd be just as vigilant. Next time she might, oh, let the dogs knock her trigger finger as they bounded in the air.

Peggy was now sniffing his hand, and he found it impossible not to let her. They were friends again. How could he ever have doubted her, his Peggy Sue? "What's the matter with Sacajawea?" he asked as the dogs now surrounded him playfully.

"Maybe it's the way you call her that. But I'll tell you what it is. We're worried, she's worried," he corrected himself, "that your mother intends on stealing the painting."

His father looked even worse than usual. His face was splotchy from drink, at least two shades pinker than the once-powerful chest visible through the opening of his bathrobe. He'd been a lifelong boozer; in the last few years, however, whatever brakes had slowed down his decline had had their padding slip.

"What's she up to?"

"How long are you here?"

"I came to visit."

"Well, I'll tell you about it. Go make yourself a drink while I put on some clothes. I'll have a scotch and soda."

"It's four in the afternoon."

"All right, make that a martini. I'll be right there."

"How about we go for a walk. It's a nice day, Dad."

His father looked like O'Malley was proposing they go over Niagara Falls in a barrel, but he just shrugged and with the dogs bouncing around him—they seemed to know the word "walk"—he left to go change. O'Malley turned and quickly straightened the painting one final time, as if to dare Carmela.

It took five minutes for his father to dress, but in that time O'Malley made a quick tour of the house. What had seemed cramped and cluttered while growing up had recently fetched his father an offer of two million dollars from a twenty-nine-year-old pollster who wanted to live in Georgetown. There were tasteful reminders of his father's service to his country, not least of which being the worn carpets everywhere that were an itinerary of his father's prime. The staircase was draped in a runner from China, the rug in the large foyer downstairs could have been in the entrance to the Shah's own guesthouse, and there were traces here of Afghanistan, there of Romania, masks from Africa, Mayan pottery from Guatemala that these days he'd be shot for trying to expropriate. The only thing of Mayan extraction his father recently had managed to get out of Central America was the warrior downstairs who'd just about wound O'Malley's clock. What he'd left behind there was his image—his cover—as a semiretired Foreign Service consultant.

Not so long ago, there had been a slew of revelations of his father's actions in that region, actions that had, completely to O'Malley's surprise, come to light during televised Senate hearings into CIA activities. He'd been watching the news one evening when his father's name came up. When he'd picked himself up off the floor, he'd rushed home in solidarity with the old man, who seemed quite genuinely surprised at the events that began to unfold around him.

It had taken an enormous foreign policy controversy to shed light on the true nature of his father's post-retirement consulting contract with the U.S. Government. Contrary to what O'Malley had believed since he was a boy, it wasn't the State Department that had claimed his father's allegiance; that was just a cover for his actual thirty-year career with the CIA. This revelation shook O'Malley's world as if someone had overturned a completed jigsaw puzzle without warning. Since O'Malley had been a child, his father had gone to various White House meetings under different presidents, the presumption being that he was some kind of elevated thinker, some guru of diplomacy upon whom presidents relied.

His father had always kept a sense of humor about what it was he did. When once he'd been asked by a ponderous bore if he was "one of the Wise Men," he'd replied, "I'm a Wise Ass, not a Wise Man." O'Malley had never once doubted the former description, not even enough to be curious. Yet, in all those years of semiretirement, his father had continued to be a more than busy spook, and when he'd left his State Department cover to become a "consultant," it proved to be a merely more lucrative continuation.

His time spent in Iran after the Second World War, O'Malley discovered, hadn't been a mission of diplomacy, but rather, covert action. His trips to Vietnam, to Kenya, to Laos, were the necessary destinations of a specialist in coups d'état. Though he'd retired his civil servant's GS designation midway through the Nixon Administration—and now O'Malley wondered why—his father had kept busy, at least if one believed the report of that Senate committee. O'Malley wasn't certain if he did, but he knew he didn't believe half of what was written about the old man in issues of *The Nation, Mother Jones,* and other journals of the counterculture.

What was hard to fathom was whether his father's passion for Mayan artifacts existed in its own right or was a cover for his trips down Mexico way. The only thing he knew for certain was his father had been warned never to show up with his passport at the airport in Miami again, not even for a trip to the Bahamas, so seriously did some worry about his safety. Though when describing where he lived, O'Malley sometimes told people his apartment was only blocks from where Reagan was shot and Orlando Letelier, the Chilean leftist, was blown up, he did not worry about his old man's safety here in Georgetown. There were plenty of larger targets about around here.

His father came to the head of the stairs as O'Malley stood in the entranceway. One thing that could be said of Carmela was she did impose a certain order on the house. It was tidy, though there were tufts of dog hair on the rugs. "Ready?" said his father. He was dressed like a child for a sledding expedition: scarf around his neck, a parka, although he had a green felt Borsalino on his head. O'Malley looked for mittens. Instead, his father had on pigskin gloves.

"Sure. Let's walk down to the river."

"Thomas, I'm prepared to walk with you to the end of the block. The river is a little ambitious."

But walk they did, into the mild winter air, on a day when the street was filled only with the occasional shopper from Maryland trying to squeeze a car too large into a parking space too small. The dogs bounded ahead of them, circling three college girls in blue jeans, all but tipping over the stooped old widow of a famous Cold War columnist who'd been hauling her groceries up this block since O'Malley was in knee pants. The woman looked up in disgust as his father tipped his hat to her.

"You were telling me about Mother's becoming an art thief."

"Yes, I was. Do we really have to go to the river? Wouldn't you rather go to the Four Seasons for a drink?"

"What makes you think she wants the art?"

"She sent me a goddamned letter, is how I know. She's got that idiot lawyer of hers threatening me if I don't hand over the Gauguin and a laundry list of lesser *objets* that I, not she, picked out." His father did not mention who had paid for them.

"But if I remember my District of Columbia marriage law," O'Malley chimed in, "she doesn't have any claim on a possession in an existing marriage. You aren't divorced, so legally there can't be a division of property."

"Right you are," his father said. "Your mother is sitting in that co-op of hers with enough art to fill the Hermitage, and she's decided to go after my art for spite. Well, I suppose, not just for spite. She'd just rather sell the art on my walls, not hers. Your mother's suffering from a liquidity crisis, Thomas. Speaking of which, are you sure you don't want a drink? She's squandered her vast gobs of money on a who's who of greaseballs, charlatans, and would-be commissars. She's always been redder than a drunkard's eyeball, but now she's decided it's not enough that she gives away her money, she wants to redistribute what small wealth I've accumulated. I'll be damned if I'll give up the Gauguin so your mother can enrich some Marxist cooperative in Sante Fe. Danny, get back here, you stupid mutt."

The dog came trotting back up Thirtieth Street, a bobbing head on a stationary tongue, his shoulders hunched in cheerful subservience, as the other two dogs stood in the middle of the street. They were blocking traffic, and an impatient Virginian in a large BMW leaned on his horn.

"Hey, you, go to hell," yelled his father, and O'Malley wondered whether or not they should go for that drink. He gently pressed him out of harm's way as the driver in the BMW mouthed obscenities from behind the glass window and accelerated up the street. In a moment they'd negotiated M Street's traffic and were in sight of the river, so he kept the dogs close to them and kept his father talking. It was news that his mother was pressing her feud with the old man into the realm of possessions, striking him in a way she knew would hurt.

"I've never been able to understand how you two could be married for as long as you were with her politics as different from yours."

"I always believed politics stopped at the bedroom door. Then television came inside the bedroom. Our marriage was doomed by the transistor. Once they miniaturized enough to make a little TV you could prop on the corner of a dressing table, the divorce rate in this country started to soar. Our marriage may not have survived the breakdown in bipartisan consensus brought on by the Vietnam War, but for damned sure, television didn't help."

"If Mother's politics were that far to the left even in those days, how did your career survive? How is it she wasn't a security risk?"

"Easy. Because any woman in those days who was so outspokenly crazy in her politics, the thinking went, didn't have the temperament for spying. That's what they thought on C Street." Then, as if remembering who he was speaking to, his father said quietly, "That's what they thought. On C Street or out in Langley. From Dulles to Helms, they found her amusing in spite of herself. If she was a spy, she certainly had the wrong cover, if you know what I mean. Name a famous house-wife from the period."

"Lucille Ball."

"No, not Lucille Ball."

"June Cleaver."

"June Cleaver could have gotten away with being a spy, but certainly not your mother."

"Well, then, how did she put up with you, if you were off knocking off Jomo Kenyatta or whatever it was you did in those days?"

"First of all I'm not going to tell you what I did in those days, even if I thought you were sympathetic. Your working for our new President leads me to believe you would not be. At any rate, it was simple. I just told her I was working in concert with John XXIII."

"I don't get it."

"I told her that everything we did was done with an eye to making the world safe for Catholicism. This was before your mother had a crisis of conscience after Vatican II, not knowing how to reconcile her interest in what today would be called liberation theology with her impulse to want to keep the Latin mass, but so long as she thought my activities were for increasing the hegemony of The One True Church, she could live with me. She would have come out against the war in Vietnam long before she did if Diem hadn't been Catholic."

"But you overthrew Diem."

"And replaced him with Catholics."

O'Malley looked confused. "Perhaps I can't explain it to you in this day and age," his father said.

"No, I understand. I'm just always marveling at how bizarre she is."

"She's one of a kind, I'll give her that. She's probably the only Catholic in America who supports the Bishops' letter on nuclear weapons, the Pope's position on contraceptives, but thinks he doesn't go far enough when it comes to support for Marxist principles. Though I think she may be in the process of rethinking her position on divorce if she's serious about liquidating my beautiful Gauguin."

They were standing in front of the Washington Harbour development, looking out on the Potomac. Chunks of ice floated toward Roosevelt Island. On the lee side wood ducks were landing. Some afternoon oarsmen threaded their sculls through the frozen obstacle course as the bright lights of Rosslyn were coming on across the river; to their left, the Kennedy Center stood like a scaled-down tribute less to JFK than to Mussolini. Memorial Bridge was a distant note of national elegance, a rarity. Near the railing above the river, they found a bench and went to sit down in it, his father's hands in his parka pockets, his hat pulled down over his eyes. They were still clear and bright, if a bit bloodshot, though the skin around them was puffy.

"How do you know she needs the cash the painting would bring in?"

"You forget that your Uncle Jake is still my lawyer."

His Uncle Jake Ingram, a good man and a powerhouse at Barrett and Cooke, continued to represent his father in the civil litigation that stemmed from his legal difficulties. Questions remained about transactions with arms dealers, offshore accounts, the laundering of funds. Some foundation in Miami that basked in his mother's eleemosynary favor continued to pester the old man with requests for depositions. The more it dragged on—the depositions, the "60 Minutes" harassment, the obligatory naming in any published conspiracy theory—the more his father seemed to give up on everything other than the booze. Uncle Jake continually tried to cheer his friend up, even if the only way to do so was to tell him the latest story about O'Malley's mother, Jake's youngest sister. And this latest one, as his father related it to him, involved his mother's having been taken by a con man who promised her "socially responsible" investments.

When his father finished, O'Malley said, "She'll be all right, Dad."

"Well, I know. The Foundation's not going to let her starve. Jake'll see to that."

"She's obviously got enough money to still be politically active. She's still taking out ads. There was one in the *Times* just the other week protesting our nuclear stockpile."

"Did that cause you any problems at the White House? I'm assuming that our new President doesn't intend on beating our swords into plowshares in his first few months in office."

"I don't think anybody other than the President knows she's my mother, and he thinks she's amusing. She ended up contributing to the campaign. But there is one problem I can see I'm going to have there."

"As a patriot, you're going to be compelled to blow the whistle on this fraud for whom you work."

"No, Dad. It isn't funny. I was arrested for DWI on the night of the inaugural."

"Oh, nertz," his father said. "Do they know?"

"Not yet."

"Wasn't drunk driving one of Hardison's big issues?"

"Yeah, well, it was after it turned out that combine driver in Spirit Lake had been indulging in ethanol or something. I have to admit, I helped draft the statement."

"So you're doubly vulnerable."

"Yeah. I was thinking maybe Uncle Jake could help."

"I'll help."

"Dad, I don't need money."

"No, I'll defend you. I'm still a member of the bar. They haven't taken that away from me yet."

"No, Dad, you don't have to do that. I just wanted you to know, is all."

"Do you want my help?" He looked like there was perhaps more riding on it for him than for O'Malley.

"Yes," said O'Malley, with a nanosecond of hesitation. "You've always been there for me when I've been in trouble."

"And you for me," said his father, and he started to laugh with more life than O'Malley could remember lately without his having a drink in his hand.

I n those rare days when there were no major speeches, when the President's addressing trade groups and Boy Scout troops was the business at hand, the speechwriters could be forgiven for getting into mischief, or at least what for them passed for it.

While Katherine Tierney kept her nose to the administrative grindstone, concentrating on the paper flow that was so much a part of her job, Colin Denholm sat in his office with his tie at full mast, a look of rapture on his face as he memorized whole pages of *Bartlett's Quotations*. Will Ames sometimes snuck away to prayer meetings, or wrote imaginary speeches for the President to deliver, calling on America to achieve a Third Great Awakening. And O'Malley? O'Malley was trying to get the White House operators to track down Thomas Pynchon.

"I'm sorry, Mr. O'Malley, there's no Thomas Pynchon in Seattle."

"Damn, have you tried Portland?"

"We tried Portland yesterday, sir."

"Boston?"

"We tried Boston the day before, sir."

"Well, this is a matter of national security. Is there any way you can get into the telephone system's master computers?"

"We can't do that, sir."

"All right," he would say after a while, and then hang up. Then, in a minute, "Operator, can you track down, I believe it's Cornish, New Hampshire. I need to speak to Mr. J. D. Salinger." The phone rang and an exasperated voice answered and O'Malley hung up. He found he didn't have a single thing to say.

T he meeting was to take place at 2:30 and Kit Bowles skipped lunch to prepare for it. It was to be a showdown, of sorts. After all the fights she'd had with Wilbur Todd, Senator Partridge's administrative assistant, today she was going to have her chance to settle things. They'd been quarreling over what issues the new Senator from Wyoming should make his own, and today, at last, would come her opportunity to argue her case in front of the Senator, just her and Todd. She had an idea that was going to surprise him, an idea for getting Partridge on the cutting edge that she hadn't bothered to discuss with Wilbur. She'd arranged the meeting so that Todd, the veteran Hill Luddite who was her immediate boss, couldn't veto her proposal just because it hadn't germinated in a right-wing think tank.

That they were some weeks into the new year without having a legislative strategy was a result of the accidental manner in which Tony Partridge had become a senator shortly after the new Congress had convened. His journey from Cheyenne to Washington wasn't the result of the voters' will. No, his ascension to the Senate seat was the result of what had occurred when Senator Warren Stone, one of the most powerful men in Washington, had dashed from the hideaway office in the Russell Building in which he sat getting snackered, in order to cast a floor vote on a farm appropriation. He'd had the bad luck to fall onto the tracks of the Senate subway system, and to the horror of the tourists, staffers, and other senators looking on, he'd groggily reached for the third rail. A blue spark had been the last bit of power this senator ever exercised, and it had been up to the Governor of Wyoming to appoint a man, not who could fill Warren Stone's shoes, for who could do that? But someone who could at least answer a quorum call and return letters to constituents.

The Governor himself had designs on the seat, which would come open in the next election. So, to make certain the person who warmed it for him wasn't a threat to his dreams, he'd appointed Tony Partridge, the Finance Chairman of the Wyoming Young Republicans, as the newest United States Senator.

That the move was transparent both to Wyoming's voters and national reporters did not augur well for Partridge's career in "the most exclusive club in the world." His being good-looking and earnest, and a bit shy in public, did not improve matters.

Two months before, Partridge had been a successful young lawyer whose twin passions were Republican politics and skiing at Jackson Hole. The photo of him in stretch pants that *The Washington Post* Style section splattered on its front page along with a snide profile didn't ease his transition to the capital. On the day he was sworn in, the Republican Leader of the Senate was asked what assignments the new senator would have. It was widely reported that the Leader's eyes darted about as he commented, "We think we'll have him teach our kids how to snowplow, though it looks like we're going to have to keep him away from our wives." Veteran reporters laughing almost until they puked wasn't a good sign.

He'd ended up with marginal committee assignments, other than Agriculture, where it was expected he would vote with the ranking Republican and not cause any trouble. What Kit Bowles liked was that he was on the Agriculture, Nutrition and Forestry Committee, a normally invisible assignment for a Republican without seniority unless the efficacy of swine flu vaccines was a subject for national debate. But she had an idea as to how Partridge could vault onto the Sunday talk shows that are the leading indicators of Washington status, and she was eager to bring it to his attention.

She'd ended up his legislative director by an unusual route. After Kit had spent several unhappy though highly lucrative years as a model in Milan and Paris, fending off Eurotrash in various ports and capitals, she'd decide to embark on a more substantive career. In spite of the time she spent with David Nicole, she'd had high grades at Smith, majoring in political science. When she was accepted to the London School of Economics, she'd dropped her modeling career and had graduated with the equivalent of a master's. Having no interest in going to work on Wall Street, where her aging father continued to hold court hoping that someday a new Republican president would appoint him Secretary of the Treasury, she'd settled upon Washington. She'd been an economist for the Banking Committee for over two years before a fateful evening when Senator Wyatt McCallum, a friend of her family's on whose personal staff she'd worked before she'd filled one of his committee slots, invited her to a dinner party at his home. It was only when the taxi left her on the gravel driveway of his large house in McLean that she discovered no one was there, not his wife or his servants, and that while dinner was to be served—from a Chinese restaurant that delivered—it looked like she was the party.

Senator McCallum was in his mid-sixties. He had a head of Central Casting white hair, and he had the courtly air required of a reformed segregationist from the Commonwealth of Virginia who'd been in office since Kit had been a child. On the evening Kit Bowles was invited to his house, the Senator himself answered the door. Rather than look as dignified as he often was when in mid-filibuster, he was dressed a little like a corpse in a clown suit. He'd slicked his white hair down and he was wearing a loud madras sports jacket that had been bought for him by his rather flashy, and curiously absent, second wife. Lingering in the stale odor of pipes, cigars, and cigarettes, which he smoked constantly from the time he propped himself up in the morning to the time he passed out at night, was the smell of a vile cologne, circa 1954, which the Senator had splashed on.

"My darling, come in."

"Uncle Wyatt, how are you?" she said, holding her breath and kissing his cheek. "Where's Aunt Molly?" she asked innocently enough. There was no one to be seen in the gaudy, large living room, and the lights were turned so low she could barely make out the furniture.

"I thought that we'd have dinner together, my dear, and talk about your future."

"My future," she repeated. "My, Uncle Wyatt."

It was after the inedible Chinese dinner and the stories McCallum told of his dealings with Chiang Kai-shek, with Nixon, with Bobby Kennedy and Fidel Castro, only then that the inevitable move she'd been bracing for occurred.

McCallum had awkwardly cleared away their dishes and bade her come sit next to him as he showed her photos from a picture album. There were scenes of the Senator at historical moments that had rocked the world, arranged chronologically, probably by someone on his staff, probably on time paid for by the taxpayers. All the while he puffed on a cigar that, in combination with his cologne, had the aphrodisiac qualities of binary nerve gas. He brought her a brandy snifter and was pointing out the photo of him leering at Martin Luther King during some confrontation in Richmond, as if this were the way into her knickers, when his cigar went out and his gold-plated lighter sparked without result.

"Damn Zippo needs a refill," he said. He went to a drawer and pulled out a can of lighter fluid, which he brought over to the table where they were sitting. It was only after he laid tip to moistened cotton pad and had the cigar puffing once more that he began to rub the inside of her thigh.

That's when Kit reached for the can, doused his lap with it, and picking his lighter up off the table, flicked up the top and said, "I think this is when you call me a cab, Senator." This was one order from staff with which he dutifully complied, protesting all the while that she'd misunderstood him.

Nicholas Bowles called him in his office two days later. Kit had taken two days' sick leave from the honorable Senator's committee office.

"Nick, my boy, how are the markets?" the Senator asked.

"Your stock just headed south, Wyatt. It appears investors discovered there were some fiduciary problems connected with your thinking with your dick. I understand all orders are to sell and no one thinks a plugged nickel is a worthy bargain for your sorry ass, unless, of course, you get real smart, real fast."

"I'm amenable to a compromise."

"There isn't going to be a compromise, Wyatt. My daughter Kit, whom we had you consider your loving niece, who labored in your fucking office for over two years, is looking for a new job on the Hill. Know of any?"

"There's that new senator coming to town, that pretty boy from Wyoming."

"Maybe you'll put in a good word for her," her father said.

But Kit would not hear of it, though she was grateful for the tip. She bade her father call McCallum back and tell him to forget the favor, that she'd get a job on her own, but she allowed her father to let the Senator think he'd be better off not blocking her appointment to any job she wanted, ever. That while she didn't need him now, he had better stay out of her way. Then she'd submitted her résumé to Partridge's office manager in the Senator's first week in town, and her reputation and qualifications were such that she landed an interview. After an unexpectedly long meeting with Partridge—whom she liked, though he clearly was a goofball—she'd accepted the offer to be his $44,000-

a-year legislative director. When she passed Senator McCallum in the hallways of the Dirksen Building, walking with some bright-eyed young aide looking self-important in a brand-new dress, it was all she could do not to call out, "Got a light, Senator?"

Today she gathered up her folders and walked into Partridge's office just as Wilbur Todd arrived. He was a burly Montanan with a gray walrus mustache and spectacles that made him look like an insurance adjuster for Allstate, spending lonely evenings dashing to the sites of twisters and locust infestations.

"Hi, Wilbur," she said breezily as he pulled up one of the standard-issue leather and oak chairs. They were a bit weak on the office amenities because the Capitol furniture supply had been picked clean by the freshmen who'd arrived weeks before Partridge's appointment. Other than the clock with its circular system of lights, which indicated how much time the Senator had before a vote, and the requisite photographs of Partridge with big-name Republicans, his office was a little disappointing. It looked like actual work might be done in it.

Wilbur barely said hello. He seemed bored by the prospect ahead. He'd been plucked from an office in the Republican Leadership and foisted on Partridge to make sure the new Senator would not be a complete embarrassment to the party, and he had to listen to a junior staffer, a woman no less, tell him what issues the fool ought to be choosing to make his mark, when making his mark wasn't something anyone was particularly interested in Partridge doing. Twenty-three years as a Senate aide, a parking space near an elevator, every junior senator's A.A. calling him Mr. Todd, and this East Coast cookie had *ideas*. Because she also had a pair of legs—quite a pair of legs, he had to admit—she was going to get her say. He'd sit through it, but he didn't have to pretend to be happy about it.

They waited in silence before Partridge came in the door, chased by some Wyomingites who'd seen him in the hallway as they came for White House passes. "Sorry I'm late," he said. He had his biggest grin on his face, which is to say his face was entirely lit up, as with joy. He still couldn't believe he was a senator. Which gave him something in common with most people in Washington.

"Now, what are we doing this for?" he asked, as he came around the desk and sat in his standard-issue, regulation senator's chair.

"We wanted to settle your legislative agenda sometime before the August recess," Kit said with a smile.

"I don't get it. It's still winter." He had a confused look on a face that could not hide emotions. His dark brown forelock lay upon his brow, which was good, because his forehead was so smooth and unlined as to make him seem vacuous, which he wasn't, Kit had come to believe, or at least hoped.

"I was exaggerating," she said, continuing to smile. Oh, boy. Wilbur Todd grunted and shifted his belly so the huge lunch he'd eaten didn't press too hard against his large Western belt buckle.

"Well, let's hear what you two think. You're the experts. I'm just a country boy from the Tetons," he said with a wink, as if this were manifestly untrue, as if this were an obvious dodge at hiding his shrewdness.

Kit decided to get right to the point. "Tony, there aren't a lot of possibilities for you to make either news or noise in this Congress, at least not if you stick to your committee assignments and just do as the Leadership tells you. Which I'm not arguing against, mind you," she said in an aside meant to curry favor with Wilbur Todd.

"One way you could make news in the Ag Committee would be if you came out wholly against price supports."

Todd coughed involuntarily at this, and for the first time, turned to look at her.

"I'm not recommending it. But I think I have a way of getting you in front of the curve, on the crest of a wave. It's said there are only three kinds of senators—beautiful people, surfers, and untouchables. B.P.'s are the senators who get face time on the networks no matter what the issue is. Untouchables are the ones who only get on the networks if they fall into the Tidal Basin in the arms of a stripper. But surfers, they're the real stars of this town, the ones who find an issue and ride it just as far as they can."

She was gathering confidence, and Partridge sat back in his chair gazing at her intently.

"I think I've got the issue for you to surf on all the way to reelection, Senator."

"Drugs," said Wilbur, impassively.

"Drugs? Drugs are yesterday's issue. It's like trade policy or the deficit. Besides, there are other surfboards in the water ahead of you on that one. No, I've got an issue, and you've got a committee assignment that matches that issue, that can get you on 'Face the Nation.' "

"Don't keep us in suspense any longer, Kit," said Wilbur somewhat nastily.

"Low-density lipoproteins," she said with a dramatist's flair.

"Beg pardon?" said Partridge.

"Yeah, what?" said Wilbur.

"Cholesterol." They didn't stir. "C'mon, think about it. The entire country's becoming health-conscious—well, everyone but Wilbur. And cholesterol affects everyone. Remember, it isn't just called the Agriculture Committee; it's the Agriculture, Nutrition and Forestry Committee. If you used your seat on it to press for labeling of cholesterol levels, education about eating habits, a move toward leaner cuts of meat, fewer eggs, there are a lot of possible actions you could call for. And you could be a hero doing it. More to the point, you could do it on 'GMA,' the 'Today' show, and the 'MacNeil/Lehrer News Hour.' "

"You ever been to Wyoming?" Wilbur was shouting. "You ever seen a steer? What do you think they do on ranches out there? Ride ponies and piss in the campfire?"

"Wilbur has a point."

"You're goddamn well told I do," said Wilbur. "That's the craziest damned idea I ever heard of."

"It's a good idea," said Kit, unflustered.

"It's a piece of shit, squeeze my French. I just knew she had some touchy-feely Harvard-type idea. I knew it, I knew it, I knew it."

"Well, what do you suggest, Wilbur? There are some merits to Kit's suggestions."

"Bullshit," he said with complete contempt for the Senator from Wyoming. "You want to get your face on TV? You go out and make a speech says you have knowledge there's high-level drug use in the Hardison White House."

"Is there?"

"Hell, I don't know. But if what you want is to get on TV, that's the way to go. People are obsessed with drugs."

"Yeah, with good reason, Wilbur," said Partridge. "There's been a murder a day here since I got here. Crack's a terrible problem. Drugs are ruining the cities in this country."

"No one gives a rat's ass about that in Wyoming. It's the question of whether the leadership of the country's smoking cocaine or snorting marijuana or whatever it is people do."

"This is sickening," said Kit. "What's he supposed to do? Say he has a list of two hundred and forty high-level Democrats who are card-carrying members of the Medellín cartel?"

"Stuff works," said Wilbur with a grin.

"Yeah, it also got Gene McCarthy censured," said Partridge with some heat.

"That was Joe McCarthy, Senator," said Kit evenly.

"Whatever," he said.

There came the familiar clicks and buzzes just before Senate bells went off. They turned to the clock to see how many lights went on. It was a vote.

"What's the vote?" he asked.

Kit looked at her notes. "It's an amendment by Senator Harkins to the National Pancake Week resolution calling for the abolition of the Air Force as well as a ten-percent surcharge on all people making more than thirty thousand a year."

"You should vote against it," Wilbur said helpfully.

"Look, I'm going to think about this," the Senator said.

"Cholesterol, Tony. You've got it, I've got it, Wilbur's going to die of it. It can be a great issue for you."

"Drugs," said Wilbur, nodding so vigorously his walrus mustache lay even with one of his chins.

"I'll get back to you," said the Senator, and then he went to vote.

fter a few months when there actually were some quiet days, they settled into a rhythm of work that alternated between merely busy and a two-minute drill in a football game. Crazed or in control, the President's schedule dictated picked-up steam, constant motion, whether he was going out on the road to sell his economic program, or merely engaging in activities around La Casa Blanca staged for the evening news. And all the time, for everyone, there was the constant pressure of living under scrutiny, whether it was under the watchful eyes of staff more senior, or for the senior staff, the constant vigilance of the media. It was something that made O'Malley uncomfortable, even after he had settled in and thought of himself as an anonymous cog in a prestigious machine, a purveyor of a commodity, in this case the words the President spoke. These were in constant, if unappreciated, demand.

There were jokes and pet phrases that made the news, throwaway lines that sometimes had a longer half-life than the substantive sentences they all labored over. Sometimes they were left to work on their speeches, have lunch in the mess, and leave for home at a decent hour. Other times they were whipped from above, waiting tensely for the reaction to the drafts they produced. There were tugs of war over what the

President would say, and sometimes they took it upon themselves to nudge him in a particular direction by offering up a text of what they thought he wanted to say, as opposed to what others—the staff, the media—wanted him to say. Because they were providing the words that were to come out of his mouth, there was a necessary conceit involved in their work: they had to will into being a connection between their fingers on a computer keyboard and the thoughts in the President's mind, the feelings in his heart. As time went on, as their fights with the bureaucracy over everything from major addresses to simple introductions had them constantly at war with one competing White House faction or another, there came to be an esprit de corps within Katherine's shop that made for a common defense. "Keeping the Assholes at Bay" were the fighting words they adopted, and even Buffy, the receptionist, was known to invoke them.

The speechwriters held a peculiar status. It was acknowledged that they were artists of a sort, but at the same time, they were viewed as mechanics whose job it was to keep the rhetoric of an administration ever on the road. Worse, they were all suspected of being closet ideologues.

O'Malley's run-in with Whitney in the Chief of Staff's office early on set the tone for the uneasy relationship they would have that first winter. Though Whitney was politic enough to pass on a note of praise for a particular address that had received high marks for the President, they didn't much like him. Still, he did not interfere with the workings of their office unless there was something that mattered to him.

For every day that O'Malley had time to indulge in his games with the White House operators, there were five in which he sweated from 7:30 A.M. until well after the evening news, days in which the speechwriters bounced ideas off each other like Tin Pan Alley songwriters. It was on an evening in early April when he had struggled all day long over a speech the President was to deliver to the Veterans of Foreign Wars—a speech viewed as important for laying down some kind of Hardison Doctrine—that O'Malley had arranged to meet Kit and some friends nearby for dinner at Primi Piatti. Though the speech was due to be routed through the Cabinet in only two days, at quarter to eight he'd switched off his computer and wandered up Pennsylvania Avenue.

There was the general roar in the cavernous dining room as he spotted Kit. He waved hello to the diminutive maitre d' and walked through the tables toward her. "Hi," he said, kissing her cheek.

"How are you?" she asked with a smile. She was wearing a bright blue suit, a bit more properly dressed than he was, wilted in pinstripes, but with a sporty striped shirt and loud tie. Because he was not worried about advancing within the White House, there being no job above his he would ever desire, he had long since ceased to care about how he was dressed, just so long as he remembered to wear socks.

"I'm beat. This VFW speech is mind-boggling. All the buttons you have to touch lest the President be declared a wimp or a warmonger."

"How did you end up doing this?"

"I'll be damned if I know. I told Katherine, I'm not qualified. But Will's working on the National Religious Broadcasters speech, and Colin's trying to put together a package for the trip to South America in May, which, by the way, they want me to go on."

"You're kidding. That's great." She seemed genuinely pleased for him.

"Even though Colin's writing the speeches, they decided—somebody decided—that Hardison's more comfortable with me than any of the others, at least on the road, so I'm going. Have laptop, will travel. Oh, the press office announced that Colombia's out—too risky—though they're rescheduling a stop in Caracas, Venezuela. Speaking of Colombia, how are drugs?"

"They're beating cholesterol, I'm afraid."

"You're kidding." He reached toward a bread stick and broke one in two. He'd had only a salad at his desk for lunch and he was hungry.

"It's too depressing to talk about it. The fat slob's gotten Jerry Jetta and Mike Humperdink in on the action, and Partridge is listening to them."

"That's terrible," he said sympathetically. Jetta and Humperdink were two Republican consultants of dubious value and a reputation for sleaze who had recently had Partridge's ear. That there weren't better operatives helping out had to do with the fact that the good image-makers were staying away in droves.

"Look," he said, "let me tell you quickly who we're meeting. Tim Skelton was a friend of mine at law school, okay. He was Senator Sam Brock's press secretary in the campaign, and he's really good, though he made the mistake of getting under Hardison's skin, which is why he's been blocked from the administration."

"That's too bad."

"It's worse than you think. He thought he was getting a job in the press office—McCurry offered him one," he said referring to the popular White House press secretary, Mike McCurry. "He went off after the election and got married thinking he was returning to a job and when he got back Hardison had blocked it. So he's freshly married and un-employed."

"That doesn't speak well for Hardison. Didn't you talk to him about it?"

"There was no use. He woke up every morning of the primary and found that Tim had a brand-new way of insulting him. He's really very good. Brock's sort of a pussy, so it was up to Skelton to do the nut-cutting. He was even tougher on Senator Bligh than he was on Hardison. Oh, here they are," he said, pushing his chair back and getting up.

"Tim."

"Hey, man," he said extending his hand.

"Hey, darling," O'Malley said to Paulina, Skelton's wife. While Skelton was merely a decent-looking oaf in a leather jacket, his wife was stunning: delicate-looking, with sensuous features and intelligent eyes. O'Malley had often kidded his friend over who was getting the better deal in that relationship.

"This is my friend Kit Bowles, Tim Skelton and Paulina . . . are you using his name these days?"

"Not if she wants to keep her job," said Skelton good-naturedly.

"I'm a Republican," Paulina confided to Kit. "It's better I not be connected to Skelton."

"There's no problem, I guess, if you're a Republican," said Skelton. "It's if you're a Democrat that I'm poison."

"Yeah, how goes the job search?" O'Malley asked.

"Sucks," said Skelton with a smile. "I got blocked by Senator Bligh from that press job with the DNC."

"Oh, Tim, that's terrible." O'Malley hadn't known he was up for it.

"No, that's Washington. I've only got two enemies in this town, but they're the President of the United States and the Senate Majority Leader."

"Not bad," said Kit.

Skelton shrugged. "You're a Republican too, aren't you, Kit? What's this, another mixed relationship, Tom?"

"Yeah, like you two."

"I was thinking more of your parents," he said to O'Malley, and as that settled over the table like a pall, the waiter came over and took a drink order.

"Where do you work, Kit?" asked Paulina.

"For Tony Partridge."

"Ohhhhhh," said both Skelton and his wife.

"He's not as bad as you've heard."

"It would be difficult for him to be as bad as we've heard," said Skelton.

"Why can't Brock take care of you, now that he's Secretary of Defense?" O'Malley asked.

"This is the part that hurts," said Paulina.

"I get blocked from working in the White House press office because Hardison hates me. Fair enough. The only reason to be involved in politics in the first place is so if you win, you get to throw your enemies in jail. I mean, if I were Argentinian or something, I'd be *disappeared*," Skelton said, drawing his finger across his throat. "Bligh blocking me from the Democratic National Committee is absolutely his prerogative. I would defend him for that. He'd be a wimp or a statesman if he let me have the job, and God knows Bligh ain't either of those things. But there I sweat my tush off for Brock for three years. I spend enough time with him in Iowa to qualify to vote there, I spend enough time in New Hampshire with him to claim it as my domicile and not have to pay taxes, and when the guy lands a job with the administration in spite of all the nasty things I say on his behalf, I don't get offered a job. It's outrageous."

"It is. Why's he doing this?"

"I asked him. I say, why aren't I welcome at DOD? First thing he says is that there are career military people who should be spokesmen there. I say, fine, I understand you got colonels to take care of. I'm not asking to brief *Defense Week* every day. But something, somewhere. It's not like the Department of Defense doesn't have a billion fucking jobs to fill. So he goes, I don't want people to think I'm running for president, and you were my campaign press secretary. So that's when I lost it. I said, You mean if you'd been elected, and you'd gone to the White House, you wouldn't have brought me with you 'cause you thought people might worry you were planning your reelection!" Skelton brought his fist down on the table so hard the waiter jumped as he came to deliver their drinks. He waited for the glasses to be still before he began to place them on the table.

"Thomas."

"That's terrible, Tim."

"Thomas," said a voice to his left, and he saw Kit's mouth open. "Hello, Kit," said David Nicole.

"David," said O'Malley.

Nicole stood next to their table with that slight grin on his face that

O'Malley remembered all the way back to his childhood. He was nattily attired in an Armani sports coat and a silk shirt, buttoned all the way up. He looked like he would have fit in better in Hollywood than here in D.C. His black hair was shorter than it had been in college, but it was still tied back neatly, with a stylishly small ponytail draped over his collar. He looked fit and was suntanned though his face had aged.

"I was wondering when I was going to run into you," O'Malley managed to get out.

"Bound to happen sooner or later. It's a small town," said Nicole. "Though I guess these days we run with different crowds."

"These are my friends Tim and Paulina, and . . ."

"And I know Kit," Nicole said easily. "Hello again, Kit."

"Hello, David."

"You're looking well."

"You are too."

"You two should come to my restaurant sometime, Thomas."

"I've been meaning to." He was now standing, talking to his old friend, and the rest of the boisterous restaurant seemed silent to him. It had been a long time.

"You should come visit me, old friends and all."

"I should, you're right."

"I understand I can reach you at the White House."

"You can," O'Malley said, and a chill went down his spine. He realized he was beginning to perspire. The notion of Nicole coming to visit him was too horrifying for words. In a second, he could see himself giving Nicole's Social Security number to the Secret Service agents downstairs, in order to get him through the door, and alarm bells whooping through the building. He had a vision of Marines, DEA agents, of astronauts in uniform called up for active duty, a bullhorn in the stairwell telling him to come out of his office with his hands held high.

"But I won't blow your cover, man. I'll call you at home."

"Maybe that would be best."

Skelton, seeing his friend's discomfort, allowed, "When I walk by the White House these days, the surface-to-air missiles track me down the street."

"You must be a dangerous customer," said Nicole with such false respect the good-natured grin was drained from Skelton's face.

"Have you been sitting here the whole time?" O'Malley interjected: a peacemaker.

"Well, my partner, Tina, and I saw you over here," Nicole said, gesturing to a table along the wall at which sat a glamorous, tall woman with a movie star's head of black hair. She didn't look like the kind of woman you often saw in Washington. There was no place in this spineless city for a woman who looked so dangerously provocative. "I couldn't resist saying hello."

"I'm glad you did," O'Malley lied. He was moments away from feeling giddy.

"I bet," said Nicole, smiling. "I'll call you, invite you to my restaurant."

"Okay."

And with that, Nicole strolled back to his table, and both O'Malley and Kit Bowles exhaled.

"Who was that?" asked Skelton.

"It's a long story," said O'Malley. Both he and Kit gulped their drinks a little desperately.

pecial Agent Harlan Bryce had a problem that went way beyond his hangover. He was supposed to interview some big-shot partner in a D.C. law firm about a speechwriter in the White House, but it was going to be a little difficult to leave home. Somehow, he was fuzzy on the details, but he'd run into a blunt object the night before—the street, a sap, his windshield, he couldn't be certain—and though he'd made it to his own bed, he had awakened with his pillow crusted to the crown of his head by a nasty patch of coagulated blood.

Normally he would simply have pulled on the same suit he wore to these interviews, made an attempt at shaving with the electric razor on the trip from Falls Church into the city, and shown up, grumpy but professional, at wherever the interview was to be held. He enjoyed the way receptionists at swank Washington offices recoiled in horror when he identified himself as being from the FBI and asked to speak to their boss. They'd all but pull wheelies in their swivel chairs and go off to fetch him. It was up to the boss to explain to the receptionists that Bryce had come merely as part of a background investigation on some partner or former employee who was up for a government job. He preferred to let them think he was about to march their boss out of there in manacles. He thought it was good for morale.

Normally he got a real kick out of this. He enjoyed his job. But today was different. Today he'd had to get into the shower with his pillow stuck to his head in order to melt the sucker off. Today he just didn't have the energy to make it into town.

Instead, he sat in his dark bedroom with his head throbbing, a bottle of Smirnoff vodka on the dresser table, and tried unsuccessfully to piece together how it was he'd come to have that pillow glued to his cranium. He was known as the best background agent in the business, but reconstructing the details of his own life this morning was more than a little difficult. Whole hours of his life had just washed away, like a seawall in a turbulent storm.

Waking up with a hangover was not unfamiliar, but blacking out like this was disturbing. It was closer to being the silhouette in the Bureau's target range than it was to being the shooter. He may have been the kind of guy who hung out at strip joints on Fourteenth Street until last call, rationalizing that only through a life of total filth could he see the dark patches in men's hearts and divine their potential risks to national security, but he did not as a general rule lose track of where he'd been. He did not as a matter of course wake up fastened to his goddamned pillow.

As he saw it, that he didn't trust a soul was a statement of his professional integrity. He just knew that someday he was going to investigate some mild-mannered, churchgoing, loving husband who was up for a Schedule C appointment and slowly unearth proof that the man was a drug-addicted philanderer who drank bourbon for breakfast and was so schizoid he reported to a neo-Nazi organization and a cell in the American Communist Party on even and odd days of the week, with KGB connections and his name on the mailing list of the North American Man-Boy Love Association.

This fellow he now was investigating, Thomas O'Malley, was working at the White House as a speechwriter. So far, he seemed normal enough, through Bryce found it curious that in each of the six buildings O'Malley had listed as having lived in while he was a resident of New York City, no one could remember him. That hardly anyone in these buildings would even open their doors to the FBI agent investigating hinted at something fishy, something hidden in O'Malley's past, and Bryce was determined to root it out. Though not today. Today was a day for a hair of the dog. He was a deliberate man with much more research to do into the potential for squalor in a civil servant's soul.

H e thought it was a fire.

From the lights flashing and the vehicles out front, he thought his dorm was burning down. And then he stood in the crowd underneath a pine tree and watched as two men wearing windbreakers on which the initials "DEA" had been stenciled in yellow letters came out of the main door with a miserable-looking David Nicole in handcuffs behind his back. Nicole wasn't squirming, but he wasn't limp, either. He walked under his own steam, not looking at anyone, and got into the car that took him away.

They'd gone to school together since they were four years old, except for the time Nicole had been expelled from St. Albans. Among parents in Northwest Washington, Nicole became persona non grata for having successfully manipulated the son of the ambassador from Pakistan into using his diplomatic immunity to import several pounds of hashish. This was over spring break, their junior year. Because Nicole's grades were consistently excellent, his skill as a football halfback renowned, and his line of bullshit so pure, he'd been able to persuade Amherst to let him in the next year. They'd roomed together, but there had been tensions, mostly over drugs.

In high school, O'Malley had occasionally smoked dope, like every-one else, hanging out in friends' houses with towels rolled up against the door, the Rolling Stones playing in muted tones while they giggled or sat with bloodshot eyes, planning their next moves. For O'Malley it was a game of cops and robbers with his teachers at school, and his parents at home, but vague threats, dupes mostly. It was a world that included books that were not on the course list, rock 'n' roll music, and evenings at his girlfriend Tawnee Marlowe's house, where he became privy to pleasures he had a vague sense others had discovered before him, but not like this, this was special.

For Nicole, reefer was religion, a ticket to the ends of the earth. He grew to know more about Oaxaca and Kashmir than the National Geo-graphic Society did. Dope was power, an influence he had over those who were as mystified by what they discovered through it, by their need for it, as they were by his expertise. Nicole began to deal seriously, volume and quality, with a B list for selling and an A list for sharing, for showing off. He developed marketing skills they don't teach in B-school. Any party Nicole showed up at revolved around who he let in on the drugs. An anointed few—mostly kids he could control—were allowed to subdivide the pounds he showed up with and make money selling ounces. He picked and chose who was allowed to deal. Rivals were either undercut or socially isolated until they couldn't have sold anything anyway and so they just gave up. O'Malley didn't much feel like being controlled, by Nicole or anyone else.

Except, perhaps, by Tawnee, who, when the boys headed north to Amherst, went to Smith, where she scandalized those on her freshman corridor by alternating nights at O'Malley's dorm with nights she had him over. That over the next two years Nicole began infiltrating the huge dystopian towers at UMass. in search of connections did not seem overly troublesome until he began to show up at the room he shared with O'Malley in the company of guys with names like Jesus and Apache who were interested in traffic that seemed a little heavy, not just pounds at a time, but whole bales of it, and not just dope but cocaine.

And then Apache, a tiny Puerto Rican with leather thongs around his biceps, turned out to be a narcotics officer and Nicole went off in a car with his hands behind his back as the bubble-gum machine up top rocked light from side to side. Kit Bowles, Nicole's girlfriend, and Tawnee were suspended from Smith, though not expelled, on the basis of no more evidence than that they knew how to spell David Nicole's name, and after a visitation by his father and his Uncle Jake, Amherst allowed O'Malley to graduate, though they were none too pleased by his presence.

Nicole spent a well-publicized year waiting for trial, but when it finally came up, he got off lightly. They celebrated in New York, O'Malley and Nicole, but then Nicole did the oddest thing imaginable. Rather than look at the experience he'd just gone through as some kind of epic warning, he began to view it as a proof of omnipotence, as validation of the line of bullshit he'd been working since they went to St. Albans. It became clear his attraction to drugs was more than a romantic quest, an insecurity, or a flawed aesthetic. While O'Malley, for survival's sake, turned his back on his dangerous friend, Nicole began a journey into harrowing amounts of cocaine that had to lead to jail or his death. The lightest sentence imaginable was a perforated septum.

O'Malley wasn't exactly headed toward the corporate world, but it scared him to think where Nicole was going. This wouldn't have mattered to O'Malley so much except Nicole began to take Tawnee there with him.

She'd always loved to party, she liked staying up all night chopping at a mound in front of her, and not long after both Nicole and O'Malley had taken up residence in New York, eventually rather than coming home from Nicole's Harrison Street loft at ten in the morning all wired and jittery and suicidal, she ended up just staying there. O'Malley, resigned, thought it didn't matter. He moved on, at least so far as other girlfriends were concerned.

And then Nicole went to South America and took Tawnee there with him, and in circumstances O'Malley at first didn't understand—though when the details were known, he vowed the statute of limitations would never run out—Nicole returned to the States without her. She hooked up with some real bad dudes, is how Nicole put it when he called with the news, and O'Malley didn't doubt it, for she'd hooked up with Nicole, hadn't she?

He went looking for her. It took O'Malley three weeks in Santa Marta with Tawnee's brother, Will, to find out that Nicole had left her in the mountains outside of Medellín for collateral for a coke deal while he went back to Bogotá to raise the money. They spent three weeks in Medellín trying to track her down, three weeks with no help from the U.S. Consulate and with every effort at finding her an invitation to robbery. If still alive, she was nowhere to be found. The trail was totally cold.

As it was when they came back to look for Nicole, and O'Malley was sick enough with hatred actually to follow through on the vengeance he had planned. But Nicole, like Tawnee, had disappeared. Eventually, the memory of Tawnee and even of Nicole receded. He certainly did not often think of them during the presidential campaign. And now he was in the White House and Nicole was in town. It was not a prescription for the kind of quiet living he needed to engage in while he waited for his security clearance.

H is father was resplendent in a three-piece tailored suit, though it was taking forever to get him in his car. All his life, O'Malley thought, this was how expeditions were begun, whether it was to go up to Vermont to go skiing or to Tysons Corner for shopping at the mall. It seemed that doing something with his father more often than not was an overly equipped disaster, and there were moments such as this that he wondered how the nation's security could have survived his father's dawdling, putzing, and inability to follow routine instructions for something as innocuous as an electrical gadget. James Bond he most certainly wasn't.

"I'll be right there. You go start the car and get the heat going, will you," his father ordered him absentmindedly, and O'Malley, who was taking the afternoon off from work to appear before a District of Columbia magistrate on a charge of drunken driving, sighed and decided not to fight. He was too keyed up.

"Dad!" he called when his father appeared to be dawdling. It sure was cold, waiting in the driveway as the exhaust pumped visibly. In a moment his father was at the door, bundled up against the unexpectedly cold April day, carrying his briefcase as if it were the first day of school. Carmela saw him off with a final glare at O'Malley.

"Got everything?" he said to his father, as the old man let the dogs bound into the back.

"I believe so. Except for an apple."

"Excuse me?"

"You should always bring a judge a gift."

"You've spent too much time in the Third World, Dad," said O'Malley, and he was about to make a reference to the D.C. government when he decided against it. He didn't want to encourage his father.

They drove from M Street onto Pennsylvania Avenue, where pedestrians huddled against the arctic air. The window in the back of the Wagoneer was fogging up from the dogs' breath, so he turned on the rear defroster. Danny and Zippy were jumping around in the back as Peggy lay contentedly near the back of their seat.

"I'm going to South America, did I tell you?"

"No," said his father. "Where to?"

"Santiago, where Hardison's going to attend the new President's inaugural."

"Oh, God," said his father.

"As a matter of fact, while we're there, there's talk that he'll witness the new President's signing the extradition papers for that DINA agent who had Letelier bombed. Friend of yours, maybe?"

He looked over at his father, who stared impassively out the window.

"Then we go to Caracas, and he speaks before the Congress. And then, and you're going to love this, we stop in Managua for a ceremony for the normalization of relations."

"Oh, spare me this crap," said his father as they stopped on the corner of Seventeenth Street, before O'Malley hung a right. He would have had his father come meet him on this corner, except it was so bloody cold, and he didn't want to have his coworkers heading back to the White House after lunch ask him what he was doing there, and besides, he couldn't trust the old man to arrive on time. By taking the whole afternoon off and meeting him at the house, O'Malley at least could guarantee they'd get there.

It was when they turned left on E Street to pass between the Ellipse and the White House that his father turned to him and told him a rare story about his days with the CIA. It was when O'Malley was a child, and his father was spending a great deal of time in Venezuela as the country developed its immense resources and flirted with the anti-Americanism that would end with the nationalization of the oil fields.

"I'd had the opportunity to deal with President Rómulo Betancourt on a number of occasions, don't ask me in what capacity, and I was staying, as I always did, at the Avila, which is still my favorite hotel, when Betancourt arrived.

"You have to love South American style—it's not like ours at all, when it comes to the movement of a leader. I was standing in the lobby about to go out to dinner when in burst El Presidente's forward guards, brandishing machine guns and looking for all the world like they were about to assault the hotel. It could only be one person coming in, so I stood there and waited for Betancourt, who I think was coming in to have a tryst with an American mistress, if I recall right. So he walks in the lobby and he goes right through it and somehow he must have seen me because he stops and walks over to where I was standing.

" 'Señor O'Malley,' he says. 'I did not know you were in my country.'

"So I said, 'I've been here for three days, Señor Presidente.'

" 'Three days,' he says, 'and you did not come to visit me?'

"So, I said, 'Señor Presidente, you are a busy man, and I have been busy.' And he said, 'Señor O'Malley, when you are in Venezuela, I am never so busy that I can't see you, and you are never so busy that you can't see me.' "

And with that his father burst into laughter and all but slapped his thigh. "Isn't that wonderful?" he said, and O'Malley had to agree. What was wonderful was his father's mood, and his level of sobriety.

They had twenty minutes to make it to court as they continued down Pennsylvania Avenue once they'd picked it up again on Fifteenth Street. It had been over three months since the inaugural evening when he had tried to squeeze in a last night of revelry. They drove by the corner where his car had been stopped by the roadblock and he'd had his run-in with the D.C. cop. There were patches of frost on the windows in the back that had been clouded by the breath of the dogs.

They stopped at a light by the old Post Office Building, and O'Malley said, "We'll just make it," and it was then that Zippy, who'd appeared more than a little agitated the whole way, could be seen in the rear-view mirror lifting up his leg and pissing a steaming, visible yellow stream all over the rear window.

"Oh, goddamn that dog," O'Malley shouted as the light went green and he pressed his foot to the floor, only it was worse than he thought, because it was so cold out, and the window was so heated by the defroster from within, that the rear window suddenly shattered, causing all three dogs to leap toward the front of the car.

There was shattered glass like cut zircons everywhere in the back, on the dogs, on the carpeting that was ruined with dog hairs, anyway. Zippy looked mournful as a stream of cold air now flooded the Wagoneer and his father in the front seat burst out laughing.

"This isn't funny," O'Malley shouted at him, as he tried to drive with some semblance of control. The temperature in the car plummeted.

But his father was laughing, and he continued to do so even as O'Malley tried to wedge the Wagoneer into a space that would have challenged the driver of a compact. They had five minutes to make it and O'Malley was not happy about this at all. But his father was, and as he bade his dogs stay in the car, telling them if they froze it would be their own fault, he reminded O'Malley that the car, like the dogs, was his.

"Loosen up," he chided him, as they headed for the courthouse on foot.

ilbur Todd sat looking smug and Kit Bowles looked down at her shoes. She'd expected what was coming and there was nothing she wanted to say. Senator Partridge told them he wanted to broaden the advice he was getting from Todd and from Kit, but what he proposed, she realized, was to narrow his advice. He wanted a consensus, he said, which meant he wanted to marshal evidence one way or another to ease, if not eliminate, the necessity to choose. Since the two people he'd called in for help were Todd's chums, she knew what the verdict was likely to be, and for that reason she was all but mute.

"Drugs are clearly the way to go, and Wilbur's right, you need to attack the White House directly."

Thus, Jerry Jetta. The son of a former Iowa GOP bigwig, he had long since parlayed his father's connections in the first-in-the-nation caucus state into a media consultancy. His lucky break in having been born in a state whose political resonance overcame his mediocrity impressed some people, and Partridge was one. That it wasn't just Jetta, but every schoolchild in Iowa who had had the chance to sit on Reagan's knee, was a point that was lost on the Senator from Wyoming. He'd known Jerry's old man and was convinced not only that he was an impressive operator, but that the acorn did not fall far from the tree.

Kit also knew Jetta from Republican circles. He often had tried to hit on her at parties. From what she could tell, he was notable only for the brazenness of his shakedown style in the months leading up to the Iowa caucuses. There were rumors that he and his father were on all seven sides before the caucuses last time, and in each case they'd tried to persuade the candidates that they needed some savvy (and incidentally, expensive) local Indian guides, such as themselves, to maneuver through the shoals and rapids in the land of corn.

Jerry Jetta was physically remarkable, other than for his albino coloration, for such absence of fitness as bordered on amoebic bone structuring. He proved his conservatism by wearing both suspenders and a belt. He had come to the Senator's office offering his services within weeks of Partridge's arrival, and with Wilbur's encouragement, the Senator seemed to fall for his blandishments.

He'd soon begun bringing his buddy, Mike Humperdink, to sit in on the strategy sessions. Humperdink, who was as diminutive as Jetta was flabby, came wooing the new Senator with a slightly different pitch. Whereas Jetta was quite openly avaricious, displaying his Mercedes-Benz as verification of his having mastered the Washington consultant's racket, Humperdink wanted to *volunteer* to help Partridge raise money, arguing it was necessary if he planned to run for the seat to which he'd been appointed, and pointing out, slyly, that if he chose not to run, he could keep any money Humperdink raised for him, and spend it any way he desired.

Humperdink, who claimed distant relationship to Engelbert, the singer, had a track record of disrupting a number of campaigns, and Kit had collected the war stories. That he sat there nodding as Jetta went on about how ridiculous was the notion of carving out turf on "this cholesterol nonsense" made Kit hate him all the more.

"Jerry's right, Senator. Cholesterol's an issue for wimps."

Wilbur looked at her when five-foot, one-inch Humperdink said this, but she wouldn't give him the satisfaction of returning his gaze.

Instead she mused on what she knew about Mike Humperdink, not least of which being what she'd been told about the way he'd almost single-handedly sunk the electoral chances of Senator Dale Carey, who had once been thought of as the likely Republican nominee in the last presidential race, before his campaign went down in flames in New Hampshire.

From what she was told, Humperdink's M.O. was to suck up to candidates with his own nice-guy act, all the while proving his worth by raising money from a tried and true list of contributors from his home state of Maryland. After a while, the candidate would find him so suffocating, he'd order his campaign staff to give him something to do, anything at all, so long as it kept him too busy to hang out with the candidate. Once inside, he was like a computer virus, destroying not so much files as relationships and joie de vivre by his constant scheming for power, and if power within appeared to be beyond his reach, he would leak to the media well-documented, albeit doctored, tales of incompetence and corruption. Fisticuffs was the only threat he understood, but Kit was too disillusioned with Partridge to deck the little worm on the Senator's behalf.

Humperdink had run for Congress a couple of election cycles before this, and lost in a Republican district by the largest margin in its history, perhaps because of, not in spite of, a war chest that allowed him to beam his televised image into households two times more often than his opponent. He was trounced by the incumbent, a slippery polyester-clad deal-cutter who'd shrugged off a multiple-count indictment.

Perhaps the low point of his campaign was when, in the midst of the drug-testing frenzy in the August of that particular election year, he allowed network camera crews to follow him into the john where he tinkled his specimen, holding it up like it was a trophy before handing it to the doctors for testing.

Which now was one of the helpful suggestions he made to Partridge.

"Tony, it was like magic. I made network television by doing it."

"It was a great move," Jerry Jetta agreed.

"And it moved the polls dramatically. You ought to think about it when you make your charges, because you're going to have to show that your skirt's clean."

"Wait just a goddamn minute," Kit interjected. She hadn't meant to say anything. "What do you mean, it made the polls move dramatically?"

Humperdink turned to her slowly. He stared myopically through the glasses that covered half his face. "The polls," he declared with some little dignity, "moved dramatically." And then he turned back toward Partridge, who was sitting there looking a little frightened of Kit starting a fight with his new chums and advisers.

"From what to what?" she asked.

"Beg pardon?"

"What were the polls at before you took your drug test, what were they after, and for the record, what precisely was the margin of defeat in your race?"

"Kit," said Partridge.

"I just want to know, Tony."

"Okay," said Humperdink. "I was behind sixty–twenty with the rest undecided before the drug test, and afterward it went to sixty–twenty-five."

"Wow. Five points moved from the undecided column."

Humperdink sat there blinking.

"Five points in a close race is a lot, Kit," said Jetta.

"Yes, but this wasn't a close race, now was it. I don't think I heard what the final margin was, Mike."

"Ninetyonenine," Humperdink mumbled.

"Excuse me?"

"Ninety-one to nine," said Humperdink.

"At least he's run for office," Wilbur Todd now kicked in, staring at her. "He didn't learn about politics at the London School of Trigonomics."

"Fine," she said. "I just wanted to establish his bona fides as a political expert on the use of drug testing to win elections."

"Kit, your hostility is really unnecessary," Partridge was saying.

"I'm not hostile!" she said through clenched teeth.

"Maybe I should postpone a final decision on this," said Partridge.

She came within a centimeter of telling the Senator, "Did anyone ever tell you you're handsome when you're angry?"

I s the defendant represented by counsel?" asked the judge. She had seemed more than a little displeased to have had his father call out, "We're here, Your Honor," as they heard his case being called when they were just inside the door. The prosecutor seemed positively outraged.

"Your Honor, I am the defendant's counsel," his father now said, rather magisterially, if, O'Malley thought, a little breathlessly. They'd gotten lost inside the building and for a moment had dropped in on the wrong courtroom, where, to O'Malley's horror, a trial of a crack dealer who'd wiped out a whole schoolyard with an Uzi proceeded with such an absence of drama, one could have been forgiven for thinking they were in Small Claims Court. It had taken them a few minutes to discover they weren't in Traffic Court, either.

"How does the defendant plead?"

"Guilty, with an explanation, Your Honor," his father began, reading from a yellow notepad he'd snatched from his briefcase. "You see, Your Honor—"

"Wait, just a minute," she said, staring down at them as if O'Malley's father had just asked for a mistrial. "The defendant was arrested driving a vehicle at the corner of Pennsylvania Avenue and Thirteenth Street on January twentieth with a blood-alcohol level in excess of legal sobriety. I've got that part right, Counselor?"

"Yes, Your Honor, but—"

"And he was argumentative with a District of Columbia police officer, is that not correct?"

"Yes, Your Honor, but—"

"And he is now pleading guilty to this charge, is that not correct?"

"Yes, your Honor, but—"

"But what, Counselor?"

"But my son, er, the defendant, comes from a good home, if I do say so myself, and is currently employed at the White House, Your Honor . . ."

He didn't just say that. They were taking on water. Oh, God, he didn't just say that. On the way up the stairs he had meant to remind his father how frightened he was that his being on the White House staff would get into the papers, and now his father had just blurted it out.

"Counselor, I don't care if he's the President of the United States. He's pled guilty to a very serious charge. I sentence him to three months' suspended driver's license, which will be restored upon the successful completion of a three-month alcohol counseling course with a counselor to be chosen by the court. I hope he gets more help from that counselor than he has from this one. Case closed," she said, rapping her gavel against the block.

"This is an outrage," his father said as they began walking out of the courtroom.

"Shhh, Dad, it's fair enough," O'Malley said. While his father complained as he drove the whole frigid way home, O'Malley having reached for his new wallet and surrendered his newly replaced license to a Clerk of the Court, he prayed that Traffic Court was too insignificant for anyone at the White House or in the news media to have picked up word of his conviction.

ale moon arc across the obelisk, circular threat of snow. Kit murmured in her sleep as O'Malley sipped his tea and pulled on his shirt. The luminous numbers of his digital clock said naptime was over and it was time to go to dinner. At Globe. With Nicole.

"Are you off?"

"In a minute, yeah. You should sleep."

"No, if I don't get up now I'll wake up at three in the morning, raring to go."

"Want a cup of tea?"

"No, if I have a cup of tea I'll be up *until* three in the morning, raring to go. I have to go home in a little while."

"That sure was fun."

Her hand reaching out from underneath the covers. Fingers touching his. The moon cast his shadow over the bed as if he were to engulf her.

He missed her the moment he hit the street and wondered what it was he was doing spending a Saturday night having dinner with Nicole. Something said it could be surgical, discrete, an evening for renewing an acquaintanceship and shutting it off all at once. And then there was the voice powered by the bright winter moon above his shoulder that told him he was getting into something he'd best leave alone.

He'd been curious about Globe long before he knew David Nicole was its proprietor. In the former neighborhood hardware store with a steel garage door, they'd constructed a high-tech bar. When the weather was warm, on those few evenings when he'd been home early enough from the campaign to wander his neighborhood, the party had stretched through the open garage doorway onto the street. He hadn't realized there was a restaurant in the back, nor an upstairs dance floor, until he'd read about it in the *City Paper*. The only thing he'd paused to notice was that there seemed to be a disproportionate number of Middle Eastern gentlemen in attendance.

He asked the Chinese hostess to fetch Nicole and waited in the cusp between the restaurant in the back and the austere black chrome bar in the front. It was a rather un-Washington clientele. Washington was not a very hip city by any means; conformity, not individualism, is the trait of the nation's capital, a company town. It was unusual to see couples in Japanese designer wear, men with two days' growth of beard in thousand-dollar sports coats, and, especially, all these Arabs.

Over the bar was some kind of metal contraption, perhaps sculpture, though from the tiny pricks of light shining from it he suspected some functional utility. He was inspecting it when Nicole put his arm on his shoulder. "Welcome to the Globe."

"Hi, David."

"Hello, Thomas. Hungry?"

"Sure."

"I've told Nguyen and Dong that tonight we're showing off. Come upstairs. Tina wants to meet you."

"What's that over the bar?"

"The spaceship they used in *Blade Runner*."

"Cool."

"I thought you'd appreciate it." His lips separated in the smile that had warmed disciplinary tribunals all through their childhood, until his luck ran out. Though it must have had some effect on the judge, since Nicole had simply walked after being arrested for selling almost five keys of coke to federal agents.

"Your customers look like terrorists."

"They probably would, to someone who works in the White House. C'mon, we don't want to keep Tina waiting."

He followed Nicole to the front of the bar, and after his former friend had removed the velvet rope and stanchion, they headed up the stairs. They came out on a wide open space with a parquet floor, where a large empty bar was illuminated by a single flute of light. A solitary bartender was cleaning glasses and Nicole walked over to the bar and began noisily flicking switches.

A bandstand forty feet to their left suddenly became visible, as did columns of speakers surrounding it. With another flick, one entire wall came to life in a sea of blue, literally: it was a brightly colored map of Africa, surrounded by ocean. Another flick, another continent, this time South America. Europe emerged with a deliberate click. The States were in the rear near the men's room.

There were sofas around the room, and another rope and stanchion segregated a comfortable area O'Malley imagined was reserved for a D.C. hip elite the makings of which would be a mystery to him, though here they would likely be hand-chosen by Nicole.

"This," said Nicole, "is the playroom."

"It's everything a boy could want, David."

"Except a girl, and she's waiting. Follow me."

There was a passageway lined by cases of beer from Third World breweries, and box upon box of distilled liquor. Nicole opened a doorway rimmed by yellow light and they found themselves in a large, comfortable living room with zebra skins on the floor, a regulation pool table, leather couches, and a black dining-room table with leaves that extended it to groaning board potential. There was another bar, this one made of oak, next to a spiral staircase that descended somewhere below. Standing at it was the glamorous woman whom O'Malley had seen with Nicole at Primi Piatti that night.

"Tina, my oldest friend, Thomas O'Malley."

"How are you," she said, showing a mouthful of white teeth as she extended a long arm from out of a royal blue angora sweater the likes of which one was unlikely to see this side of a Brian Ferry album cover. She was wearing a pair of faded jeans, but it occurred to O'Malley that jeans might not ever have been so perfectly utilized before, that he was in the presence of the apogee of an American art form, and should treat this like a patriotic occasion.

"I'm impressed," said O'Malley. "With your nightclub."

"Thank you," she said demurely. They stood eye to eye and he kept her gaze locked, fearful that if he allowed his eyes to roam, it would be all over. He would betray a weakness on which Nicole would swoop like a fighter pilot. "We worked hard to get it to work. You wouldn't have believed what a dump this was just a few months ago."

"No, I would. I live in the neighborhood."

"Where do you live?" asked Nicole. "And what do you want to drink, by the way? I was thinking martinis."

"Not for me. I'll have a beer," he said brightly, thinking of the judge and the course on the ravages of alcohol to which he'd been sentenced.

"You think Hardison's going to be anything less than a disaster?"

"You think your restaurant's going to survive?" Hardison and his prospects were the only things O'Malley wanted less to discuss with Nicole than how close he lived to Globe, and to its owner's orbit.

"Tom. You've always had fight in you. Come, sit over here, make yourself at home. You're family, Thomas. It's been way too long." Nicole sat down on the couch near the pool table, patting its leather cushion. There was a commotion in the spiral staircase and Tina went over to it, where hands materialized, passing her a bowl of taco chips and salsa. She placed them on the dining table.

"I think Hardison's going to do okay, but then I would," said O'Malley. Having to be a shill for the administration in every social setting was tough enough. If he were a mechanic, he doubted he'd have to vouchsafe Mr. Goodwrench at every bowling tournament he played in. Discussing politics with Nicole made his spirits sag.

"The guy strikes me as something of a moralistic wimp. I can't believe he's going to normalize relations with Nicaragua just like that, nothing in return."

"When did you become a right-winger?"

"When did you become a speechwriter?"

"Not long ago, but I had my politics established well before then."

"Maybe my politics have been tempered by spending a little time in other countries. And it has made me suspicious of people like Hardison."

"Except when it comes to law and order."

"Thomas, to begin with, Hardison's no different on law 'n' order than the Republicans. He's for it. Secondly, look around you. I'm a businessman. I may not be the actual permittee here, predicate felons being unable to get liquor licenses even in the District of Columbia. But I'm a tax-paying businessman, and I could never have supported your candidate for president."

"What's he like?" Tina asked, coming over and leaning against the pool table.

He considered. For Tina, he would consider. "He's a great guy. I spent a lot of time with him on the campaign. I'm not going to pretend these days I sit around and rap with him, but I believe in him. That's important to me."

"Thomas comes from a rather cause-oriented family," Nicole said to Tina.

"You believe my old man?" O'Malley said laughing.

"It's great! All that time we thought he was just a foreign policy nerd."

"What's this?" asked Tina.

"Thomas's father was identified by the Select Committee on Intelligence Abuses as being a prime offender, having set up whole airlifts of illicit materiel to the contras."

"Hmm," she said, looking at him seriously. There was something about her that struck O'Malley as being perhaps just a little bit overly carnivorous. But he liked her. "Excuse me," she said, and went over to the spiral staircase, which she descended.

Nicole leaned back in the couch with his beer resting upon his baggy wool pants. He looked prosperous in his expensive shirt, buttoned all the way to his neck in a style that on Harry Truman had been gauche, but on him looked hip. There clearly was some serious money behind this venture, and where it came from, O'Malley could only guess.

"So what do you think?" he asked.

"I think she's incredible."

"I mean the restaurant, but I see how your mind works. You're dating above yourself as well. I can't believe Kit's working for that doofus, though I guess the trustees of Smith College are relieved."

"Okay. The *restaurant*'s magnificent, David. You've got a good thing going here."

"I've got a good thing going with Tina. We met in Sinaloa two years ago."

"I can't imagine what you were doing there."

"Not what you think. At least probably not precisely what you think. She was with this bad-ass who treated her like his bauble. She gave up everything when she left him for me, but now she's given me everything I've got. She's tamed me. She's made me healthy. I subscribe to the Berkeley Wellness Letter. I eat oats."

"I'm pleased to hear it." He was. He felt his opposition to his old friend crumbling. There were eighteen years of friendship preceding what went wrong, though when it had gone wrong, it had gone very wrong.

"I'm proud of you, making it to the White House. That's a big step up from, what was it you were doing the last time I saw you?"

"Bartending."

"Smokestack's Lightning on West Broadway."

"Right. I quit the day after I witnessed three Chinese kids shoot an old man in the street right in front of it. I called UVa. the next day and told them I'd be attending law school after all."

"Jesus, a lawyer, in the White House. Who would have thought you'd go legit."

"And are you?"

"Legit?"

"Yeah."

"Mostly. I dabble. Tina keeps good track of me. I'm only allowed to get out of hand on Saturdays near the end of the month when the moon is full. You know what that means?"

"No."

"Tonight's the night."

"Not for me, David. I'm so boring these days it bores me."

"We'll see."

"No, we won't, David."

"We'll see," said Nicole.

he elevator doors opened on the fifth floor of *The Washington Post* building and the two weary Metro reporters stepped in. Cale McTeague and Steven Bronstein stood in the fluorescence as the elevator descended, brains numb from haggling, their Saturday shot from reporting and writing, but excited at the prospect of a page-one story in the Sunday paper.

It had started on Friday when the news desk received a tip from D.C. Traffic Court that a White House employee had just pleaded guilty to Driving While Under the Influence. This alone was reason to scamper down there to find out who it was. That the luckless speechwriter was represented in court by the notorious CIA bagman and *agent provocateur*, Robert O'Malley, added spice to thin Metro section gruel. That said convicted White House speechwriter, Thomas O'Malley, was the son of the spook lawyer, gave them an interesting angle. That he was the speechwriter who, according to political reporters, was responsible for having written Hardison's statement condemning drunk driving as the candidate extended his publicity bonanza at that twin disaster two summers before in Iowa gave them a rare opportunity to argue for a front-page story.

When Steve Bronstein had reached Thomas O'Malley at the White House the day before, he'd been inclined to drop the piece. In fact, he couldn't be sure, but he may have led O'Malley to believe that was exactly what he was going to do. He'd been moved by O'Malley's argument that he hadn't been on the White House staff when he'd been arrested, and that while he regretted his actions and knew they were wrong, it had happened on a evening for celebrating the culmination of two years' work.

"What arc you, some kind of wimp?" McTeague asked him when he mentioned his inclination to give the guy a break. And McTeague, he realized, had been right.

"Look," he'd argued with his editor, "Hardison used drunk driving as an issue in his campaign. This guy, O'Malley, wrote the statement that made it an issue. He was represented in court by a very shady lawyer, who just happens to be his father. I smell a rat."

Bronstein nudged him.

"We smell a rat," McTeague repeated. "Don't forget, Watergate started as a second-rate burglary."

They'd been given their shot, and they'd spent the day reporting and writing, managing to fill twenty inches on O'Malley's having been a bartender, on the use of the new sobriety as a political issue, and had given the usual run of political commentators an opportunity to defend or pile on, depending on where they sat. White House press secretary Mike McCurry had said that the President did not know about the conviction and would not comment on it. On background he'd tried to kill the story, but the argument that boys will be boys didn't cut it with McTeague.

The elevator deposited them in the lobby. For a moment they stood on Fifteenth Street as the full moon shone above the Madison Hotel.

"Pleasure doing business with you, Steve."

"Yeah, you too, Cale," said Bronstein, though he wasn't so sure whether they'd been completely fair to the poor bastard, who seemed like a nice enough guy on the phone.

"This could be our ticket out of Metro, you know," McTeague said, as if sensing his partner's discomfort.

"I know," said Bronstein with a grin.

he had the keys in her hand and was about to lock the door when Kit heard O'Malley's phone start ringing. She might have left if she hadn't thought that maybe Tom was cutting dinner short and wanted to get together with her.

"Hello," she said.

"White House operator for Mr. O'Malley."

"Who at the White House is calling?"

"It's William Tiswell calling," said the pert voice of the operator. "Is Mr. O'Malley there?"

"He's not, and I don't know how to reach him. Is there a message?"

"Hold, please."

Then, after a thirty-second delay in which she tried to imagine what the White House could possibly want from O'Malley at this time of night on a Saturday, a harshly obnoxious voice came over the line.

"Who's this?" it asked.

"Who's this?" she said firmly.

"It's Bill Tiswell. Where's O'Malley? Out drinking?"

As a matter of fact, she thought, he is. Instead she said, "He isn't here, but I can leave him a message."

"Tell him he needs to read tomorrow's *Post,* and he needs to call me when he does so. Preferably tonight. I'm at the White House."

"Does he have the number?" she asked innocently, but Tiswell had already hung up.

homas O'Malley, who had intended a perfunctory social call with dinner thrown in for good measure, sat with the heel of his palm propping up his jaw. Nicole had just sprayed part of a second magnum of champagne in an arc that had creased the pool table. Nicole giggled.

Dinner had been wondrous, O'Malley admitted, though he would never get used to the fad of putting flowers in a salad. By now the stir-fried swordfish Tina had served on blue corn tortillas had settled agreeably, though his stomach swelled on a rising tide of champagne bubbles. O'Malley giggled too.

"What the hell is that?" he perked up and spat out as the strange sounds of a band gently rocked into the room. "Is that samba music?"

"Sure is," said Nicole, a little tipsy from the champagne and having trouble with the weight of the magnum and the accuracy that pouring required.

"What happened to rock 'n' roll?"

"Nothing happened to it that I know of, but we play World music here: Afro-pop, salsa, samba . . ."

"Bulgarian folk music?"

"As a matter of fact."

"You mean, I don't have to go to South America to hear this crap, I can just walk up the street."

"Oh," said Nicole. "You're going on that trip to South America."

"Yeah, David, the first time I've had to go there in years." He was in a good mood, he was liking Nicole, and especially, his friend Tina. But the opportunity had presented itself, though Nicole wisely ignored it. O'Malley's remark cast a shadow across the table.

Though not for long. "It's a Saturday night."

"You said that already, David."

"And Tina has a treat for us," he said as Tina already began unfolding a small plastic bag in which O'Malley could see a dirty gray chunk of what looked like the old rock.

"I don't do coke anymore, David. Champagne is fine."

"Why not? Start chopping, Tina."

"I just don't do it anymore, David."

"Because you work in the White House?"

"That has something do with it, but not everything. I just don't. Don't push me." He was tempted, but not overmuch. The sense of well-being, the confidence, he missed. But not the urge to overdo, the lack of control, the dilemma between putting all the logs on a fire at once and basking in its blaze, or the strategy of placing small logs on, one at a time. Either way, the fire raged and when it was over you felt a coldness that was worse than merely cool, it was the absence of heat you desired in ways that undermined you. He did not need it. No thanks.

"That's fine, no problem," said Nicole, though Tina had cleared a space in front of her and was shaping two thick lines as Nicole pulled out a silver tooter. He leaned over near her, his shoulder resting against hers, and quickly scarfed up the blow that she'd chopped.

"Because I was thinking, Thomas, that you're in a very special position."

"That's right, I'm vulnerable."

"Not vulnerable," Nicole said sharply, picking up his stem of champagne. "Omnipotent. You could do great things. You could make both of us rich."

"What are you talking about?"

"South America."

"I don't get it." He sat looking at his friend's cheeks pulse in the swallowing motion, though nothing was going down his throat. That was some line he'd just snorted, and he couldn't imagine Nicole doing anything but the best.

"Your bags don't get checked," Tina said calmly, and then dipped her nose to the tooter.

"You just get on Air Force One and fly to Andrews Air Force Base. No customs, either leaving Venezuela or landing in the States."

"And you could get fifteen, twenty keys easy in a laptop case, presuming that's what you use."

"You two have presumed a fuck of a lot already, I'll tell you," he said, throwing down his napkin.

"Thomas, don't be upset. We're businessmen. And you and I are old friends. And you owe me."

"Owe you? I don't owe you anything other than the bill for this meal, which I want, right now, please." He stood now as Nicole leaned back in his chair, thoroughly relaxed from the cocaine. Tina was staring at him with a face he suddenly realized was more than carnivorous. As beautiful as she was, her face bordered on cannibalistic.

"You owe me for the way I covered for you, for your interest in our business."

"You've gotta be fucking kidding me, David. What did I get out of it? I sold the occasional lid you left around the room when you weren't there. I got some spare change out of the deal, spending money. But I wasn't your partner, you can't give me that shit. I don't owe you. Jesus Christ. What about Tawnee? You left her with a bunch of cocaine cowboys. You just left her there, she's dead, or worse, and you say I owe you? I can't believe what an asshole you are." He said this last linc quietly.

He was standing with his hands squeezing the chair that he'd been sitting in, and he didn't know what he would do with it. Tina sat there as calmly as if they were discussing mutual funds. But Nicole now leaned forward, engaged.

"Thomas, there's no risk."

"I don't care. I'm not doing it."

"You're very vulnerable, you're right. There are all sorts of news organizations that would love to find out a speechwriter for our pro-hibitionist President once was nearly indicted for selling drugs."

"First of all, I was never almost indicted."

"You don't know how close you came. Apache could have made you easily for all the times you were in the room. You could have been part of a conspiracy, but I protected you."

"Are you trying to blackmail me, David, or what?"

"I prefer the 'or what.' "

"Fuck you, David. Don't call or write, and I'll see my way out."

With that, he turned and walked swiftly for the door. He heard Nicole shouting behind him, but then the door was open and the loud sound of a bad samba band was coming from the dance floor. The club by now was packed with college students, hipsters in sports jackets, women in miniskirts he bet they did not wear to their government offices, though they probably didn't work in government offices: everyone here seemed part of an alternative D.C. He wasn't thinking about anything other than getting out of there as swiftly as possible, and given the amount of champagne he'd been drinking, he bounced off people effortlessly. He tumbled down the stairs as couples were making their way up them, and he didn't mind that people had to flatten themselves against the railing in order to get out of his way. After this evening he didn't think anything would surprise him again, though he had a dim sense of remorse at being so stupid he hadn't seen this coming, hadn't remem-bered what Nicole was really like. But he was surprised when he got to the bottom of the stairs, surprised to see Kit standing there looking miserable, her eyes darting around at the entrance of the bar as if she were looking for someone. It was amazing. Downstairs was crawling with guys with leather pants and chains around their necks, men who would have looked at home in the Oman Hilton. They were staring at Kit somewhat hungrily. "Kit," he said loudly and there was relief in her eyes when she saw him. He noticed she was carrying a thick Sunday *Washington Post.*

T hey were sitting in Katherine Tierney's sunny living room when Will Ames's little girl upchucked on the couch, and the commotion left talk of O'Malley's woes far, far behind. Colin Denholm was there, along with his prim and proper wife, and Katherine, whose new boyfriend was the Deputy White House Counsel, was making breakfast tacos in her gleaming kitchen. They could have been any cluster of Bloody Mary–drinking suburbanites, except one of them had his arrest photos arrayed on the front page of the paper as if he were on the lam and you just might spy him, cold-eyed and foul of breath, while you waited in line for your packet of stamps.

"Are you okay, sweetie?" Kit Bowles was asking, and the little girl was shaking her head.

"Quit your barfing, Mary," said Will's tough farm-girl wife, wrenching their daughter off the floor and rocking her in her arms. The girl may have been about to behave, may have been on the verge of qualifying for polite society, but such was the construction-worker wrench with which she was picked up, she now began to wail. If Will's wife had a lasso, she would have roped the girl in and lashed her to the leg of the dining-room table, that much was clear.

Will didn't even bother to look sheepish, as if this sort of behavior was to be tolerated, like that of a boorish teenager with high SAT's. He just sat in Katherine's recliner and drained his Bloody Mary. He made no motion to clean up the mess, and neither did Madge, his bouncer of a wife. Seeing that otherwise it would not get done, O'Malley wandered into the kitchen and returned with a dish towel with which to gently clean the dark green leather of Katherine's quite elegant couch. It was that kind of a morning.

The brunch had long been scheduled, though he'd planned on passing it up. But having read about himself on the front page of the *Post*, the notion of being with his friends and colleagues seemed attractive to the point of necessity. Having refused to return Bill Tiswell's phone call last night, he would need Katherine's protection at work the next morning. So he came, prodded by Katherine's 7:00 A.M. phone call. Her checking in on him ostensibly was to commiserate, though he detected an underlying urgency. She questioned him—grilled him, is how he put it to Kit—about whether or not this was something that as his boss, she would need to dust off her old sociology texts to get a handle on. "You don't have a drinking problem, do you?" And O'Malley, who had not had a great evening, scraped off whatever it was that coated his tongue and croaked into the phone, "Of course not."

Now here they were in her Cleveland Park home, which looked dumpy on the outside, but which inside perfectly reflected her personality. It was a little prissy, and ordered in a thoroughly adult fashion, yet while not exactly colorful, there was the odd discordant element— in this case, the long nude above the fireplace, resembling, it had to be admitted, Katherine in a younger day. Anyone who'd ever seen her in jogging shorts could identify that haunch.

"Help yourself, everyone," Katherine now announced above the din of Will's wailing little girl. O'Malley was prepared to ignore Madge unless she hit the kid, and then he was going to drop-kick her out the back door to the tiny garden. If he drowned her in the bird feeder's solitary inch of brackish water, he didn't think Will would mind.

Kit, who had been up early while O'Malley slept away his troubles, stood in line for the tortillas with Rod Gardener, Katherine's new boyfriend. Hunger was the only thing that would have brought her into any kind of line with him. He was tall and pompous, with a jaw carved by some comic from a sketch of Dudley Dooright, and he was more than a little impressed with his position. "Nice to meet you, son," is how he'd greeted O'Malley, who may have been older than he was, when they entered Katherine's house. "You're in a heap of trouble."

For now the Deputy White House Counsel was silently intent on filling up his plate while the rest of the guests were so foolish as to dawdle. Had Katherine not reached across the table and tapped his hand with a spoon encrusted with egg yolk, he might have scarfed up the contents of a bowl that was meant for the nine of them.

"Wait a minute," said O'Malley in amazement. "So you're the guy," he said to Gardener.

The Deputy White House Counsel stood at the head of the table for a moment and paused to face his accuser, although not without taking one large frayed twist of almond pastry and stuffing it into his mouth. "What," smack, smack, "guy?" he said with a very graphic exposition of mammalian chewing patterns. Between his eating habits and the eruption of the little girl, Kit thought she would just stick to the Bloodies.

"I've been in the mess behind you. You're the guy who wipes out the salad bar, aren't you?"

Gardener's eyes moved slowly back and forth. "I didn't know jailbirds had mess privileges," he said haughtily.

But it was true, O'Malley was certain. He was in the presence of the mystery man who depleted the salad bar within moments of the White House mess's doors opening for lunch. He'd seen him at one of the circular tables, mauling the lazy Susan, but he'd never connected him with the panic in the eyes of the Filipino waiters. He'd always assumed that the salad bars were wiped out by a crowd, and that the waiters were made nervous by Chief of Staff Harold Whitney and his yellow-tied janissaries, not by this six-foot-four terror of All You Can Eat nights at the local Howard Johnson's.

Their plates full, even Will's daughter had reclaimed her sea legs and sat on the rug pulling an almond pastry this way and that. Colin had not said a word, and his wife seemed more reticent than he. They were dressed for church in the Assembly of God parish they attended someplace out in one of the Virginia satellite communities, and had arrived from there with Will and his family. However, where Will was dressed in the same suit he wore to work at least three days a week, and Madge was in a not unstylish combo, Colin's wife, Dorothy, dressed in what looked like a black smock that had some kind of a doily stitched around the neck.

The talk turned, as was usual these days, to the latest machine gun murders in the crack wars of D.C. O'Malley's drunken episode shared the front page with what was becoming an ordinary sight: body bags at a junior high, in this case, a picture of four children in Southeast who'd been mowed down in a crossfire while they innocently shot not smack but hoops. Hoops in a weekend playground.

"There was a body found in the woods behind our home in Burke," was the first thing Colin had said since he walked in the door.

"Drug-related," his wife pronounced with wide-eyed certainty. In her Grant Woods getup, you had the feeling that drug-related killings were an abstraction whose recent introduction to her exurban neighborhood had the psychological effect of a world closing in.

"You ever read the crime report in the *Post* on Thursdays?" Kit now was asking. "It's horrifying. I wish I hadn't discovered it was in there, 'cause now I find myself looking forward to it, which is pretty sick, don't you think?"

"I read about a crime in the paper today," said Rod Gardener, a smirk on his face as he stared at O'Malley. Katherine went, "Rod," and then Will, who'd downed a couple of Bloodies, jumped in.

"The randomness of violence is a precursor to the Apocalypse. These are signs, unmistakable, clear, easy for anyone to see, if we choose to."

It was, in fact, a sign of the times that no one corrected him. It was a sign of the times that the Deputy Counsel to a Democratic President of the United States now said, "There's nothing happening in the District of Columbia that the death penalty for dope dealing wouldn't cure."

"Rod!" Katherine now said with vehemence. "You think some child of the underclass who turns to drugs and supports himself and his habit by selling crack or whatever should be murdered by the State for his actions? 'Cause if you do, I'm going to have to wonder what you're doing working for this President." She was a strict guardian of the President's conscience, at least as expressed through the words he used; she had not been heard previously by any of them to have extended that concern to personnel policies, or to her boyfriends. The implication was she was going to have to wonder more what she was doing sharing her bed with him than what it was he was doing in his position at the White House.

"I don't think there's anything wrong with the District of Columbia that a strong dose of order couldn't cure."

They looked at each other as if there were a Republican in their midst. Kit looked back at each face as if to say, Don't look at me.

"That's interesting, Rod," said O'Malley. "I'm not certain I disagree with you, but you raise an interesting point. Here all of us came of age in a time when drugs were tolerated, okay? And here we are with an epidemic of lawlessness and murder. And the most recent Republican administration had a policy of 'maximum intolerance' toward drug use. Yet, and I'm just thinking aloud here, I'd bet that all of us at the very least have friends who used to, oh, you know, smoke the occasional joint. What do you think the White House's position ought to be with regard to our pasts? I mean, how long should we be judged for, say, our actions in college?"

"Forever," said Gardener.

"You're kidding," said Will, who among them might be suspected of vying with Colin for the most upright existence. "I did a lot of things B.C. I don't do now, but I don't think they have relevance to my present behavior or to the job I can do for this President."

"B.C.?" Katherine asked.

"Before Christ," said Madge, smugly.

"The slate's wiped clean when you're born again," Will said with evident relief.

"The White House sets a tone, or is supposed to," pronounced Rod

Gardener as if they all were stupid for even bringing this up. "I don't think it should countenance immoral behavior." He was again staring at O'Malley.

"Nor do I," said O'Malley directly. "But we're not talking about behavior while we're employed there. We're talking about *past* behavior."

"All right," said Gardener. "Should we allow an embezzler to work at Treasury? A murderer at Justice?"

"Of course not," said Colin, perking up and taking this seriously. "But Tom's point's different. We don't look at drug use the same way today that we did in the sixties and seventies, partly because the results keep showing up on the eleven o'clock news in footage of ambulances leaving the scene of a murder. What he's asking is whether the things we did in a different environment are to be held against us today."

"I would have been sitting on the edge of my seat waiting for old Rod here's answer if we had had this conversation last week," said Will with a smile. "But my FBI clearance came Friday."

"It did?" asked O'Malley. "I wonder when mine's coming. I don't even know if they've started it."

"They've started it," said Gardener.

"I haven't been told whether I've passed," said Colin.

"I wouldn't worry about it," said Katherine. "Mine hasn't come yet either. Though this whole subject scares the hell out of me, not so much because of drug use as politics. Sitting for ten minutes in a meeting with Communists could have ended up haunting you for the rest of your life not so long ago. And Jesus, when I was in college, I sat in some meetings the minutes of which would probably get me fired if I didn't first die of embarrassment. Now I wonder whether being identified as having sat back then in a room where a joint was passed could have the same effect on my job as being identified in rooms with Bernadette . . ." She looked at Rod Gardener. Her own boyfriend. "With some of the kooks I used to know."

"Well, since none of us have to worry about any of these things . . ." Will chimed in to laughter from everyone but O'Malley, Kit, and Rod Gardener.

"O'Malley wants to know the answer to this question because he was arrested on the very day before he came to work," Gardener said like a chess player savoring checkmate.

"That *is* cutting it a little close, Tom," said Colin.

"No, I'm asking," he said as the phone rang, "because I wonder about our generation's assuming positions in government. There are real questions about what constitutes acceptable behavior in a particular environment, and how that behavior is viewed . . ."

"Tom, it's for you," said Katherine from the kitchen. "It's the Signal operator."

O'Malley felt his cheeks flush. Gardener was studying him. White House Signal had tracked him down here, which must mean someone important was looking for him. He doubted someone needed a speech. There were only a couple of possibilities as to who it could be. He rose as unself-consciously as he could to go take the phone from Katherine's hand. They all made as if they weren't interested in who it was, all except Gardener, who stared at O'Malley as he walked to the kitchen.

"Mr. O'Malley?"

"Yes, this is he."

His cheeks hot, he waited for whoever it was who was calling. He suspected he knew.

"Hold for the President."

Oh, God, not here. He moved into the kitchen as far from the crowd as he could get, and he fell in love with Kit all over again when in the time it took for the President to come on the line, she began tickling Will's little girl, and loud shrieks of joy covered the sound of his conversation with the President of the United States.

om Donilon, a partner in the law firm for which O'Malley had worked, was as busy as O'Malley was, so over breakfast at the Art Gallery Grill he delivered just the relevant facts.

"I had a visit from an FBI agent today."

"Oh."

"Sleazy sonofabitch. He wanted to know whether you were loyal to the United States of America."

"And what did you say?"

"Don't worry, I covered for you. He asked if you'd shown hostility to any ethnic or racial group. I told him you seemed less than enthusiastic about the Nation of Islam. Anyway, he seemed principally to be interested in whether, when you were an associate here, we saw signs of drug or alcohol abuse. I told him you seemed pretty normal to me, that we'd closed a couple of bars together in our time, but that no one here thought there was any kind of problem."

"You saw the *Post*, I suppose."

"Oh, yeah, sure, and so had Special Agent Bryce. My advice to you?"

"Yeah."

"Get to all the people you can think of who might be contacted by them and make certain that no one, no one at all, even hints that there might be a problem . . ."

"There isn't a problem . . ."

"Hey, I know that, pal. Just make certain that everybody sings off the same choir sheet. Remember, these FBI reports tend to be unanalyzed trash bags of innuendo. And Tom?"

"Yeah, Tom." After having been called in to see the Chief of Staff, he didn't have much humor for advice.

"If you have any skeletons out there rattling around, slam the door on them tight."

"I appreciate it," he said, though the thought that sprang to mind was just how wide that entranceway was to David Nicole's restaurant just up the hill on Eighteenth Street.

 here were many ways to think of the White House—the home of the President, the center of power, a building as symbolic as a wedding cake—but O'Malley chose to think of it as a campus. His having been called in to see Harold Whitney was less a visitation upon his boss than a summoning to meet with the headmaster.

He'd had to wait in the West Wing lobby like any other visitor to the White House. But that was okay, there were worse places to wait. Because President Hardison was a New Yorker, arrayed upon the colonial coffee tables were the *Daily News* and the *New York Post*, papers that probably had not graced this particular room during previous administrations. He was trying to stay calm, and in fact did not think there was much to worry about, in that the conversation he'd had over the phone with the President the day before found him concerned, non-judgmental, and actually rather kind about the predicament O'Malley was in. But it was nervous-making being called in to see Whitney, especially when everyone he'd seen in the Old Exec this morning had stared right through him like he wasn't there, like they did not expect to see him around the White House much longer after the coverage in the Sunday *Post*.

He liked being in the White House, found that for all the inherent tension of being privileged to work there, there was a beauty to it, a patriotic grace that felt like a reward. No matter what was to happen with Whitney, he felt cheered by his surroundings. So he reached over and picked up the *New York Post* and found his equanimity was a shattered conceit. This must be what it's like to be President, he said to himself. You can't even pick up the paper.

"HARDISON AIDE'S PARTY HARDY: Speechwriter's Words Come Out Slurred." After the headline, the story was something of a disappointment, a slightly incoherent rewrite of what *The Washington Post* already had. He was in the midst of it when Whitney's receptionist entered the lobby and coldly bade him walk the plank to the Chief of Staff's office.

"Thomas, sit down, sit down," said Whitney affably when he walked into the room. He was grateful he'd thought to wear his most starched white shirt, his most inoffensive rep tie, his shiniest tie shoes underneath his grayest suit. The only thing that might be wrong with the way he organized himself sartorially is it matched the way Whitney was dressed, to the regimental stripe. "Glad to see you're dressing better," said Whitney, as he motioned him to one of the facing Hepplewhites. When O'Malley sat down in his, Whitney alighted regally, like he was prepared for a photo op. Still, it was a more pleasant gathering than the last time he'd been called there.

Within a minute, the hard-faced assistant who'd been his Sherpa to the heights of such power reentered the room with a tray on which there were two cups of coffee along with a creamer and a sugar bowl with the Great Seal of the United States. He all but cooed in thanks. This was the full treatment. Whitney was looking like a tolerant uncle.

"The President and I spoke about your . . . situation," he began delicately. O'Malley nodded and went, "Uh huh."

"He's very fond of you, you know."

"I know."

"Thinks you're very talented."

"I'm honored."

Whitney looked at him as if he were crazy, or at least a kid who didn't know the value of the President of the United States taking an interest in him. He looked at O'Malley with what could only be wonder, as if he didn't realize the significance of the White House Chief of Staff, and not just some toady, actually going out of his way to be concerned for him. "The President wants to do what's best for you, which means, unfortunately, there are some questions I need to ask you."

He thought, Uh oh, though he said, "Shoot."

"God knows," Whitney said with a chuckle, "there've been some moments when I've gotten behind the wheel when I shouldn't have. There was this one time leaving Bohemian Grove . . . , well, that doesn't matter, I guess." He blinked and looked confused, as if being avuncular with staff did not come naturally. It was uncertain whether chumminess was required of him, one more of the behavioral booby traps he'd been either dodging or walking into since he moved to Washington.

He was a striking man whose most notable features were his silver hair and eyebrows, and there was an element of competence to him such that when he gave you his full attention, it was clear he was capable of understanding what you were telling him, even if this was so outside of his ken as to qualify for the vagaries of life. And he didn't much like the vagaries of life, that much was apparent. He now fixed O'Malley with the same gaze he reserved for Pentagon generals who dreamed of death rays disguised in acronyms, scientists researching AIDS. It was the gaze he'd learned to reserve for senators whose petty wish list of White House goodies ought to have been met with the kind of scorn Whitney once had meted out to recalcitrant mailroom clerks, but which now were accorded with the flexible respect that went along with this crazy turf God alone had ceded to him as part of his destiny. He'd seen it all, Whitney had, and it was worth it when measured by the dollars he had made and the power he'd accrued, but that didn't mean he had to enjoy meeting with the likes of O'Malley. To his credit, he gave the kindness the President had devolved unto him really his very best shot.

So he adjusted his cuffs with their presidential links—he would not take his jacket off in his own office out of respect for the building they were in—and decided to bore in.

"The President wants to know if you have a drinking problem."

"He asked me that yesterday and I told him I did not." This was the part where he felt like he was in the headmaster's office. Admit nothing, deny everything, the schoolboy credo, only in this case what he was telling Whitney was the truth.

"If I may ask," said Whitney with a delicacy that had developed very late in life, perhaps in the last few minutes, "how then is it you were arrested for driving while under the influence?"

"It's one of those things. I shouldn't have been driving, but it *was* the night of the inaugural. It is not a condition I either find myself in with more than the customary rhythms, nor do I drive drunk. I've told this to the President."

"You understand what the rules of behavior for the White House staff are, don't you?"

"Actually that's something I don't exactly know." He sipped his coffee and stared over the cup at Whitney, who was doing his utmost to be stern and understanding all at once, and you could tell from the way one eyebrow crushed down like a caterpillar jogging toward his nose that stern understanding was a personal oxymoron to the Chief of Staff, like bland exuberance.

"Well, there's something in the regs somewhere about it, I can't remember exactly what, though I suppose I could have Bill Tiswell look it up . . ."

"I'm happy to take your interpretation, sir. Whatever you think is fair. I mean, whatever it is you and the President want," he said, slightly emphasizing the word "president" as if to rub in the fact that Hardison had called him personally to offer his concern.

"We want you to go into treatment, to begin with."

"And I am, already. I have to do it to fulfill the terms of the court."

"Good," said Whitney, and he seemed lost as to what came next. He looked a little panicked, as if this were the moment he would have relied on good staff work for the second condition and there was no good staff around. "And, well, no more embarrassments to the President of any kind. Do I make myself clear?"

He didn't, but O'Malley threw up his hands like a surrendering prisoner. He wasn't certain what "embarrassments of any kind" entailed exactly—the definition could stretch from a phrase in a speech the media jumped on to a full exegesis of his life—but he knew, in Whitney's terms, what the bottom line was. He couldn't afford such drama as a parking ticket. He was on double, secret probation.

I t was the week the Senate seemed to stay in session for bloody ever, a week when frayed nerves and bags under eyes had the whole place a little spooked. Kit Bowles waited one afternoon in the entrance to Senator Partridge's office, the receptionists and two caseworkers whose desks were near the doorway waiting at full alert. "Here he comes," said Kit excitedly, and within a moment Mike Humperdink, whose most memorable campaign tactic was to pee into a bottle for doctors to examine, had entered the office, along with his balding chum, Jerry Jetta.

It was precisely on cue that Kit, Cheri, Shirley, Debby, and Dotty all raised their small specimen bottles and swiftly drank down the apple juice they had in there, and then, in a fashion they'd practiced, went, "Ahhhh," in satisfaction. Jerry Jetta looked like he thought they were crazy, but Humperdink had the perfect response. He just gulped.

W hen the Secret Service agent who normally joshed with him on his way out the door would barely acknowledge his smile and wave, O'Malley knew it would be a while until things settled back to normal. If ever they would. Usually as chipper leaving work as he was arriving in the morning, he wandered up Connecticut Avenue like a kid who'd lost his dog in a flood. Things had gone from bad to worse when the President himself had returned through the interoffice mail a speech O'Malley had written with a note in the President's inimitable scrawl at the top: "Doesn't anyone back there have a sense of humor?" That the President did not, this week at least, may have been attributable to the brouhaha up the Hill. That it was O'Malley who had received the rather rare lash from the President was a sign, he was convinced, of just how far his star had fallen.

He hadn't seen Kit since the brunch. He'd needed to, but the battle over the new President's new Commerce Secretary—she'd gotten on the wrong side of the animal rights movement—had degenerated into the kind of choreographed drama that had senators baying endlessly into the night, wearing their best ties in case they got face time on TV, and otherwise behaving like they were on the set of "Masterpiece Theatre," when at best what they were doing would qualify for a tawdry miniseries with the usual ingredients: power, infidelity, and Jane Seymour.

He was numb through this particular minuet, not only because of his own travails, but because his work load had piled up. He'd made his mark with tragedy, that emphatic hug Hardison had given to the victims of the Spirit Lake disasters almost two summers before, and so naturally it was O'Malley who conjured up official grief on behalf of the administration whenever they were called upon to lend a sorrowful shoulder to anything more dramatic than a three-car pileup on the interstate. Plane crashes he had down cold, especially ones that involved famous youngsters: spelling-bee champs, skaters, child stars. He was particularly adept at fires, tornadoes and storms. That this week there were children who drowned in wells, an explosion on an oil platform, and a terrorist attack at an overseas servicemen's club kept him busy but did not improve his mood.

So he wandered through Dupont Circle on his way home, a little too preoccupied for the younger bums cadging quarters to even attempt to bother. And what was on his mind wasn't how much trouble he was in at the White House. It wasn't on the size and shape of the doghouse that may as well have been constructed on the White House lawn, so publicly did he feel his current disgrace. It was on David Nicole, as it had been all week, and the question of whether his attempt at blackmail was Nicole's best shot, or just the opening round in a game of chicken, in which Nicole would attempt to get what he wanted, and either succeed or inflict pain, up to and not excluding death. This was not a joke. It had been years since he'd seen David in action, but he had always had a single-mindedness to him, not to mention a craftiness about how to achieve his ends, that made anyone discounting him an eventual loser in their run-ins. Nicole was a serious person about the things he wanted, not to be trifled with. He'd long since had his Marquis of Queensberry rule book dropped in a back-alley dumpster. And O'Malley couldn't even guess what Nicole had been willing to do to achieve his ends in the intervening years since he'd last seen him.

The success of Globe, Nicole's newly elegant style of dress, the brazenness of his blackmail attempt: all this bespoke Nicole's having crossed a line somewhere. Sometime in the last few years he'd forged beyond mere manipulativeness and into the territory of professional criminality. O'Malley was as sure of this as he was scared by it.

He tended to doubt Nicole would give up on his blackmail attempt, especially since he'd clearly already calibrated the profit at stake. Getting O'Malley to smuggle back a bucket of coke must have seemed to Nicole to be an obvious and easy accomplishment. There was nothing the White House or reporters or anyone else could do to him that matched this potential for disaster.

H umble if not exactly contrite, O'Malley watched the video with alarm. Hal, the counselor he had been ordered by the court to visit, sat working at his desk while the four of them watched a movie which graphically depicted alcohol's assault on the liver. The Before picture was ugly enough; the After was appalling. He did not want to be there, did not think he should have to, but from this first session he began to look at his sentence here as the psychological equivalent of chicken soup: it couldn't hurt.

A mixed bag, his three fellow attendees each had been picked up by the D.C. cops in varying stages of disrepair. Michael, an Episcopalian minister, had driven his Chevy into the shoals of Rock Creek. Loreen, from Texas, was gratefully fleeing from tequila. Dirk was, like they all were, required to go through the three-month course, but unlike the rest of them he almost cheerfully acknowledged his alcoholism and genuinely wished to get the monkey off his back. O'Malley stared over at him with some admiration, an obviously troubled man who'd judged his own degree of difficulties and was determined to do something about them.

It was while he shielded his eyes from the view of the diseased liver swelling to elephantine proportions that O'Malley hit upon the notion of his therapy here as a purgatory out of which he might be able to spring not himself but his father. But first he'd have to get him here. It was a project he deemed more and more necessary. The destruction continued before his very eyes.

David Nicole, early in life, understood the mechanics of marketing. No reefer he had ever sold had the same name as the last batch, especially since it often *was* the last batch. New and improved was a notion he'd stumbled on as if he'd invented it. Bad at math, he'd never had much trouble deciphering the supply and demand equation.

Hashish that had been rubbed in Rawalpindi had been reborn in Nicole's hands as Khyber Black; cocaine that was jazzed up with the odd chemically manipulated lump or two was by a miracle of verbal alchemy converted into the legendary Pink Flake. He read his Coleridge, researched his absinthe, and memorized passages from De Quincey's *Confessions of an English Opium-Eater.* So intoxicating was his spiel, people had walked out of his room in college higher than the substance they'd shared could possibly have leveraged them, and their word-of-mouth endorsement sent others scrambling to his door, where he greeted them like a high-class tailor, offering made-to-measure rushes, aphrodisiacs, and hallucinations. He understood one-stop shopping, and how a wholesale merchandiser needed to keep his hand in at the retail level.

Early on at Amherst he learned the advantages of giving free drugs to socially active, pretty coeds from the neighboring institutes of, as he loved to put it, higher learning. They circulated through the community like targeted direct mail, and the business in their wake was gratifying. It was through such manipulations that he stumbled upon one of the tricks he used to make Globe a hot spot.

When Tina leased the space on Eighteenth Street and secured her liquor license, it was natural that Nicole would figure a way to make it successful. First thing he did after the *Blade Runner* spaceship was strapped above the bar, the thin, tall stereo speakers were disguised as metallic cactus plants, and the upstairs was furnished in its map-room motif was enter into an agreement with the Capitol Offenses Escort Service to provide him with young women he instructed in the following manner: "Find the biggest loudmouth at the bar and take him home with you." Since they were paid handsomely to do so, the escorts went about their tasks, often hitting upon guys who seemed mortified that their fondest dreams were, completely to their surprise, coming true, and in front of their friends.

When within a matter of a month Globe became known as a place where beautiful women were walking out with men they'd just met, the place was overrun, and not only on weekends. In order to keep the place from quickly resembling a guildhall on stag night, he'd then gone about the business of entering into a contract with one of Washington's few modeling agencies, and for a fee, while contravening several civil-rights statutes, determined which of the males on their roster were heterosexual. These were then hired under contract to come to Globe on specified evenings and simply hang out, to do with themselves as they wished. If they found women with whom they wanted to leave, so much the better, so long as other women witnessed the transaction and came to believe that pick-up parity existed there. The only time things got out of hand was on those evenings when the good-looking male models walked out the door with the escorts Nicole had hired. It was a waste of his money, in the narrow sense, though the aesthetic example of handsome men and attractive women meeting there added a gloss to the place that ensured continued business.

There were few things he would not do to make certain his business was successful, and though he had to be extraordinarily careful about it, being a predicate felon and all, he never entirely gave up on the business that had almost landed him in jail. He still circulated in a crowd that moved drugs, still knew people with names like Big Carmine and Cosmo and Joey the Goat who were ever on the lookout for import-export opportunities. In fact, on this particular morning when he broached the subject of bringing into the country on a one-shot basis a package of pure cocaine, his friend John Santangelo had told him the material could be picked up anywhere in South America he wanted it. "You could have it in Caracas in May?"

"I could have it in Patagonia in April," said the well-dressed, Cadillac-driving businessman from Baltimore who from time to time stopped by Globe on mornings such as this.

They sat across from each other in the empty bar, cups of cappuccino steaming in front of them, a frothy white mustache of speckled cin-namon and milk on John's lip. There were evenings when John came to Globe and hung out right here near the bar. One such evening David Nicole had instructed an escort who happened to have been there that night—a winning lottery ticket ready, literally, to drop into some un-suspecting guy's lap—to take John home with her. That John owned a portion of Capitol Offenses and was, in fact, going home with an employee was something Nicole had never let on. It had made John's week and Nicole knew it.

"I'm talking about bringing in something like twenty keys, I'm not certain exactly how much."

"Twenty would be nice." John was a large man given to understatement in his dress and his means of expression. He wore black suits with white shirts and no tie, and his only sartorial distinction was hair slicked back straight. He was a calm man, very deliberate, whose shuttling between Baltimore and Washington like any other franchiser did not reveal the faintest hint of desperation. He had his fingers in several pies, and when opportunities arose, he acted on them. That David Nicole, whom he knew to be an equally serious person, seemed to think he had someone who could successfully mule twenty kilos of cocaine from Caracas to Washington was a business opportunity he thoughtfully considered, though he'd long since learned that the gap between reach and grasp, especially in these things, was the difference between a home in the Bahamas and a federal pen. "What makes you think you can get it here? And why Caracas? It's a shitty place, you ever been there?" John prided himself on his knowledge of South America.

"I think I can get it here 'cause the guy I'm dealing with isn't slowed down by customs. And if you read the *Post* this morning about the upcoming travels of our President, you'll see why I'm talking Venezuela."

There wasn't a glimmer of expression on John's face. They might have been talking about aluminum siding. He just drank this in, like the cappuccino. "This could be interesting," he said after a minute passed. "You realize if I do this, you take responsibility until you place something in my hands. You are liable for whatever you have delivered to your person down there, which we'll provide, at cost, at the point of transfer."

"Fine. What I want to know is what my reward is for making the delivery."

"You put this in my hands, I'll give you one hundred dollars."

They looked at each other over the table. The vague reek of draft beer was everywhere, and in the absence of the stereo that blasted through the bar at night, there was a hollow stillness to the place.

"Too small by half," said Nicole. "My guy's taking the risk."

"You seem to be telling me there is no risk."

"Touché. One hundred fifty, John. I know what the math is on this one. And fuck the mule, *I'm* taking a big financial risk; I'm responsible for the cost of the material down there, which, by the way, is?"

"Twenty keys down there?" said John, thinking. "You take responsibility for seventy-five dollars."

"That sounds about right. So when I deliver, you give me one fifty."

"Deal, and if you don't deliver, you're into me for seventy-five bucks."

"Don't worry," said Nicole. "The guy I'm working with is very responsible. He's my oldest friend. He doesn't know he's going to do this yet, but he'll come around. But I'll tell you, John. He's very responsible."

"He better be, if you're into me for seventy-five bucks."

"He'll do the right thing, my man. Put your mind at ease."

I t was not of the order of a surprise cameo by Halley's Comet when his mother showed up at the White House, but neither had she called him to tell him she was coming. It was *The New York Times* that served like some DEW station on the Bering Strait, issuing the first report that she was on her way. O'Malley happened to notice the culled item in the White House News Digest. It spoke of several well-heeled emissaries on behalf of the Sendero Luminoso who, inexplicably, were making the rounds of Washington, from the Office of Public Liaison to the Papal Nuncio, though they apparently had been all but thrown down the steps of the Peruvian Embassy.

His mother's name was mentioned—as in, "Barbara O'Malley, known in liberal circles as 'Saint Jude,' in honor of her patronage of lost causes"—but still she didn't call. Other than the notion that he was beyond the pale, and that she had the tendency to breeze in and out of National Airport without so much as a courtesy call, the only reason he could think of for her ignoring him was that she was planning on being arrested, which was her usual M.O. on a trip to Washington. O'Malley's mother seemed to like getting arrested, and he wondered if, however, out of some sliver of maternal concern, she thought that perhaps this wasn't the best of times to involve her son in an area where she had a lawyer who already had the posting of bail bonds down to a two-step procedure.

So when Buffy, who had taken on an unbecoming air of confidence, walked into his office chewing gum, a ditsy smile on her face, and pronounced that the Service had a woman out front who claimed to be his mother, he logged off his computer and put on his jacket and tried to get reservations at the mess. It was noon on the Friday of a horrible week and he felt more than a twinge of relief that his mother was there, though taking care of him was something of which she was almost pathologically incapable. The likelihood is it worked in the opposite direction as well.

"I'm surprised they aren't wearing brown shirts," she said audibly enough when he came to the desk and escorted her through the metal detectors. He pretended not to hear that since the two white-shirted Secret Service agents sneered knowingly at him anyway. "How are you, Mother?" he said as she offered her cheek. He wondered what the Senderos—high upon the Andes, their cheeks stuffed with coca leaves, their AK-47's swinging across their backs as they prodded their pack mules up the incline, their Little Red Books or whatever Maoist garbage they swilled like cheap wine cluttering up their rucksacks—could possibly make of his mother here in her Chanel outfit and bulky overcoat— no mink, in deference to animal rights—as she came to the White House to petition on their behalf.

"I'm fine, though you meet the most wretched people in Washington, don't you? I'd forgotten just how terrible people could be."

They were walking along the corridor toward his office, past the Vice President's office, past the Office of Political Affairs, in front of which, with another visitor, he might have stopped to chuckle. Her heels tapped noisily against the black-and-white checks of the floor and he realized they must have cut a sight, his mother still glamorous with her jet black hair. At fifty-eight, she had the body if not of an aerobics instructor, at least of a woman who put in her hours gliding down slopes with a kamikaze grin, taking swipes at the lawn with a savage six-iron, returning dink shots with the white-skirted best of them. She was fussing with her White House pass to make certain it hung beside her pearls just so. "I was surprised to hear you were out front."

"I didn't know if I'd be able to see you, and I didn't want to disappoint you," she said with such an absence of vanity it would have been rude for him to laugh.

"I would have understood if you couldn't see me. Perhaps I could have stopped by to see you."

"Yes, you know where the District jail is now, don't you?" she said drily.

"I do know where the Hay-Adams is. Would you like to lunch at the mess?"

"I suppose so. I don't see the Papal Nuncio until two-thirty. He's probably on the phone with Opus Dei, getting his orders, even as we speak."

She allowed herself to be led downstairs and out across West Executive Drive. If the White House was a campus, this was even more terrorizing than parents' weekend, only the terror came in reverse. Rather than fearing that his mother would meet his teachers and she would think terrible things about him, in this case he feared his teachers—the senior staff—would meet his mother, and *they* would think terrible things about him. This was not the week for a further display of eccentricity.

Inside the double doorway, the entrance to the mess was a little backed up, filled with hearty deputy assistants to the President and their grinning, almost giddy guests. Even the assistant secretaries, over from the agencies, had rubber necks in the expectation that the President or Chief of Staff might walk in or out of the narrow corridor that stepped down to the mess, and in that time they might press upon either of them that intricate, seemingly intractable policy initiative so bottlenecked in the Cabinet Council. The number-one strategy for people walking in was to look like they belonged, and for people walking out, to fill their pockets with White House matchbooks and, in deference to President Hardison's fetish, to scoop up a handful of the Reese's Pieces that he had revived as effectively as a return visit from E.T.

"Oh my," said his mother, a mite too loudly. "I didn't know so many yellow ties were on sale this year."

"Hello, Mr. O'Malley," said Manuel, the maitre d', his lone supporter on the White House staff, or at least the only person who had not been noticeably cooler to him on Monday than he had been the Friday before. He'd wondered whether Manuel simply didn't read the *Post*, but that was ridiculous. For whom were court intrigues more important? And then he'd realized that Manuel had been around long enough not to be put off by the initial blistering attack; he knew that either there were many more to come, and that he'd best be nice until the aide was out the door, or else that the aide was the victim of that peculiarly Washingtonian inversion of Andy Warhol's fifteen-minute rule, in which everyone is infamous for one news cycle. "Your table is waiting," he said, passing him on like a baton to one of the Filipino waiters.

They headed left, though his mother would not know that in the caste system at work, this meant he was of secondary importance. As they were shown to a table along the wall, and he noticed a variety of staffers look up from their soup, his mother shifted into even haughtier gear for an entrance into the small, wood-paneled dining room. They would have stared at O'Malley anyway, at least this week, but his mother truly was a sight. Embarrassed, O'Malley took the seat with his back to the room, which would prove to be a mistake.

They ordered iced tea, and he had a club sandwich while his mother simply stuck with the navy bean soup. "Don't you want more, Mother? It's Mexican day," he said, and in so doing realized once again how intimate he was with the schedule of the kitchen, how easy it would be to think of the presidential quarters upstairs as if they were simply the prime locale in a very large dorm. But his mother, not untypically, refused to eat more. She just tapped an ersatz sugar packet against the palm of her hand and nervously looked around the room.

"Very important people, I can tell they think," she said too loudly for comfort.

"Shh, goddamn it, I have to work here, Mother."

"Yes, well, what? Making Hardison sound less like a fool than usual? Although, I must say, I didn't expect him to be holding out that olive branch to Nicaragua. That's awfully good of him."

"I'm going on the trip," he said sunnily, as if there were no black clouds hovering over the image.

"Are you? Then you'll meet Rosario Murillo, Ortega's wife, I'm sure. She's a little cheap, but she's certainly energetic."

In another age, his mother would have said of Krupskaya, who had the personal misfortune of being married to Lenin, "She could stand to shave and have the warts removed from her chin, but otherwise she's a lively conversationalist."

Her soup arrived, as did his sandwich, and he noticed she was bug-eyed over something. He turned and looked over his shoulder as subtly as he could. There, in a double-breasted gray suit, bright pink shirt and loud tie, was Lemlow Motrin, the supercilious National Security Council specialist on South America. He had recently been hoist by his own petard on the front page of the *Post* when a memo he had written came to light. In it, he had argued that the administration ought to be lending assistance to the new Peruvian president in his struggle with the Senderos, and succor not just of the humanitarian sort but the full nine yards: Stinger missiles, M-16's, Huey copters, uniforms indistinguishable from snaky lianas. Everything but a regiment of North Carolina beagles and Kentucky mules. He'd gotten the usual treatment for his proposal: it had been leaked by someone either in the White House or on the Hill, and he'd had the customary references to Vietnam, Nicaragua, and Oliver North brandished, if not as blunt instruments, then

at least as a wet newspaper to pummel him upside his think tank—
nurtured noggin.

"Don't even think about it," he said to his mother. She looked at
him with all the innocence she could muster. "Just whatever that
thought is, lose it. I mean it," he said, holding up a carrot stick and
pointing it at her.

She fluttered her eyelids theatrically, as if his suspicions were beneath
him. Behind him, Motrin sat down at one of the large communal
tables, disdainful of his colleagues, but also innocent and unaware of
this terrorist, O'Malley's mother, in their midst.

"Now look, I have to ask you something. Are you trying to get Dad
to hand over his Gauguin?"

Shocked, she said, "That is between your father and me."

"No, actually, Mother, it affects me too, because I'm the one who
still lives here. I'm the one who has to make certain everything's okay
in his life, and I'll tell you, your trying to take it has him in a tizzy."

"To begin with, it's my Gauguin. I wrote the check for it at the Wally
Findlay Gallery in 1957. My accountant still has the stub."

"I believe it, but Mother, you don't really need the money, do you?"

"I need the money more than that band of peasants he wants to
support in Guatemala."

"Beg pardon?" This was going to be good.

"Your father and that Inca of his—"

"Mayan," he corrected.

"Are in the midst of funneling arms to some right-wing guerrilla army
perched outside of Guatemala City."

"That's ridiculous."

"It's not ridiculous. Why don't you ask Motrin over there whether
it's true. Your father, who is either bored by not having any revolutions
to play with or else has just finally, once and for all, gone completely
nuts, is up to his rump in it. All I'm trying to do is make certain my
painting doesn't buy bullets for some greedy little right-wing colonel
trying to become the Somoza of his day."

He was speechless, an odd condition for a speechwriter. "I'll check
on this," is all he could muster. They finished their meals rather quickly,
his mother resisting his entreaties that she try the John Marshall pie.
He was so eager to get out of there that he neglected to remind her one
final time not to make a fuss as they passed Motrin. His mother, it was
clear, couldn't help herself.

"You're a disgrace," she hissed as they walked by the poor bastard, who looked up and flushed all at once. His face was the color of his tie, though the expression was as bland and resigned as a sheep in its final descent toward the clippers. O'Malley thought he would die at this contravention of mess protocol. He could barely speak to her he was so mad as they walked across West Exec back to his office, where for an hour she amused herself in theological discussions with Will Ames before heading for her appointment with the Papal Nuncio.

o middle manager on his way to happy hour could so loudly have mouthed the words "Thank God It's Friday" as O'Malley did as he straightened his desk and his tie and prepared to leave for the weekend. And that's when the phone rang and he grabbed it, all the while struggling to put on his jacket.

"Yeah," he said, expecting it to be Kit, whom he was to meet at a restaurant on Connecticut Avenue.

"Hello, Thomas." It was Nicole. "Did you have a good week?"

"What do you want, David?"

"Just checking in to see how you're doing. I guess this must have been a rough one."

Not as rough as it could be, he almost blurted out.

"Leave me alone, David. We've got nothing to talk about."

"But that's not true, Thomas. We've got lots to talk about. For example, do you read *Newsweek?*"

He refused to answer, just stood there, breathing into a phone he'd had pressed to his mouth this week like it was a regulator and he was underwater.

"Because my understanding, Thomas, is that there might be a Periscope item in it Monday on the dope-dealing background of an unnamed 'high White House official,' if you know what I mean."

"How could that happen, David?" he asked calmly as he could be.

"Oh, I have a great many customers at my bar who I treat awfully well. Why, there are some reporters who think of me as a regular dating service, and they know that a man in my position picks up an awful lot of good gossip, *capisce?*"

"Talking like a thug is so beneath you, Nicole. You've got the mannerisms and the rhythm down, I admit, but it is so unbecoming as to genuinely depress. And anyway, you destroy me, and you definitely ruin whatever chance you have of getting that package brought in."

He'd said it. He'd allowed Nicole to think there was a chance of it.

"Hey, buddy, I'll back off," said Nicole with obvious triumph in his voice. "Don't worry about *Newsweek*. We can stop the presses."

"I'm not going to help you, David," he said, as if there was a need once again to put it on the record.

"That's fine, I'll talk to you later."

"No, don't," he was saying when Nicole hung up.

He stood there a moment and looked at the painting of George Washington that was hanging over his fireplace. "Now what am I going to do?" he asked aloud. George wasn't talking.

it and O'Malley walked in silence. He couldn't explain to her how vulnerable he felt, and how confused he was. He couldn't tell her he was being blackmailed. It was too disturbing to bring up. He was going to have to figure out on his own the way to brazen through this problem. The thing of it was, if Nicole began to unleash all his considerable craftiness against him, well, O'Malley was in a position where a sniper hiding in the bushes could just about destroy him. This was the common thread connecting lives in the public arena—and as ridiculous as it seemed, even a low-level job at the White House qualified as such. An FBI background investigation going on, *The Washington Post* having come down on him like a hammer, his relationship with the President the only thing that kept him from having been fired at the White House: his problems were a bit beyond the order of simply detesting what was in his lunchpail every day. And risky as it was, he was on the verge of deciding that in so many ways the only way out was just to succumb, to go along with Nicole and bring in the drugs.

Nicole was right. From what information as O'Malley had been able to garner, a presidential trip was a moving, almost hermetically sealed series of motorcades and escorted lift-offs in Air Force One, protected from street life, demonstrations, the dislocation of being in a foreign land. You could ring up Domino's from a moving car in Moscow, and the White House Communications Agency was working on a way to get the pizza delivered via cellular fax right there in your limo. You moved en masse and neither the masses nor troubling individuals could get through to you—unless you wanted them to. And once he was in possession of the package, it might as well have been delivered to him in his apartment a few blocks from here: by being inside the presidential cocoon, he was in the territory of the United States. So long as he received the package without a hitch, there was no way he could get caught. And once he was back in the States and he'd taken care of Nicole, he could go back to the business of being an adult. Whatever slate there was to clear between him and his former friend, it would be cleared, he'd make sure of that. But first he had to get Nicole off his case.

Of course, it would be best if he could shut the bastard down. But he had no idea how that could be accomplished. How dare Nicole disrupt the life O'Malley had struggled to put together?

But then, Nicole's particular thuggish personality included a talent for sensing when someone was vulnerable. And the newspaper coverage this week had certainly tipped that hand.

"You're awfully quiet," she said to him as they reached the top of the hill at California Street. Behind them, down Connecticut Avenue, a neon sign that said "Tokyo" advertised a Japanese restaurant. Cars and pickup trucks from Maryland heading toward Dupont Circle flashed by with revving engines. The ruby eyes of the Washington Monument flashed upon the White House, which was hidden from view by the downtown buildings and the intervening space. She didn't know what it was, but she could feel there was something wrong from the way he now clung to her. She instinctively told him it was all right, though her guess was it probably wasn't. Her guess was that it probably had to do with David Nicole, and that she'd better find out what was going on.

That cover story in *The New Republic* was a real humdinger. Comparing President Hardison to Neville Chamberlain was a good way to get the White House's attention. "Mr. Hardison makes Vidkun Quisling look like a one-man Civil Defense League," is how *The National Review* so subtly put it. Even the *New York Times* editorialists, on the whole supportive of what the administration had done to date, allowed themselves to quibble publicly with the mission of his first State visit, implying he was out of his depth. That Hardison was going to Nicaragua while Daniel Ortega had the deposed Mrs. Chamorro lingering under house arrest was considered quite an affront. It was clearly falling to the speechwriters to pull a rabbit out of a hat, and while grumbles and groans were occasionally heard around the building, they attained a new status, even O'Malley. People clearly were rooting for them.

The speeches Colin Denholm had drafted were being edited by committee, and the effect on them was similar to that of a story making its rounds of a large table at a party. What started out coherent returned to them quite garbled. What was a statesmanlike rendering of realpolitik when the routing sheet first was attached to it returned to the speechwriters with conflicting instructions. The State Department wanted the references to American interests dropped in favor of a declaration of the brotherhood of man. The Pentagon, in contrast, wanted the speech beefed up with an elegy to American weaponry, from cudgels to the Big One. Treasury wanted each of the speeches to sound like they were being given by a smiling banker in a boomtown, a free toaster hidden by the podium. OMB's changes would have made the President sound like a stern father, cutting off a drugged-out teenager from the last of his allowance.

Since much was riding on what the President was to say, and as there appeared to be gridlock in the approval process, Katherine cut a deal with Harold Whitney himself, in which new speeches would be quickly worked up and approved by a rump group, which would include Whitney, the President, and the Secretary of State. It appeared to be the only way to get the show on the road. While the administration argued, while stories were leaked about particular versions of speeches that already were two generations old, the assignments were handed down. Katherine herself would take on Nicaragua, thus assuring the United States would get the better end of the bargain. Colin would create a new version of the Santiago speech. And O'Malley was coaxed out of the doghouse with instructions to come up with a brand-new speech for Venezuela.

It was early yet, so Globe wasn't blaring with gaucho music, Polynesian polkas, or punk down from the steppes. Neither was there Gypsy disco, Celtic surf music, or hillbilly salsa. Kit thought no harm could come from stopping by for a single glass of wine and a conversation, though with Nicole nothing was ever as simple as you planned it. Once upon a time she'd had to leave America to turn off the relentless arguing, mind games, and vaguely threatening pressure he'd applied as she'd tried to disengage from him, and this when he was distracted by such minor events as a grand jury up in Springfield deciding whether or not to indict.

There were a few solitary young gentlemen whose studied slouches and ties at a happy-hour half-mast belied the alertness with which their eyes followed her entrance. With a little luck, she would find Nicole before any of them slithered over to her. She walked in past the bar area and all the way back to the hostess in the rear, and before she even got there, she was impressed with the care with which the woman had choreographed her look. Here was a six-foot-four black woman calmly organizing the backlit screen on which she kept track of her waiting stations with pastel-colored wax pencils as if she were the head of naval operations and the tables were the vessels of war, yet what was most remarkable was that this clearly intelligent professional had chosen to dress like a Zulu, replete with straw skirt and ankle cummerbunds of a decidedly jungly origin. Kit reminded herself she should never under-estimate Nicole's ability to persuade someone to do precisely what was not in their interest.

"Is David here?"

"David?" the hostess asked, her nostrils flaring, as if David were the name of everyone on this particular planet, or as if Kit had asked for someone named Vishnu or Boris.

"Your employer," Kit said with the steel of her class she often was reluctant to reveal.

"And you are?"

"Kit," she said, forming the word in her mouth and cutting it off at the end as if her tongue were a guillotine.

The woman, obviously used to taking precise instructions, walked back toward the kitchen. Kit was in luck, for the woman returned with Nicole.

"The clientele of my restaurant has risen immeasurably." He kissed her hand, clicked his heels, and mock bowed, showing off his glistening black slicked-back hair and ponytail. "Have you come for dinner?"

"I thought a drink."

"Dinner, no?"

"No."

"Okay, a drink then, come." And with that he was grabbing her hand and moving her, pulling her along with him to the bar. One of the reasons she had made such an effort to stay away from even seeing him now that they both were in Washington was because this was the way it always worked: thirty seconds in his presence and you were heading where he wanted to go. Even if where he wanted to go was where you wanted to go, the feeling was of floating with a powerful current.

They took a seat at one of the chrome tables and the bartender came all the way around to take their order. "Bass Ale for me," said Nicole politely, as if he were a passerby who'd stepped in to get out of the cold. "White wine," said Kit, and then she turned to her former boyfriend. She put her hand underneath her chin and looked up at him. He was still remarkably cool-looking, far more handsome than he had been when she first knew him, his skin cleared up, his hair receding at the temples in a not unbecoming way. He certainly dressed better than he had in the days when flannel shirts and a leather jacket had been his idea of haute couture, when often he went shoeless just to show how tough he was.

"You've turned into a wonderful-looking grownup," he said charmingly.

"I was thinking something similar about you."

"Who would have thought you'd be a power operative for a GOP senator. I'm not putting you down!" he added quickly.

"I know you're not. Jesus, I wouldn't have predicted it myself."

"Wall Street, I could have seen. Hollywood, absolutely. Or, continuing to make millions as a model. I used to see you in ads for Henry Grethel . . ."

"You remember those!"

"Sure, I used to tear through Vogues looking for you. I'd get up to the head of the line, you know, at a Drugfair or something, and I'd manfully plunk down the packet of condoms and the pipe cleaners and the Clear Eyes, and then sort of embarrassedly, if that's a word, slide the latest *Vogue* across the counter as if, any second, someone was going to mutter, 'What a perv.' "

"It seems like my glamorous existence was long ago."

"You're still leading a glamorous existence."

"Wrong. Working for Tony Partridge does not qualify as glamorous, by any stretch."

"I buy that," he said, smiling. He was being nice, the charming Nicole, the Nicole her parents had adored before they'd read in *The New York Times* that their daughter's longtime boyfriend had been arrested for selling drugs to a federal agent. "You have a nice life, though. I'm happy you're with Tom these days."

"Are you?" she said softly, not challenging him so much as simply curious.

"Oh, Kit, darling, yeah, of course." He grasped her hands on the table. "Look, two of my favorite people in the world. Of course I'm happy for you. And I'm proud of him. God, talk about surprises. You know, Tom O'Malley in the White House. That's one of those class-reunion shockers that make people . . ." His head and upper body shook as he looked for the word. "Believe in God. You know what I mean?"

She smiled, played a little with the stem of her wineglass, rolling it this way and that on the smooth, black tabletop. "What happened when he came here for dinner, David?"

"What do you mean?" In a second, he'd dropped his expansive self for this one. This one was suspicious, and very, very quick. She'd seen it before.

"There's something going on, David, that I want to know about."

"Something . . ."

"Cut the crap. Something between you and Tom that has him upset, and I want to know what it is."

"Hey, Kit. If there was something going on that you should know about, you think either of us would keep it from you?"

"You just said that so artfully. 'Something going on that you should know about.' Tell me, David."

"Hi," said Tina as she walked up to their table.

Nicole made to stand in honor of his partner, though Kit stayed where she was. Tina held her hand out, a thin hand, extended from a long arm, and in a second Kit had determined that Nicole's new girlfriend was probably three or four inches taller than he was. She carried with her the faint contrivance of the kept woman with a daily report on her bank balance.

"You know Tina, right, Kit?"

"We haven't actually met." Kit imagined this was using up much of Nicole's five-minutes-a-year allotment of visible discomfort. She made it easy on him. She smiled at Tina, and the smile she received in return was anything but guileless: it was the professional smile of the Las Vegas hostess, the dope dealer's mistress. She didn't like her.

"Excuse me," she said to Tina, who now sat down with them and motioned to the bartender for a drink. "We were right in the middle of something." Tina made no move to leave and Kit made no move to invite her to stay. "Tell me, David."

"It sounds to me like this is more a question of what's going on between you and Tom than anything between Tom and me. I mean, if you think Tom's hiding something from you, that's between you two. I'm just an old friend of his who misses him. Nothing more."

"Your innocent act sets off alarm bells. I am not without a memory chip."

"Hey," said Tina.

"You stay out of this."

"You can't tell me—"

"Girls!" said Nicole. Then, "Kit, if Tom's upset about things, that's natural. He's undoubtedly got some troubles at work, being accused of having a drinking problem and all . . ."

"He doesn't have a drinking problem."

"Of course not. I was just thinking of the *Post* article and him being in trouble. But I'm not adding to it, his problems, that is."

"All right," she said, obviously not believing him. She pushed away from the table. "Let me just tell you this. If you mess up Tom's life the way you messed up your own, I'll do whatever it takes. Senate investigators, the DEA, D.C. health inspectors. Whatever it takes, David."

"Kit gets her gun?" he said mockingly. Tina burst into laughter as Kit got up to leave.

"Stay, Kit." Nicole seemed quite sincerely disappointed she was leaving.

"Hurry back now, ya hear," said Tina with mock gaiety as Kit retreated.

hen the trip was two weeks away, O'Malley labored on the speech the President was to give to the Venezuelan legislators. He became so immersed in the history of U.S.–Venezuelan relations that when he slept, the dream conversations he had with Simón Bolívar were on a continuum climbing up his daily learning curve, high as the Andes, without, unfortunately, the breathtaking views. He wished he'd taken South American history at Amherst, though given the amount of time he spent studying in those days, he would have forgotten it all, anyway. Perhaps it was better this was all new, though it was taking rather a lot of energy to absorb what he needed to in order to make the President sound, all at once, fresh with understanding, cogent of argument, lambent of wit, and felicitous of phrase.

It was tough being a speechwriter when you felt looking over your shoulder opposition congressmen who would be quick to hoot and holler, editorialists waiting to pounce, not to mention the audience, which could be quick to take offense. It was difficult not to think of each phrase in the context of history, and as ideas rolled off his fingers and into the computer, he saw a diver go off the high board, the degree of difficulty pronounced, the judges delayed in their response. Depending on what he wrote, the President would be viewed as a graceful success, or else all of Washington—all of the Americas—would be talking about his painful bellyflop.

Such was his concentration, he had told Buffy to hold all calls except those from the researchers attached to the speechwriting shop; the advance team who were to fill in those quirky little touches of verisimilitude so that the audience could think the speech was written truly with them in mind; and his contacts in the State Department. These last ones in particular were professionals; they didn't mind his calling them regularly and asking them seemingly dumb questions about balance of payments, minutes of OPEC meetings, and where he could find reference books to poetic metaphors that seized upon the Orinoco. Had he wanted them to, the Library of Congress could have arranged a private screening of *Aguirre, the Wrath of God*. In a fairly mellow mood, the pressure notwithstanding, when he wandered out on this Tuesday morning to fill up his mug with coffee and overheard Buffy talking on the phone with Tim Skelton, he motioned that he would take the call, and retreated to his office for her to send it in.

"Hey, man," he said, his feet kicked up on the table beside his computer. It was the first time in days he had so rested.

"I've got great news," said Skelton.

"What's that?"

"My long national nightmare is over."

"You've got a job."

"You got it."

"Where?" he asked, and when Skelton told him it was as Deputy Assistant Secretary for Public Affairs at the Department of Agriculture, his heart sank—what a dump for someone of Skelton's talents to land in—though he sounded a buoyant note. "That's terrific," he found himself saying.

"Look, we both know it's terrible, but Paulina and I have bills to pay. So I'm going to do it. I'm going to have to learn about crop rotation, payments in kind, grain storage, and winter wheat, but, hell, it's honest work, I guess."

"Just think how much you'll be able to show off the next time you're in Iowa for the caucuses."

"That actually is one of the reasons I called."

"Oh."

"I had a visit from an FBI agent. Uh, about you."

"Tell me." O'Malley felt the hair on the back of his neck begin to go squirrelly on him.

"He wanted to know whether it was true that on the night Hardison won the caucuses, you danced naked on the piano at the Hotel Savery."

"Jesus."

"Don't worry, I told him you had your pants on."

"Tim . . ."

"Tom, I couldn't lie. He said he had multiple witnesses, some of them placing me with you—though God knows I didn't have as much reason to be cheerful that night. And I'm up for this job at Ag and all. But don't worry. He asked the usual questions about drugs and alcohol, and I told him he was barking up the wrong tree. Said you were simply celebrating the fact that you never had to go to Iowa again."

"That has the virtue, as Henry Kissinger would say, of being true."

"Only problem with that is Special Agent Bryce is from Iowa, or so he allowed when we did a little small-talking. But I don't think he'll hold that against you."

"That's a relief." O'Malley immediately thought of the advice he'd gotten from Tom Donilon about the imperatives of no one giving the FBI even the slightest encouragement to delve deeper into his life.

"Don't worry, Tom. He asked if I knew of anyone who would have more information about your drinking problem, and I told him that I didn't know a soul who would talk to him."

f the air hadn't been so soft as to reverse engines on even the most plummeting of manic depressives, he might have been thrown into a funk. But Kit looked particularly lovely this evening, they both were in spring clothes, and when they rang the doorbell at his father's Georgetown house, he could hear the dogs serenade them and bounce off the inside of the door like jumping beans in a jar. "You ready?" he asked.

"As I'll ever be."

And then they were standing in the warm light of the entrance, even Carmela having in advance agreed to negotiations to be on something less than war footing. She had her hands full anyway as she tried to control the leaping dogs, but O'Malley detected the slightest glimmer of a smile at the corners of her mouth. His father came to the head of the stairs and descended them with the grace of a man who knows how to make an entrance, which of course was spoiled when he tripped on the last step and was nearly thrown headlong, though he recovered nicely with his head practically wedged between Kit's breasts. "Dad, I'd like you to meet . . ."

"We've just met, Tom, I assure you."

And then they were heading up the stairs to have a drink in his study, because Kit wanted to see the Gauguin.

"Martinis, Rob Roys?" his father pitched giddily.

"White wine for me," said Kit with a smile.

"I'll have a Perrier, Dad."

"Perrier," his father pronounced. "Hell of a drink for a social engagement."

But he went about his chores as bartender without complaint, actually with relish, at one point walking to the staircase and calling in Spanish for Carmela to "bring a bottle of that piss water from France."

"It's lovely, Mr. O'Malley." Kit stood underneath the Gauguin, which admittedly, with the drapes to the window drawn, the single spotlight shining on it, the rest of the room with its oak bookshelves, its mammoth antique desk, and the couch that as a boy O'Malley had curled in, waiting, usually in vain, for his parents to read to him, gave the room an aura of peacefulness. If O'Malley closed his eyes for a moment, he might believe he was in a home filled with beauty, comfort, and love, not a halfway house for escapees from Senate Select Committee Hell.

If he cared to think about it, the emotion that sprang to mind from his childhood here was, first and foremost, a sense of loss, though the condition he remembered most was boredom. The loss was over his parents' obviously faltering relationship—it died before his eyes, he was the one who witnessed it—though the boredom was a condition he imagined was wholly of his own device.

"Come sit on the couch, Kit." It was as if O'Malley was hardly there. His father had on this absurd ascot and was trying to look like an English gentleman. "I understand you work for Senator Partridge."

"Yes, sir, I do."

"Seems like an impressive young man. Do you mind if I smoke?" His father already had a cigarette lit, his third since they entered the room.

"Not at all," said Kit, and O'Malley was hard-pressed to distinguish whether she was responding to Partridge's impressiveness or the fait accompli of the old man's smoking.

"My loving son took after my wife politically. I suppose not entirely. He hasn't offered State's evidence against me. But how nice it is that he's with such a lovely woman with such sensible politics." He made to sip his martini.

"Yeah, Dad, Partridge wants to support right-wing guerrillas in Guatemala, too."

The stream of his father's martini spewed nearly across the room, scaring Zippy to jump up in a yelp.

"Beg pardon?" His father was looking at him with something less than a poker face.

"I had lunch with Mother, of all people, at the White House mess. She told me."

"Her latest fabrication," his father said, recovering. "Now Kit, tell me about what you do." He turned his entire concentration, his entire red face, toward her, ignoring O'Malley and what he'd said, though O'Malley was left to wonder throughout the excruciating evening how a man so easily spooked could have been one.

T he easy part was getting through to the office of the speechwriters. From there it was tougher to actually speak to O'Malley. Nicole paced on the zebra-skin rug in his upstairs office cum poolroom, the phone cord trailing behind him like a rat tail, waiting for his friend to come on the line. He was on hold for what seemed like forever.

"Still there?" came the perky voice on the other end of the line. She was nice, absolutely wooable.

"Yes, ma'am," he said chucklingly. "Just waiting for Thomas." If he could have reached out and playfully tapped her shoulder, he would have.

"He'll be right with you."

And then he was back in motion, rolling balls around on the green felt table, as down the stairwell he could hear Nguyen and Dong, his two Vietnamese chefs, boat people from Hue, scream at each other, an afternoon ritual that, just as couples follow fights with forgiving, quite marvelous sex, often preceded their outdoing themselves on the wok.

"Hello." He sounded harried.

"Thomas."

"This is a really rotten time to call."

"I can call back."

"No, this is as good a time as any. What do you want? I've just had a speech returned to me with more red marks on it than those Latin papers we used to have to do for Mrs. Wieschert."

"She was something, wasn't she?"

"What's up, David?"

What's up? He scrunched up his forehead and shook his head for a minute. "I was just checking in, Thomas. Ten days until you head to Chile."

"I bet you know the whole itinerary, don't you?"

"It's been in the *Post*, Tom."

"Has it? I've been too busy to notice."

"And I was just wondering . . ."

"If I'm going to do it, right?"

"Yeah, when you put it so directly. I'm a more subtle guy than that. But yes, that's what I was wondering. Are you?" He hated having to be so direct, at least over the phone.

"This is a hell of a way to talk about it," said O'Malley.

Ah hah.

"The answer is no," O'Malley quickly added. "There's no way."

"C'mon, Tom. C'mon. Don't be a pussy. This thing is so easy. There hasn't been an opportunity to do something like this ever before. This is an historic opportunity."

"You're exactly right. 'White House Aide Arrested,' I can see the headline."

"You've already had that headline, haven't you?"

"I guess I have, David, and that's why it doesn't make much sense to talk about this anymore."

"Well, I don't know, things could be real uncomfortable for you if your unofficial Amherst transcript were to be leaked to *The New York Times*." Nicole felt his face get hot as he said that, and he felt unaccustomably foolish. This wasn't the way he'd been planning on the phone call going. In advance, he'd envisioned charm and persuasion, not snarling one-upmanship.

"I'm really tired of this, Nicole. Somehow, don't ask me why, I expected better of you. Please don't call me, okay? I'm asking you, man. I'm not going to take your calls anymore."

"All right, all right, all right. I hear you, buddy. Be seeing you around the campus," he said and hung up before O'Malley could say another word.

O'Malley thought: The campus? The White House?

Nicole thought it was almost time to phone his friend John and tell him to prepare for the delivery to Caracas.

T ony Partridge, in his thirty-ninth year, was not enjoying life the way he ought to have been. Alone in the nation's capital, unsure what the dating dos and don'ts were for a U.S. Senator, he was a highly eligible bachelor whose extra-man invitations from a variety of social choreographers were more of a nuisance than an opportunity. The women he met at Washington dinner parties tended to be appalling.

He was lonely, if the truth be told, and greatly missed his dog, Spam, who had not made the journey on the big bird east from Stapleton Airport in Denver. While he imagined Spam on his brother's ranch near Casper rolling in sheep dung and doing other fun things, here he was after a long day of trying to parse the political implications of a variety of absurd amendments, a day of watching others jousting and showing off on the Senate floor, and rather than watching nighttime soaps at his rented house out near the Maryland line, he was sitting through an endless dinner party in which the woman to his left appeared to be intent on devouring his ear while her husband kept tabs with an evil eye, and the senile old biddy to his right kept blinking and marveling that he seemed too young to be a senator.

He'd missed the entire ski season, some smart-ass magazine in New York had put him down as a late entry in the Dumbest Senator sweep-stakes, and life as a freshman of little consequence and no legitimacy was a grind. *The Washington Post* had had their fun with him, and when his name had come up on some television show in which Washington journalists sat in a sandbox and threw spitballs at one another, the five of them had erupted into barking sea lions who could barely stop laughing long enough to clap.

So now he sat through this dinner party in which the famous right-wing editor across the table regaled the nine of them with amusing tidbits about eccentric Cabinet secretaries in administrations gone by, from the one who had his cuspidor installed in his office to the one who evaluated civil servants according to their prowess on the touch-football field. Cigars were being passed to the menfolk, which made him feel a little nauseous, and he would have tuned out the editor, would have ignored the pompous lobbyist who was notable for little else than his having converted a house in Rock Creek Park into an imitation Versailles, would just as soon not have listened to the hostess, Clarissa Lowery, a heavily made-up, overdressed benefactress of the Republican party who'd insisted, *insisted* he come to her party. His mind was wandering to the threats he was receiving back home, clearly from the Governor, in which elements of his college days were seemingly being scrutinized for potential embarrassments. But then, just as he was tuning out the entire boring affair, he felt a hand moving up his thigh, which made his eyes widen a millimeter for every inch it roamed.

He stared straight ahead. He did not dare look down. Now it was the turn of the former intelligence agent to keep them enthralled, or at least he would have if you could have understood precisely what he was saying. The combination of his Eastern lockjaw and the copious amounts of claret the white-gloved servant had not for an instant allowed to disappear from any of their glasses made Tony strain to hear him. And he was already under strain, his eyes bugging out of his head.

The pink-nosed man from the CIA had some amusing anecdotes about the sophistication in banking methods required by the new breed of Latino military men—it seemed that bribery, imitating life, was dependent on computers and the fax—and while he seemed to want the good Senator from Wyoming in particular to listen up, every few seconds his eyes flitting from one person to another with a rare American jadedness suggesting a working knowledge of punji stakes and other elements of torture, it was in a form of pain akin to the rack that Tony Partridge did not throw his napkin on the table and forcefully remove the hand that now was working its way up to his lap. For the worst thing was happening. Worse than if his molester were the middle-aged, overly made-up, probable seducer of swimming-pool attendants and maintenance men to his left, the woman whose hand was now rubbing his crotch with what seemed like a fur-lined glove was the old crone who'd marveled at his age. One lone bead of sweat leapt like a single lemming off his brow and into the remains of his crème caramel.

At that moment, the cat that had clawed his way up Partridge's pant leg came grappling out of his lap, caught on to his tie, and with an act worthy of a Siamese pole-vaulter, managed to parlay its way onto the table, where it was met with oohs from the ladies and a shriek from Tony Partridge he instantly regretted.

"I'm sorry," he panted. "I thought it was . . ." And then he didn't know what to say.

"Oh," said his hostess with mock sympathy. "Did Haldeman give you a scare?" The cat pawed the linen tablecloth while the humans stared on bemusedly, all but Partridge whose pink cheeks, given to flushes in the most uneventful of moments, now took on the coloring of the crustacean they had devoured as their first course. Another cat leapt up from the floor into the lap of their hostess, the Republican sugar mommy who had blackmailed the new Senator from Wyoming into attendance with vague threats about his prospects for fundraising when he actually ran for the seat he now held. "Did Erlichman miss Haldeman?" she asked, kissing the cat she held in her arms.

Partridge threw his napkin on the table. It was time to get out of there. At least in Wyoming the animals who surprised you were legit-imate varmints, at the minimum a prairie dog.

"I'm terribly sorry," he said to his hostess as he pushed his chair back and stood up. "I have a committee hearing first thing in the morning."

"Of course, of course," said the old editor who nominally was the hostess's date. "You must be terribly busy."

There didn't seem to be any mockery in his statement. Tony made his way over to where his hostess was sitting stroking the cat in her lap, and he bowed in mock apology. "It was delightful. I enjoyed this."

"I'm so glad," she said with utter falsity. Up close, he had noticed over cocktails, her face had the quality of a bruised fruit, and there was something insolent about her confidence that she could summon mem-bers of the United States Senate with the inducement of her contri-butions. He'd met social climbers in Washington, he'd met matriarchs in Wyoming, but he'd never met a woman who seemed as greedy for her name to appear in reports to the Federal Election Commission as in gossip columns. "So nice you could come," she said with sulphuric emphasis on the word "nice." He thought it best that he quickly get out of there.

"Nice to have met you," he said to the editor. With the patch over his eye and the dandruff on his blazer, somehow it didn't seem unlikely that the old fart would finish his career as a columnist for a newspaper run by the Moonies. He put his cigar between his teeth and grasped Tony's hand with both of his. "A delight," the older man said, quite sincerely.

The lobbyist was unctuous. "I'll call your legislative aide in the morn-ing. And I'll make sure you get that check messengered over. Not that there's a quid pro quo!" he announced happily to the group. Partridge shook his hand and tried to remember what it was the man had needed to talk to his staff about.

His dinner companion who had nearly licked his ear gazed mean-ingfully into his eyes and told him that she was depending, not hoping, depending on seeing him again. Her husband shook his hand with manful brevity and a tight smile, a born cuckold if ever there was one. Tony bent over to say good-bye to the old biddy, who asked him one more time if he really was a senator, and as he started to leave, the retired CIA agent said he would see him out, even as he rose a little uncertainly from the table.

The butler held the door open with great ceremony, clearly a man who took his work seriously, and Partridge and the elderly spy walked out onto the Georgetown sidewalk. You could smell humid earth in the air, Dumbarton Oaks estate across R Street a living, breathing organism. Somewhere in the distance along the trail toward the mosque on Massachusetts, he thought he could hear the hoot of an owl, which, given they were in the middle of a city of several hundred thousand people, was a charming possibility. The recent cherry blossoms had provided them with a psychedelic landscape, giving life in Washington a dramatic softening, as if your consciousness had a fringe on top. The old man lit a cigarette and they paused for a moment. Tony could tell there was something he wanted to tell him, and so he waited with him while the butler jogged around the corner of the house to fetch his car, though just being near the pixilated drunkard made him wonder for a moment if they both would explode from the alcohol fumes and his lighting a match.

"I really," the man said a little unsteadily, "appreciated your writing me that letter."

"Hey, happy to do it," he said, thinking, letter? Was the man a constituent, and did this thus prove the mail system in his office worked? The new Senator from Wyoming waited in front of Clarissa Lowery's Georgetown home as the tipsy spy now stared at him from amidst a wreath of smoke.

"You might not remember," he said astutely. "But you wrote me saying you were ashamed that I should be branded a criminal for simply trying to help the cause of free—" He burped, and smoke came pouring out of his mouth from some inner recess. "—dom."

"Oh, so you're *Robert* O'Malley," he pronounced with amazement, and the older man made a vaguely Arabic hand gesture of acknowledgment. "Of course."

He remembered now. When it looked as if O'Malley was likely to be spending much of what remained of his life, if not making license plates at a maximum-security federal pen, at least puttering around the manicured lawns of Allenwood, he'd written him a long letter one night filled with references to chins being kept up, bastards not getting him down, and a variety of other collegiate motivations. "Pleased to meet you," he now said, holding out his hand to him once again.

Senator Partridge's bright blue 1969 Porsche now was pulled up in front in a first-gear roar and a noisy screech that culminated in the pulling of the hand brake as if the vehicle had come to the end of its tether. The butler popped out and stood holding the door for him. This was service.

"Can I give you a ride?"

"Thank you, but I live just down the hill. Clarissa and I are neighbors of a sort."

"I wish I'd realized earlier who you were. I just didn't catch your first name. I'm a terrible politician," he said, grinning.

Robert O'Malley shrugged graciously, as if there were no way that Partridge could have known, though they clearly had been introduced, and though his infamy had been celebrated in full color in *Time*, and nightly on Brokawjenningsrather.

The car was gently vibrating, and occasionally a cough shot out of the tail pipe. The butler still held the door open.

"It was a pleasure meeting you," the young Senator told the older spy, taking his hand and pumping two, three times. Then he turned and shook the butler's hand, though the man looked at him as if he were crazy, and got into his sports car with the Wyoming tags. He flipped on the lights, which illuminated R Street all the way down toward the cemetery over Rock Creek Park. He turned on the radio, and the harmonies of the B-52's caterwauling about some private Idaho drowned out the roar of the engine as he accelerated, one hand on the steering wheel, the other waving at that notorious patriot with whom he'd just had dinner. Robert O'Malley walked down R Street, though he quickly faded in Tony Partridge's rearview. It wasn't for a block or two that the new Senator realized he didn't have the slightest idea where he was going.

 mperial Bedroom was being grazed by the laser in his CD player, though the room they were in was anything but. They floated like Sunday sailors in a sea of lapping newspapers. The Outlook section of the *Post* was next to *The New York Times Magazine*, and arrayed on the floor were coffee cups and three-fourths–eaten bowls of oatmeal. Kit was in the bathrobe she'd brought over to his apartment, the lone signal that their lives were somehow joining, though they still kept the shuttling rhythm of individual berths and negotiated sleepovers.

The news concerned the President's lack of success in moving his legislation through the increasingly hostile Congress, and the fact that the Republicans, so recently the majority in the House, were exercising their prerogatives upon having finally taken power. On the television screen, one of the Sunday political talk shows that in Washington qualified as services of the church of information was turned on silently, talking heads ponderously analyzing each of the events of the week. They were sitting on his couch, each with a different section of the paper, O'Malley with the Book Review, Kit with the Sports section, when Kit looked up and addressed him. "Tom?"

"Darling," he said without looking up.

"Is there something I ought to know about you and David?"

"Sweetie, I only have eyes for you. What do you mean?" He still wouldn't look up, but she sensed she had his attention. She'd learned he had a pretty bad poker face.

"I'm just wondering what's wrong, and you'll forgive me if I think it has something to do with David."

"Nothing's wrong except I'm busy at work. And anyway, why would you think that?" He was looking up at her now. He blinked his eyes slowly, and she knew he was trying to hide something from the way he had his teeth clenched, his face on full sentry, guarding against whatever it was she was about to say. It was a good thing he wasn't a businessman, or an arms-control negotiator.

"Just wondering."

"Don't," he said looking back down at the Book Review.

She didn't press it, but she hoped whatever it was, he didn't have to deal with Nicole face-to-face.

He thought *Newsweek*'s Periscope section should actually have been called the Torpedo section, for that's what it felt like. He felt like he took it in the boiler room.

It was the following morning that the perilous edition of *Newsweek* hit the stand, though the A.P. wrote off it from the copy their New York bureau received on Sunday. When O'Malley saw the Periscope item, he marveled at how that submarine of a political gossip column had him in his sights, and no amount of depth charges could reveal precisely where the story was coming from, though you didn't have to be a member of Mensa to guess.

The item was fewer than fifty words long, but by mid-morning he had it memorized, and he wasn't the only one. The reference was to a top White House aide with a druggy past, and he supposed, in another moment of detachment, that he should be complimented by his rise in status. Not surprisingly, the item was of interest to more than a few souls, including the President of the United States.

At his morning briefing, White House Press Secretary Mike McCurry was forced to state that the White House believed the story was "a load of hooey," but that given the serious nature of the charge, they would conduct an internal investigation, "despite the fact that we believe it to be a particularly nasty rumor with less basis in fact than we usually find in gossip columns."

His brave demeanor, the nonchalance with which he went on to other subjects despite the interest of the White House press corps, did not reflect the internal telephone traffic going on at that moment between the West Wing and the Department of Justice. Nor between a pay phone in the basement of the Old Exec and a restaurant on Eighteenth Street, Northwest.

Nicole either was genuinely unavailable, or else was toying with him, not taking his calls as a way of making him sweat further. It was hard for O'Malley to imagine himself sweating further. Though he tried to remain calm, and though there was very little work for him to do now that the Venezuela speech was more or less settled upon by the rump group formed to judge it, he was convinced, even as he walked with the agility of Frankenstein down the hall to the men's room, that everyone knew it was he who was the subject of the item. After a while, it made sense for him simply to crawl behind his computer and exude preoccupation with work, and not a fixation on survival.

Nearby in the office of the White House Counsel, Rod Gardener was sitting at his desk, two Danishes and a bag of Cheetos beside him, with a stack of FBI reports piled two feet high. Harold Whitney himself had called White House Counsel Rumson Dickering and ordered him to have his staff immediately begin a review of their collection of the dreaded Office of Personnel Management Standard Form 86's, A.K.A. the Questionnaire for Sensitive Positions. Since Dickering was a notorious handwringer, and was at this very moment calling his handlers at the ACLU to decide whether it was proper that he should do as asked, it befell Gardener to do the work. He had no more squeamishness doing this than anything else, but he didn't much like today's task for one particular reason. If he were to do a thorough job of leafing through each White House staffer's Form 86, he would have to work straight through lunch, and this was pasta day at the mess, his favorite meal of the week. He frowned and dug in, first to the pastries, then to the paperwork.

That the document on which political appointees were to list their experiences with drugs and alcohol was called Form 86 was either quite a terrific coincidence or evidence of a bureaucratic sense of humor not often invoked. And either way, it was lost on Gardener. For to be "86'd" was to be removed, in the parlance of restaurants and other institutions, and to guarantee your removal from a top government job, all you had to do was mishandle your Form 86. One wrong admission, one sudden surge of confessional enthusiasm, and you were done for. Perhaps the bureaucrat who dreamed up Form 86 was simply a very practical fellow who thought there was no point in coming up with another number for the form whose most extreme consequences were expulsion from government service. Either way, Gardener was forced to leaf through more of them than he cared to, in search of the mysterious White House druggy. He left Cheetos fingerprints on the corners next to question 24, "Your Involvement With Alcohol and Dangerous Drugs, Including Marijuana and Cocaine." He admired the scope of interrogation, to wit, "Do you now use or supply, or within the LAST FIVE YEARS have you used or supplied, marijuana, narcotics, hallucinogens, or other dangerous or illegal drugs?" He chuckled through his Cheetos. What kind of fool would say yes? He immediately leafed through until he got to Harold Whitney's.

It was with particular relish that he looked at the White House Chief of Staff's and his butt boy Bill Tiswell's answers to the yes/no option relating to the question, "Do you now use, or within the LAST FIVE YEARS have you used, alcoholic beverages habitually to excess?" He suspected their negative answers to be lies.

While Gardener bore down trying to get through his task before lunchtime, down in the Office of Political Affairs, over in the Office of Public Liaison, some of the younger staffers were on the phones with friends around town, a peculiar nervousness evident on their faces. In the corridor outside of the Vice President's office there seemed to be two completely different levels of confidence exhibited by staff members, according to one's age, though even some of the older members were on this morning known to head with furtive rubbernecks to the men's room, clutching bottles of Visine with which to mask signs of last night's scotch and soda debauch.

Downstairs in the gym, joggers changing for their runs along the Mall nervously joked about how dull the Christmas parties were going to be this year. Upstairs at the Office of Management and Budget, the elite civil servants whose spread sheets and computer models routinely toted up the billions the government spent, carried with them on this day more than ever an air of superiority.

Around the grounds, the Secret Service, who were known to enjoy their days off, seemed particularly cranky today. They took longer than usual to call names up on their screens at the entrance, and they were more contemptuous than ever of senators and congressmen who arrived for their weekly leadership meetings, even though some of them had been coming every week for years, in war and in peace, through good administrations and bad. When one granite-faced agent with the voice of a Texas Ranger insisted Senator Nelson Bligh, the Majority Leader of the Senate, break out his ID while his car was stopped at the Southwest gate, his aides immediately noted that the President's legislative program was in even more trouble than was generally thought. They got to a phone in the West Wing lobby and said as much to the *National Journal*.

The press office was abuzz with *Newsweek*'s revelation, not least of which because reporters, unsatisfied with what they saw as a brush-off from the Press Secretary, came barging in through the briefing room, two and three at a time, to try to pursue it. There was a sense of revolutionary justice about, and no one, neither the staff in the press office nor the reporters themselves, now knew what the rules were about one's past use of drugs. At any given moment, the portable gallows could show up outside their own front door, and they could be called out. The particular problem with this, as with all instances of revolutionary justice, was the notion that summary executions for fault could be decided upon by someone equally flawed in character, if not more so, and that there was no appeal. Some of the younger reporters were the last souls in America who could afford to have people judged for past drug use, but there was a spore in the air, a fever about, that made them float this way and that, asking tough questions and then arguing among themselves as to whether it was fair that they even brought this up.

When one young television reporter managed to persuade Deputy

Press Secretary Paul Begala to do a stand-up with him on the front lawn, Begala's truculence reflected the mood among the President's public-relations men.

"Have you ever smoked pot?" the blow-dried, slightly nervous new network correspondent asked. The White House was over Begala's shoulder, as were about five other camera crews and correspondents doing their own stand-ups underneath the President's quarters.

"Sure," said Begala, "haven't you?"

The correspondent looked at him for a second, and then lowered both his microphone and his head, though the cameraman kept shooting.

"I can't use that, Paul. My mother watches me when I'm on the air," the correspondent said a little despondently, and with that, Begala wandered back to work, humming, "I Shall Be Released."

At lunchtime on K Street, reporters, lobbyists, lawyers, and pols marveled over the brush fire that was sweeping from the White House. To their credit, a number of the reporters now dining at Duke Zeibert's had earlier in the day seized upon those members of Congress who headed for the radio and television gallery in the Capitol to demand a top-to-bottom investigation of the White House staff, and asked them if they were confident that their own staff could withstand such scrutiny, and for that matter, if they could. One tousle-haired young senator with a sculpted forelock and the voting record of a small-town deacon was stopped dead in his tracks midway through an assault on the White House with a demand for details as to his every action as an undergrad at Duke, class of '71. When the news conference was derailed by his blustering about the Vietnam War, in which he had managed to elude duty—by all accounts, avoiding it was the one thing he'd applied himself to, other than coeds, beer, and dancing the shag—the reporters had gone back to work with a sense of achievement. The ritualistic invocation of squirms was an important part of their job.

At the CBS bureau on Twentieth and M, producers were on the phone, calling up footage of Woodstock, the Chicago convention, and other such artifacts. One producer, perhaps a little too ambitious to actually get a piece on the air by 6:30, was trying to assemble archival footage on Prohibition and other moralistic upheavals in the nation's past, from Carrie Nation to Mothers Against Drunk Driving. Over at the *New York Times* bureau on Eye Street, the Nexis machine had been properly coaxed to cough up not only candidate Hardison's pledges to make America a drug-free nation, but also his admission, three weeks later, that yes, while a student at Columbia in the 1960s, a number of them had tried "boo" before heading downtown to see Peter, Paul and Mary sing "Puff, the Magic Dragon."

Naturally, the *Post* was at full battle stations. Their reporters were proceeding at ramming speed, or at least some of them were. Though there would only be three articles on this the next morning, and though the Style section would produce a rather snide piece about the panic that had suddenly struck an entire generation of Washingtonians, it was no secret that they were determined to be the news organization that discovered exactly who it was their sister publication had been alluding to when it claimed that a "high White House official"—the exact phrase Nicole had used to threaten O'Malley a week or so before—had been involved in the drug trade.

There were many who did not take this seriously, who thought this was a typical Washington tempest in a teapot. While three thousand miles west across the continent the writers for Johnny Carson got down to work, here at the *Post* newsroom, however, Steven Bronstein and Cale McTeague were sitting at their desks in the Metro section, gazing at the action over in National. An outside observer might think that the newspaper's National Desk stars were just socializing with one another, clustered around particular desks, swapping tales. McTeague and Bronstein knew that their compatriots were engaged in the symbiosis of creative tension, one-upping each other and deciding how to set the trap that would snare the White House druggy. And the thing is, they thought perhaps on this one they started out with a better idea than any of the hotshots they could see twenty terminals away.

"Do ya think?" asked Steven.

"Hey, man," said Cale. "Where there's smoke . . ."

"There's smoke?" asked Bronstein.

And then each of them picked up their one-hundred-twenty-two-dollar sports coats and prepared to go investigate.

Because it was a lovely warm day, the main entrance to Globe was open, even though the lunch trade was over. David Nicole sat in the front of the bar with a glass of Quibell mineral water, imported all the way from West Virginia, fizzing on the table in front of him. While Hector and Julio helped the gentlemen from Arcadia Distributors lug in the cases of Canadian beer, Nicole was huddled with his friend John Santangelo, discussing details of a quite different delivery, with an FOB charge that was quite high indeed, its port of embarkation exotic.

"Today's drop dead day," John said, all matter-of-fact.

"That's fine," said Nicole. He hadn't bothered to tie his hair in the customary ponytail, so it was arrayed on the shoulders of his plain oxford shirt.

John was slumped forward on the twin pillars of his arms, a huge hand stirring the sugar in his cappuccino. He looked like he carried the weight of the world, though his shoulders could handle it, and there was a faint edge of melancholy to his demeanor.

The phone next to the cash register at the bar rang once, twice, before somewhere, someone picked it up. Hector and Julio were speaking nonstop with absolutely no inflection in their voices. The street traffic was filled with what qualified in Washington as alternative society, artists, some students, some white-collar workers on their day off, slumming it.

"David, it's for you," called a waitress who'd been sitting smoking cigarettes in the back of the restaurant.

"Who is it?"

"Tom O'Malley."

"Tell him I'm not here," he called.

"Isn't that your friend?" John asked him with a touch of surprise.

"Yeah."

"Shouldn't you take that call?"

"Not yet. I'm going to wait until after the evening news," said Nicole. John Santangelo shrugged. How Nicole conducted his business was up to him. But by the time he got back into his car to drive to Baltimore, from that moment on, they had a deal, and the business they were conducting was serious. He liked Nicole. He was a stand-up guy. But if he didn't come through, he'd be treated like just another small-time bookie with a fistful of losing two-dollar stubs.

he wanted to know what was going on. "Has all hell broken loose down there the way it has up here?"

"Have you seen CNN?"

"No, but I've seen what's on the wires, and I've read *Newsweek*. Tell me, Tom," Kit said firmly. "This is Nicole, isn't it? He's doing this to you, isn't he?"

There was a strong impulse to tell her the truth, but the schoolboy code—Admit Nothing, Deny Everything—was too strong to tamp down. So he told her the closest thing he could to the truth. "I don't know."

"Listen to me," she whispered into the phone. Even the legislative director had to share her office with members of her staff, and Kit had by now grown used to talking to people with her voice hushed. "I've got a senator who doesn't know what he wants to do to make his mark here in Washington. He's got advisers, other than me, outside advisers who are prodding him to make his mark by saying he has lists of White House staffers who, I don't know, smoke crack in the Situation Room. And if Tony Partridge is thinking about doing this, can you imagine what some two-bit congressman from Orange County, California, is thinking of?" She paused to let this sink in. "This is an environment in which you can get hurt, Tom."

"I'm probably a little bit better aware of that than you are, Kit."

"Don't be defensive. I'm just trying to spell it out for you. Have you heard about your FBI clearance yet?"

"No," he admitted, though by now both Colin and Katherine had, and he was beginning to feel a little forlorn about being the only one in the office left hanging. He'd tried not to think about it, especially today.

"Okay, and you've already been a cause célèbre for your drunk-driving conviction."

"I'm aware of this, Kit." He wanted off the phone with her, and fast.

"I'm just trying to point out to you that this whole thing is a disaster for anyone our age who works in the White House, but given your relationship with David Nicole, you could be . . . eviscerated by this. Even if they aren't out to get you, even if they're just trawling, you could easily be the person caught in the net."

"Do you think I'm stupid?"

"You are if you're lying to me about Nicole."

"Good-bye, Kit, I gotta go."

"Don't be a jerk, I'm trying to help. I'm trying to make you *think*, Tom. You know, this is a time for anyone to keep his head down, especially you."

"I gotta go," he whispered. "Really, sweetie, I've got-to-go."

"I'm just trying to make you think," she repeated.

And she had. As he sat there in his office with his head pressed against his computer screen, he was thinking, all right. He was thinking about Nicole's ruthlessness, his single-mindedness when it came to getting what he wanted. He was thinking about his own precarious perch at this desk in the White House, his past association with Nicole endangering him due to the present atmosphere. He was thinking how badly he'd exposed himself to the very pressures Nicole was applying.

Nicole wasn't going to give up this nonsense. He knew him too well, and it was terrifying to think how far he'd go. Under no circumstances could he afford another planted story. The only thing he could think to do was to tell Nicole that he'd do it.

pecial Agent Harlan Bryce, who had some time to kill, ducked into Mr. Eagan's for a quick one. Just a pop, he said to himself with all good intentions. He still had a five o'clock appointment with a former neighbor of his quarry, someone who over the phone had talked about loud fights that might have been the result of drunkenness, and there was something about furniture and other possessions having been thrown out the window and ending up in the alleyway out back. He thought he'd mull this over with a drink. It was his favorite kind of tale: domestic violence. Not even subversion scored those kinds of debilitating points on your career scoreboard anymore.

There was a Ventures song playing on the jukebox and the surf was certainly up for the ten or so souls who'd left the bright midafternoon sunshine of Connecticut Avenue for the understandable want of liquid refreshment. Once responsible society was somewhere outside of the door that closed behind him, he felt safe. Felt pretty good, in fact, as the young bartender poured him a shot of Stoly on ice without the slightest hint of judgment. Just a pop, he reminded himself.

And so he sat there, musing over the beauty of that poured first shot, and thought back, as happened quite often, to his wife's description of him shortly before she became his ex-wife: "A golf ball with its rubber bands about to blow." Jesus, he said to himself, and took a good shot of cool Russian vodka. She had a mouth.

"Bartender, another one," he said without even looking up. He remembered for just an instant the one time he'd come close to getting fired from the Bureau for daytime drinking. It had been around the time that Christina had left him for a Secret Service agent whose only accomplishment, near as he ever could tell, was that he could bowl his weight. That and the bastard once had wrestled to the ground some girl from the Manson family after she took a shot at Gerald Ford, who was Harlan's idea of a first-rate president.

It wasn't a fond memory, and thankfully it passed quickly, but what happened was this: He's sitting around 11:00 A.M. in a bar at a strip joint near the Bureau, deeply in need of a snootful to steady his hands, though his whole person was relieved by just the prospect of the drink in front of him. Just then, as he remembered it, Delano Roosevelt, the only black supervisor in the whole goddamn building, and a man whom Harlan considered an ally, walks in and takes a seat right next to him. "Hello, Harlan," said Roosevelt.

"Delano, how ya doing?" he asked all unimpressed, as if he were a regular 11:00 A.M. drinking partner. He asked it as if Roosevelt's having a drink with him was purely his choice.

"Whatyahaving?" Roosevelt asks with equal nonchalance.

"Oh, had a rough one last night, wife and all. Thought I'd have a vodka."

"I see," says Harlan's boss, and of course, when the bartender comes over, he orders a Coke.

The problem, near as he could remember it, was that his hands were shaking so much he couldn't get the drink to his mouth, and that was under the best of circumstances, which, his boss beside him, these weren't. So the best he could do, and now he chuckled thinking about it, it was a painful memory, but he had to laugh at his craftiness, what he did was turn to Roosevelt and say, "Do you remember Tad O'Meara?"

"Can't say I do, Harlan."

"Sure you do," said Harlan. "He was the guy used to drink during the day all the time, until it got to the point where he couldn't even get the drink from the bar to his lips, his hands shook so much. So sometimes you'd find him and he'd have to lean over," and with this Harlan leaned over, "and sip from his drink," which Harlan now did, his lip affixed to the rim of glass, his nose hanging over the edge almost level with the bar.

He got that first sip down, and from there it was a cinch to drain the sucker. He walked out of the bar trying to persuade Roosevelt that he didn't have a problem other than his wife's departure, and he thought he had him swayed, because Roosevelt, who was actually kind of a good guy, told him that he had to clean up his act, and then left it at that. Three weeks later, some congressional investigation named Roosevelt as having been particularly zealous in the surveillance of left-wing groups and next thing he knew, Harlan's boss was being transferred to Little Rock. He never saw him again.

He smiled thinking about it, and looking at his watch, saw that he had time for just one more. There was a guy in a three-piece suit sitting next to him who looked at him out of the corner of his eye when he contemplated ordering another. "If the White House can do it, you can, right, buddy?"

"Right," said Harlan, agreeably, though he hoped the guy didn't try to engage him in conversation.

The bartender came over, and after Harlan signaled him by lifting his empty glass, the fellow to his right said to the bartender, "You got any good connections at the White House, Mike?" The bartender grinned.

"Used to be you could get 'ludes from the White House doctor back in the Carter years." The bartender said it like he'd lined up outside the security gates for his scrip.

"Ancient history, man," said the guy to his right, and Harlan agreed. What were these guys talking about?

Just then, on the television above the bar, which Mr. Eagan's usually had connected to a basketball game they brought down from the satellite dish, he saw the somber face of a Cable News Network anchor mouthing silently while the graphic said "White House Drug Investigation," and then they were shown a stand-up on the front lawn itself.

"What's going on?" he asked the fellow next to him.

"You haven't heard? They say there's some guy dealing drugs out of the White House. Just between us," he said confidentially, "I hear the quality of the stuff is primo." And with that, the guy winked. And with that, Harlan was paid up and out the door, leaving his drink on the bar untouched.

"Oh, well," said the fellow he'd left behind. "No use letting it go to waste. Salud."

 here were times when his runs made him feel like he was an expensive ten-speed gliding down the autobahn at a hundred kilometers per. And then there were times when he felt like a rusty old dump truck lumbering down a logging trail. Tonight, fortunately, he felt like a greyhound, and the mechanical rabbit he chased brought him down from the heights of Adams Morgan to the Mall at about a seven-minute pace.

There were hundreds of tourists visible on the bluff as he turned up toward the Washington Monument, the powerful lights heralding the obelisk like it was the middle of an air raid, or the opening of a movie entitled *Springtime in Washington*. The cherry blossoms that rimmed the Tidal Basin were no longer visible. They'd been shredded by rain and insulted by a sudden cold snap that had come and left with manic indecision. The expanse of the long Mall between the Lincoln Memorial and the Capitol Building was breathtaking even to someone whose oxygen intake was rhythmically paced to a metronome set on high.

He was trying to purge fear and anxiety, to pound it out, as he ran up the hill toward the monument. The winds whipped the circle of American flags, and the heroic lighting revealed the line of tourists who gathered each spring evening at dusk for a chance to internally ascend the highest point in the federal city.

He was a little out of breath when he got to the top of the hill. He'd been pushing it because he had to be back, showered, and changed in time for his weekly court-ordered counseling cum A.A. meeting, and the one good thing that had come out of the day, the one thing that if he looked back upon this day from the vantage point of later years— and he would, there wasn't a doubt about that—was that his father had agreed to come along with him.

So he slowed, allowed himself to catch his breath though it was in contravention of the runner's catechism. He walked for a minute across the flat top of the hill underneath the spire that rose like the national lightning rod. In front of him was the Capitol, rising far more magisterially than it deserved, considering the kinds of activities that took place in it every day it was in session. To his right, across the Tidal Basin, was the perfectly proportioned white marble dome of the Jefferson Memorial. Behind him, down the hill he'd just run up, was the austere Lincoln Memorial. O'Malley wondered sometimes if the rectangular Reflecting Pool in front of Lincoln's perch might be called that for more than one reason: it was the clearest, most meditative spot in the capital city. And now here he was on top of the hill that rose from it, looking down toward the polite, compact monument he could see off to his left across the Ellipse, the White House. He couldn't help thinking it was the most singular piece of beauty in his sight. He wondered what it said about him that he was now willing to break the law in order to keep from being locked out of it. He hoped it said he was someone who wanted to do good things for his country, who was forced to engage in a criminal act as his price for that.

He stopped short, pulled up. What you are doing is wrong, and only incidentally, very stupid, he said to himself.

There was nothing admirable about his desperation to stay working in the White House, which rankled mightily. There was nothing romantic about his caving in to Nicole. He looked at his watch. It was time to get pounding again, time to think only that he was breathing minute by minute, in his quest to quash the trouble in his system and be home in time to keep his life moving forward.

I t was meta-journalism time in Washington. That is, the only thing to write about was journalism itself. Since no one as yet could take the story in *Newsweek* further, within a day, as rumors broke everywhere that this publication or that was set to roll with the inside scoop on crack rings in the Oval Office, reporters had nothing to write about except for the efforts, and frustrations, of their colleagues. They could not legitimately report rumors, but they could, with forced bemusement, write about the problems their fellow reporters were having in tracking those rumors down.

In so doing, they were able to get into print and thus perpetuate all manner of crazy tales, legitimizing them to the extent that they could be written about anew. It was a neat trick.

While one newspaper would print every last long shot their reporters had been told, in order to give the nation the flavor of the Washington rumor mill, another would muse on the tortured consciences of those poor younger journalists put in the position, alas, of having to write about a subject which, had the tables been turned on them, they would have been loath to discuss. When "Nightline" went on the air that Tuesday with its discussion of "Rumors and the New Reportage," a variety of editors clucked about how terrible it was, though what were they to do? They then gave voice to the most outrageous of the tales that were circulating Washington, only to hold up their hands in protest and hasten to add that, so far, these were, of course, nothing they'd been able to prove.

By end of Wednesday, the furor appeared to have died down, partly because there were skillful backgrounders from the White House allowing that they were deeply concerned about the stories, investigating mightily, but with assurances thus far that everyone from the FBI to the National Security Council was convinced that the Periscope item was a plant by hostile Republicans, out to embarrass Hardison on the eve of his first trip abroad. This precipitated a round of discussions about whether or not the media were being used by skillful practitioners of the malignant leak.

By Thursday, there was an anti-Periscope backlash evident, especially from reporters for *Time*, who huffily declared that they'd heard some of the same things, but that they had the obligation to *prove* their stories, to make them *factual* before they could get them into print. They would then go on to say they couldn't, as yet, prove that, let's see, Harold Whitney had long been an abuser of methaqualone, that the Secretary of State had returned from his years as Ambassador to Pakistan with a vicious opium dependency, or even that there were cocaine and cough-medicine parties regularly taking place among assistants to the President and women from the West Wing at Friday night poolside soirees. Word-of-mouth party patter was that even the *Post* was frustrated in its attempts to show that the fact-spewing and unkempt Director of the Office of Management and Budget, a notoriously hardworking and suspiciously slim numbers-cruncher whose résumé revealed the indicting fact of his having graduated from Berkeley, actually had a quite monumental metamphetamine habit, though an analysis of his behavioral patterns could lend circumstantial credence to the charge.

The story the White House reacted to Friday with great umbrage was that the First Lady had been an experimenter in hallucinogens when she was a student at Vassar, class of '66. White House Press Secretary Mike McCurry was given high marks for the lecture he delivered to the assembled press corps that things were getting out of hand. He did, however, have to release a chronology that showed that at the time the First Lady had been at Vassar, the notorious Timothy Leary had already been run out of nearby Millbrook by G. Gordon Liddy. The White House was rumored to have tried tracking down either Liddy or Leary, who were said these days to be fast friends, in order to have them issue a statement that Mrs. Hardison had neither tuned in nor turned on. It was demonstrable from her transcript that she had not dropped out.

In the midst of all this, the White House was trying to prepare for Monday's departure to Santiago. They carried on briefings as if all were normal, skillfully managing the expectations for their journey. The inauguration of the new Chilean President was being heralded as a great moment for Democracy in the Americas, and the stop in Venezuela was seen as a strategically important effort on the new administration's behalf to grapple with the problem of Third World debt. The most controversial aspect of the trip—the renewal of upgraded diplomatic relations with Nicaragua, replete with Most Favored Nation trade status—had by this time been argued round and flat on all the talk shows. It was clear that in the atmosphere of rumor that had settled upon the nation's capital, the fortuitous timing of the President's trip was a lucky diversion. Though it had been set into motion by a combination of the President's wishes and O'Malley's insert into his inaugural address, on the Sunday before Air Force One was to lift off, there was the story in *The New York Times* about Harold Whitney's masterminding the thing from the beginning. At least there was something O'Malley could laugh about that week.

e couldn't just show up. That would be too simple, too logical. Too much to ask.

Somehow it made perfect sense to O'Malley that his father would come to a meeting of Alcoholics Anonymous with a lawyer. "Da-ad," said O'Malley when they met in the lobby. Upstairs was where the small

group he was required to attend each week met with Hal, their counselor.

"I suppose you know my lawyer," his father said formally. He was
dressed in a bespoke tailored suit and his shoes had been shined by
Carmela. He looked like he was set to make another appearance before
a select congressional committee.

"Hi, Uncle Jake."

"Hello, Tom. Shall we proceed?"

"If by that you mean get on the elevator, why don't we."

So they walked over to the ornate elevator and O'Malley pressed the
button. They had to wait awkwardly in silence for the operator to swing
it back down to the ground floor to pick them up. His Uncle Jake, an
immense man with a courtly manner and a bushy gray mustache, held
the door open for them and his father entered first. He slid to the
back and wouldn't look at O'Malley as they ascended to the third
floor.

It didn't go much better through the counseling, or later, in the
nearby meeting of A.A. His Uncle Jake, whom O'Malley knew to be
a half-quart-a-day man himself, kept up his end by prompting his client
with asides of "You don't have to answer that," when he was asked the
most basic of questions. Hal's equilibrium seemed to be thrown off by
the sight of the two older gentlemen in their Savile Row suits sitting as
erect as senior civil servants on the tube to Whitehall. When he turned
and asked Robert O'Malley if he felt he had a problem abusing alcohol,
Uncle Jake barked "Objection!" so loudly the Episcopalian minister
attending the session with them visibly jumped, and then moved with
sidelong glances down the couch.

O'Malley's instant reaction was to say, "Drinking isn't a problem,
Hal. It comes easily to him." And with that, he didn't just have his
father to reckon with, but his father's lawyer as well. In short order he
was accused of badgering the witness, and it was only with a non-
aggression pact negotiated by Hal that the group could continue.

Afterward, when they had gone through the A.A. meeting in the
basement of a downtown church, O'Malley cringing the whole time at
the notion that, anonymity or no, he would see a coworker, the three
of them went to Duke Zeibert's for a late supper. His Uncle Jake worked
the room like a ward heeler. The two older men were relaxed and jovial
as they were served martinis and then a fine bottle of Chardonnay with
their fried clams. O'Malley sat there as his Uncle Jake got plowed and
occasionally reached over and gave him a good whack on the shoulder
to show him how much he loved him. It was infectious, and at some

point he ceased sipping Perrier and joined in on the wine. As soon as he did that, Uncle Jake ordered another bottle. By the time he got home he'd had a grand time and for the life of him couldn't have said what was the purpose of the evening.

I t was clearly embarrassing for him to have to admit this in front of his staff and advisers, but this was the time to put his foot down and he did so. "I can't do that, Jerry," Senator Partridge was saying, and Kit's heart was beating so hard she was certain Wilbur Todd must be able to hear it. Her boss's bad fortune with the *Casper Star-Tribune* just might save O'Malley from another broadside.

"Tony," said Mike Humperdink, and with Jerry Jetta having made his pitch first, he was clearly lined up as the number-two punch, "even if the Governor says you're a child molester, there's no reason you can't ride this one all the way to reelection. This is drugs, Tony. Drug use in the White House. Electoral kryptonite."

"It's election, Mike, not reelection, so let's be straight about this. I don't have the same slack cut for me as someone who's been in a term or two. And when the largest paper in the state is willing to print this," he said, tossing the newspaper that was on the desk over to Jerry Jetta, who was closest to him, "it's pretty clear there are some charges I can't just drop and then hope to brazen through. What are my negatives?" he demanded of Kit.

"An upwardly creeping thirty percent."

"Yeah, see, it's not going to work."

What he was pointing to was a fifty-column-inch background declaration of vulnerability that could only have come from a prepared brief pieced together by political consultants, research staff, people with the goods and without shame. It had taken up a large portion of the front page of the Sunday paper usually devoted to farm yields; hot news from the Interior Department; and from Yellowstone, biologists' analyses of coprolitic bear droppings. The Governor's fingerprints weren't quite visible in the light, but if you turned the paper to the proper angle, the shadow of the bastard giggling was clear to see.

What the story said was that "Wyoming GOP sources" were "concerned" about Tony Partridge's weaknesses as a candidate should he actually begin to think that he'd been placed into the Senate as anything other than a temp. In fact, reading the piece, the image Tony thought of was one of those mink toilet seat warmers he'd seen advertised in the Neiman's catalogue. Even the most favorable sources allowed that while Tony was a good guy, he was in a bit over his head. This might not be the case had Tony applied himself in school, but he hadn't. There for the world to see was his grade-point average for the nine semesters, yes, nine semesters, he spent at Colorado College. He blushed when he first read that one, even in the privacy of his office. The implication was strong that if he hadn't spent as much time in Aspen hanging out in a house that was later raided by Colorado state troopers investigating marijuana traffickers, he might not have had to attend his junior year one and one half times.

Then: the strong whiff of adultery in his relations with his former law partner's wife—it seemed he'd come *that* close to being named a co-respondent in the divorce—and there were numerous on-the-record quotes from bartenders around Casper who thought they were doing him a favor by attesting to how often he got lucky at the various happy hours and wet t-shirt nights it took to get through the long Wyoming winter.

And now here was Tony Partridge having to tell the operatives who wanted to run his campaign that perhaps he was an imperfect vehicle to run a moralistic assault on the White House, and Kit was all but set to cheer. Her eyes gleaming with admiration was in marked contrast to the agitation evident by both Humperdink and Jetta, though Wilbur Todd looked remarkably impassive, like a man who simply punched the clock and tore pages off his calendar to mark the time.

"You're not going to let a newspaper article spook you out of the race, are you, Tony?"

"No, I'm not."

Kit thought she could sense a palpable wave of relief from the two sleazoids who, whether they knew it or not, viewed getting O'Malley's scalp as the tangible first act in Partridge's campaign. Whether the Senator won or lost, they would nonetheless collect fat fees, especially the way they worked up their contract, which called for them to have a sizable chunk of the media buy. She knew they were motivated toward victory, not because they cared about Partridge, but because having never been involved in a genuinely successful race, they sorely needed one. This made them dangerous men.

"You realize, then, that you may have to do some things you don't want to do." Humperdink said this like he was lecturing a child about homework.

"I realize it better than you. Just take my word for it, will you please, that with this as the background," and he pointed to the paper, "I'm not in a position to make any charges about drug use. Do you need me to spell it out for you?"

"No, but—"

"Save it. Okay, Kit, bring me your file on cholesterol. And ask Billmire to get in here with the files on Guatemala and multilateral development banks."

"Boring," said Jetta aloud. He looked wounded in his chair.

But Partridge wouldn't hear of it. "No, Jerry, not boring. Safe."

It was all Kit could do to keep from yelling hooray as she walked out the door. She was about to call O'Malley when she remembered they weren't talking, and by the time she was back in the office, she had on a suitably serious frown. Cholesterol was a serious issue.

H e let him stew for three whole days before he took the call, and even when he took it, he pretended for a long couple of minutes that he didn't know what O'Malley was talking about.

"Um, Tom, could you get to the point? I've been too busy to read anything this week. There was something in *Newsweek*, you say."

"Just tell me where you want me to meet you, preferably not at your restaurant. I shouldn't be seen with you."

He didn't have the heart to tell him that since it was O'Malley who was going to come back into the United States with a goddamn duffel bag of contraband, it was O'Malley, in fact, who was the dangerous one to be seen with. They set a time and a place, and for a moment when he hung up the phone, he felt like a bastard. For a moment.

W hile Tom O'Malley was un-
furling his umbrella and hop-
ping from puddle to puddle
on his way home to change his clothes, with several hours to kill before
his rendezvous with Nicole at the 9:30 Club, Kit was the last one left
in her office. The Senate office quiet but for the rain lashing at her
lone window overlooking a dull stretch of Maryland Avenue, she was
working on the Partridge-Leach Healthful Diet Act, and was far too
engrossed in the prospects of vanquishing the nation's low-density lipoproteins to feel even a little bit blue.

She had this one so well worked out in her mind, she doubted she'd
even have to submit it to Legislative Counsel for the cursory constitutional checkup. Rather than having had to spend her time wheedling
over the phone with other Senate-side legislative directors, as word of
mouth spread about Partridge's first initiative, cosponsors were calling
her. Judging from the bipartisan response she was getting even before
the wording of the bill was in her computer, she thought it likely that
Partridge-Leach would be fast-tracked through the system, and there
were other staffers who had said aloud over the phone, "Why didn't we
think of that?" She was far too pleased with Partridge, with herself, to
think for more than an instant about the downward roller-coaster rush
that marked this week's relationship with O'Malley.

While Kit worked in the Hart Building, rain was lashing the Capitol,
rain was washing Washington. Great rivulets were dividing Constitution
Avenue and chasing after the huddled taxis at the bottom of Capitol
Hill. The light changed and they broke into an expanded cluster of
smeared red taillights in the canyon between the East Wing of the
National Gallery and the Canadian Embassy. The jogging paths on the
Mall were being pocked by the springtime downpour, and on the South
Lawn of the White House the tulip beds were being shredded. No
sooner had they emerged from the last vestiges of winter than the Maryland monsoons had swept in, and when they left, if ever they left, it
was quite likely that the District would be in the full steamy clutch of
summer.

While O'Malley wrestled with his bumbershoot and was drenched,
a few blocks away on Fifteenth Street *The Washington Post* was witness

to Steve Bronstein and Cale McTeague pitching their editor once more to let them pursue the hunch they had about who—if the *Newsweek* item continued to be believed—might actually have dealt drugs before going to work at the White House. It was a tough sale. They had no direct evidence, nothing even indirect that was really all that interesting, and there was a jurisdictional dispute the editor would have to grapple with, for they were dealing with the White House, the most elite of beats. But they were persistent fellows, they marshaled their evidence well, and they thought they could sense the tide was turning.

Outside, there were great aquatic sprays scattering bystanders as cars turned the corner onto Eye Street. A straight shot to Georgetown would have brought a driver within drenched blocks of Robert O'Malley's townhouse, where the aging agent was listening in disbelief to his brother-in-law, as he told him that divorce papers were being prepared in New York and were to be served within a matter of days. He sat in his slightly messy den as the dogs moaned and tried to hide under his desk while the thunder rumbled and the sheets of lightning over the Potomac lit up the Virginia sky. He would not have been any more surprised had a blue electric charge come out of the phone itself, and when the conversation was over, he rose slowly, convinced that if ever there was an occasion when a man deserved a drink, this was it.

Cocktails were being served in the screened-in porch of Clarissa Lowery's nearby Georgetown manse, and while cats were seen swaying midst the potted plants, the hostess's earthy voice was in low chuckle at the remarks of Senator Chester Berretta, for whom she had gathered the twenty or so lobbyists and conservative activists, their checkbooks in hand. It was a fundraiser she was hosting, though the sardonic Senator had no opponent, no race anytime soon, and no fear that one would develop. While a butler circulated with stems of champagne, Berretta regaled the group with the latest rumors about President Hardison himself sending aides out to the many D.C. drug markets to make purchases for his Camp David recreation. "Why do you think," the Senator asked, "he's made South America his first destination?" And there were nods and knowing smiles around the room. What had before been a somewhat stiff gathering now became a free-for-all of abuse heaped on the recently inaugurated President. Berretta certainly knew how to break the ice.

Straight down R Street and cascading over the cemetery's edge into the engorged Rock Creek, the water rushed, though Tim Skelton sat in his car across a narrow strip of grass in the traffic that moved in jerks. Attempting to exit up the hill on Massachusetts Avenue, he was stopped in his car with the radio playing, while the rain poured down and his mind was all but blank, deadened from a long day of talking on the phone to the Land O' Lakes Radio Network, the Watertown, South Dakota, *News Argus*, and other such major radio outlets that regularly followed the actions of the Ag Sec. The only thing at all that stood out in his mind, other than the prospect of soon being home with his wife, was the ominous phone call he'd received from the FBI agent who already had questioned him about his friend Tom O'Malley.

He would have been hard pressed to say—though he had no intention of telling anyone about it—what disturbed him most: the questions that the guy asked him, or the mere fact that he called back as if he knew Skelton wanted to be helpful to him. He supposed he should let O'Malley know that the guy had called twice, and especially that he asked if Skelton had even the slightest indication that O'Malley had, in an earlier life, been involved in the dealing of drugs. But his friend had reacted so strangely when he'd told him weeks before that he'd had the first conversation with the G-man, he didn't know what to do. The FBI agent didn't seem to know anything, he was obviously fishing, but even that was a frightening thought. Just then the traffic broke as the light must have changed out of sight up on Massachusetts, and Skelton gunned the engine of his subcompact and made it halfway up the hill before being stopped anew. He sat staring at the water that was pouring off the back of the Japanese Embassy and rolling down the road to the roiled Rock Creek.

Downstream at the Watergate, cars were turning off onto Virginia Avenue and heading toward the White House, where Rod Gardener and Bill Tiswell were going over the report that tomorrow would be handed to the President. The room was a mess, with dozens of piles of FBI reports, Form 86's, containers of carryout food, and transcripts of interviews the transition team and the Personnel Office had conducted with would-be White House staffers. From this they'd assembled their package. They had a list, a little list, of suspects that they deemed likely as any to have been the one that *Newsweek* had in mind. These included an assistant secretary for policy who had beaten Tiswell at tennis the summer before, and an assistant press secretary who had cut in front of Gardener in the line for the salad bar at the mess. Also included were a variety of staffers who just seemed odd, having risen through the ranks to their positions at the White House through a variety of coalitional organizations neither Tiswell nor Gardener much trusted. These were abortion rights activists and other feminist fronts, think-tank grads and Ivy League professors, farm organizers active in the Iowa caucuses, not to mention civil servants who had long worked with Hardison when he was a Cabinet officer, and thus had no need to appropriately kowtow to Tiswell. They were about to hand their little project in to the secretary they'd asked to stay late when a quick conference went like this.

"O'Malley?"

"Yeah, sure, he's a jerk."

"Okay."

By such deliberations, he was chosen to be included in the collection of offending 86's that were to be forwarded to the Chief Executive. Later, when the floodgates opened and O'Malley was all but washed away, this action would be but salt in the ocean, just one more element that nearly swept him under.

For now, he was standing outside his apartment door, drenched through, his shoes ruined. He shook his umbrella and left it to dry, but it would prove useless to protect him from what was coming down.

The wall of sound was not the only obstacle to entrance, there was also the matter of ID. "You have to be kidding," O'Malley said to the pale, long-haired bouncer who was blocking his way into the 9:30 Club. "No way, man," came the reply, and so O'Malley, who'd celebrated his twenty-first birthday at least a couple of presidents ago, fished in his pocket for something that would vouch for his age.

"Would you accept a White House ID?" It was worth a shot. His driver's license having been suspended, directly the result of his last visit here, there wasn't anything else he could find other than an American Express card that might attest to his good standing in the world of adults. And if he was a member in good standing in that world, what was he doing here? This was a very good question.

The doorman stared myopically at the card. "C'mere and look at this," he said with what passed for excitement to one of his t-shirted cohorts. Now they were passing it between them as a small crowd backed up at the doorway, and within seconds his White House ID was being circulated and O'Malley was standing there feeling like a jerk.

"This good enough for you?" he said, grabbing it back from a girl who was gazing down at it like it was a map to an alien world.

"How do we know you aren't just an intern?" the doorman asked, but it was clear from what passed as a smile on his lips that he was toying with him, and within a moment, O'Malley was in the door as the Pixies' "Wave of Mutilation" reverberated playfully around the room.

He searched the crowd near the bandstand for Nicole, but couldn't find him. It was early yet, and he wasn't worried. There were buzz-saw chords from a band he couldn't identify ripping through the speakers, and the Jetsons cartoons on the interspersed videos lent the place a rec-room ambience he quite enjoyed. He went into the hallway to the back door to look for his coconspirator, and when he couldn't find him there either, he pulled up a chair and ordered a beer.

Having some time to contemplate what he was doing there wasn't what the doctor ordered. Here was the familiar feeling he'd had in any number of situations when he knew if he just got up and walked out the door, he wouldn't get in trouble. Somehow the unifying element between those events and this one was Nicole. He stayed glued to his seat and thought how his life had been permanently changed by that freshman philosophy class he took at Amherst wherein he learned of the principle of causal determinism. Cause was sufficient that he be there, therefore it was necessary. That was that.

No, that wasn't that. It wasn't passivity that had brought him here. It was fear. Of that maniac, Nicole.

"Thought I'd find you back here," Nicole said as he slid onto the empty stool next to him. He seemed not to notice O'Malley tense up on his arrival.

He was surprisingly low-key for the adult Nicole, wearing a simple leather jacket and a t-shirt. If he'd been shoeless, he could easily have passed for the Nicole of their college years. "I haven't been here in a while."

"Is this Macy's checking out Gimbels?"

"You picked the place, chum. And, with all due respect, this isn't competition to Globe."

"If you say so, David," said the grisly biker of a bartender who came over and noncommittally slid a Heineken in front of Nicole. He didn't appear to expect any money for it.

"How you been, man?"

"Good," said the bartender. "Long time."

"You know where to find me."

"I'm being a good boy these days. I'm out of the business." And with that he sidled down the bar where two kids with dyed-blonde Mohawks were bouncing like they had to go to the bathroom. There was a twenty-dollar bill pressed between the fingers of the male of the species as if it were a flag. As he hung on to the bar, trying to get the bartender's attention, he and his cohort pogoed to the beat.

"Old friend?" O'Malley asked, nodding toward the bartender.

"Old customer. I haven't seen him in a while."

"Customer at your bar?"

"Not quite."

"Oh, great. I thought we were going to meet someplace where neither of us was known."

"Settle down, Thomas, will you. You never used to be this jumpy."

"I've never been blackmailed before, either. This is uncharted territory for me. I guess probably not for you, huh."

Nicole just took a sip of his beer and looked around the room. The place was getting crowded, it was getting time for the band to come on, and there were students from George Washington and A.U., some local 9:30 Club regulars, and a handful of congressional workers out for an evening either pressed against the walls looking at the monitors or else choking the hallway from the dance floor to the bar.

"Just tell me," Nicole said softly. "Are you going to do it?" He was staring straight ahead at the bottles lined up underneath the posters of bands that recently had played there, and his face was almost utterly devoid of emotion. Ten years before, O'Malley would have been delighted to have been sitting in a club with him, even on a school night, out later than they ought to be to see Richard Hell and the Voidoids, the Raybeats, Eight-Eyed Spy.

"Let me ask you this, then." He was trying to match Nicole's softer demeanor, but it was hard. His resentment fought its way to the surface, and O'Malley had to work to wrestle it under control. "Are you going to be more specific in your next plant? Is the next article going to say that a White House staffer who went to Amherst and whose initials are T.O. is the person reporters and the FBI should look into?"

"I guess if I have to," Nicole said, and this time he looked at O'Malley. Pure defiance. An attitude like that of any kid who'd walked through the doors of this place with a ripped leather jacket looking for a fight.

In the background they could hear some local band plug in and quickly tune their instruments before plunging into their first, fast, pretty awful song. As kids moved into the room with the bandstand, the bar nearly emptied until it was the two of them sitting near the end of it, almost by themselves.

"What kind of person are you? What have you become, David?"

"I'm your best friend."

That didn't qualify as an answer. "Great." And then a shadow came across his face. "You leave Tawnee in Colombia." Nicole made to protest, but O'Malley raised his finger to stop him. "You just left her there. I never even found out what happened to her—no one did. It's a mystery to the Consulate, or actually, not that much of a mystery. She's just abandoned by you. And then I waste time trying to track you down so I can kill you—I swear to God, I was going to kill you, David— but you're nowhere to be found. And I looked, I really looked. You were off in Mazatlán or something and I was kicking myself, until finally I decide to get a little serious about life and I get my act together. And now you come back into my life after I've grown up and have some vulnerabilities and you blackmail me. I really want to know, where did you get so far off track?"

"I could ask you the same thing, pal. You were a very interesting guy. You were a wonderful writer, one of the most creative people I ever knew. You can blame me for it, but the fact is, you're the guy who made the decision to be a lawyer." If he were any more contemptuous, he would likely have spat on the floor. "And a speechwriter. Hack professions."

"Okay, but I grew up, David. I'm not caught in some fantasy out of an Eagles song." Then, softer, "I'm not hurting anybody."

"Are you going to do it or not?" He made it seem as if his vast reservoir of patience had been exhausted.

"Yeah, David, I'm going to do it. And then I want you to stay away from me for the rest of my life. And away from Kit, too. We don't want anything to do with you. Not a Christmas card, not a postcard from Kathmandu."

"You're just so superior, aren't you. Both of you, with your perfect little D.C. careers."

"Okay, okay, enough. Let's just go over the details of this." O'Malley drained his beer and smacked it down on the bar, letting the rings of suds slowly melt downward to the bottom of the bottle. He turned to his tormentor and waited for his instructions, which were delivered while the feedback from the band's guitar masked their conspiracy. He was going to commit a felony. He was going to do something he knew was wrong. At this point, there was no turning back.

After a while they made their way toward the front of the club and watched a band put in the kind of performance that years before they would simply have marked down as having been worthy of their time. Nothing special, just worthy of their time. This on the premise that time was immeasurable.

Time was running out and he was only half packed. His face flushed, he stuffed socks into the side pocket of the Gurkha bag that passed for his suitcase and roughly divided underwear into days on the road, having to stop for a moment to count out loud. The phone rang and he ignored it as long as he could, gathering his laptop and the laser printer he was bringing along should there need to be revisions in any of the speeches the President was to deliver on the trip. Suits? In the hanging bag. Toiletries? In the kit. Kit. He looked at his watch. She was going to pick him up and take him to the White House in exactly ten minutes and he still had much to do. They were pushing it if he was going to make it in time for his ride in the convoy out to Andrews. He picked up the phone.

"Thomas, it's your father."

"Hey, Dad, I'm really crunching here. Can I call you from the airport?"

"This will only take a few minutes. It's important."

"I'll call you."

"But—"

"No, Dad, I got to move."

He was lugging the computer equipment to the front door when there was a knock. This was going to be good. He had mere minutes before Kit was expected downstairs, which could only mean that standing outside his door was an encyclopedia salesman with a guaranteed long-winded rap, the unintelligible Salvadoran janitor who beset O'Malley with his problem with the "womens," or some variation on the theme of bill collectors and bureaucrats who made house calls. He flung the door open with the expectation of having to shoo whoever it was away. And the person standing in the hallway looking like something out of a dream was Kit Bowles.

"Darling," he exclaimed, surprised. She was dressed in a spring skirt that clearly had been invented with her legs in mind, and the shirt she had on was a rather elegant tee, not particularly suitable for working in a Republican office unless you were feeling secure on the cusp of puckish.

He hadn't seen her in what seemed like too long. Over the phone, even arranging her chauffeuring him to the White House, they'd been snippy and arch in the particular manner of the overly educated in the midst of a fight, and yet the communication it was instantly obvious she was interested in here was decidedly non-verbal. She walked in with her face pressed to his and pushed him, their mouths joined, toward the bed, though he was tripping over bags on his backward tango. When he thought he could afford a free-fall, he landed square in the middle of the unmade tangle of sheets with Kit crashing down on top of him, and their mouths never broke contact, either then or as she wrestled his pinstripes down below his knees. He couldn't see what she was doing with her hands, but what she was doing with her tongue hadn't been legal in this country until at least midway through the Kennedy Administration, of that he was sure. Soon, he was an inflated raft on the deep blue sea, and the swells, which rose and fell to a tempo determined in the heavens, gently washed them home.

o O'Malley it was part and parcel of the lack of justice in life that Kit had her license and he did not. She couldn't drive. Rather, she drove remarkably fast, with the aggression of a prison escapee, which was needed right about now, given how late he was. There was, however, no evidence of her ever having seen the movies they show in Driver's Ed in the hope of leaving an indelible impression on soft, adolescent minds.

He hung on and closed his eyes as she went through the tunnel under Dupont Circle at a pace that would have scared him on a thruway. And then cars spilled into the funnel of Connecticut Avenue at about N Street and things ground down to a halt. "Sweet Mother of God," O'Malley said in prayer.

"Relax, Thomas, if you get to the White House too late for your ride, I'll run you out to Andrews."

"Have you ever been there?"

"No."

"Do you know how to get there?"

"Not really."

"Ohhhhhhhh," he intoned, like a sick dog, and thinking of dogs, he remembered he had to call his father. In fact, his father would know how to get to the Air Force base. If the traffic didn't break, and they arrived at the White House with the convoy that was to head out there already gone, he'd get to the pay phones on Seventeenth and Pennsylvania and find out from his father the fastest way out. But he hoped he didn't have to do it. With the entire White House senior staff particularly conscious of protocol—he had no doubt there were people who hadn't slept last night when they received their packets from White House Advance and found out where they were seated on the plane—it wouldn't be helpful to have to arrive at the guard tower at Andrews in a screech and jog with his computer equipment.

Then the traffic broke at M and they were able to make it all the way down to Pennsylvania in one invigorating shot, Kit weaving in and out of taxis in a manner that had the cabbies shaking their dreadlocks in wonder. "I love you," he said to her when she let him out across Seventeenth Street from the Old Exec. He nuzzled her face with his and looked at his watch all at once, and presumed he would just make it. He was exhilarated, exhausted, and on the verge of getting weepy all at once. But then he picked up his hanging bag and Gurkha, his laptop and his crudely boxed printer, and as he staggered through the rush hour traffic to get across the street, he watched her zoom off as if this separation were a common occurrence and didn't have the potential for a terrible permanence.

t was a lucky break, but it made perfect sense, that the last person left for the shuttle of Chryslers was an assistant press secretary, Max Pearlman, with whom O'Malley had been friends since before the giddy days of the New Hampshire primary. It made sense because, other than O'Malley and a handful of advance men, Max was the lowest-ranking White House official to make it on the manifest. He too had thought he was going to be left behind, and so there was a palpable sense of relief when the plainly dressed Army aide who was part of the cadre of White House drivers took his bags and placed them in the trunk of the car along with O'Malley's gear.

"Didn't think I was going to make it, man," said Pearlman with a grin. He was the nicest of guys, a slightly balding diminutive sort who once, in a bar in Atlanta on the Super Tuesday night they'd won eleven primaries, allowed as how he was working for Hardison to get a novel out of the experience—and upon puffy-eyed reflection the next day had all but begged O'Malley to forget he'd ever said it. Even in Washington, you weren't supposed to announce your kiss-and-tell intentions before the consummation.

Now they got into the Chrysler as their silent driver waved to the Service agents at the Southwest gate and gunned it onto E Street. Within moments they were riding over the Memorial Bridge as the sun sparkled on the Potomac and the distant spires of the Cathedral loomed over a bend in the river that was Georgetown. O'Malley sat back and let the sun warm his face and just felt silly.

He chatted with Max, who had similar tastes in music, and thought he noticed the Army aide's eyes flash in the rearview at the mention of the Gang of Four, though they stayed on the road as he and the assistant press secretary reminisced over the Fall. As the name of Echo and the Bunnymen reverberated in the car, they were heading north to Maryland discussing the relative merits of Magazine and Mission of Burma, Pylon and the Plimsouls. And so on through Pere Ubu, the Buzzcocks and the Minutemen. When they were pulling into Andrews and the guard just waved them through, Pearlman was in a rapturous state describing early shows at the Rat by the Del Fuegos. O'Malley wondered if they would fly over Tierra del Fuego at any point in their journey, about which, suddenly, almost in spite of himself, he was excited. His rapture came to a rapid end when they arrived at the small Air Force terminal and the Army aide pulled the car to a halt like an old cavalryman reining in his horse. He gave O'Malley and Pearlman an overly familiar glance. It was as if he suspected their discussion of rock 'n' roll bands was clearly a code for something treasonous. This would go in a report. O'Malley stood in the sunlight, in trouble again.

hile dogs sniffed his equipment as if looking for a bone, he commandeered a cellular phone to check in with his father. There was a general excitement among the White House aides who were gathered waiting to be called onto Air Force One, and at the same time, a looseness that reflected the absence of Harold Whitney and other top honchos, all of whom were choppering out with the President. O'Malley turned his back to the collection of his colleagues, and the pool reporters teased Max about the closeness with which he cut his arrival time. This was something they were used to, how close to the edge of permissible White House convention the assistant press secretary continually pressed.

"Dad, it's me," said O'Malley.

"Hello, Thomas." He sounded down.

"What's up?"

"It's your mother."

Uh oh. "What's she done now?" He didn't like the sound of his father's voice on this one. This didn't sound like any of the crises that his father regularly ratcheted up from a skirmish on the field to full-scale nuclear assault, from an annoyance with muskets to DefCom 3. This sounded real.

"She's filing for divorce," he said miserably. It sounded like this mere formalization of a condition that already existed was more than just a shock to his father. It sounded like a disillusionment.

"Oh, Dad," O'Malley said softly. Behind him the sound of the pool reporters laughing uproariously nearly drowned out his connection to his old man. He could hear a young Air Force aide announce they could load onto Air Force One, which was pulled up on the tarmac, glistening, a hundred yards from the gate. "Do you know what's precipitating it?"

"Some such nonsense."

"Jesus, I never thought she'd do it, Dad."

"Well, she is."

He could now hear the distant flat stutter of the helicopter blades carrying the President toward them to his jet. O'Malley knew that Air Force One waited for just one man. "Oh, Dad, I'm so sorry. And I'm sorry I have to go."

"Go," he said, rejected.

"It's just the President's about to—"

"Go," he said, inconsolably.

"Sorry, Dad," he said almost in a whisper. And then he picked up his bags—the computer equipment was already being loaded by one of the Air Force aides into the compartment above his seat—and staggered out onto the tarmac to follow the procession toward the plane.

T heir late breakfast at the Hay-Adams was winding down, and it's possible that the discomfort on the waiter's face was a reflection of how close they were coming to cleaning out the larder. The combination of White House Counsel Rod Gardener's second breakfast of the morning with that of Mike Humperdink's All-Star appetite was enough to give the breakfast chef an ulcer. They'd cleaned out the grapefruit, the oatmeal was but a crust on a metal pail, and the lunchtime ration of eggs for sea-urchin omelettes was as endangered as any snail darter.

Gardener's 7:00 A.M. entry—a not unusual event—was something the kitchen could handle. What was a little strange was his return trip two hours later with the tiny Mike Humperdink. The visitation ought not, on the face of it, be a direct challenge to the kitchen help. However, when it became clear that Humperdink could match Gardener muffin for muffin, as if Mutt could outdevour Jeff, the waiting staff's usual haughtiness of demeanor perished along with the stewed prunes, corned beef hash, and bowl after bowl of Rice Krispies.

While the maitre d' wilted and expressed sotto voce wonder about where the two relatively lean men put all the food they packed away, the Democrat lawyer and Republican political consultant got down to business.

"So what do you need, Rod?" Theirs was a mutuality of interest, an informal alliance that for the one brought access to the White House, and for the other access to Republican politicians. That neither could provide that much of either commodity didn't matter; brandishing access, not necessarily possessing it, was the whole point in Washington.

"We could use some help on the foreign-aid appropriation bill. You're close to Senator Berretta, aren't you?"

"We talk from time to time. I could talk to him." In truth, neither Berretta nor anyone on his staff could stand Humperdink, recognizing him for what he was: a would-be influence peddler and campaign consultant devoid of talent, if not of balls. That was the rap. But Gardener, who aspired to peddling influence in his post–White House incarnation, and whose secret plan was to rewrite the Ethics in Government Law until it allowed him to cash in immediately upon his resignation from the White House, didn't know that.

"Good, because Congressional Relations is getting nowhere with him. He throws them out of his office, from what I can tell. If he could be persuaded that the foreign-aid package the President's going to announce in Managua is just the carrot and that we have plenty of sticks in our arsenal if Ortega doesn't shape up, maybe he'll back off a little."

"I doubt it," said Humperdink. He rummaged in the muffin basket— their third—and when he found it empty, began to pick up crumbs from the table and drop them in his tiny mouth. He peered through his glass at his White House acquaintance. He'd assiduously courted him back during the previous spring when it began to look as if Gardener's candidate, William Hardison, was actually going to make it to the White House while Humperdink's would perish in the primaries. That Humperdink had later wormed his way into the debate preparations for his party's nominee and then succeeded in getting a copy of the official briefing book into Gardener's hands had cemented a relationship that was, if not friendly, certainly useful. And these days it was something he practically could bank on: he could get access to the White House for his lobbying clients, and in turn he was a Republican ally to the White House outside the usual channels. It worked profitably, neatly, and it was always a pleasure to eat with someone whose appetite was similar to his own. They ate together every month or so, and so long as Gardener didn't mind the chance that they would be seen together, Humperdink certainly didn't; in his world, it could only help to be known to occasionally break bread with the Deputy White House Counsel.

"I don't think," Humperdink allowed, "anyone buys the notion that Hardison's going to use a stick against anyone. Anyone other than our allies, I guess."

"Maybe not. But you could find out what Berretta wants from us. If we were to try to find out directly, it would look like we were groveling."

"He likes it when the White House grovels. It may be the only pleasure he gets out of life. He's a miserable man."

"We're finding that out. So far, I don't think Congressional Relations has a clue about what it would take to get Berretta to play ball."

"I'll try to find out, Rod. There's a chance he might object to what you're doing in Nicaragua because he has convictions." They looked at each other. "Nah, I don't think so, either," Humperdink said. "Now let me ask you a question."

"Shoot." Gardener began picking at the tablecloth. The waiters were in hiding, and behind the swinging door to the butler's pantry, the breakfast chef was almost in tears.

"There anything to this *Newsweek* story? I noticed it calmed down today with the President getting out of the country. But is there anything to it?"

"I can't tell. I went through every goddamn FBI report and personnel questionnaire. I can't find anything. Neither could the FBI."

"I may have to cause some mischief with it. It's too good a story not to have Republicans have a good run at the Democrats over it. You understand, don't you?"

"Yeah, sure." And he did. He was a pro when it came to partisanship. He never complained when Humperdink encouraged a savage assault on the President. Always just assumed he did it to cover himself for his regular acts of perfidy against his own party.

"If, um, a Republican were to try to get a little mileage out of this, okay? Make a few charges about drugs in the White House and all that, where would you be least uncomfortable with the charges being hurled?"

Gardener looked down his long nose at the tiny Republican operative. He thought for a moment. "Don't go after the NSC."

"Ah, of course. Without question."

"And not after the President."

"Hey, look, I'm just trying to get some mischief going. A little drama. I'm not looking to bring down a government."

"Or the First Lady." It was the noblest moment of Gardener's life.

"Naturally."

"And who's going to be making the charges?"

"Maybe Partridge."

"Partridge! That asshole!"

"I said maybe, Rod. I didn't say definitely. It's just that this is too good a story not to have a little fun with it. Just tell me what direction I should nudge reporters."

"The press office. That's an obvious one. And the speechwriters, other than Katherine Tierney, I guess." His nobility knew no bounds, considering how unceremoniously Katherine had dumped him. As far as Gardener was concerned, all he'd done in a midnight refrigerator raid was eat the birthday cake she'd made for her niece's party the next day. She made it sound like he'd committed murder or something, though she broke it off with him with a professionalism that suggested either she'd done it a time or two before this or she had missed her true calling before the bar.

"Of course," said Humperdink. "I should have thought of them." He looked at his watch. "Waiter, the check."

The waiter jumped, almost whimpering with glee that they were getting out before the help had to go up the street to the Capital Hilton and borrow some victuals.

"After all," said Humperdink, continuing his train of thought. "How can you trust wordsmiths and those people who actually enjoy talking with reporters?"

"My point precisely," agreed Rod Gardener.

The pressurized cabin was not like the ones in the little jets they used to fly in, sometimes just Hardison and him. It was difficult to imagine, but there had been, once upon a time, entire trips to New Hampshire and Iowa and places like South Dakota where it was only the two of them and the pilots, banking in a Learjet, landing on runways where you had to watch out for cows, taking off in snowstorms where the pilot had deiced the wings by rubbing them down with the sweater off his back.

Now the President was up front in the First Family's cabin with a prophylactic seal of Secret Service and senior staff preventing any debilitating contact with either lesser staffers such as himself, or worse, the small pool of reporters who were granted entrance in case the President had a heart attack or let slip a major pronouncement. There was no place the President could go with the exception of Camp David where the press pool wasn't in close proximity.

Given the conditions, sometimes they wished they weren't. While the jet had been chopped up into comfortable suites for the President and his most exalted advisers, the reporters were segregated in the back of the plane, in seats that seemed to be designed as a punishment, and the constant refrain one heard from them, other than calls for Bloody Marys, was that, at the very least, they knew they were sojourning on the best-maintained 747 in the world.

During the campaign, O'Malley had flown so often with candidate Hardison that each time they crossed the continental forty-eight he could look up from a newspaper and know which state they were over by its topography, its degree of dryness, population density, its verdancy and incline. He could tell where they were from their proximity to coastlines, the way the shadows of the jet fell large as lakes. Shapes of buttes, fields of monotonous rhythm, gradual rises from delta to source: to his eye, all these delineated place as much as lines on a multicolored map. He could *sense* whether this river was the Platte, that one the Snake, the Potomac, the Pedernales; knew by intuition that that was Mount Shasta, this was Mount Hood, that the orange arm on the dark horizon was Chicago.

Back then, the plane would not have taken off if he hadn't been on it. Now it was a miracle that he made it on the manifest. The only reason he was there was because Katherine, concerned for the integrity of the speeches the President was to deliver, had the good sense to demand the presence of the person with the longest history of dealing with him under the pressures of the road.

Outside of the phone call he'd received on the day that he made the front page of the *Post*, O'Malley had barely had any contact with him. He had not spent any time in close proximity to him since the evening before the inaugural when he'd been called out to the President-elect's house. He wondered what, if anything, the President thought of him these days. Was he a nonentity, someone who'd been a part of the road to power, a blocker who'd helped batter down the doors to the palace but now, for no reason other than he'd accomplished what was needed of him, was to be left in the vestibule? Or worse, someone who helped get him across the threshold but who had subsequently revealed himself to have the kinds of personal problems that outweighed whatever talents that might have been put to use?

He wanted to give his chum, the President, the benefit of the doubt. After all, his time spent with Hardison, giving him advice whether it was called for or not, helping to shape his inchoate thoughts into rhetoric that conveyed itself on television, throwing himself between Hardison and the people whom Hardison needed protection from, whether they were advisers or the media—all of these things, he had thought, provided them with a special bond, though of course he knew that in the big-league world of politics there were no special bonds save between a politician and his ambition. This usually was covered by the perception that the bond was between the politician and the voters, but really it wasn't. It was always between the politician and his ambition.

So now as the jet headed toward New Orleans, where there would be a rally at the Superdome designed to give the President a big send-off before he represented the United States on the other side of the climatic mirror, on the other side of the Americas, O'Malley sat in the half-world of airplane consciousness, tempered by the hiss of the engines and the flow of the processed oxygen. And what he most wondered was whether there was a small part of his having caved in to Nicole that had to do with hoping to get caught, hoping to, through his spectacular bust—for that's what it would be—somehow hurt the President who wasn't paying enough attention to him.

O'Malley was able to convince himself that what he was doing was making a final payment to a past life, settling all debts, though it was typical of his bargaining style that he felt Nicole owed him, and yet it was O'Malley who was making the payment. In its own way it was worth it, because it was an explicit rendering of a discrete payment after which he could be free to move on with his life, knowing that Nicole never could come back to him with the leverage of pending business. This was it; it was understood. And even someone as amoral as Nicole lived by the code of precise terms. Even Nicole honored his contracts.

By wrestling with this, he was able to enjoy the flight, or at least the fact of his being on it. There were groups of his colleagues standing in the aisles, their jackets off, their ties pulled down like a pressure valve slightly loosened. The ties would be cinched to attention soon enough when they moved en masse to the rally. Then the entire crew of advance men, policy aides, Secret Service agents, even reporters would give the appearance of high purpose that settled onto people's faces the moment they were in public with the President. There was a *gravitas* conferred on those who were part of the President's official movements that often crossed the border into pompousness. For now, however, O'Malley sat back and on occasion glanced out the window to measure their progress by the cities he just automatically identified—that there is Knoxville, this here's Birmingham—and snatches of conversation floated over to him.

Up the aisle and talking with his hands was Willy Barnes, the bald-headed, good-natured, though street-smart political operative who had risen from being Hardison's campaign manager from his first Queens congressional race to now be the Assistant to the President for Political Affairs. He'd been there every step of the way, Hardison's Senate A.A., his chief of staff when he was a Cabinet officer. It had been Barnes who had been publicly eased out as campaign manager when there had been the need to bring in Harold Whitney as the chairman of the campaign, if for no other reason than to express to the elite news organizations and to the establishment that paid attention to them that someone versed in the management doctrines of the Fortune 100 would be there during the transition from campaign to the reality of managing the White House.

Whitney's arrival had been perceived as a declaration of Hardison's acceptance of the inevitability of victory. Once Hardison had been elected, however, it was clear that Barnes was the behind-the-scenes political adviser who mattered. He was dapper, charming, and too tough to be rolled, and he was the only African-American in the President's retinue of senior advisers. He kept a very low profile, spoke to the press only on background, and stayed out of the day-to-day minutiae of managing the White House in order to concentrate on the President's long-range political strategy. He was, in short, something of a miracle—the White House aide uninterested in becoming a media star—and O'Malley admired him for it. Now he was chatting with Rumson Dickering, the President's bow-tied and fastidious counsel, by all accounts the most worthless member of the senior staff, a real 'fraidy cat, in Willy Barnes's private assessment. There would have been no way of knowing, from seeing them together, just how contemptuous Barnes was of Dickering. They seemed to be getting along fine, chatting with their glasses of orange juice crimped close to their shirts like they were standing on the lawn of a garden party somewhere in McLean. "Your whole personnel process is completely fucked, Rumson, you know that, don't you," Barnes was saying with a grin.

"Of course, of course," Dickering agreed, because Dickering always agreed. That he then blamed someone else was easily predictable. "Of course, we're only following the guidelines set down by the FBI, many of which are constitutionally questionable, from a civil liberties stand-point."

"Yeah, well, when there was that section of the form that asked me to list every place I'd lived since 1950 . . ."

"Oh, it's not that bad, ho ho ho."

"It's that bad, Rumson," Barnes was saying with a smile. "I wrote down, 'If you FeeBees are so smart, you figure out where I've lived since 1950.' "

"Ho ho ho ho ho."

Across the section of seats within earshot Molly Ethridge was talking to Bill Tiswell, and for once, Tiswell was trying to act like a human being. No, it was worse than that. He was trying to be cute.

Tiswell had the broken-nose good looks of a tennis pro, though the hours he was putting in at the White House were beginning to show in a certain softness of belly. Ethridge had the silk-bloused, blow-dried perfection of the White House Woman, not a hair out of place, in perpetual motion, very good-looking, but with all of the sex appeal of an Irish setter. Each could have used about two weeks of sleep, could well have benefited from someone tapping them on the shoulder and wooing them to a dayroom couch where, clothed, they could lie down and get refreshed.

But here they were, on the perpetual edge of exhaustion from the hours they put in keeping up with the demands of their White House importance, Tiswell the primary aide to Harold Whitney, Ethridge the Deputy Director of Public Liaison, and seeing the two coo and flutter, the mating rituals of an iguana and a gila monster, just about made O'Malley lose it.

"So then what did you tell him?" Tiswell said a little encouragingly, the opposite of his usual demeanor.

"I said, 'I don't care if you're the Assistant Secretary for Policy and Planning, if that doesn't come out of my shop, it sure as hell doesn't come out of yours.' "

"Good for you." Tiswell looked smitten. It was a horrifying sight, no less so because the emotion appeared to be genuine. Idi Amin feeding an ice cream cone to a child didn't make his presence any more pal-atable.

"Then I told him to check his budget requests for the next FY and just see whether OMB gives him the okay without a fight, know what I mean?"

"Oh, Molly."

O'Malley, on the verge of reaching for the motion-sickness bag in the seat pocket, tuned out their conversation. Behind him and sprawled around a semicircle of seats in disarray were several of the reporters who made up the pool, and Max Pearlman, who was their baby-sitter, had their attention by telling tales out of school. The reporters sat with the eager faces of Cub Scouts being told a ghost story while sitting around the campfire.

"It was a dark and stormy night."

"Ma-ax!" Allison Hardy of the *Los Angeles Times* squealed. Her reportorial shtick depended on excessive friendliness and flirtatiousness, which, coupled with expressions of difficulty in grasping even the basics of points, gave the feeling that you were helping a blind person across the street. Of course, the usual feeling in print was of being hit by her striped cane right between the eyes. But Max was a sucker, Max lived dangerously, and Max continued.

"The Libyans were getting particularly uppity, threatening the destruction of everything in the world that's nice: Italy, baseball stadiums, Disneyland."

"We're talking February," Michael Quirk of the A.P. added to no one in particular. He was a sandy-haired preppy with wire-rimmed glasses and a nervous demeanor who liked to stick to the facts.

"The President was upstairs in the family quarters preparing to have the first private dinner with the First Lady in the first term, or at least in many a moon, when who comes riding up the elevator but Harold Whitney."

"Businessman extraordinaire," Quirk ID'd him. "Most powerful chief of staff in White House history, or so it says on his résumé. Go on."

O'Malley leaned back in his seat and listened, hoping for all the world it didn't appear like he was enjoying this if, for some reason, Bill Tiswell turned his attention to Max Pearlman and caught him ratting on the Chief of Staff.

"The elevator doors open on the third-floor landing and the presidential dogs come running out of the dining room to greet the grim-faced Chief of Staff."

"Lincoln, Jefferson, and Spot," Quirk said quickly.

"Lightning crackles across the sky behind the Washington Monument."

"Lightning in February?" Allison asked.

"He's a press secretary, Al," Julie Porter of *The New York Times* said quickly.

" 'I have grave news,' the Chief of Staff announces. 'And so do I,' says the First Lady. 'Get OUT. Come back when dinner's done. I don't care if the missiles are flying. This is the first dinner we've had together in months.' And so Whitney, steaming, gets back into the elevator and has to ride downstairs and wait in his office until he's called for," Max concluded.

"So that's the start of the feud," Quirk said with wonder.

"It's not necessarily the precise start of it, but it's one of the epochal moments, you'd have to say."

"Jesus, Max, that's interesting," said Allison. She all but curled up in his lap where he was sitting in an aisle seat.

"You guys gotta protect me," Max said with worry.

"Don't worry, we'll cover you," said Julie Porter, which immediately registered with O'Malley as one of those great lies, up there with the check in the mail.

It was almost precisely at this moment that Whitney, who had been sitting near the front of the cabin chatting it up with Lemlow Motrin and various other NSC types, stood up in the aisle, stretched his legs, and began to march toward them. He swayed on his feet as the plane hit a brief patch of turbulence, and then steadying himself, glad-handed his way down the procession of staffers. He was clearly upbeat about the trip he had long since persuaded reporters he'd masterminded. It was clear that as he projected his nice-guy image, shocking some advance men and Secret Service agents to whom he'd never said a civil word, it was with the intent of impressing the small cluster of reporters he'd spied in the back of the plane near O'Malley.

O'Malley took a brief glance at the reporters, who froze and stared with something that bordered on contempt at the Chief of Staff as he stepped down the aisle toward them. Max Pearlman looked for all the world as if he hoped he could just melt into his seat. O'Malley took out his folders with speech texts and busied himself with the appearance of concentration, managing at the same time to find his Walkman and slip the headphones over his ears, though he didn't turn it on. He wanted to make Whitney think he was working so hard there was no point in talking with him as he made his way down the aisle to the john.

By the time he got there, Whitney ignored O'Malley because he was close enough to the reporters that they commanded his attention.

"Harold, what's the significance of the Chilean inaugural?" asked Michael Quirk directly. They had their pads out and the next thing you knew, there was a mini news conference going on in the back with Whitney looking uncomfortable, like he had to go to the bathroom or something.

"Well, Mike, we think this signals the fruition of the democratic impulse this President is attempting to foster in the Americas," Whitney began. Willy Barnes stopped looking at Whitney, and Bill Tiswell went back to his flirtation with Molly Ethridge. Whitney was on his own.

O'Malley couldn't bear to listen to the canned foreign policy expertise. Not knowing what cassette was in there, he turned on his Walkman. The sound of Sonic Youth made his sitting on Air Force One an instant incongruity. He sat there listening, pretending to be working on the speech text, a reluctant subversive. They flew on.

T ina had this thing about catalogues. Running the restaurant and helping Nicole with his other business were full-time jobs, and who had time to shop? Rare was the weekday when she could head down to the fancy stores on Connecticut Avenue, and there was something about the suburban malls on weekends that made her skin crawl. When she spent time in them, walking up to counters in her usual uniform of blue jeans and a sweater or light jersey, she was consistently patronized by heavily made-up sales clerks who seemed to recognize her, as if she were somehow similar to them, as if she were the wife of some Maryland pool contractor or used-Mercedes dealer. It wasn't worth the effort to put them in their place. Not when she could just take out a pen and order. Catalogues weren't judgmental.

With catalogues, all that mattered was that you got the information right and that your American Express was fully charged. That, and that the delivery truck could find where you lived. Nicole was embarrassed to have been told by the UPS deliveryman that their Wyoming Avenue condominium was the only non-commercial stop on his route. For stop the UPS man did, delivering a steady flow of boxes from which, once the plastic stuffing was removed, kitchen appliances, knickknacks, freeze-dried steaks—as if a restaurateur needed steaks from Chicago delivered to his home!—and item after item of clothes came pouring forth. There were times when he was glad they didn't have cable TV in this part of the District. He feared what would happen if Tina discovered a more upscale version of the Home Shopping Channel.

Once, when they returned home after a busy evening at the restaurant and found the entrance to their apartment free from the usual maze of boxes left by UPS, his initial impulse was to call and find out if the delivery truck had broken down. She slugged him in the arm when he said that, but the thought that something had happened crossed her mind.

On this particular morning, Tina was dreaming big. Nicole was showering, and so she sat out on the deck overlooking the variegated Adams-Morgan landscape as birds soared above the Masonic temple down on Sixteenth Street. The sky was free of the turbulent spring clouds that had so steadily rained upon them, and it felt good to be reclining in the turquoise chaise longue (American Detail catalogue) and drink coffee poured from her Swedish thermos (International Products catalogue) into her Christian Dior tiger-pattern mug (Home! catalogue), all the while leafing through the Big Score catalogue she and Nicole had automatically started to receive when they had been the only people in their zip code who re-upped for a three-year subscription to *High Times*.

Though they didn't come right out and say it, it was clear the Big Score catalogue was for people who made heavy-duty dope deals and had an excess of cash. Those people who didn't want to pay with credit cards could wire payment, either directly to Big Score's offices in, where else, Miami, or else launder the whole thing through a series of conveniently located banks in the Bahamas, the Netherlands Antilles, or the Turks and Caicos islands.

And what could your cash procure? Used Learjets and Gulf Streams with sophisticated radar detectors and rather intricately designed cargo hatches were five-deep in the inventory. There was a whole batch of devices that could detect bugs in telephones and even in the walls of the average dealer's ranch-style home. One device was said to be able to detect when your windows were being microwaved for sound, and there was an intriguing gadget that turned your floppy disks into mush the moment someone tapped into your system and failed to punch the code. But what particularly held Tina's fascination this morning wasn't the range of kidnap-proof BMW's with oil-slick projectors and bullet-proof shields worthy of a production line in M's little workshop. She had no interest in the scales so accurate that a gnat alighting on a rock of cocaine would be picked up first by its aura. What she got all dreamy-eyed and warm just thinking about was the page that was dedicated to islands for sale in a variety of locales that read like a list of spices.

She remembered the golden days of the Sakowitz catalogues and the islands they offered for sale, but those were always dumpy sandbars off some oil derrick in the Gulf of Mexico, with about as much privacy as a tree house in Central Park. Here, however, Big Score showed an island off Nuku Hiva in the Marquesas that had everything a girl could want: its own airstrip, the protection of a coral reef, and a neat little fixer-upper with oceanvu just begging to have a satellite dish installed. Or else, if she was interested in risking the political climate in Fiji, there was a nifty little island in the Bligh Water off Vatia Point that had regular mail service and four-day-old copies of *Le Monde* delivered every Tuesday and Friday. The previous owners of one island paradise in the Kingdom of Tonga had built a comfortable two-bedroom co-op in the fuselage of a Japanese bomber that was advertised as coming with enough foliage to camouflage a battalion. Additionally, it had a stereo system that could rock the neighbors two atolls away.

By the time she got to the pages that detailed the nitty-gritty of currency conversions and living permits in the Seychelles, the bonded risk analysis of mercenary-led coups in Mauritius, and the helpful hints from some entrepreneurial Gilligan who'd been cast away and lived to tell the tale, she'd made up her mind. Nicole walked out onto his deck, drying his hair with a towel, and found her there with a grin on her face that could only mean she wanted to order something from a catalogue. Did she ever.

 They were playing cat and mouse, and Kit knew she couldn't appear too eager or the guest-grabber would turn on her like *that*. "I'm just calling to see about Congressman Partridge's availability," the woman said noncommittally, maddeningly.

"Senator Partridge does have a breakfast," Kit said in reply, but knew she sounded ridiculous. The breakfast would have to be with the reborn Elvis to justify missing "Good Morning America," and in that instance, she hoped "GMA" would take both of them, seriatim.

"Don't cancel your plans," the guest-grabber said as in, Don't hold your breath.

"No, no, of course not. Do you have any idea when you'll know?"

"Probably by sometime midday tomorrow. We'll call you," she said dismissively. Then, "And are you the person we should do the preinterview with?" She asked it like the question was whether Kit was the person who could make the animal do its trick on cue.

"That's me."

"Okay," said the guest-grabber, somewhat perfunctorily, though she quickly warmed. "Hey, listen, I've been eating bran cereal recently. Do you think that will lower my cholesterol?"

"I'll tell you the morning of the show. Bye-bye, now." She hung up just as the receptionist was buzzing her with the word that "Today" was on the line. There was no doubt about it. Cholesterol was a winner.

icole had his hair combed and spread across his bare shoulders drying in the warm morning air. Where Tina reclined, the sunlight glistened off her teeth, perfect teeth she'd had capped when she was living in Laurel Canyon with the Rock Star. That was the way he divided up her life before she knew him. Either she had been with the Rock Star or else she was with the Dealer, and in either instance he knew she paid a heavy cost for whatever benefits she'd derived.

With the Rock Star, her capped teeth weren't even partial compensation for having to attend to him when he'd done so much coke and so many 'ludes he'd crawl on the floor and bark like the sick dog he was. There were plenty of teenage girls who had veterinarian impulses, and she left him with one. Unfortunately, thought Nicole, until she met him, she had a bad habit of choosing nasty cool bastards who were invariably the exact wrong person with whom to make long-term plans. Though she was far from a victim, hardly helpless.

With the Dealer, she was cut in on the money that had eventually helped stake them to Globe, Tina and Nicole, to their new life on the East Coast. The cost for this was having to witness his increasing cruelty with subordinates, his gradual unhinging and lack of respect for life. That, and the uncertainty about when the Dealer would return to the States and exact a horrifying revenge on the two of them for the sin of having escaped. There were bad nights when she had chain-saw dreams, and it wasn't for decoration that she kept a Doberman with a spiked collar in their two-bedroom condo.

It was when the Dealer was laying low in Mexico planning to kill an informant set to testify in federal court that Nicole met Tina and under epic conditions of escape they'd set sail together from Sinaloa to San Diego, wondering all the while if, when they arrived, the Dealer would be waiting to slit both their throats. He wasn't. He'd been nailed by Federales in the meantime, but it was some journey, sailing in the open seas, not knowing if their arrival home would be their very last act. Actually, you couldn't beat it for a romantic start to a relationship: clear Pacific nights with sky stretching across skeletal blue stars, Nicole and Tina and a case of California wine snug in the back of the customized sloop. Still, these days Nicole thought it was a terrible thing to have to worry whether someone could come out of your past to exact a price you were no longer willing to pay, at least not at the same terms you entered into in a previous life. He thought it was just a terrible thing.

He chose not to think about the role he played in the Federales finding out where the big gringo dope dealer was hiding, nor was it customary for him to dwell on the way, with Tina's avid assistance, he had lightened the Dealer's stash of those greenbacks with the portrait of Mr. Franklin. Nicole's sailboat, the *Miss T.*, was thoroughly searched by the customs agents when they entered the territorial waters of the Estados Unidos, but those were the days when the dogs were trained only to pick up a whiff of drugs, and not the smell of cash, which is what lined the hull. The false bottom to his boat was stuffed with the packets of hundreds the Dealer had taken with him to Mexico in case he got in trouble. Nicole regularly hoped the twin circumstances of his acquiring that load and simultaneously turning the Dealer in would ensure the bastard stayed in some Mexican hellhole for a long time to come. In the meantime, Nicole was in his own version of hell, though its greatest symptom was simply a chronic case of the hidden jitters.

He couldn't deny that, as careful as they'd been to return to the East Coast without allowing too many of their California acquaintances to even know they were in the country, there were evenings when, walking down the alley behind Globe to get to Wyoming, or just staying in the lights of the building as he walked to his parking space, he wondered if that particular shadow was It. He caught his breath more often than he would ever tell Tina, jumped for just a moment in worry that this was the time the Dealer was going to exact his revenge. It was the way shadows loomed that spooked him, though he could as easily be thrown by the bark of a dog, by a stranger's particularly dry cough, by the crunch of a twig in innocent woods. He didn't tell this to Tina, but the bartenders each had been shown the old photos of the Dealer that had appeared in *Time* when the two of them had been safely at sea and DEA agents were celebrating the bust made by their Mexican bros. The 32-caliber Walther PPK he kept in his office wasn't there in case the place was robbed. The place was robbed, they had insurance. The gun was there for a different kind of insurance, against a particular calamity, an infestation he knew he deserved according to Old Testament rules of revenge.

So when Tina, the light of his life, sat there in the warm morning sun as he exhaled smoke from his first cigarette of the day, sat there and went on excitedly about the notion of their escape to their own Pacific island, he listened.

"Yanggeta Island in the Yasawa group is a veritable steal for Fiji," she was saying to him as she leafed through the catalogue.

"My."

"And if you're up for the Solomons, there's an old Japanese fort on Utupua that sounds like it could use a little decorating, but otherwise is okay."

"Wow."

"I'm serious, David." She was so pretty, lying there in the sunlight, while he sat there in a slowly dispersing wreath of his own smoke smiling at the thought of the two of them marooned by their own choosing on some volcanic rock. But she did have a point. If the Japs could last as long as they did on Okinawa, the Dealer would have to mount quite a raid to get them. He thought of aircraft carriers and long gray frigates, the catapult launching F-16's off the deck. Maybe Tina was on to something. It wouldn't have been the first time. He leaned over and began to leaf through the catalogue.

"What are the terms?"

"Of purchase?"

"Yeah, and ownership."

"Where?"

"Someplace warm, with a steady breeze, stable politics, and a supermercado just a pirogue away."

In a moment she had it. " 'Tehutu Island,' " she read, " 'just outside the reef surrounding Tahaa, Eastern Polynesia. The living quarters are bungalow-style, with fresh running water and an electrical generator installed in 1978. Two bedrooms, two baths, stunning view of Raiatea, supply boat available alternate Thursdays. Comes complete with wine cellar, thatched-roof guest hut, and much, much more. Has to be seen to be believed! Asking eight hundred and forty thousand dollars, with clear deed and title to be superseded only by France's participation in war. Extradition treaty with the States.' " She looked up. "David, I love it!"

"It does sound pretty nice. But baby, you do realize how rough it could be living on some speck in the middle of the ocean?"

"I don't care." Her eyes were bright, the way they got whenever she found something in a catalogue she had to have. "I could move tomorrow."

"Whoa there. First of all, that's a lot of money." He ground out his cigarette and lit another as a cloud came in front of the sun and cooled him. He shivered for just a moment. "We couldn't do it . . . right away."

"We could if this deal with O'Malley works out." Her face was set in its hard, businesswoman countenance, which to others might have erased what attractiveness they found in her; to Nicole it was this look above all he couldn't resist.

"No, we wouldn't be close. All my money's tied up in Globe."

"We would be if he did it a few times."

"Tina, I told O'Malley this was a one-shot deal."

"What if it works?"

"Exactly. A one-shot deal, easily accomplished, and then he's off the hook."

"If it's easily accomplished, it could be done again. If it works, we could do it whenever the President goes anywhere. He could as easily bring back smack from Asia or the Middle East as coke from South America."

"No, honey, I told him this was it."

But then there was Tina, leaning forward with a smile on her face, kissing the end of his nose. "Please, David." She kissed his eyes, his forehead. "Oh, please," she whispered. "Cookouts on our very own beach. Rides on our own pet dolphin." He smiled when she said that, and was still smiling as she began to kiss his neck, and then his chest, until he would have bought her the island of Oahu, if O'Malley made enough trips.

he event in the Superdome did not go precisely on cue. When later they did a postmortem on the disastrous trip, it was New Orleans that got the blame for things going so far off track.

O'Malley found himself standing in front of the camera platform as the eight or nine thousand people the Louisiana Democratic party had rounded up and ticketed for the event made their way in. If there had been a spot check of the city of New Orleans's municipal offices, you could well have found a great many people coincidentally taking "personal days" this afternoon. Today was less than a perfect occasion to get a Louisiana driver's license.

Near as O'Malley could figure it from where he stood, the stage was set up perpendicular to where the goal lines ought to have been, with the bulletproof podium, replete with Great Seal, placed exactly on the fifty-yard line. Normally reserved for Saints, the program today would have its full share of sinners, as evidenced by the presence of former governor T. John Thibodaux, who had been invited by the White House to serve as emcee.

For the fourth time in twenty years, Thibodaux was the party's nominee to retake the governor's mansion. The last time around, he'd reentered office full of remorse and debt, with the state's economy booming, the mood buoyant. His remorse was for how few were his second-term accomplishments, and his debts were from gambling. Then, after the four years of his third term, he'd thought better of reelection, leaving the state's economy a shambles, roads and bridges collapsing all over the place, rumors of indictments as thick as gumbo. Somehow Thibodaux was able to celebrate his liberation from the hard work in Baton Rouge with a much-publicized two-week, million-dollar spree at the gaming tables in Monte Carlo—and by the time the former po' boy from Acadia returned with briefcases so stuffed with cash a representative of the IRS met his chartered jet, the state's mood, at least toward him, was admiring verging on worshipful.

Broke again, it now seemed there was nothing for him to do to replenish his bank accounts other than run for governor. He'd been asked whether he thought he could win an unprecedented fourth term, and his reply to the reporter had been, "Cher, there's one t'ing bothering me. Ah haven't been indicted for a t'ing. Me, I'm used to three or two indictments every campaign. How'muh supposed to win without indictments, eh, cher?"

Now the combo on the stage was giving way to a more traditional New Orleans jazz band, and the crowd, which was predominantly black, continued to file onto the floor and find the seats they'd been assigned. In the pen that held the news media, Willy Barnes was standing with a cluster of reporters and O'Malley, for want of something better to do, went and stood beside him.

Jack Carthage of NBC News, as pleasant an airhead as had face time on TV, was insisting on telling Willy Barnes a story he clearly didn't want to hear. Pressed next to him was Wyatt Phillips from CBS, Jenny Giopolli from *The Washington Post*, and a couple of other reporters who were new to O'Malley.

When the story was over, and it was a stupid, tasteless tale with a racist undertone, Barnes just stared at him. "Excuse me," he said, and walked toward some other reporters, greeting them with a smile.

"Oh, God, do you think I offended him?" Carthage asked Giopolli and Phillips. The two just looked at him and then at each other before heading away. Carthage was left there to loosen his tie for a second and primp before a pocket mirror.

"I thought it was a pretty good story," Carthage now said to no one in particular, before popping his hands from his cuffs and adjusting his jacket for show time.

Which it was soon to be. O'Malley walked in front of the camera platform, the dozens of tripods placed atop the section marked off for them with duct tape by White House Advance, the sound men jumping on and off to check the connections to the mult box. Techies from WHCA were adjusting knobs to make certain the sound was crystalline when the time came for the President to make his remarks. O'Malley saw Mike McCurry surrounded by reporters who appeared to be badgering him about something or other, but such was the life of the Press Secretary. It made sense that with all the daily hassles of McCurry's life, rather than ride with reporters, as he had during the campaign, on the first leg of this trip McCurry had sat in the front of the plane, no doubt meditating and trying to get his blood pressure under control before having to face his charges once again. He hadn't stopped by to say hello to Max and the pool reporters in the back, which was okay. Lion tamers weren't expected to keep cats at home.

The band was being shooed off the stage now, though they ritualistically played "When the Saints Go Marching In" while Governor Thibodaux moved playfully toward the podium as if he were Johnny and this was his "Tonight" show. "Ahem," he coughed into the mike and it was a marvel to behold, the way the crowd suddenly stilled in the presence of Their Master's Voice. The powerful spotlights dilated momentarily, then focused in on the plump, white-haired scoundrel who was standing there in front of this circus, chuckling. Reporters who wouldn't pay attention to the President unless he was declaring war were looking up now at this phenomenon, looking up at something you did not see in Washington anymore: the colorful pol with his own personality and the guts to express it. There was nothing about Thibodaux that had been squeezed out and washed of the full range of hues. Compared to the homogeneity of Washington pols in the modern era, T. John was a raw hunk of stinking goat cheese, and now the old goat was set to go in his role as today's emcee.

Just the week before, it had been brought to his attention by a reporter that in the final months of Thibodaux's last reign as governor, his girlfriend—a twenty-four-year-old former Miss Louisiana—had been on the state payroll to the tune of sixty thousand dollars a year. "Cher, you don't say," Thibodaux had said, looking from the reporter to the camera with genuine surprise. "Sixty thousand, huh?" The reporter allowed it was so. "So talented, she is, too. I didn't know da filly was so poorly, pitifully underpaid. When I get back into office I'll have to give the poor little thing a raise."

The reporter had stepped back, visibly shaken. "A raise? To what?"

"To whatever," Thibodaux had said with a shrug and a wave of his hand, and then gone on about his business, leaving the reporter's head shaking, but Thibodaux's grip on the electorate no less secure.

Now his grip was on the podium, and when he said, "Mesdames, messieurs, I'm T. John Thibodaux," a crescendo of applause ripped across the floor of the Superdome, engulfing them all, reporters and the White House staff who stood near them alike, which was hard to do in a hall this massive.

As O'Malley marveled at the way Thibodaux treated the audience of eight thousand as if they were his grandchildren gathered for a family reunion, Manny Slung wandered over, his brow glistening though the air conditioning was perfect, bags under his eyes as if he'd been up all night preparing for this event, which he probably had.

"Hey, Tom." He always just sidled up in his long-suffering manner as if he weren't deserving of notice, announced himself pathetically, and stood there waiting to be whipped. There was no way of knowing, looking at his slovenly dress and the wide polyester tie that invariably had a prominent soup stain on it, that Manny was a terror on the details, for whom no balloon drop was insignificant, no simple blue drape backdrop adequate. He was considered the best Big Event man in the advance trade, and could whip up a crowd with whatever it took, which often was cash. He hadn't gone to the White House when the campaign ended, though he was called in to put together some of the more overtly political rallies, and had recently stage-managed the President's five-city tour in support of his budget.

"Nice event, Manny. Looks really good."

"It looks like shit. We oughta done the thing inside an aquarium or something, a hotel lobby, maybe. I'd take the proverbial phone booth, make it look like a rousing send-off. Twenty thousand people here get swallowed up like Tiananmen Square, fifty thousand, it still looks empty. But the geniuses at the White House know what they're doing, right? So look what we did," he said, showing off his handiwork. "We built the platforms in a semicircle so the bastards won't be able to pan to any empty seats."

"Good move."

"Yeah, it came to me at two A.M. Media squawked all to hell, but you know what to do with 'em if they can't take a joke, know what I mean?"

"Sure do. You holding up?" They went back a ways, having spent weeks on the road together during the campaign. The joke had always been that Hardison's advance team was whoever was the first person out the car door, but in actuality, Manny's cadres of local volunteers had grown every step of the way, and there seldom were the kinds of screw-ups you pay for on the nightly news: parade routes empty, shots of the candidate arriving at the factory as the workers are bolting for their cars, or the surprise of inadvertently insulting the locals by not knowing a particular detail about their lives, such as their being more concerned about environmental restrictions than about, say, acid rain. It was Manny's job to make sure the candidate knew that acid rain was Plattsburg, yesterday, and that freely polluting smokestacks were the livelihood here in Youngstown, today. He did it well.

"I'm fine, Tom, tired. I've been back and forth to Venezuela three times in three weeks. I go back in three hours. I'll be glad when this trip is over, I'll tell you."

"How's it look down there?" O'Malley asked, and suddenly he too was sweating, air conditioning or no air conditioning. It had been hours since he thought about what it was he would be doing in Venezuela; he'd had the terrors under control. Now the mere mention of the country made him feel a little dizzy, and the sweat started streaming off him like Angel Falls.

"It'll work. It's simple enough. It's the inaugural in Santiago to worry about, but for some reason they don't want me there. They're worried I should insult people with all the other foreign heads of state there. Something about protocol." He shrugged.

"See you in a couple of days, then."

"Sure, Tom. You know where you go when this is over?"

"Back to the entrance, right?"

"The buses will be there," Manny said as if this were the only thing in life you could count on, and then he headed off like a man with a couple of things to attend to.

Rather than wait through T. John's speech, O'Malley waded through the crowd to find a phone. He wanted to call Kit. He made his way back along the aisles toward the entrance. The empty bleachers rising all the way to the top of the Superdome made the crowd here on the floor seem insignificant, and if Manny was able to prevent cameras from panning the vast, yawning statement of indifference the building would make as the President entered, he would be worth every dime he'd pad on his expense account.

O'Malley found the wall of pay phones near the escalator and punched in Kit's number, followed by his digital credit code. He had to wait a long minute for her to come on.

"Hi." She was on the line and he leaned his head into the metallic well of the phone module. "How's it going?"

"Okay I guess. Do you have the nation's veins unclogged, cleared of fatty deposits and debris?"

"Oh, Tom, I think 'Good Morning America's' going to have Partridge on, on Wednesday."

"That's wonderful."

"He's never been on before. Wilbur Todd's just walking around shaking his head, hoping that none of the ranchers coming to our fundraiser in Cheyenne next month cancel. He didn't really like my idea of what some of the cattlemen should consider raising instead of steers."

"What did you suggest? Dental floss?"

"Free-range chickens."

"I can see why he's upset."

"They have a free range out there, Tom."

"Listen, I was calling to tell you how much I missed you. You surely made my day."

He could hear her smiling across the wires.

"I've been sitting at my desk worried about your dance card being filled with beautiful Chileans named Consuela and Isabel."

The innocence in her voice stabbed at him. How could he betray her? Not for the first time, his cowardice—no, worse, his complicity in a criminal venture—gnawed at him. He knew he had to say something to her, and he was about to, when he had a sensation that he used to get on the campaign trail. It was a sensation that in the room where the speeches were taking place, there was a hush, the dog that didn't bark. Something was going wrong. "Kit, hold on for a second, will you?" He cupped the phone.

"Now, the President, he's a good man. He's a nice guy," Thibodaux was saying, drawing out the last two words. "This trip, though, this trip to Nicaragua, I can't support it. If the President was standing right here, I'd say to him, 'Mon cher, I just don't know. There's the poor and the disadvantaged just two miles down the road in Algiers. And you know how I feel about the poor and the disadvantaged.' He's a nice guy, for a guy from New York, but I'd tell him, 'I just don't think we need to help the communists in Nicaragua when we got the poor here, eh, cher?' And it pains me, it truly does, to have to say that I can't support my President on this petting, and brushing, and stroking the communists like they some kind of pet. The President well, I wish that. He knows that. But should we see him off on this trip of his?" As soon as O'Malley heard the suddenly negative response of the crowd, he knew they were in trouble.

"Kit, we got problems."

"You *are* planning on finding some Chilean beauty?" She sounded genuinely hurt.

"No, not you and me. The President."

"What is it?"

"I think T. John Thibodaux's about to lead a walkout before the President speaks. Look, I'll call you as soon as I can. I may be able to call just before we get on the plane."

He began quickly to jog back onto the floor of the Superdome, all the while listening to Thibodaux's siren call over the enormously loud, slightly echoing speakers that were aimed multidirectionally toward the tens of thousands of empty seats. "I know that you feel the same way that I do, I do, I do," came the triplicate reverb of Thibodaux's message as O'Malley turned the corner and tried to press his way through orange-jacketed, beefy security people, all of them now turned toward the drama unfolding on the stage. He rushed toward the camera platform around which reporters were scribbling furiously as producers jumped on and off, waving their crews to pan down on the crowd as it got riled up from Thibodaux's call of agitation. There was a row whose view was slightly blocked by the camera platform, and which because of that was less crowded than others, so he stood his ground there to see what would unfold.

Thibodaux's speech was the strangest thing O'Malley thought he'd ever heard. Alternately remorseful and hostile, it was like the monologue of a psychopath moments before he kills the hostages.

"Now, we love this President, don't we?" He looked like a tender preacher before some riverside baptismal. Then he brandished the snake.

"So we have to save him from the fool advice he obviously's been getting, eh?" The crowd responded with a full-throated roar as those members of the White House staff who were standing in the pen braced themselves for an assault. This was a crowd that was getting set to do something nasty.

In the White House staff area, Willy Barnes was looking on in horror, knowing that whatever embarrassment Thibodaux caused the President would be laid at his doorstep, for as the Assistant to the President for Political Affairs, it had been he who had signed off on Thibodaux being the emcee. His reasoning for wanting him on the stage was sound; he was the most popular politician in a state the President had lost in November, and a favorable association with him would send the signal that the President was consolidating his control over the party even in areas that he hadn't been able to deliver. But no matter what the reasoning, if this thing turned on them, the assessments in the press would be unkind to Willy Barnes, other White House staffers would see to that. He would need a rowboat to stay afloat from all the leaks.

"So, with sadness, to my President I have to say, me, I can't wish you well in Nicaragua. I might could wish you well on your trip, but for the sellout to the communists. But when we have our children to take care of, Mr. President, we can't see you off on this little junket of yours. We're going to be leaving right now, and have ourselves a little party outside. Because perhaps some of you can't afford the food, I've arranged free of charge some food. And beer and wine. Let's go! *Laissez les bons temps rouler!*"

And with that he stepped from behind the podium and was helped by a ring of assistants who had expected this, who were waiting for him, who helped him down off the stage and into the surge of people who were now stomping and hollering in support of his secessionist cry.

On the camera platform, there was panic. Crews tried to break down and wade into the crowd to get footage of Thibodaux as he was picked up and carried on the shoulders of this black giant who'd been waiting at stage left to hoist the little ex-Governor like he was nothing heavier than a sack of red beans. The crowd pressed in and let him lead it, all at once. The White House staffers were looking around wildly, advance men all seemed to be spitting into their walkie-talkies, and then the crowd turned on the lot of them and it was like a scene from "Rawhide" when the lightning crackled and the cows took off. This particular stampede now swept back toward the long camera platform and within seconds was toppling it, as tripods and the heavy Ikegamis that were perched on top came crashing down on producers and correspondents, with moans erupting, tough female reporters screaming, and fights breaking out.

It was amazing how quickly the crews reacted compared to their more glamorous on-air colleagues. It was as if the correspondents had gotten so used to their steady diet of handouts, and to the manipulations of sources they talked to all the time but hardly ever saw, that when news reared up and tipped them over, they didn't know what to do. Their crews did.

O'Malley, whose row intersected an aisle which had yet to get clogged by the backward motion of this angry procession, watched as a large cameraman used his tripod as a baseball bat, felling two of Thibodaux's legionnaires who were climbing over the lot of them like this was the way up San Juan Hill. The sound it made was something he'd never forget, about what would happen to a watermelon dropped from a second-story balcony onto an asphalt driveway. And then the cameraman was jumped from behind and O'Malley couldn't see him anymore.

On the stage, the band was striking up "Hail to the Chief," and O'Malley prayed they didn't have the stupidity to bring the President on now. Any fool, even an advance man, could see the crowd was being sucked in from all sides, chaotically swelling beyond the upturned camera platform as Thibodaux headed toward the door. Row upon row of folding chairs collapsed, only to be tossed about like so many Pop Art paper clips. There didn't seem to be a particular focus to the anger of the crowd; it just continued to swell and moved, an ugly juggernaut, toward the entrance, the upended camera platform and tipped-over reporters more a consequence than an object of its destructive motion.

He could see Thibodaux bobbing up and down in the distance, atop the tentacles of clutching admirers, the whole living organism picking up speed. As people crowded around him to wish him well, they fell into the procession nearing the edge of the floor, nearing what would have been the sidelines if this were a game. It wasn't, though it would be replayed over and over again on television screens tonight, there wasn't a question about that.

A few feet away from him, where the media was straggling to collect itself in the wake of genuine news, a particularly disheveled Jack Carthage was trying to do a stand-up, though he was bleeding from a small cut above his eye. "In a stunning rebuke, a crowd here at the Superdome in New Orleans has turned their backs on the entrance of President Hardison and rushed to get away from him." Just then, some stragglers who were trying to catch up to Thibodaux's entourage barreled into

Carthage from behind, sending him to the floor like just another tight end flattened by a linebacker.

The White House staff was in disarray, with terror on the faces of those whose position there protected them, they had thought, from the rabble of Democracy. There were among his colleagues people who O'Malley just knew had thought victory in the November election meant never having to deal with real voters again.

Then, wading into the crowd from the stage was a phalanx of uniformed Secret Service agents who had been dispatched like the cavalry to relieve the last redoubt, which in this case was Willy Barnes. He was fuming, itching for a fight, though by the time he reacted to the melee, it was rolling beyond him and out the door. From O'Malley's solitary position out of harm's way, he could see Molly Ethridge all but sobbing as one very large agent now gently pulled her from where she was standing into what would be a protected convoy toward the stage area. Willy Barnes was arguing vociferously with one of the agents, but then he too went gently, and the lot of them, advance men frozen in walkie-talkie babble, staff assistants wild-eyed with fear of the crowd returning, a couple of Barnes's deputies from the political office shouting at each other, no doubt assigning blame; the whole lot of them began to follow the flying wedge of agents as they pulled them to the safety of the stage.

The reporters weren't so lucky. There was a fight still going on where the cameraman had whacked his double. Lingering, taunting pockets of young toughs were threatening members of the Northern media, some of whose response, bless their souls, was to try to analyze their anger, and for broadcast. "Perfect," shouted a correspondent from ABC as this tall, pale white kid with an unintentionally punk haircut spat at him. "Why the hostility?" he said, proffering his microphone. The kid's response was to slap it away and move in to pummel him, though the cameraman quickly dropped his camera and came to the rescue.

Those who weren't chasing the melee loaded up their equipment and made to get the hell out of there. O'Malley could see that Thibodaux was now off the floor and, he hoped, making his way into a waiting Black Maria. The crowd pooled up around the exit waiting to drain through behind him, and they seemed to be in boisterous good cheer, as if this were nothing other than a slightly more entertaining than usual afternoon off from work. Those who remained in the hall were either lazy, unmoved, or, in the case of the young, mostly white gang who continued to surround the toppled camera platform, hostile. It was time to get out of there.

The President of the United States hadn't even made his speech. O'Malley stood there for a moment and stared at the crowd as it made its way out of the portals following their Cajun Pied Piper. Is that it? he thought. Had the hundred-and-twenty-day run the President had been on come to an end by this display of disrespect? Had what authority as Hardison had been granted by the voters six months previously just rolled on out into the parking lot to drink beer and let the good times roll?

There was no time to answer his own question. It was time to move it, and fast, to get out of there. He fought his way through the crowd and up the escalators to the outside.

No one paid attention to him when he stepped into the humid New Orleans air, and so he put his head down and kept moving. It sure was hot, the sun by now out brilliantly, not a cloud to be seen. The tall buildings down Poydras toward the French Quarter were sparkling in the afternoon light. He took off his jacket as he walked and draped it, Sinatra-style, over his shoulder. Of course, as soon as he'd done this, he was no longer visibly wearing his lapel pin that identified him as a member of the White House staff, so that when he got to the sawhorse barricades, the policeman there wouldn't let him through for just that crucial moment it took for him to see, completely to his horror, the motorcade suddenly begin to move. He pressed the pin in the jacket he held almost up to the cop's eye until the bastard let him through, and then, since the cars were beginning to roll, had to start jogging toward them.

"Oh, no," he said out loud. His feet seemed stuck, nightmare-style. They just couldn't move fast enough, though he was relieved to see that once the cars and minivans, even the ambulance, had come to the entrance to the street itself, for some reason they stopped, even though this subjected them once again to the chanting crowds who had stayed outside in the sun the whole time, not in on the joke, unaware of what had happened to the President inside the building. Some of the more marginal demonstrators might actually have called off their protest if they'd known the insults to which their President had been subjected at the hands of a common enemy, T. John Thibodaux.

He began to jog with confidence that he'd make it, though by now sweat was streaming down his face, his shirt drenched. No matter. He didn't suppose that too many people on the plane now would be worried about aesthetics. Air Force One, all at once, began to seem like the safest spot on earth, and it had air conditioning, too.

He didn't know why the cars remained stopped where they were until suddenly, as he jumped off the edge of a concrete ramp to the street where they were waiting, he heard the roar of motorcycles. He turned and in the second it took for the cops on motorbikes to skid around him and the driver of the presidential limo that was accelerating up the ramp to spot him and jam on the brakes, he learned indisputably that your life doesn't pass before your eyes that moment before death.

The brakes squealed. He wasn't run over. It was clearly the decoy car because here was Bill Tiswell with the door open shrieking, "Get in here, you asshole." This he did, gratefully. He found himself in the car with Tiswell and Harold Whitney, who was sitting there in the back paying him no mind, just leaning forward with his elbows on his knees, kneading the pink flesh of his forehead. O'Malley instinctively looked through the back window at the second limousine where the President was sitting, no doubt not very pleased about any of this. It wasn't a very good start to the trip. For either of them.

As darkness fell in Washington that night, the season's first softball games were played out on the Mall. It was an evening for cookouts, the official start of the grilling season. In a good mood, flush with spring fever and the prospect of making a lot of money for no work, Nicole took a turn as bartender at Globe when they got shorthanded, and the business spilled out into the street.

He was standing talking to two pretty interns whom he probably should have asked for ID before he served them their drinks when the phone rang by the cash register. "Globe," he shouted over the noise, still smiling at the pretty young things as they obviously flirted with him.

"Yeah, David Nicole there?"

"This is Nicole." It was John Santangelo, and he'd been expecting the call.

"Did you see the news tonight?"

"Missed it. What's up?" he asked, cradling the receiver on his shoulder and pointing to a fellow who was leaning over the bar. The guy mimed the motion of drinking from a bottle, mouthed the words Dos Equis, and raised one finger to signal how many. Nicole turned his back to him and reached underneath the register into the vast, long cooler.

"Looked to me like this trip's already all fucked up."

"How so?" Nicole asked with nonchalance as he unwrapped himself from the telephone cord and took the fellow's money. The customer immediately began to hit on the two interns, who now nervously lit cigarettes and began to talk to him.

"They had some kind of a goddamn riot at the Superdome. The guy on CBS said they were considering just going down to Chile and then coming straight back so the President could address the nation, or something like that."

"What are you talking about?" Nicole stood very straight, ignoring the customers' clamoring.

"I'm saying that CBS said," John repeated slowly, "that the White House was so shook up by what happened in New Orleans, they were thinking of going to Chile for some big party, whatever they're going there for, and then coming straight back so that Hardison could address the nation on television."

"But what would they do about the rest of the trip?"

"They'd blow it off and reschedule, is what I heard."

"That's ridiculous," Nicole blurted. At this, an artificially tanned fellow in a black unconstructed jacket with the sleeves rolled up snapped his fingers. People were backed up two deep from the bar. Customers could have set themselves on fire and Nicole would not have noticed.

"It better be, David. I got people who are out on a limb on this one. Your guy doesn't get to bring things home to Daddy, you may be buying an airline ticket yourself."

"Don't worry, John."

"I'm not worried, David. I just know you're good for it. Make sure your passport's in order."

When John hung up and Nicole went back about the business of being a bartender, he ignored the guy with the tan and filled the orders of the first three guys wearing suits. "Any of you fellows know what happened to the President in New Orleans today?" Their answers were vague, but it sounded like it was close to being a disaster.

T he White House staff could but lick their wounds as they flew on Air Force One. By the time they crossed the Isthmus of Panama, it was thoroughly dark off the end of the wing, just a mango slice of sky visible on the horizon. O'Malley sat with the air nozzle still directed at his face, though the perspiration had long since dried. He was rumpled and dazed, though at least he had the luxury of being left alone, something denied poor Willy Barnes. Willy was being taken to an airborne woodshed in the front of the plane.

Only half of Max's charges in the press corps had made it to the plane on time for takeoff. As soon as the motorcade had driven up underneath the wing, they prepared to leave, abandoning not only the pool reporters who were supposed to fly with them but the press plane itself. It would just have to find its own way down the spine of the continent. They were likely to hear about this. Their clippings would reflect this evidence of disarray.

Harold Whitney had started out the flight in his seat up front, almost catatonic. Only with reluctance had he been coaxed up to the President's—and the First Lady's—cabin. He'd emerged characteristically imperial in manner, but altogether fouler of humor than any of them had seen. Ever. It was clear a bureaucratic struggle was taking place in which Whitney was trying to foist all blame for the trip on Willy, which might be a little difficult to do if Max was correct. Max Pearlman spent the first twenty minutes of the flight quietly briefing some of them that just before the event, Harold had been taking credit for the Superdome rally. By so doing, he had inadvertently taken the public pressure off Willy Barnes. No wonder he was depressed. He'd alibied the designated scapegoat.

Santiago was a disaster, too. When countries whose inflation rate soars beyond their national IQ giggle editorially, you know you've screwed things up. When petty empires whose greatest art form is the epaulet worn on the junta's shoulders stare down their noses at the Estados Unidos, things have gone awry. When revolutionary leaders whose last bath is celebrated by a national holiday second in importance only to the previous recorded moment they trimmed their trademark beards, there's something wrong with this picture. And that was Santiago.

It was probably a setup. The junta stepping down couldn't have been all that pleased by Hardison's insistence during the campaign that they do so, nor could they have been all that happy about his having taken credit for their ceding power. And the earnest young college professors being allowed to assume what power the junta gave up couldn't have been all that happy with them, either. It had taken several administrations for the Colossus of the North to get the generals to take their boots off the professors' necks and let them go about the business of ruining the economy. Or such was the impression reporters conveyed when they caught up with the presidential party.

The reviews from New Orleans were slipped under O'Malley's door in the Holiday Inn they were staying in on Avenida Bernardo O'Higgins, having been faxed early in the morning through the White House Communications Agency. They were not good. And worse, the reporters who accompanied the presidential party through the symbolic day of cutting the chain and padlock that had held the National Congress closed since the coup that killed Allende, through the swearing-in of the new President and the handing over of keys to the presidential palace from one mustachioed man in uniform to an indistinguishable brother in a barely presentable suit—the reporters made certain they rubbed it in. Their resentment at having been left behind made them eager to say how badly they thought the President was doing in his first venture outside of the twelve-mile limit, and how they looked forward to pointing this out via satellite or in their papers.

By the time the President arrived, it was so late that the symbolic regiment of military men and civilians who were to greet him had left to go to the other end of the airport, where Fidel's plane was arriving on time.

"Another instance of a crowd rushing to get away from him," was how Jack Carthage, bandaged and bleary-eyed from having flown most of the night to get there, greeted the viewers of the "Today" show that first morning.

"Jack?" Bryant Gumble interrupted when he was signing off his piece.

"Yes, Bryant." His wounds notwithstanding, he stood in tousle-headed and Burberry-ed perfection in front of the "Today" show's set along the Río Mapocho, the Andes rising magnificently behind him on one of the rare autumn mornings when the smog of Santiago did not sock the city in.

"What do you attribute this ineptitude to? And is the White House embarrassing the United States in the eyes of the world?"

"Well, Bryant, the answer to your second question is, not yet. One foreign diplomat told me there's a certain goofy charm to just how badly the White House has done in their first few hours here. And as to why the White House hasn't quite gotten their act together, most people believe it has to do with the lack of a vision, the President's failure to communicate clear goals for his administration."

Jack was thanked by Bryant for his insights and quickly descended upon by a gang of roving spin doctors, who'd been awakened and deputized as soon as the senior staff realized they had some problems. Even O'Malley was brought in. Along with the clips, there had been talking points slipped under his door, and by 6:30 A.M. he'd been contacted and told to report to the staff room by 7:00. For the rest of the day, his instructions were to talk to reporters and assure them that the White House was "proud to participate in the dawn of a new era in American-Chilean relations, an era ushered in by the strong emphasis President Hardison made on a return to democracy during the campaign."

"Is that democracy in America or Chile?" Wyatt Phillips, not unreasonably, had asked Harold Whitney at the morning briefing he held in the room set up by the advance team to resemble in every significant detail the White House briefing room. Phillips somehow had found, or been slipped, a copy of the White House talking points, which he would hold up to the camera in his piece that night. His piece would focus on how the White House was inept even when it was trying to control the message its own staff put out.

They didn't look much better throughout the rest of the day. The suspicion that either the new rulers or the old were pissed at the United

States was confirmed when, as the motorcade rolled toward the symbolic reopening of the Congreso Nacional, they were cut off by the motorcade carrying Castro and held in position in the Plaza de Armas. During the long ten minutes in which they had to watch the rival motorcade glide by in long Zil limousines, the Secret Service agents nearly exhibited zip-gun pique at the smirking conspiracy of Cuban thugs who took their Spanish-language cues from grim Chilean soldiers in green fatigues, white belts, and caps with patent-leather rims. By the time the motorcade was allowed to pass, the President was late. Rather than take his position on the reviewing stand between Mrs. Thatcher and Chancellor Kohl, he was wedged between González of Spain and Castro, who exacerbated the President's problems by hugging him with excitement when the new Chilean president cut the link and allowed the doors that had been closed for many years to swing open. As the thirty thousand people pressed in the plaza broke into cheers and the F-16's of the newly subordinated Chilean Air Force shrieked with dipped wings across the sky, the cameras of the Western media concentrated on Castro's Soviet-style embrace of Hardison. The President patted him on the back, twice—he was obviously just trying to be polite—but that acquiescence to the old dictator's embrace would be seized upon by Hardison's enemies as, at best, a symbol of weakness, and perhaps an admission of an ardor far worse than that. Castro looked like he was trying to hump him. It was the riveting moment, and no amount of talking points, no velocity of spin, could change that snapshot of Castro, his eyes closed, his beard pressed against Hardison's shoulder. Their bad luck continued.

 atherine Tierney read the *Post* with despair, though it wasn't her biggest headache. The op-ed page was filled with hoots about the trip's more boorish episodes, but it wasn't the trip that was bothering her. The speech Colin had written for New Orleans had never been delivered. There was no mention of the remarks Hardison was to have given last night upon his arrival in Santiago. That was understandable, given the news that by the time he got there, the only people waiting for the President's arrival were American advance men, no doubt standing in the darkness in pinstripes and sunglasses. No, what was her biggest problem was the rumor that the White House aide with the dope-dealing past was one of her speech-writers.

Ralph Thicke of *The Washington Times* had told her. "I've been given a tip that the dope dealer's someone in your shop, Kate," he had said that morning. She had thought he was phoning to ask about the speeches, which was why she hadn't just bucked the call over to the shell of a press office that remained there while most White House staffers were with the President. But she knew Ralph, knew him to be well meaning, if crazy, always chasing down long-shot stories the *Post* wouldn't touch, and so she'd returned his call. And found that it was her speechwriters who were being assaulted by Republican operatives.

"Are you still looking for that phantom?" she asked Ralph with a nervous laugh.

"I wasn't until I got this tip. But I got it from a good source."

"A source within the White House, Ralph, or a source trying to give us trouble?"

"A source who's usually reliable, Katherine, that's all I can tell you."

"Okay, but let me just tell you. If it isn't someone on the White House staff who's directly working on our investigation, or someone in the FBI, your source doesn't know anything, and if I were you, I would begin to suspect his motivation. The rumor I hear is that *Newsweek* got the tip from a bartender. And I got *that* from a good source. So if the person who told you this is a Republican, Ralph, you don't have a source. You have a character assassin."

"It's a Republican," Ralph began. "But one I believe has very good information. And he made it clear that the person the White House is concluding has the problem is one of your speechwriters. He specifically said the person was not you, okay? So you can relax. He specifically said it wasn't you."

"Oh, great. Thanks a hell of a lot. That still means you think it's one of my people. And Ralph, let me tell you, I know where our investigation's going, and from what I hear, our internal investigation— not *Newsweek*'s, though having printed it, they're as concerned about whether it's true as we are—our people are concluding the whole thing was a rumor concocted by Republicans who knew the White House would go crazy trying to run it down. What I hear is that the reporter from *Newsweek* couldn't produce a credible source to his editors after they began to run the story down. I hear he's admitted he was told it by some guy who runs a bar in Adams Morgan. That's what I hear. And with all due respect, if there was something to it, don't you think the *Post* would have broken the story by now?" Oops. But she couldn't resist.

Ralph acted like he hadn't heard it. "Katherine, I like you. I'm sorry about this. I thought I'd see if you could tell me anything. But I've got enough to go with this story."

"You don't have anything," she all but shouted into the phone. "All you have is a rumor. And you can't print rumors."

"Actually, I can," Ralph said before ringing off.

But that wasn't what disturbed her. What disturbed her was the fact that Ralph's Republican source had specifically exempted her from suspicion. Which meant that unless that source was just making the whole thing up, swinging wildly and seeing where his punch landed, he had talked to someone in the White House who was protecting her. Which could only mean Rod Gardener, who she knew was working on the internal investigation. And who she knew couldn't stand Tom O'Malley.

 is heart was beating like a bass drum solo at a heavy metal concert and it wouldn't let up. He thought for a moment it might be the sight of the bonfires in the plazas throughout the city, the crowds he could hear chanting what turned out to be the cheer for a local football team, as it grew dark and cold. "It's chilly," he said to Max at one point as they tried to forge their way against the crowds on the Alameda, and Max fell to giggling as if they were stoned teenagers in a sixties-style street demonstration.

The crowd, a hundred thousand strong, swarmed up Santa Lucia Hill in celebration of the junta's end. They could hear a pretty fair rock band play "Jumpin' Jack Flash" somewhere in the wooded park that led up toward the fortress. Students swayed boughs wrapped in burning rags and the Chilean flag. When O'Malley began to flash on what a genuine celebration this was, the people in the streets, not just fat cats in tuxedos, it depressed him about the inaugural he'd lived through only months ago. This in turn made him think how that inaugural, and his impulse to celebrate it in a fashion similar to the way these students drinking wine out of goat sacks did now, had indirectly put him in the position he was in. In a foreign country far, far from home. Planning on smuggling cocaine on Air Force One. Thump thump thump thump thump.

"Let's go back," he said to Max, depressed. His heart was beating faster than the pulse of the crowd, faster than he thought he would be able to stand if it kept up at this pace until he was back in the States two nights from now. They went back to the hotel and joined a party in progress. In a restaurant that was absurdly situated around the swimming pool, they found some of the advance men eating with reporters who weren't assigned to cover the official dinner at the Congreso Nacional.

"I'm glad we're not in the pool," said one producer from CBS who looked weary from the strain of covering the day's events.

"You are in the pool, mate," said a drunken reporter from the *Times* of London, standing up and pushing the hapless fellow from his chair over the edge. The producer had just enough of his wits about him to grab on to his tormentor, and the two cannonballed in together, the delayed-reaction surge of spray hitting the table as if splashed by a flip of Orca's tail at Ocearama. With that it became a free-for-all, and it was only Max's and O'Malley's momentary good luck that they had pulled up chairs on the end farthest from the pool that allowed them to get out of there without going in.

He went back to his room, regretting he would miss dinner. But how could he have continued to sit with the group of reporters without their hearing his heart beat so loudly? He put his hand over it, Webelo-style. His heart was bound to give him away, which made it beat all the harder.

Kit went over the points the Senator was to make one more time, even though it was early and she well knew he wasn't a morning person. The much too cheerful ABC guest-grabber brought him a cup of coffee in the greenroom—Kit refused any, she was too nervous—and he sat there clearing his throat a little obnoxiously, as if there were something terrible down there he could get at if he just tried hard enough. She knew he had allergies in Washington, maybe *to* Washington, knew he sometimes had to coax up phlegm, and annoyingly, in the middle of meetings, get up and walk into his private bathroom to spit into the sink, but this sound was horrible, like an auto mechanic revving the engine of a sick Italian car, high-strung and gut-shot. Worse, she felt he wasn't paying attention.

Senator Partridge leafed through the newspapers arrayed on the coffee table, and at one point Kit caught herself about to snap at him for fixating on the sports page highlights of the basketball play-offs instead of reading any of the briefing material she'd stayed late at the office preparing. She sat on the couch, staring at her shoes, and realized she was twice as nervous as he was, and she wondered if it was because she took this, his first appearance on a network talk show, twice as seriously. Why should appearing on "Good Morning America" be different from anything else in her dealings with Partridge?

"You read the paper?" he suddenly asked.

"In general, or this morning?"

"This morning. Anything in them I need to know about?" He sat there craning his neck and straightening his tie. In a moment he'd start making that noise again, that terrible sound of trying to clear his throat.

"Nothing I could tell. Uh, the White House is claiming no conclusions should be drawn from the President hugging Castro down in Chile. Other than that, there's nothing pressing in either the *Times*, the *Post*, or the *Journal*."

He nodded his head and she couldn't believe he was being so casual. They led him off to makeup where the lady remarked on how smooth his skin was and Partridge flirted, politely. Then they walked him down the corridor into a small room lined with books, some of which no doubt were left by previous guests who'd gone on "GMA" to pitch them. For the most part, they were White House memoirs dating to the Reagan years, as well as a number of Watergate exposés. Kit pressed herself against the wall as a technician snaked the microphone up underneath the Senator's shirt and out around his necktie, which she noticed approvingly was a simple pattern of alternating rep stripes, red and television blue. Partridge sat there and let them check the levels and then stared into the camera with a loopy slight grin on his face. The guy was a natural.

"Now, remember, no matter what Charlie asks you," she said as if she and their interlocutor were chums from way back, "get the subject back to cholesterol."

"What's the name of the bill again?"

She wanted to shoot him. "It's the Partridge-Leach Healthful Diet Act."

"Education, labeling of cholesterol contents, Just Say Vegetable." By George, he had it.

The down side to her being in this tiny room with him, other than comfort, was that she couldn't hear the show. There was a tiny monitor along the opposite wall, but right now all it showed was Charlie and Joan looking grumpy and faintly uncomfortable as the camera swung out of control, shooting this way and that. Either it was an avant-garde advertisement or else it was just near show time.

"Yes, Charlie," Partridge suddenly barked, as if he were hearing voices. He was, though the earphone wasn't pressed in perfectly and he took the time to squeeze it in. If he were to graduate to that level of Washington media figure who went on these shows often, they would have to have him fitted for his own earplug, which they would simply connect to the audio when they arrived for these shows. She would have to remind herself.

"Okay, I'll be talking at about this level, three, two, one. Uh, Tony Partridge, three, two, one," he said like a child practicing lift-off on some mission to Mars. And then, in a moment, she could see the graphics on the screen and they were under way. Partridge sat there with his face toward the camera, though one eye was cocked to the monitor a quarter turn to his right as they went through the introductory portion of news, and occasionally, as they replayed the footage of the President and Castro hugging like Warren Beatty and Diane Keaton at the end of *Reds*, Kit's mind flashed to O'Malley. She hoped he was enjoying this trip, though it was turning out to be a first-class bust. Then, the news was over and Joan was running down who was on the show, and suddenly the red light above the camera in front of Partridge was on, and his face came momentarily on the screen. Thank God he wasn't picking his nose. Or revving up the engines in his lungs. Instead he looked terrific.

The cameraman went, "Two minutes," when they went to the ad, and he held up his fingers in the victory sign. Partridge, panic-struck for just a second, hissed to Kit, "Partridge-Leach Diet Act?"

"Healthful Diet Act," she corrected. "Just keep it on cholesterol."

And then in his earplug he could hear a voice saying, "Thirty seconds," and he stared in the camera and suddenly, a tiny voice, with none of the urgency or importance one would associate with national television, was saying his name, and introducing him as the author of a bill being introduced today that was aimed at reducing the unhealthy level of low-density lipoproteins in the blood. "Good morning, Senator, and just what the heck are 'low-density lipoproteins,' anyway?"

"Good morning, Charlie. Well, low-density lipoproteins are the bad cholesterol, which shouldn't be confused with the good cholesterol. They're the fatty deposits in the bloodstream that clog up, um, things, and my bill, the Partridge-Leach, uh, Good Morning America Act is aimed at working to ensure that we educate people about the difference between high-density and low-density, uh, the good and bad cholesterols, and also to label, um, food, as to the levels of . . ."

Kit's heart had positively stopped. She couldn't hear the question Charlie interrupted him with, though the Senator heard his disembodied host now ask him whether his bill wasn't a threat to the beef industry of his home state of Wyoming.

"Why, not at all, Charlie. Beef is good food, and should be a part of people's diet, uh, taken moderately, and not to excess. It's the egg ranchers from dairy states, not Wyoming cattle farmers, who should, um, be less happy," he said now with an inappropriate if handsome grin.

"Senator, I don't mean to switch gears on you, but there's a report in *The Washington Times* this morning that says that sources in the White House report the person or persons there who have ties to drug dealers appear to be members of the speechwriters' office. Have you read this story?"

"Uh, in *The Washington Times*," Partridge began, and Kit slumped against the wall. What was in *The Washington Times*? "I haven't seen that article, Charlie, but you know, drugs are bad for people's health. Why, some people say you should Just Say No, but I say, Just Say Vegetable. Uh, you should say no partly because drugs are bad for your health. Sort of like cholesterol," he said and she could see his brow wet with perspiration. What was he babbling about?

"Senator, we don't have much time. Do you think there should be a special prosecutor to look into these accusations of drug dealing connected to the White House?"

"Uh, sounds fine to me, Charlie," Partridge allowed. He shrugged good-naturedly and waved his hand like it was no skin off his butt what the Justice Department did. And with that she could see the camera pan back on Charlie and Joan sitting together as they went to an ad, and Partridge was free to go. What sounded fine? Kit wanted to know. Certainly not Partridge's performance.

"Kit," he said excitedly. "I stuck to the script! I got cholesterol in, didn't I?"

She had to admit he had. But what *had* he been babbling about?

L eaving Santiago was a relief for all, except for O'Malley and his percussive heartbeat. The airliner picked up speed and then was launched, veering right upon takeoff toward mountains that were like bugle blasts upon the flattened plains. Sunlight was spun through their windows, illuminating all of their faces if only for a second, and O'Malley prayed that when the light was on him, his looks didn't give him away. His mission ate away at his well-being.

The plan as Nicole had related it to him at the 9:30 Club was very simple. While the President and members of the senior staff were at the State dinner at La Casona, the presidential palace, the rest of them had been given the evening off. O'Malley was to beg off from any social engagements, pleading a last-minute rewrite of the speech the President was to give the next day. At precisely 10:00 P.M., he was to expect a knock on his door, only what would be rolled in wouldn't be the Yanqui Special room-service club sandwich, it would be twenty kilos of freshly processed rock. Somehow this would have wended its way from the vegetable kingdom in Bolivia, over the Andes, with a stop for refining in Colombia. The airplane O'Malley flew on would roughly approximate the drug's journey before they rendezvoused in Venezuela. He wondered if he could peek through clouds and see the mule train.

It was a simple plan, and he kept reminding himself that all he had to do was accept the package, and squeeze it into the small Hewlett-Packard printer he had carried onto the jet two days before. The Secret Service was by now used to his lugging his laptop and the printer everywhere they went; there was no reason to think this would become a problem Thursday when they headed to Managua and then home. His mind tried not to flash on Venezuelan security forces searching his room while they were at El Capitolio for the President's speech, their finding the guts of his printer removed and stashed underneath the bed. He had a vision of jackboots marching Nazi-style into the capitol building, their hauling him off before an audience of surprised Venezuelan legislators and the assembled press corps. As clearly as if it were on the movie screen at the front of the plane, he saw his inert body as he was dragged by his armpits to a waiting Venezuelan prison.

What was the redeeming side to his ten-year stay in a Venezuelan jail? His Spanish would certainly improve. If they allowed him to have books and they gave him a pen and some paper, he would complete his education and write a book, a novel that perfectly matched South American fabulism with the poignancy of a Gulag memoir. It would be a very moral book. It would spell out how he got himself into this mess. It would be a lesson to others.

S he knew something was wrong from the congratulatory glee with which Jerry Jetta and Mike Humperdink greeted Partridge's return to the Hart Building. While the Senator had been able to drive underneath the Capitol to park, it had taken Kit ten minutes to make it in from the satellite lot to which she was assigned, and by the time she got there, Jetta and Humperdink were surrounding the Senator and all but patting him on the back while the switchboard lit up and Michele, the press secretary, appeared to be drowning from the press calls. Wilbur was sitting on the couch in the Senator's office with a smug grin on his face, and Jetta began to walk around going, "Excellent, excellent," punching the air and talking to inanimate objects such as bookshelves, desks, and the decorative head of a Teton mountain goat that was mounted and hung on the wall.

"We've got calls from CBS and CNN, boss," young Michele burst in and told the Senator, who was standing by his desk, a little shocked by the stir he'd created.

"What do they want?" Kit asked.

"They want to know if he'll say the same thing to their correspondents that he said on 'GMA.' "

"What, they're doing pieces on our cholesterol bill?" With that, Jetta and Humperdink burst into laughter, and Wilbur rolled back on the couch and kicked his short legs in the air like this was the funniest thing he ever heard. Kit hated being the straight man.

Michele, who didn't have much of a sense of humor, filled her in. "Weren't you there? Tony called for a special prosecutor to investigate the White House dope dealer."

"Oh, Tony, you didn't." So that's what it had been all about. When they were walking out of ABC, he was too proud of his remembering to keep everything on cholesterol to have been able to tell her what Charlie had asked him at the end. There went their cholesterol headlines. And then it hit her. Partridge had just become O'Malley's inadvertent tormentor.

The soldiers were everywhere in their red berets and shiny metal helmets, through the ceremony at the airport where the two presidents greeted each other and waved to the cameras before getting on the helicopter, throughout the long ride the staff and the press corps took from the airport into the sprawling metropolis. Every mile or so there were new formations of troops gathered around personnel carriers and jeeps, and as they began to whiz by the hovels and shacks that rose from the highway up into the hills in an amazingly congested and horrifying clutter, children peered at them from the roadside with the mute incomprehension that suggested that by age six there was nothing in life that could surprise or amaze them.

There was none of the prosperity and temperate cleanliness of Santiago here; Caracas sprawled with shacks on the surrounding mountains like litter that had been dropped and never cleaned up. They entered the city proper and there was a dense pack of traffic being held up at the circles, roaring in the tension that built in the heat as the army kept them back until the convoy of buses and the American cars dispatched from the Embassy went by. When they did, the cars hit the circles in a growl of scraped bumpers and epithets. The large buildings that had gone up in the oil boom of years gone by rose in gleaming spires through the congestion, though it looked like a minor earthquake could make a real mess of things. There was little apparent charm to the city as they made their way and were dropped off at the high-rise Hilton where they were to stay the night. Where O'Malley was to receive the goods. Where the most evil transaction of his life would take place. If all went well, he'd be in the convoy tomorrow when they turned around and fought their way back out of the city, under the diplomatic immunity of the United States, under the watchful eyes of the army. If all went well.

Special Agent Harlan Bryce all but cackled in the conference room. Called in to an interagency review of the Form 86's that had been pulled and sent over from White House Personnel, he announced gleefully to the assembled crew that he had the mystery solved. He'd cracked the White House's most vexing public-relations problem and the biggest challenge to the investigative capabilities of the federal government, the single largest blot on their record in the new administration. "I have the little fucker," he announced.

There was a handful of their Most Wanted list who looked more respectable than he did. He still had to flash his ID to the guards downstairs, though he'd worked there for almost twenty years. It didn't help that every Monday his hands shook a little more than they had the week before, that more often than not, when he took the time to shave with a razor at his home, the white foam would be enlivened with splotches of pink blood, the residue of the shakes. But he was a hell of a sleuth when it came to these Form 86's, that was the word on Harlan. He could never actually have passed one himself, but that didn't matter anymore.

"Okay, you got said White House aide with his Form 86 pulled by Gardener and Tiswell over to the White House, see." He lit a cigarette with a blowtorch-sized flame from his Bic. He took three big puffs and continued. "Now, said White House aide, Thomas O'Malley, seems to have been the countercultural type. He appears to have been a rebel, a liberal who went boho after college, mayhaps as a way of getting back at his father, an American patriot you of course remember worked for our sister agency in Langley." The six heads around the table, representatives of the Secret Service, the White House Counsel's office, and some preppy from the Justice Department who was known to be hostile to the work of the Federal Bureau of Investigation, nodded.

"Now, I've traced him to New York where he appears to have been unable, really, to either hold down a job or stay for more than a year in any one residence. None of his neighbors will admit to having known him." Harlan looked up from his notepad to let that settle in. "At the bars where he worked, he was known as a fun guy, and I quote, 'He liked to party, he was always organizing groups to go to the clubs when our shifts ended.' Now, I don't suppose I have to tell you what kind of clubs we're talking about. Places with bands named, and I am not kidding you, the Dead Kennedys, Devo, and Iggy Pop." He looked up from his notepad as if there were nothing more to say, as if this were enough to indict the guy and send him up the river for life.

If he had to guess where he was with his jury, the six grim white men around the table, Harlan would have been hard-pressed to say. Impassivity was the good agent's protective mask. He proceeded.

"His mother is Barbara Ingram O'Malley, well-known benefactor of left-wing causes, including, in the early seventies, the National Organization for the Reform of Marijuana Laws. She has long been active in support of South American radicals, including, according to her file here at the Bureau, the M-15 guerrilla movement in Colombia, which, as you know, trades cocaine for weapons. In fact, Thomas O'Malley made a trip to Colombia shortly after graduation from college, and even paid a visit to our consulate in Medellín." With that Harlan raised an eyebrow and looked at each of them individually, a cold group, except for the young preppy from Justice who looked as if he was beginning to get excited.

"Why did he visit the consulate in Medellín, Har?" It was Rigby, Harlan's immediate superviser, and since he was known to be one of the most skillful bureaucrats in the Bureau, he must be voicing the question others had. Rigby knew how to please these guys. Rigby could fill out forms and make them read like country-western songs.

"Seems he was looking for a girl who went native on him. According to the report the consul filed with DEA at the time, our Mr. O'Malley came looking for a girl who had vanished onto one of the plantations owned by the cartel. The consulate believed she was dead."

"You have anything more current than ten years ago, Agent Bryce?" It was the preppy from Justice. He must have misread him. These political appointees were a pain in the butt, that was for sure, the Democrats worse than Republicans.

Harlan looked at him with a scowl as if to say, Wha? If they weren't ready to ban the little fucker from any branch of government more sensitive than a park ranger, what was this place coming to?

"He admitted smoking pot within the last five years on his Form Eighty-six," Harlan said, as if offering up his trump card before he had wanted to.

"That's it?" the preppy asked.

"He got into fights with a woman he lived with out of wedlock. Sounded to the neighbors like there was serious drinking going on, though he didn't put that down on his form." They looked skeptical. He sweetened the pot. "He was arrested for DWI in January. After leaving a club where a band called, get this, the Feelies, was playing." A king. "Today in *The Washington Times*, there's a front-page story that says the guy we're after works in the office of speechwriters. So does O'Malley." An ace.

"It also says that this is something we've concluded, Agent Bryce. Unless I'm wrong, this isn't something we've yet concluded." Harlan began to suspect the preppy must be a friend of O'Malley's, unless he was just automatically defending him. This might have something to do with class, with people from the same colleges protecting each other. O'Malley would do the same for him, and so forth. The Washington Buddy System. He sat there seething. He didn't have any buddies.

"Yeah, Harlan, is this it?" Rigby asked.

There was more, but Harlan knew he was up against a stacked deck. No need to continue with this group. He gave a wave of his hand that was supposed to imply nonchalance, but came perilously close to giving the finger to the preppy.

"Then I suggest, if that is all you have," the preppy was saying as if he were in charge, though Harlan knew no reason why he outranked the mute representative from the White House Counsel's office, "I suggest you find out more before we just have him hauled off in manacles and sent to Sing Sing, okay, Agent Bryce?"

It was Lorton Penitentiary, in Virginia, though he didn't feel like correcting the jerk. Boy, what did it take these days to get someone nailed as an undesirable? Harlan sat there scratching his face as the rest of them got up to go.

momentary sense of well-being settled upon O'Malley as he stared out his window on the Hilton's twenty-third floor and looked upon Caracas. It was vast and far more orderly than it had seemed in the midday jumble of honking horns and slick, litter-strewn streets. From here, there was a cosmopolitan shape that must once have seemed premeditated before it was overrun by overbuilding, by the traffic that moved in a continuum of Ford Festivas acing out old Chevy Novas as they rushed along avenues that once must have seemed grand. The cars played chicken as they veered to the circles around fountains that were dwarfed by billboards. Municipal structures from the thirties bore the relative stamp of history in the facelessness of modern kitsch, in the shadow of architectural impermanence that implied these new buildings would all wear out when the money did.

The money was gone, though the city still seemed vital. In the distance he could see a cable car ascending a green mountain that alone among the hills surrounding the city was free of the clutter of shanties. He turned from the view momentarily to actually check on the business at hand, to look at the speech the President was to deliver tomorrow just a few blocks from here.

There was, in addition, his assignment to come up with a tougher statement for the President when he got to the announcement of renewed relations in Managua. Because of the currency of that footage of the President with Castro, the White House was cutting short the Nicaraguan segment of the trip. Rather than having the President attend a series of events in downtown Managua, the plan now called for him merely to get out of the plane for an airport ceremony, in which he would deliver a brief statement O'Malley was assigned to massage from the rough outline presented him by Lemlow Motrin into something memorable, poetic, and able to stem right-wing criticism, all at once.

As if tugged toward it, he wandered back to the window and put his face against the glass. Caracas was actually very beautiful, the way the mountains ringed the center. He saw that now. There was no way you would confuse this with the United States, though there was an obvious New World vitality to it. There was a marvelous chaos to the city sprawl that overtly stated its American independence, that announced its shape came as the result of a determinism that wasn't just the post-colonial collapse of African cities he'd visited with his father as a child. He suddenly found he liked it here. It would be nice to be here, perhaps with Kit, without the responsibilities of work. Without having put everything at risk because of his inability to stand up to David Nicole. Because of the fear his former friend inspired.

W hen the Mayor of Washington, after much maneuvering, went and flunked his drug test, Steve Bronstein already was bored with his beat. That the Mayor then was bloodied by thugs for failure to pay his debts to Jamaican crack gangs landed McTeague and Bronstein a page-one story, but it wasn't the story he wanted to write. He wanted to write about much bigger crooks. He wanted to write about Congress.

Unfortunately, it was easier to transfer to the National Desk at the *Post* from some small-town daily in Missouri than it was to move up from Metro. This was why, months before, Bronstein had made his pact with the devil, as it were, and agreed to team up with Cale McTeague.

Where Bronstein was a fairly laid-back reporter—there were questions he was ashamed to ask—he was a first-rate stylist, and could organize his pieces with cohesiveness, clarity and, he'd been told, that special feel for nuance that alerted editors to the journalists who would make their marks. Unfortunately, while he might end up the greatest stylist in Metro section history, this would not land him on the National Desk unless he got a lucky break. Tom O'Malley was his lucky break. That's what Cale McTeague said. He was convinced of it, though Bronstein wasn't nearly so sure.

Cale, long-haired, irreverent, frequently broke, had on more than a few occasions come within an inch of being bounced, usually with cause, usually for insolence. He did not suffer fools. He was bold. He had an intuitive grasp of where a story was going such that, for example, when the news spread that the Mayor had been found outside of that discotheque in Southeast, clutching his busted ribs and claiming he simply had danced too vigorously to the Go-Go music, Cale had by the next day been able to stitch together a package complete with graphics that showed how much the Mayor owed, to whom, and what threats he'd been living under.

Unfortunately, Cale couldn't write worth a damn, which was where Bronstein came in. The Bronstein and McTeague byline was directly the result of mutual benefit, a division of labor like so many others, based on an understanding of the difference between manufacturing and packaging. They were getting noticed. They were being talked about as the team that would be sent to Richmond to cover the Virginia Legislature when the next session came to order, though the only thing either of them could possibly imagine as being worse than that would be to have to move to Annapolis to cover the Maryland Legislature. They wanted National, talked about it at lunch, talked about it increasingly on weekends they spent together, working at the paper, going out for beer and pizza at A.V.'s afterward, plotting their great leap forward.

Unfortunately for Bronstein, all this ambition and hard work didn't leave much time to meet girls. McTeague didn't need time; there was something about the energy with which he threw himself into every argument, every phone call, everything he did, that women found attractive, and he had no dating scruples. They went to interview the Mayor's Special Assistant for Narcotics Control the day after the Mayor flunked his drug test, and that night McTeague went out dancing with the guy's secretary, who couldn't have been twenty-one. Amazing. The Metro section softball team played the Circulation team on the Mall, and McTeague walked off with the receptionist for whom people purposely got lost just to get a glimpse, just to have an excuse to ask her for directions, people who'd worked at the paper for years. And he did this while her boyfriend was waiting for her over by the National Museum in his pickup with the Virginia plates and his engine running. The kid was a phenom.

Bronstein, constantly amazed by his partner, was slower in this as in other things, though he was also more discriminating, and he had a certain style. Tonight, for example, he'd been invited to be the guest of Mandy Drabb at the Republican Progress Council's big cocktail party at the Marriott. Though she was a little too Republican for him, though he felt certain that rather than having spent her teenage weekends out cruising malls and getting in mischief in Firebirds and El Dorados, she'd probably played doubles at country clubs that would never have let him in to clean their pool, he had an enormous crush on her. He could hardly believe his luck at having met her one Friday night a few weeks before at some sports bar in Georgetown where she'd been surrounded by giggling girlfriends and he'd been with McTeague.

This was one instance where being with McTeague had helped, since Mandy and Cale had gotten into an argument within minutes of his trying to pick up one of her friends. Steve had been the peacemaker, and by the end, it had gotten ugly enough for her to have told Cale he was an asshole. He thought she'd given him her phone number almost as a deliberate affront to McTeague, but hey, whatever works, right?

Since then they'd had brunch on the Sunday when his and Cale's piece on the Mayor's troubles with that Uzi-toting gang of crackheads had been front-page news, and his contempt for the Mayor had given them something—perhaps their only thing—in common. He'd sat in the sunlight of the outdoor cafe, hardly watching his eggs Benedict congeal, mooning at her and just listening to her precious laugh. And now she was taking him to Clarissa Lowery's big fundraising cocktail party on behalf of the PAC that was the old fraud's vehicle to Republican sainthood, if not an ambassadorship. They'd already made plans for dinner afterward. Perhaps tonight was the night.

He sat dreamily in front of his computer screen, thinking about the evening's possibilities. There was something about Mandy that made him visualize her in riding jodhpurs and boots, naked from the waist up, in one hand a riding crop gently tapping the other palm. He barely acknowledged Cale, as his partner worked feverishly to track down the story in *The Washington Times* about the White House druggy being a speechwriter. Somewhere in the back of his mind he doubted that Cale would ever let desire get in the way of a story. But then, Cale didn't have to.

The crowd began to surround the hotel around five o'clock. He could hear the chants when they were still blocks away. His eyelids snapped back, his heart was beating fast, and the back of his neck was clammy even though the air conditioning was going full bore, an aspect of North American engineering that had been transplanted along with the Hilton logo. O'Malley's nap was over and he'd fallen deeply enough asleep to have awakened with the momentary start that the mob was coming for him, to wonder if he was its purpose. He saw: Jacobins, guillotines, the DEA.

He hadn't meant to sleep; he'd meant to go out into the roar of the city streets with their diesel stench, their vendors, and their crowds. Instead, having decided to lie back on his bed and rest his eyes for a moment, he'd plunged a fathom under. Now he wanted coffee, and a shower, and to be home, with everything all right.

He stood by the window and thought it maybe best he head down to one of the staff rooms to find out what was going on. He was going to have to act as unobtrusively as possible if he was to avoid telegraphing his worries to the rest of the staff. But the crowd, chanting what he could imagine only to be anti-American slogans, now began to press into the broad avenue below, wreaking havoc on traffic that made Times Square at rush hour seem like a pleasure ride in the White Mountains. Horns blared, there were hundreds of men in open shirts, leaning from their cars and shouting, to no avail, at the crowd that just kept getting larger. Looking down upon it, he thought of a tipped-over ant farm. Feeding on its own energy, it had the force to make the traffic come to a stop, which given the sheer volume of cars that began to back up on the Avenida México, was a correspondence of immensity. It was at least as powerful as the force of soldiers that had this afternoon brought the city to a snarling, revved-up stop for the length of time it took to get their motorcade from the outskirts to the whirling center. O'Malley stood there, waking up, amazed at the forces here that were beyond his control. And these were just the forces he could see.

illy Barnes prowled the staff suite cursing to himself. The fax machine on a table by the TV set was spitting out clips with beeps and a high-pitched whine. The news wasn't comforting. Every major paper in America had carried photos on its front page of the President and Castro hugging. The stories weren't unfair—they made it clear that the old dictator had mashed the unsuspecting President. But that in itself was problematic, at least when the reporters used the word "blindsided." Quarterbacks got blindsided. Rookie candidates got blindsided. Presidents weren't supposed to.

There was the notion about that the President was some kind of innocent, as out of his depth in the world of foreign affairs as he would be on a dive for the *Titanic*. Willy grimaced when he had that thought. Why was he thinking in disaster metaphors? Maybe because in a situation like this, someone usually took a fall, and he'd worked with Hardison for almost twenty-five years.

A couple of staffers from the political office were on the phones with the White House getting verbal reports. The networks apparently were playing the events of the previous twenty-four hours in fourth place, just behind the news about the employment rate—down—and the Commerce Department's figures on new housing starts, which were up. Once again Hardison had gotten a lucky break from an air disaster, in this instance a 767 that had skidded off a runway and burst into flames at O'Hare, and Willy breathed a sigh of relief. No one was killed, but there was just enough suspicion of pilot error to have made it the lead on the evening news. The footage of flames was so spectacular, it pushed coverage of the President's mostly uneventful day in South America beyond the first commercial break.

Most of the pieces the correspondents had filed from the welcoming ceremonies at Aeropuerto Caracas were interspersed with analyses by so-called objective observers in the States. A regular viewer of the news could predict what each of them would say, based on their past performances of mostly trashing the President.

The networks invariably went to the usual suspects—Democratic pollsters for candidates Hardison had beaten in the primaries, Republican media consultants who wouldn't have a nice word to say about Hardison if he discovered the cure for cancer. It was infuriating to hear his staff run down the list of whom the networks had interviewed back in Washington, and it made him wonder why, with all the resources the networks had, they relied on such a thin Rolodex of talking heads. They had on auto-dial the same group of blowhards who were set up to tell the American people what they ought to think about events already skewed by correspondents who invariably put the administration's worst foot forward. If he could have laughed about anything right now—and he couldn't, it had been that kind of trip—he would have at least gotten a slight chuckle over how differently one began to look at the news when one sat inside the most scrutinized building in the world.

The thing that was perhaps most problematic, as it was reported to him, was that Senator Tony Partridge, who Barnes thought was perhaps the biggest airhead in the Senate, had responded to some story in *The Washington Times* by calling for a special prosecutor to take up an investigation of the alleged White House drug dealer. He'd thought that particular demon had been put to rest.

"Gimme those clips," he said unhappily to his assistant. She tapped them into symmetry against the edge of the desk and handed them over. Willy took them over to the window. Twenty-two floors below, the demonstration against Hardison and President Pérez was continuing with leftist chants and metallic insults squeezed through megaphones, as if the locals couldn't distinguish between the president they'd elected and the Norteamericano oppressor they would hate even more if he turned off the spigot of credit that kept their bankrupt nation afloat. Or so Willy, who was not in a generous mood, thought as he looked upon them. Damn, that was a lot of people beginning to surround the hotel.

He quickly came across the clip from *The Washington Times* and taking out his half-frames he glanced down upon it. "Crazy man," he said aloud.

"What, Willy?" his assistant asked.

"Nothing," he muttered. But it was true. Ralph Thicke, whom he'd dealt with a time or two over the years, was certifiable. And this clip before him was right out of a madman's oeuvre. No sources quoted by name; he just hid behind what *The Washington Times* had "learned," as in, "*The Washington Times* has learned the earth is flat." In this instance, Thicke claimed they'd learned that the White House had learned that the FBI had learned—goddamn, thought Willy, Washington was an educational place. Everybody was learning everything.

The bottom line was an advanced degree in accusations at once non-specific and just precise enough: someone was fingering the speech-writers. Which was typical. It was never the functionaries, never the MBA'ed dullards with their cost-benefit ratios and their charcoal gray outlooks. It was always the creative types who were thrown to the wolves in times of generalized suspicion. His inclination was to fight this one, not out of any sense of loyalty to the speechwriters. He thought them as spoiled a bunch of troublemaking prima donnas as Harold Whitney probably thought they were. But it was clear to him that if they went after the speechwriters, it was a hop, skip and a jump to their going after the political shop, and the next thing you knew, there would be intimations coming from that group of Ivy League dipshits that, of course, it was the black man most likely to have been involved with reefer.

This whole thing was ridiculous, and the fact that Tony Partridge had seized upon it to call for an independent counsel told him everything he needed to know about that right-wing yokel. He stared down over his glasses as the sun turned brilliant red over the mountains and began to descend upon the rickety skyscrapers. The mob was chanting for someone's head, and he was impressed by the universality of human needs. There was a knock on the open door behind him and he turned to the entrance to the suite. It was Tom O'Malley, the speechwriter. "Why, Thomas," he said. "Come on in."

He almost went through the roof. It was only Willy Barnes's calming influence, his horse trainer's instincts, that kept O'Malley from rearing up and going all skittish. In the time since he read the clip that had been faxed from D.C., his face had filled with blood, and he'd moved around the room in agitation. He was trying to calibrate how much non-specific outrage he could safely show without Willy, who was a pretty savvy guy, thinking that there was a reason—other than the obvious one— why O'Malley objected to the speechwriters being listed as the targets of investigation.

"Sonofabitch," he said over and over, leaning on the edge of the air-conditioning unit, the sky going dark behind him, the crowd screaming for blood.

"Oh, don't worry about Partridge. No one takes him seriously."

"What about Partridge?" O'Malley's eyes were like a deer's in a head-lamp.

"Didn't I tell you? He called for a special prosecutor to investigate the whole thing." Willy chuckled; he was obviously not taking the story all that seriously.

O'Malley did. And it wasn't Partridge he was worried about, though that the idiot had done this surprised him. There was one particular handler Partridge must have slipped. No, the sonofabitch O'Malley was thinking about was Nicole. How, why, had he done this?

"Tom, let me give you some advice. I've lived through this before. I was in Hardison's office during Abscam, I was in town when they investigated Ham Jordan for supposedly sniffing coke at Studio 54. These things have a predictable life of their own, and if you don't have anything to worry about, you don't have anything to worry about." For someone as sharp a dresser as Willy was, he did have his avuncular side.

O'Malley tried to get himself under control, to make Willy think his was just understandable outrage. But he could feel the blood in his face, and his pulse was going like a rhythm box. This was going to be hard to pull off. His knees felt spongy, his armpits moist. He had to get out of there. He had to think about what it was that Nicole had now done. It didn't make any sense for him to plant a story now. He was on the verge—within less than four hours—of doing what the bastard had set him up to do.

"You don't have anything to worry about, do you, Tom?" For the first time in his life, O'Malley cursed his bad luck in being born white. If the tables had been reversed, he knew that Willy wouldn't be sitting there blushing like a newborn babe.

N ormally the notion of going to a fundraising cocktail party would have soured Kit's mood, but tonight her mood would have disintegrated a strip of litmus paper, anyway. The only thing salvageable was that, somehow, the idea of downing a couple of glasses of wine while lobbyists, senators, and operatives made talk so small it bordered on Lilliputian appealed to her sense of the absurd. She would say rude things. She might make a scene. She could not be held responsible for her actions, not after the day she'd had.

When Partridge had been coaxed to the radio and TV gallery to stand before the pale blue backdrop with the silhouette of the Capitol dome and repeat his call for the special prosecutor to investigate the White House, he'd jumped in a single instant from a legislator of dubious value but some potential to a media star with the kind of cachet that sent guest-grabbers and talk-show hosts into frenzies. It was over, as far as she was concerned. His potential as a solon of consequence greater than mere headlines was done. Now he was a creature of sensation, an unguided missile seeking the heat of the television lights. It was clear he liked the results of his morning goof, for by the end of the day he was upping the ante, telling a reporter over the phone that the President's failure to have the Attorney General appoint a prosecutor was a sign of guilt, and what was the President trying to hide?

Kit despaired. How do you keep them talking about cholesterol when they've made the networks? Humperdink, Jetta, and Todd watched the news broadcasts with Partridge, and while the Senator basked in the glow of his televised image, blinking in nervous recognition that things had changed for him today, the operatives beside him rooted and hollered like they were watching a rodeo and he'd just brought down a frisky steer.

So now, in a dark mood, Kit fought her way through the traffic on Pennsylvania Avenue toward the Marriott, where Clarissa Lowery was hosting her annual shakedown of lobbyists and PAC directors who were expected to pony up for Republican candidates.

It was a pleasant evening, not yet steamy, though summer would soon be upon them. The streets were beginning to fill with the white bread–fed, plump tourists, the kind who trekked through the nation's sacred buildings in tank tops, jogging shorts, and sandals with black socks. She turned up Fourteenth Street and, parking her car in a garage next to the National Press Building, she allowed the monstrous Marriott doorman in his pith helmet getup to do his thing. She knew she looked good, in spite of having been up at six o'clock to get Partridge to "GMA," and straightening her hair, she headed down the steps through the Babylonian lobby.

At the bottom of the escalators, there were cameras and producers with boom mikes ready to assault the famous. This was the kind of event that in Washington passed for glamour. Kit pressed her shoulders back and strode by with the professional air of someone who knew she could make more than a few of the bystanders do a double take. That there was residual recognition of her from those days, five years ago, when she'd been in the pages of *Bazaar,* from the days she'd learned to walk down runways with the haughtiness she now summoned, was something she took in the same long strides with which she entered the room.

It was jam-packed with stuffed shirts, and if you calibrated the man-hours that had gone into coloring, curling, and combing out the various Republican wives' hair, you could set up your own department in the Bureau of Labor Statistics. Kit stood at the threshold, tremulous with contempt. Fortunately, the first group she ran into included Michele Davis, who was always a portrait of derision at these events, even when she'd arranged them, and they were able to compare negative attitudes to the point where pleasure could be taken in noting just how bad the whole affair was. "Do you believe how awful this is?" Michele, whose job it was to baby-sit Republican governors when they were up for reelection, asked with her subversive smile.

"I don't know. How bad is it?"

"Wait until you see the dancing dollar signs," she said enigmatically, and then moved off for more champagne. Kit thought she was joking, but then, a few minutes later, when she had been roughly pulled into a group of not unamusing lawyers of her acquaintance who were cutting up their hostess behind her back, one of them danced right before her. "Ohmygod," she said aloud.

"You hadn't seen them?" Woody Fiedler asked with surprise.

"No way," she replied, in awe. For walking through the crowd with a silver tray on which flutes of champagne were there for the taking was this creature with long legs in a tight little cigarette-girl outfit and her own glittering prison cell of double bars stuck to an S, the top swirl of which was neck-high, the bottom swirl ending at crotch level. Kit didn't want to go near the semiotics of this one.

"Clarissa certainly thinks of the little touches, doesn't she?" George Roberts was as amazed as she was. He and his two friends stood there and watched the woman with the painted-on smile try to maneuver through the crowd, her hand folded back carrying the tray, her mobility affected by the twin S's of her sparkling sandwich board.

"Wait until you see the ice sculpture," Jack Hawkes said. With the air of a magician's helper he motioned to the stage, upon which was a near life-sized elephant, its tusks beginning to wilt, dripping with the heat coming from the crowd.

"I have to admit it, I am amazed. If this don't beat all, and all that." George Roberts pressed in close to her with his half-smashed leer, which was the way he got most times he was around her. His bow tie sprouted from a blue shirt that was speckled here and there with perspiration, his brow glistened. He always followed up on these occasions with about two days' worth of invitations to lunch or dinner, followed by silence until they ran into each other again, his ardor not so much having cooled as moved on to more available prey. He was a somewhat dissolute FEC lawyer who constantly was quoted in the paper when some politician had pushed the outside of the ethical envelope a little too far. Invariably it was George who had to explain on the politician's behalf that it was all *quite* legal, even though, he would cheerfully acknowledge, it *looked* terrible. George had recently been advising Partridge on the kinds of honoraria he could keep. If you were a Republican senator, you just automatically went to George Roberts. As a Federal Election

Commissioner, George had written the laws, and now that he was back in private practice, he'd all but written the book on avoiding them. This was a tried-and-true transition.

Now he grabbed two more glasses of champagne from the dollar sign as she walked past, and handing a glass to Kit, he pressed her into their conversation. "We were just discussing whether or not Hardison does the drugs with the rest of his staff."

"Oh boy," said Kit.

"I say absolutely," Jack Hawkes confided.

"You can tell from his actions, huh?" Kit said.

"How did you know I was going to say that?"

"Because it's so lame and it's just like you." She sipped her champagne.

"That's our Kit," said Woody Fiedler. He was used to her bluntness, in fact he seemed to enjoy it when they ran into each other at parties, sometimes steering her toward a particularly pompous person, usually a politician, whom she was expected to deflate. "Don't you just love her subtlety?"

"I love her shoulder blades," George Roberts said.

"Gentlemen," she protested, but she liked the attention.

"Seriously," said Jack Hawkes, a young lobbyist whose firm was comprised of political operatives who elected Republicans to office and the lawyers who would then shake them down on behalf of corporate interests. He was a plain-looking, impeccably dressed, prematurely powerful thirty-year-old who was rumored to own a piece of everything, including the President of Panama. Or perhaps it was the other way around. "Do you think they're going to nail Hardison on this drug rap?" He looked to the three of them seriously, as if his portfolio were dependent on their answer.

The ballroom was filling and they were getting squeezed into a smaller circle. Kit could see several prominent congressmen, and the repeat offenders you always saw at these events, whoever they were. Though it would be hard to say precisely what it was these people actually did, it was clear they were part of the Washington support establishment of lawyers and operatives, would-be campaign managers and that special class of the prosperous who went under the general heading of "governmental relations" experts. Somehow it was imperative that they be present at all intersections of legislators and money, preferring in particular those where the covenants were open, those where the Washington press corps was present, ostensibly to cover the event as observers, as ethical regulators, though in reality, the reporters were largely there as components of the scene, players in their own right who wished to be part of this as much socially as professionally, with the advantage of distance and the expectation of free drinks.

She saw reporters whose expense accounts freed them up to eat like kings, take rhythmically alternated week-long side trips to exotic ports of call at the end of every much-complained-about six-week stint covering politics, and still dress, not like the ink-stained wretches of a generation ago, but in a double-breasted fashion indistinguishable from the wealthy operatives over whom they sat in judgment, commenting on their greed.

"Unless Hardison's smoking crack in the residence," Woody Fiedler said seriously, his glass of wine crimped close to his chest, his glasses and thinning blonde hair giving him the donnish air he sought to affect, "there's no way this thing is going to hit him."

"What if he used to be a big doper?" asked George Roberts, playing along.

"No, the rules are they have to catch you in the act of something. You can't just get nailed based on your past life." Jack Hawkes was certain of this. "Maybe during the campaign, when you're exposed. But once the guy's president, are they allowed to keep digging?"

"The rules are, there are no rules. They," said George, "are allowed to do whatever the hell they want to do, chum. Don't you forget it."

Kit was tired of the conversation, this preoccupation with Washington's latest rumor. Gossip may well be a universal obsession, but in Washington, it was an object of policy. Rumors about womanizing, homosexuality, drug addiction, wife beating, financial woes, shady deals, alcohol problems, loss of power, social faux pas, and disfavor from on high were as relevant to one's status as one's actual job. In a certain way, all these *were* one's status, at least on this circuit. It was faintly toxic.

And yet it was irresistible. There were people engaged in gossip *in this very room* who'd spent long hours counseling the particular object of a nasty, subterranean rumor on how to bring that rumor to the surface and then strike it down. It was like coaxing a gopher from a hole so you could behead it. Disproving a negative was a Washingtonian endeavor.

"Maybe you can't get nailed, Jack, but you can be made awfully fucking miserable in this town based on your past life."

"Feeling guilty, Kit?" Jack asked.

"Yeah, aren't you?"

"I wake up in cold sweats from a dream in which my college transcript is being pored over by Senate investigators."

"They wouldn't need to go back that far. I saw you at the Palm on Saturday. A snapshot of that and you'd be banned from government service for life." Woody grinned from ear to ear.

"You were there?" Jack was blushing.

"You don't remember?"

"How do you do, gentlemen." It was Clarissa Lowery, working the room.

"Darling," said George Roberts, kissing her hand.

"How are you, Mrs. Lowery?" Kit asked politely. "It's a lovely event." She felt like a hypocrite being so nice to the old shrew, but she was a creature of her upbringing.

"It is, isn't it," their hostess said.

"This should be very successful, Clarissa," Woody Fiedler said with his most charming smile.

"It will if you pay for your ticket, Woody."

"I'm faxing a check to your office as we speak."

And then she was on to the next group of partygoers. Jack Hawkes waited until she was out of earshot to insult her. That was another thing about Washington, thought Kit. She could think of no place she'd been since high school where there was so short a time between turning your back and people saying what they thought about you.

e couldn't get to the hallway quickly enough. It had the carpeting and lights of any Hilton, Des Moines distinguishable from Caracas only by the humidity in the hallway. He pressed up against a wall, his back to the room where Willy Barnes was no doubt puzzling over his performance, and exhaled. Then, breath caught, he rushed toward the elevator bank, certain of only two things: that he needed to get to his room to think about what that *Washington Times* article meant, and that whatever chance he had ever had of getting through this had been vastly reduced. He felt radioactive, and surely they had Geiger counters on Air Force One.

He punched the button for the elevator and waited impatiently. He didn't want to see any of his colleagues, certain he wouldn't be able to hide his panic. He needed to think, needed to think, to think, think. Light popped into the numbers above the elevator, left to right, eighteen, nineteen, twenty, twenty-one. And then the door slid open and it was Manny Slung standing hunched in the incandescent corner. "If it isn't Tom O'Malley," he said, a crooked grin on his plump face. In this light, his flesh tones were curiously green.

"Hey, Manny," O'Malley said grumpily. Better it be Manny than Bill Tiswell.

O'Malley pivoted as the door closed, noticing that the orange rectangle for the twenty-third floor already was lit. They were going to the same floor. He knew it was odd behavior, but in the moment it took for the elevator to lurch upward and then come to its stop, he didn't have a thing to say to his friend. In but a second, the door was opening again and Manny was walking out into the hallway with him. "So how are you enjoying things?" he asked good-naturedly in his adenoidal accent. He didn't seem to notice O'Malley's stiffness.

"Just fine," he answered in a voice about an octave too high.

"Yeah? Neat city. I'd like I should come here sometime when I don't have an event to pull off, and I don't normally think that." Manny fell into step with him as he began to walk down the the corridor to his room.

O'Malley waited until Manny unlocked his door and entered his room before he closed his own door, and with his back pressed against it, exhaled, sliding to the floor.

teve Bronstein was smitten with his date, though he couldn't believe the way Republicans behaved. Even without McTeague there, he knew these people were guilty of something. That melting elephant on the stage was just a slightly more benign version of the eagles that hung above Nazi bacchanals. Those women in the skimpy dresses and the dollar signs went beyond camp into territory he could analyze only if, at college, he'd paid more attention to Jung. And the immensely self-satisfied men, the aerobicized women in their expensive coiffures and stylized dress code so that any four of them together seemed as perfectly matched as anything Busby Berkeley would ever have put together: all this was a far cry from the Democrat social events he'd been to where there was a decided lack of women with shaved legs, or men who'd missed a meal in about ten years.

Truth is, he felt even more out of place here than he'd thought he would, though what was more troubling to him than his feelings of inadequate elegance was the sight of Georgette Chutney, the Style section's Valkyrie scourge, snooping around, unctuously barging in on conversing guests who scattered in her considerable wake, her notebook held up high so that anyone who doubted she was a reporter would at least be assured she was a Central Casting imitation of one. He didn't want her to see him. Those hotshots from National could be seen here—for them, schmoozing wasn't just in the job description, it was the job itself—but he was nervous about the notion of his being here on a date.

Mandy was introducing him to people whose names he recognized from the paper, people he would need to know if he should ever make the grade and be able to cover anything other than the pathetic City Hall of the nation's capital. So this was work, sort of. He didn't know precisely what the rules were for fraternization, but he smiled to all, trying to indicate that just because he worked for the *Post*, it didn't mean he necessarily wanted to put them in jail. Yet.

Over there was Clarissa Lowery, whom he was pretty sure Georgette Chutney was getting set to skewer. Her status as funneler of money to Republican causes was documented by a whole branch of the Nexis library, by a whole chapter in the Select Watergate Committee Report.

Standing in a circle nearby were a number of lobbyists to whom the nation's inequalities and social ills were directly attributable, and they were so hunch-shouldered joyous, so animatedly pleased with this opportunity to tell jokes or make pitches to GOP legislators, it was possible they wouldn't even bill their clients for the time spent drinking here.

He saw a pair of New Right leaders—who a while back were ubiquitous on TV but had fallen on hard times in the intervening years—over at the table spread with salmon, cheeses, and entire orchards of fruit. They were stuffing their mouths and their pockets, all the while looking over their shoulders to see if anyone realized how long it had been since they'd had a meal. He guessed direct-mail fundraising solicitations sure must be off.

A couple of political operatives he'd seen excoriated for their negative tactics stood benignly, one-upping each other about a Republican primary they were currently competing in. "Tell you what," he overheard snappily dressed Pierre LaRoque telling his Southern rival, Harvey Car-rick. "I'll let you know when we're going on heavy attacking you guys, and then you persuade that rich idiot you're working for that he needs to spend more on TV. Then you can cut me in on the buy and we both make money, no matter who wins."

Harvey Carrick, a Nixon protégé who was as noted for his poker face as LaRoque was for his clothes, stood there with his crocodilian eyelids slowly opening and closing. "Ah could do that. But it would be wrong." Then the two of them cracked up.

Bronstein made a mental note to tell one of the National Desk editors of this exchange; it might prove useful to them and, by extension, to him. He could see the headline: "Republican Consultants Collude in Governor's Race."

He watched Jerry Jetta and Mike Humperdink, whom he had seen show up at the paper trying to sell reporters on some rumor that smeared either Democrats or their Republican rivals—it didn't seem to matter which—come over to Carrick and LaRoque, greeting them as col-leagues. But the two more established operatives quickly excused them-selves and escaped into the crowd.

In the heels she was wearing, Mandy was a little bit taller than he was. She was a portrait of tanned perfection, utterly at home. She stood near him, introducing him to people as a reporter, as if warning them to be careful what they said, and fending off the flirtations of prominent politicians, money men, and operatives of questionable moral com-passes. Whenever she could, she would lean into his shoulder and give him the skinny on whoever was close.

They saw James V. Cottonthorp, the widely heralded new Republican National Committee chairman, who was currently the darling of Bron-stein's colleagues for his simultaneous political acumen, erudition, and his playing first violin with the National Symphony Orchestra. His elegance, *gravitas*, and manifest integrity were good for the Republicans after their having been wiped out by Hardison in last fall's election.

Mandy pointed out Woody Fiedler, who was perhaps the Republicans' best fundraiser, standing with George Roberts, the well-known lawyer who helped defend GOP politicians from all manner of sleazoid ac-cusations. Completing their group were Jack Hawkes, who Bronstein knew was Number One or Two on the *Post's* Most Wanted list, and a strikingly beautiful woman who caused a reaction in Mandy. "That's Kit Bowles," she told him. "I went to Smith with her. She was a senior when I was a freshman. She was suspended when her boyfriend at

Amherst was arrested for, like, being only the biggest dope dealer in the whole Northeast. Now," Mandy sniffed, "she's working for Tony Partridge. What a transition."

He had to agree, it was quite a long way from Point A to Point B. He stared at Kit for a moment longer. He would likely have done a double take anyway—she was exceedingly attractive—but there was more to it than that: her looks were somehow familiar. He filed away the story about her and her former boyfriend. After all, it was Partridge who'd called for an investigation of the White House aide with a more than casual relationship with recreational drugs. Fairness and symmetry dictated that someone on his staff should be looked into as well. Not that in the newspaper business tit necessarily deserved tat. Even Bronstein, who viewed his calling as one of the last outposts of purity in a corrupt world, knew that politics played a role in what got assigned. He smiled at Mandy. Hanging out with Republicans could provide him goodies to impress his editors. He'd found out things tonight that could help his career and get Cale off his back.

 'Malley paced while the crowd outside began to push against the white shields of the riot police. It was getting ugly out there. The lights of Caracas were faintly yellow, as if slightly less voltage burned through them.

He went over and sat on the edge of the bed and found that his hands were shaking, and it was only a moment before he found to his tremendous relief that what bothered him was not the fact that things had been made more difficult. What bothered him was that this whole sorry venture was wrong.

By leaking more incriminating material to the news media, in this case *The Washington Times*, Nicole may have been thinking he was sealing the deal, keeping the pressure on. Instead, he made O'Malley come face-to-face with what he was doing. He suddenly found he couldn't go through with it. He was as certain of that as anything he'd ever been certain of in his life.

"I am much more than just an idiot," he said aloud, and then put his clammy hands under his arms to keep them from shaking. Outside the noise of the crowd suddenly swelled with cheers. He got up and walked over to the window. They'd turned over a car and it had burst into flames, illuminating them with dangerous flickerings. He turned his back to the window and leaned against the air conditioner.

Whether he went through with it or not, and he knew now he would not, he still had the same question in his mind. How do I get out of this? Not the smuggling, for he wasn't going to engage in that, but the consequences of his conspiracy. The conspiracy was still in motion, whether he participated in it or not, and the critical thing was to be as far removed from it as possible, like getting into a bunker when you know a bomb's set to explode.

There was a vast difference between asking himself, How do I get out of this? and asking himself, How do I get away with this? It was the difference between being able to live with himself and not.

It was clear that were he to go along with what Nicole wanted him to do, he might get away with it. Probably would. As conspiracies go, it was not unintelligently planned. Yes, and he might even be able to get Nicole off his back, though the lingering suspicion that this would only whet Nicole's appetite was ever there. But even if he got away with it and Nicole receded from his life, never to bother him again, he would know that he'd done this, and he realized with bittersweet certainty that he would not be able to carry this on his conscience.

Thus, a floodwall broke; he was awash with all the things wrong with his engaging in smuggling over forty pounds of pure cocaine into the country on the official aircraft of the President. It wasn't merely an abuse of his position, a corruption that would stain the very office of the President. It was both more and less complicated. It was simply wrong. You didn't have to live in a city as wracked by crack as the District of Columbia was to realize how things had changed from the days of his youth when smuggling drugs into the country was a high calling, no pun intended, since it was a game no more serious in the larger questions it raised than moonshiners versus "revenuers."

But it was not a game, and if ever it had been, it no longer was a noble calling. He wasn't plotting on bringing in a batch of Gold Colombian for college kids to smoke while they listened to the Dead; he was bringing in a potion that amateur chemists baked into poison.

How do I get out of this? By this, he meant Venezuela. He'd figure out later how to deal with having failed Nicole. In a moment, it came to him.

He reached over to the phone on his bedside table and called Manny. "Hullo," Manny said, resigned in advance to any request coming his way.

"Manny, it's Tom O'Malley," he said as evenly as he could.

"Yeah, Tom," his friend said, warming noticeably, as if this was one request it would almost be a pleasure to comply with.

"You hear this street demonstration?"

"What do you think? I have ears."

"I, um, have to rewrite the President's remarks for the ceremony in Nicaragua, did I tell you?"

"No."

"They want me to change the tone and make it tougher. They don't want to be as friendly as they were planning originally. Lemlow Motrin's given me some language I'm supposed to incorporate. Anyway, I can't concentrate in this room. Any chance I can get a room on the other side of the building, facing away from the demonstration?"

Manny was silent for a long moment. Then he let out the sweetest sigh O'Malley thought he'd ever heard. "I suppose so. I've got a couple stashed. Let me check and get back to you in a few minutes. Hey, you going to eat before you work?"

"Sure, you want to grab a bite?"

"Yeah, let me just play with the rooms a bit and I'll call you. I have to switch some people around, but this should work out."

"I'll be here," he said, and hung up. Then, breathing three quick, deep breaths, he lay back on the bed with his eyes closed tight, hoping when he opened them his life, somehow, would begin to get back on track.

hen he'd moved into the room Manny provided him, three flights up and facing the quiet side of the building, he dressed for dinner and met Manny by the elevator. They went downstairs to the dining room and sat at a table that replicated itself like cells. By eleven o'clock, the speech he allegedly had to work on forgotten, they were one long, interconnected party, with the White House staffers the beneficiaries of the drunken goodwill of the dozens of reporters. Even they realized it was no good even to think about going out into streets that were on the verge of riot in order to eat in a more romantic setting. The first-floor restaurant of the Hilton would do.

It had been like a game of sardines. Once Manny and O'Malley had collected Max Pearlman, reporters had begun to gravitate toward them in the cluster of elevators that shot up the center of the building, in any of the several bars that branched petal-like from the lobby, in the cold glare of the reception desk near where they stood, their faces pressed against the plate-glass entrance to the building.

A phalanx of soldiers with machine guns protected them from the snarling crew with such a visible beef as to make the crowd unleashed by T. John Thibodaux seem benign. Though in an odd way, that event in New Orleans reduced the news value of this crowd here; so long as the President wasn't directly affected by the threat of violence, reporters seemed to have perfunctory interest. Jadedness stemming from previous international travel, weariness from the road: whatever it was, most reporters seemed to respond to the events outside the doors merely as an impediment to their being able to spend their employers' dollars on a memorable meal. If bullets began to fly, that would change things. But from O'Malley's vantage point, there was a sense that the reporters expected nothing less than Venezuelans taking to the streets to protest the American President's visit. Low expectations, low news value. It was simple.

Before too long, they were joined by Wyatt Phillips and Jenny Giopolli, who made it clear that relations between CBS News and *The Washington Post* were awfully cordial. They were followed by some of the advance men who had carefully gone through tomorrow's motorcade routes enough times to feel comfortable taking a break and having dinner. Even Willy Barnes was coaxed downstairs to join in the merriment, and though he and Jack Carthage circled each other like dogs before the fight—Willy taunting the NBC correspondent when he bravely, drunkenly, threatened to go out and try to interview some of the demonstrators as to just what was their gripe with the gringo President—the group was in good spirits. Max whispered to O'Malley that he thought the trip, for all that it had been somewhat less than the triumph they would have wished for, had cemented overall good relations between the press corps and the White House staffers who'd gone along with them. Whether it had helped the President with the American people was of secondary importance to this more immediate need.

A moment of tension came when a contingent of reporters argued with the maitre d' that he should divide the check for all the tables that had been pulled together by the number of reporters who whipped out their company credit cards, and let them split the bill evenly. It was clear that the man had never heard of such a division of responsibilities, that having lived his life in Venezuela, he had seen every means of wealth redistribution under the sun, but that this was a new variation on an old theme. Normally, it was the Venezuelans who liked to expropriate the foreigners' wealth to be divided as the Venezuelans, not the foreigners, saw fit. He went off muttering, only to return with a smile and a superior who solemnly took the cards and checked each one individually with the local offices of American Express.

The exchange took forty minutes, and by the time it was over, the group had repaired to one of the bars. O'Malley, feeling considerably loosened up by the bucket of beer he was putting down, by the goodwill of drinking with their adversaries, the reporters, by the evening of relaxed defenses, thought only rarely about what it was he was avoiding upstairs. Though when he did, he was instantly sobered.

Then they were stumbling, giggling, into the lobby at two in the morning, and they saw some agitation on the faces of the machine gun–toting policemen who were assigned to keep the building secure. That they were maniacally comparing notes with some clearly pissed Secret Service agents seemed in keeping with the crowd still visible, though vastly diminished, in the street outside, with the broken glass from the entrance that was shattered on the floor. O'Malley and Manny Slung had to keep Max Pearlman standing as the elevator ascended from the mess in the lobby, and it was only through Manny's reminder that he thought to get out onto the eighteenth floor. He said good night as the doors slid shut behind him and then stood there for a moment in the hall, wondering if there was some connection between the agitation of the agents downstairs and the deal he'd called off by not being where he'd agreed to be when the moment of truth came. "Nah," he said to himself, aloud. And then he shambled down the hallway to his room on the quiet side of the building, and was asleep within a moment of pulling the covers up in protection from the air conditioning. It was almost as if he had a clear conscience.

he hotel's unpredictable alternation between hot and cold running water had a surprisingly therapeutic effect on the hungover O'Malley. He twitched and dove for cover whenever ice water was followed by the stuttering of hydraulic gears, the scalding stream that commenced to burn paint off the tile, a must to avoid. After a half hour of such torture, he was ready to face the mirror. He looked about the way he deserved.

The television was on with a rapid-fire announcer racing the clock to provide a soundtrack to the pictures of the pretty harmless damage the crowd had chalked up the night before. Toweling his hair, he looked out the window and saw that brilliant daylight left Caracas looking pretty close to normal: hazy with smog, growling with cars, alive with the bustle of a large and busy city. There was no sign on this side of the building of any damage from last night's crowd, though the television showed some tipped-over cars burning, and the sight of rocks being thrown at the white shields of the riot police. He got the impression that both sides had played out their roles, and that pedal-to-the-metal aggression had never been the object of either side's desire.

His remembrance of the night before was depressing. Working backward, all the mirth he'd felt partying with reporters and coworkers was drained of the sustaining bonhomie, as if the goodwill that had kept them afloat had, by morning, dumped them on a sandy beach, a little bruised, and desirous of fresh water, caffeine, and a more comfortable sleep. This was one of the first times since he'd been arrested for drunk driving that he'd actually gone out and caroused, that he'd thrown himself against a wave of alcohol as if to see if he could remain standing. The result wasn't edifying, not when he could see in his mind all those movies they showed in counseling on alcohol's effect on the liver, not when all his bad jokes from the previous evening were played back on a hollow laugh track. And certainly not when his motivation for partying had been to escape from his rendezvous with Nicole's deliveryman, to escape the consequences of his conspiracy to commit evil.

He dressed quickly and packed, and now that he no longer had plans to pack drugs inside his printer, he didn't have to pretend he needed it wherever he went. Now he could simply put the printer out in the hallway along with his suitcase. He would just barely make baggage call.

Life seemed better already, whatever was going to happen now. How he ever thought he could have gotten away with it was beyond him.

Breakfast was an infirmary. Jack Carthage had the pallor of a Bowery bum augmenting his slightly smashed-up face. He did not look pleased with life. The general mood of the press corps was grumpy, though Willy Barnes seemed to have perked up for the first time; reports out of the President's dinner last night were that President Carlos Villalobos had engaged in such a panegyric that the pool coverage on the morning shows back home was triumphant. It was the first successful event of the trip, and no one had mentioned on air that perhaps Villalobos's praise was to be expected. He was, after all, waiting to hear whether the United States was going to further extend credits and forgiveness of current debt. The answer, yes, was contained in the speech O'Malley had written for the President to deliver this morning.

O'Malley feigned good spirits, and in fact the mango and papaya and the rich Venezuelan coffee had the desired revivifying effect. He sat at the table with Allison Hardy of the *Los Angeles Times* and Michael Quirk of the A.P., both of whom had been in the pool the night before and had missed the revelry.

"Seems like you all had a good time," Allison breathed.

"Too good a time," O'Malley said. That's when both reporters tried to persuade him to let them have an early glance at the text of the remarks the President would make at El Capitolio. The remarks would officially be released at 11:00, and the speech was to begin at 11:30; any edge they could get on the competition would make their day easier. It was a convenience. It wasn't essential.

"C'mon, Tom. I don't know anything about Third World debt. You have to give me the speech because otherwise I'll just never understand enough of it to write intelligently." She fluttered her eyes as she said this.

Quirk was more direct. "If you give me a copy and the speech goes over well, I'll make certain you're praised by name."

O'Malley looked at him like he was crazy.

"It's my best offer," said Quirk. "Take it or leave it."

He left it, paying his check. The two reporters attempted to get it for him in a last-ditch effort at currying favor. But O'Malley's mind was made up. He wasn't going to mess with the Press Secretary's prerogatives—McCurry guarded them closely—and one of them was the release of the texts the President would deliver.

He felt a wave of irrational excitement about the notion of getting in the car to which he was assigned for the ride to El Capitolio. Once the motorcade left the building, he would no longer have to worry about meeting up with Nicole's connection. He would be back in the protective envelope of the presidential party until he was out of the country. By evening, after a brief ceremony at the airport in Managua, he would be safe and sound at home. Then the only thing to worry about would be Nicole. He resolved to have the resolve to deal with him when that time came. Once he was on U.S. soil, his major problems would just melt away. He would no longer have to worry about what could have happened if he'd acted on the insanity of actually going through with the pickup and delivery of twenty keys of cocaine, and the carrying of it into the country less than thirty feet away from a president who'd been elected, in part, on an anti-drug platform.

He was smiling and feeling increasingly relieved after having checked out. He stood in the lobby waiting for his colleagues and their charges, the reporters, to gather.

Other than the sheet of plywood that stretched from the revolving door to the wall, covering the window that had been shattered, there was very little sign of the demonstrations of the night before. Oh sure, there were more than the previous number of soldiers in green uniforms and red berets with nasty-looking machine guns hanging out. He wouldn't want to be trying to skip out on his hotel bill this morning. Other than that, there was no sign of anything out of the ordinary.

When the lobby was packed with hungover reporters, the signal came for all of them to move to their assigned cars, the media heading to their buses, the staff to the vehicles with their names on the white paper taped to the inside of the windshield.

"I feel like shit," Max said as he sidled up next to him in the humid air outside the doorway. Early morning Third World smell of leaded gas and hibiscus, the sun already lifting off from the green, elephantine mountains that ringed the city. The buses heaved a diesel sigh, there was the ubiquitous honking of horns, and the reporters, as usual, sounded like children fighting for position on a field trip from school.

"You should. You were pretty blotto last night."

"Blame it on the press. Those nattering nabobs of, what was it?"

"Negativism."

"Yeah, that's it. They ply me with alcohol to get me to spill my guts."

"From what I've seen, Max, they don't have to fill you with booze to get that result. Coffee will do."

"Water would do it," Max said helpfully.

"Compliments might do it."

"You think I'm going to get in trouble?"

"Only if the reporters screw you."

"I'm going to get in trouble," Max insisted.

"Here's our car," O'Malley said, as the Chrysler pulled up to the curb where they stood.

From out of nowhere, Bobby D'Amato, the head of the Secret Service detail, was standing next to O'Malley. He was a small but mean junkyard dog with a refined manner of speaking that did not match the fierceness

214 STATUTE OF LIMITATIONS

of his demeanor. Standing suddenly on the other side of O'Malley was a taller fellow in a cheap gray suit and reflecting shades who had Secret Service—or worse—written all over him.

"Hi, Bobby," O'Malley said reflectively, knowing something was wrong the moment D'Amato was beside him. It took him a second to realize that whatever was wrong had something to do with him. There was something powerfully wrong if D'Amato wasn't with his primary responsibility, if he wasn't with the President himself.

"Yeah, Tom, you wanna get in this car over here," the Secret Service agent said, and with but a glance at the goon in the glasses next to him, O'Malley did as he was told.

"Tom," said Max, a little frantically. He was standing by the car they had been assigned to before this change of plans, alert enough to know this detour spelled trouble for his friend. In the second before he was hustled into the car that pulled up—gently, they didn't try to push him—O'Malley knew his cover had been blown. He knew his worst fears were all about to come true. For yet another occasion, the thing that rang through his head was the schoolboy maxim: Admit Nothing, Deny Everything. He wondered how far it would take him this time.

He wasn't sleeping deeply anyway, so when the black, turtle-shaped phone Tina had purchased through a catalogue began to trill politely on the bedside table, he had the thing snapped open and up to his ear in one motion. "Yeah," he said, squinting toward the digital alarm clock that only this week had winged upon the mail currents and arrived from Sharper Image. It was not yet 6:00 A.M. "You really fucked me, David," said the voice on the other end of the line.

"Wha . . ."

"Your guy wasn't where he was supposed to be." It was John Santangelo, and to his credit, Nicole immediately thought, he wasn't raving. He had that calm tone of voice Nicole had heard when John was planning a busted kneecap for some deadbeat who hadn't paid his gambling debts.

"What happened?" He sat up in bed and now Tina stirred beside him. She lay with her head on the pillow looking up at him, knowing something was wrong. And given their nerves over the return today of O'Malley, there was only one category of potential disaster that could get Nicole going at 5:47 A.M.

"I just got a phone call from a friend of mine. He says that when a friend of his went to visit a friend of yours, the gentleman wasn't where he was supposed to be."

"Oh." What had O'Malley done?

"Oh," said John, sarcastically. "My friend tells me his friend stood knocking on your friend's door. He was a little late, apparently, so at first he thought your friend had fallen asleep. So he knocks a little harder and when the door opens, some little bastard's standing there, and when my friend's friend tries to come in, he gets the impression the guy doesn't know who he is, or what he was doing there."

"Yeah, and?" He was wide awake now, the shapes of objects in the room materializing from out of darkness that was lifting in pace with his consciousness, his realization that things were very much awry. Outside the bedroom door, the Doberman was shaking herself, thinking it was time for her walk. He suspected instantly the natural order of their lives was going to be off today.

"And my friend's friend starts to go through with our transaction, when the fellow in the room starts to call security with a walkie-talkie, David. A walkie-talkie," John repeated, as if waiting for it to sink in. This was as animated as Nicole had ever heard him. "What kind of person sits in a hotel room in Caracas with a walkie-talkie, David?"

"Go on."

"He gets out of there pretty quick, you can imagine. He has to hightail it down, I don't know, twenty flights of stairs, and when he gets out, there's a veritable army waiting for him. What am I saying? There's a literal army waiting for him: they got the army out, for Chrissakes."

"I'm listening."

"Yeah, I should think so, David. So he runs, I don't know. Somehow he gets out of there and blends in with a crowd outside the hotel, I don't know, fans of our President, whatever. Only, and you can see where this is heading, somewhere along the way he had to drop his satchel to lighten his load. You getting this picture?"

"It's gone."

"Well, yes, David, it's gone. Which should be more troubling to you than it is to me, and it's plenty troubling to me. After all, my friends did what they were supposed to do; your friend didn't. I'm going to leave aside for right now how troubled I am about what happened and just skip on down to the bottom line."

"I know the bottom line, John, you don't have to tell me."

"Humor me. I'm going to tell you anyway. You need to come through now, David."

"Right."

"Seventy-five dollars."

"I got that part."

"Yeah, you got that part in cash?"

"Let me figure that out. Let me get to my office and figure that out."

"All right, David. I'll call you at nine o'clock. You think you can get to your office by then, or are we talking different office hours? I only got into this thing because I think you're a stand-up guy. Don't go disappointing me. I've had all the disappointments for one day I can take."

"Yeah, me too," said Nicole, snapping the little turtle shut, his eyes blinking in the early morning light.

here not having been any rain in Caracas for several months or more, an oily buildup on the streets made the roads slick. When the convoy of buses, minivans, and small Chryslers turned the corner onto Avenida México in the shade of the Parque Central towers, it was a good question as to whether they were going to slide right over the curb and go accelerating through some vendor's fruit stand. But it wasn't the driving that made O'Malley nervous. It was the dude with the mirrored glasses leaning over the front seat as if to talk to him while Bobby D'Amato sat impassively at O'Malley's side.

They rode in silence for the first two minutes as troops kept the intersections clear. It was a bright, perfect morning, and the workers on the sidewalks making their way to their offices hardly gave them a glance as they whipped by, sirens blaring, slipping and sliding on the slick streets. Bobby leaned toward him confidentially, as if it were just the two of them in the car, as if there weren't a guy in the front seat turned around and staring at him as if he'd always wanted to know what a chump looked like. "Oh, Thomas, what are we going to do with you?"

"I was wondering that myself." He smiled, but the guy in the mirrored shades looked ready to growl when O'Malley said it. He had a broad, pink face, the kind that didn't respond well to the delights of the tropics, the kind that never tanned, but instead just got pinker and pinker, as if stubbornly proving its foreigner's status at every reference point of deviation from the Northern Hemisphere's climatic norms.

"Let me tell you a story, Tom." Bobby was casually looking out the window as if this were only one of several motorcades of the day, as if this were Akron and Columbus were yet to come. Only instead of passing through some dull Ohio industrial town, they were whipping along the Avenida Universidad underneath buildings that, while tall enough to exude the prosperity of a major city, still appeared to be held together with chewing gum. They passed by a construction site and it was as if toothpicks held up the building's various floors. Even under these circumstances, O'Malley was exhilarated by the city's very foreignness. But Bobby, who seemed too small to be a Secret Service agent, and especially not the one who led the detachment assigned to the President, Bobby was as calm as he ever was, calm as he would be even if there had been an attempt on the President's life and they were discussing the assassin that still lurked out there. He fixed O'Malley in his gaze.

"I checked into the hotel last night after the State dinner, Tom. I went to my room, and it was a little messy, like someone had stayed there for a few hours without the maid service cleaning up after him, know what I mean?"

O'Malley's stomach, which was sour this morning to begin with, began to churn like a washing machine. He began to get light-headed. He knew instantly where this was going.

"I take a shower, and I'm sitting on my bed relaxing, when I get this knock on the door." Bobby was talking to him like a friend, and he was a friend, although how much of a friend he was at this moment remained to be seen. They had spent hours face-to-face on dozens of trips throughout the fall campaign, and he knew that counted for something. It was probably the difference between already being grilled in some DEA office at the Embassy and being in this car.

There was something disorienting about the kindness in Bobby's voice, his friendly demeanor, and the rough-and-tumble character of his pockmarked, tough-guy face. It was more in O'Malley's experience that this worked the other way around, the strangely tough voice added to the smooth, smiling face. The car slowed.

"I answered the door, Tom, and there was this fellow I know I never saw before, babbling at me in Spanish as if I were expected to take this canvas bag he's proffering." Bobby was looking at him with a curious expression. "The only thing I could think of is that it's a bomb, you know. Not that he looked like a bomber. He looked like a slightly down-at-the-heels Venezuelan, a Caracan Willy Loman, okay? A Latin gentleman who found himself a bomb in the elevator and he's been tipped off that I'm the head of the detail. Swear to God, Tom, that was my very first thought. I must have been logy from the heat or something. However, when I went to radio for the bomb squad, the guy panics on me, and it's about then that I think to myself, This guy's here for something other than to turn in the bomb. You tell him, Carl."

"Bastard was carrying," Carl said laconically, and O'Malley pretended he didn't know what the fellow meant. His spitting out a single phrase had been such an exertion for Carl that his face was newly pink.

The motorcade was slowing, being hand-motioned by soldiers through a well-secured checkpoint into an area in the palm-shaded, green grass fringe that surrounded the old brown capitol. There were soldiers everywhere, though precious few people were allowed into this protected area for them to guard against—except perhaps the point of soldiers in such places is as much to guard against other soldiers as anyone else. Whether the authorities had learned from the night before, or this was standard practice, he didn't know.

There was a nasty-looking tank down at the end of the open street, and the atmosphere among the troops was a little nervous. This was the way O'Malley imagined soldiers behaving in the hours before and after a coup. The car was coaxed softly to its spot, and O'Malley instinctively reached for the door handle.

"Not so fast," Bobby said. "We're just going to sit here in the morning sun and have ourselves a chat, Tom."

"Huh."

He turned his full attention back to Carl the Dude. "What was he carrying?"

"What do you think?" Carl asked this as if the next obvious word in that series was "asshole."

"A gun?"

"He was carrying eighteen kilos of pure cocaine, Tom. We found the satchel where the guy dropped it in the stairwell."

This was all happening so quickly, he barely bothered to record the fact that they must have been short-weighting him by four and a quarter pounds. Either that or someone had taken a scoop between the time the bastard dropped it and the time it was weighed.

"All right," he said quickly, as if he was trying to be helpful. "So the guy who came to visit you was carrying drugs. Did you catch him?"

"Do you care?" Carl was set to pounce like Sherlock Holmes. It was obvious to O'Malley that if he answered "Yes," Carl would say "Ah hah!" His face would be twice as pink from exertion.

"Who are you, anyway? And Bobby, what the hell does this have to do with me?" Was this the time to be indignant? Is this the way an innocent man would act? It crossed his mind that if he were truly innocent, he would have fainted along about now.

"Well, that's the question, Tom," Bobby D'Amato was saying not unkindly, staring at him from behind his flat, intelligent eyes.

O'Malley looked from the impassive Bobby to the eager Carl and back again. Their driver sat rigid as if prepared to drive off, to take O'Malley to jail probably, at any second. "Wait a minute." He looked from one to the other. "You guys think I had something to do with this." He said it as if it were a revelation, something to be considered, not something that spelled the kind of trouble that changed your life.

"You're catching on," Carl said with a troubling smile on his face.

"We're curious, Tom. Why'd you check out of the room?"

"I was told I had to rewrite the President's remarks for the Managua stop. It was a madhouse outside, and I asked Manny if he could get me another room. That's, you know, all there is to it." He said it as if he at least was convinced.

The limousines were now pulling up with their motorcycle escorts and the military was swinging into action, shouting out orders, snapping to attention. The twin flags of Venezuela and the United States went limp the moment the limos stopped. O'Malley would have needed to check with the mini schedule provided by the advance office to know who was in the contingent of extremely nervous Venezuelan legislators waiting to welcome the two Presidents and their First Ladies, but the head of the greeting party was bound to make it in some of the photos taken by the nest of stills, for he was comical, the way he stood there perspiring in the heat, wringing his hands in anxiety, his lips moving as he obviously rehearsed his prepared words of welcome.

Then the door to the lead limo was opened by a military aide and the rather elegant President of Venezuela stepped out, bowing graciously to the welcoming legislators. He turned and, first things first, helped his wife out of the car, a tall redhead in a Chanel outfit O'Malley doubted had been bought in this hemisphere. She had such saucy good looks that if O'Malley were the President of Venezuela, he would have kept very close tabs on the palace guard. Caesar's wife did not look like Caesar's wife.

The four of them in their little Chrysler, the driver, O'Malley and his two interrogators, sat for a moment and watched as the President of the United States got out of his car while the brass band played a vaguely salsa version of "Hail to the Chief." And then there was Hardison and Mrs. H being introduced by the buoyant Venezuelan leader to the contingent of legislators in their best suits. The official greeter, his hands wrung dry, bowed and said his spiel, which must have been awfully florid, for the State Department translator who stood like a valet at the President's side was sucking for air as he tried to keep up.

The President stood there listening, then leaned over and in a friendly fashion just tapped the fellow one on his right shoulder, and pushed the First Lady before him, as the group made their way toward the capitol steps. The President's sylphlike translator, scores of Secret Service agents, their Venezuelan counterparts, and legislators pushed backward and then pivoted toward the doors. Bringing up the rear were Harold Whitney and Bill Tiswell, the Ambassador, and Doug Poole, the President's personal aide. Somewhat more discreet, though O'Malley instinctively looked for him, was the military aide carrying the Football, the President's Wrath of God mechanism that could launch the ICBM's. It was sobering to see, but not much more so than Bobby D'Amato who was sitting next to him, and who now turned and said, "Where were we?"

"I was telling you I'm innocent of whatever you're charging me with. What are you charging me with?"

"Probably stupidity," said Bobby, his friend.

"I was going to say conspiracy to import Class-A narcotics," said Carl, who clearly was not.

"Bobby, c'mon, you know me, this is ridiculous."

"You hear about *The Washington Times*?"

"Willy showed me the fax."

"Says it's one of the speechwriters who deals drugs," Carl said.

"It said no such thing. That whole dope-dealing story is an absurdity. It's one of those Washington parlor games, it's the rumor du jour. And even if there's something to it, it has nothing to do with me."

The media could be seen moving from the pen they'd been held in for the President's arrival. Max and the press advance men were frisky as sheepdogs, allowing no one to stray. They were all going to go in and see the President deliver a speech O'Malley had written. He longed to be going in there with them.

"If there's nothing to the story, then what was that gentleman doing in my room? Circumstances look bad, I may as well as say it." Bobby was maddeningly calm about this whole thing. But then that was the way Bobby always appeared.

"It beats me, Bobby. I don't know why he picked that room. Maybe he was looking for Lemlow Motrin."

"Why do you say Motrin?" Carl whipped off his glasses at that one. Tiny, ratlike eyes. But O'Malley knew he'd inadvertently scored by referencing the NSC's Central American liaison who was known to be friendly with various contra holdouts.

"I don't know. He's the guy who has all the connections, isn't he?" He knew from when they'd checked in that Motrin had the room next to his.

"Forget about Motrin," Bobby said, but O'Malley knew he'd introduced some doubt. He could see it by a faint softening about Bobby's eyes and mouth. "What about this arrest for drunk driving?"

"I was celebrating the inaugural. Jesus! What's that have to do with this?"

"It came up on the computer."

What computer? "Yeah, what else came up?" This was interesting.

"We don't have to tell you that," said Carl, that prick.

"Bobby."

"You're on the list of people the White House suggested be investigated when there was that rumor going around about the drug dealer."

"So, I would bet, is everybody other than Harold Whitney, and you can't be sure about him. If I told you I saw him zonked in the ITT dispensary, you'd have to put it in his FBI report, wouldn't you? And, Bobby, you don't believe that, do you? I mean about me."

But Bobby wouldn't say anything.

"What do you think? You think I was, what, sitting there waiting for some Venezuelan to come deliver drugs to me? Sheesh, that's good." He chuckled, as if it were the funniest thing imaginable. A hoot.

"You don't want to know what I think."

"Oh, I do."

The head of the Secret Service detail locked him in his gaze and it was withering. "I think you really blew it this time, Tom. That's what I think."

"Bobby!" He began to perspire, could feel his face turn red.

"There's going to be an investigation, Tom. A serious investigation, when we get Stateside. I'm going to have to turn this over to others, though I need to keep on top of it because I don't know if our security was breached. I really hope for your sake you're clean. I mean that. Right now, kiddo, you're in the basket being loaded directly into the deep fryer."

O'Malley's armpits were drenched. Bobby was right. He could feel the heat.

T hat mail-order island was beginning to look like a better investment minute by minute, even as it shimmered, receding from view.

Nicole rooted through his rolltop desk in the brightly lit office at Globe, searching for bank books, safe deposit keys, hockable valuables. Completely to his surprise, he came across a couple grams of rock cocaine he'd been missing for months, assuming the cleaning staff had either thrown it out or used it to help them merrily along their way. A moment's credit-card chopping and rolled-dollar snorting gave him a whole new slant on the day.

No euphoric agent could change the mess he was in. The tally was pretty dismal. If liquidation was what he was forced to do, he could probably lay his hands on about 40K, which got him just over halfway home. Goddamn O'Malley. What had the bastard gone and done? This was a massive fuck-up, even for him.

Nicole went searching through drawers, found the deed to the condo, which he would just as soon not have to sign over to John Santangelo, though if it came to that, John was not to be trifled with. He did business with people for whom violence wasn't an abstraction.

Nicole yanked out drawers looking for a number of IOU's that, though none of them was greater than two or three grand, could move him further on his way. Even if he couldn't find the paperwork, Nguyen owed him a couple grand for the Toyota Nicole had unloaded on him. The car's having broken down in the middle of Eighteenth Street at rush hour, only two hundred miles after Nicole handed him the keys, didn't mean Nguyen was off the hook. Goddamn O'Malley!

It was then that he pulled open the bottom drawer and came across the Walther PPK. He picked it up and felt the cold metal indentations of its grip, the solid steel of its barrel, the mechanical workings of its six-shot clip. He straightened his gaze as if he had a vision of what the last resort looked like. It did not look like an island paradise of palm fronds and coral reefs. He put the gun flat upon the table and continued his search for resources.

T hroughout the afternoon, as CNN telecast over and over again Daniel Ortega getting down on his hands and knees and throwing his arms around the President's legs, Steve Bronstein tried to make McTeague come to his senses. It was tough even to get his attention.

"You believe how snakebit this whole trip's been?" McTeague asked him with a big grin. He whirled in the busy newsroom back to the television, as the sober anchorman went to an analyst to try to make sense of things.

"Well, Lew," the smarmy expert was saying, "it's clear Ortega was trying to *embarrass* the President, and he's done a *heck* of a job of it. Ortega's very sophisticated both at playing American public opinion and at embarrassing American presidents. It wouldn't surprise me in the least to find that Ortega decided, so long as the President was going to cut short his visit because of the repercussions of his having been hugged by Castro, well then, Ortega would make him look twice as bad."

They cut back to the anchor, whose mouth was open, as if in shock, causing one of those split-second television eternities where it's obvious the script isn't being followed. His hand rising to his earphone where he obviously was hearing screams from his control room, the anchor blinked and intoned, "The Senate takes up consideration of a bill that would force supermarkets to label the cholesterol contents of the food they sell. CNN's Capitol Hill correspondent . . ."

"Cale, I need two minutes of your attention. Do you have it, or is this a thirty-second day?"

McTeague looked over to him. "Shoot."

"I'm told that one of Partridge's key aides had a boyfriend in college who took a major-league fall for dope dealing." This was the most direct attention Bronstein had been able to get from his partner all day, even though their desks were next to each other and it was the middle of the afternoon.

McTeague just looked at him. "I don't give a rat's ass if the guy's boyfriend is an ax murderer. What's that have to do with our catching the bastard at the White House?"

Bronstein rolled his eyes. "It's a girl, Cale. Her name's Kit Bowles. I'm told that her boyfriend's bust was a big deal at the time. There aren't that many Amherst College students who get indicted for conspiracy to distribute narcotics. And now she's the key legislative aide to the Senator who's calling for an independent counsel to investigate the White House. Doesn't that strike you as a little hypocritical?"

"Sure, but where's the news in it? Hypocrisy's a dog-bites-man tale in this town. We're not going to make it out of here," McTeague said, lowering his voice and leaning forward, "just by catching some Senate aide who years ago went out with a guy who sold a few baggies of pot."

"That's exactly how we're planning on making it out of here, Cale. I mean, give or take."

"Yeah, only we're talking White House. That's how we vault over the competition into National. You want to cover the Virginia-Legislature for the next two years?"

"No, but I think that Senator Partridge's hypocrisy is newsworthy. I'm surprised. I would have thought you'd want to jump on this." The footage of the President with Ortega's arms around his legs must have come on again because it seemed like half the newsroom was pressed around the television sets. Great gales of laughter swept from National to Metro.

"Look, buddy, how else do I say this but, keep your eye on the ball. The White House. Drugs. That's the ticket." And then he turned and picked up his phone, no doubt to track down another lead. Or set up a date. The guy was relentless. But he was wrong. Bronstein would show him. He picked up the phone to call Mandy, and not just to hear her voice.

R obert O'Malley let loose the latch to the kitchen door and the dogs bounded into the yard. It was a small patch of withered grass and the remnants of a flower bed to which he'd been too weary for years to do anything. It wasn't even June and already the yard gasped for breath, could have used a glass of water. He wasn't feeling particularly generous of spirit. Let it choke, he thought, and looking up into the afternoon sun that burned down upon this swamp of a city, he knew it would, it surely would.

The dogs were now through the hedge and no doubt tumbling into the street. He turned and made sure to lock the door, which was something he hadn't had to do for a long time, not since Carmela had moved in. It took a minute to find the precise key—he'd almost forgotten he had keys, it had been so long since he'd left the house without someone inside to let him back in—and by the time he did, as he'd feared, the dogs could be heard surrounding some passerby, barking with good cheer. "Goddamn it," he said, twisting the lock. "Christ on a goddamn Chris-Craft."

"I'm coming, I'm coming," he shouted, moving as spryly as could a man who hadn't broken into anything approximating a run in the three years since he'd been put out of business by the meddlers in Congress. He hadn't exactly given exercise much emphasis in the three years since his forced retirement from a thirty-year career as spy, agent provocateur, agit-prop, gunrunner, and all-around model of cloaks and sharpener of daggers.

By the time he got to the street, he found precisely what he'd feared. The dogs had surrounded Mrs. Heseltine as she walked home from the Social Safeway with her trolley of groceries. There was a history here: the dogs didn't like Mrs. Heseltine, none of his dogs ever had. Years ago, when her husband was alive, the prominent columnist had not only threatened to expose O'Malley over the actions of his dogs, but had acted upon his threats. It seems Stewart Heseltine, dean of correspondents at *Time*, had even asked JFK at a news conference after the Bay of Pigs if, now that he'd said he would get the dogs of war back on a leash, there was not something that could be done about the animals belonging to a certain CIA operative living next to him in Georgetown.

The reporters and Kennedy had laughed, but when he was called at home and informed of the exchange, Robert O'Malley hadn't. The Bay of Pigs was disgrace enough without bringing his dogs into it. He understood the President was annoyed when he'd gotten the phone call from his brother, the Attorney General, asking him if there wasn't something he could do to prevent Stewart Heseltine from leading the charge against the administration. "Uh, I think, Mr. O'Malley, that if you uni*later*ally stopped the crapping on Mr. Heseltine's lawn, it might stop his crapping on the President's foreign policy." At that stage of his career, he wasn't one who ignored the Attorney General, and O'Malley temporarily banished his dogs to the farm he and his wife owned in Middleburg, although this so affected young Tom that he forever favorably associated the Johnson Administration with the return of his dogs. It may have encouraged his definition as a Democrat.

Now, a different generation of dogs circled tiny Mrs. Heseltine, and he flapped and clapped his hands in an effort to bring them under control. He knew she had no shyness about calling the pound, and the name Heseltine still counted for something on N Street. "Sorry, Eunice, I'm a bit shorthanded these days."

But old Eunice Heseltime, who had to be about a hundred years old, just fixed him in her weather eye and yanked her trolley with its small sacks of lettuce, birdseed, and celery soup.

He bowed as she passed, yanking Zippy by his collar to be sure the old widow passed in peace, thinking that if she sold her townhouse to one of the endless succession of yuppies looking to move into the neighborhood, she could retire in comfort to Palm Beach. She could certainly afford to have someone else walk the half mile to the grocery store each day. We all have our problems, he thought, as the dogs jumped and twitched and otherwise were a nuisance.

Since being slapped with notice that Barbara was divorcing him, naming Carmela as a corespondent in an adultery action, he'd proved himself to be quite thoroughly helpless. Oh, sure, having the house to himself again had an up side. Since Carmela had been packed off to visit her sister in Houston—far from the view of inquiring lawyers, though the damage was done, that much was clear—he'd been able to stumble into the kitchen to eat ice cream at midnight without her screeching. He wasn't scolded for napping. But then, the house was a mess, a total pigsty, truth be told, and he missed her. Though Jake had been correct that until things could be worked out with Barbara, it was best Carmela not be around, he wished she were there, and not just to walk the dogs.

Something had to give, he thought, as the dogs trotted up Thirtieth Street, heading toward the tennis courts and English garden of Dumbarton Oaks. The dogs instinctively headed toward the oxygenating forest, whereas Robert O'Malley would have gravitated toward an air-conditioned tavern. Thomas would fix things, he said to himself. Thomas would come through for him. And with that thought he tagged along as the dogs chased their shadows toward some semblance of nature in the heat of the city.

I n fact, Thomas was a wreck, though on this point indistinguishable from any of the others on the President's dismal return flight. As Air Force One entered American airspace, the cabin was nearly silent, and not just from fatigue. It was like the return trip from an away game in which they'd been outscored by opponents they'd been expected to rout. No one was certain what the reaction was going to be back on campus. O'Malley in particular had to worry about his trip to the headmaster's office, his disciplinary visit with the dean of students.

Upon his release by Bobby D'Amato and his associate, O'Malley had been able to move freely throughout the speech in the Venezuelan capitol, and throughout the flight to Managua, and it was hard to tell once they were in Nicaragua whether the scrutiny he felt himself to be under was distinguishable from the extraordinarily tight security. There was an electric current of tension throughout their two-hour stop on the tarmac strewn with the debris of an air force of flying jalopies that the Sandinistas hadn't bothered to clean up. The clouds gathered and clutched their skirts, looming over the palm trees as if a downpour were inevitable, and the approaching storm made them hurry the ceremony. This gave the proceedings the faint, jumpy acceleration of a comedy being wound through the projector at a speed too fast.

There were moments when he was convinced that Harold Whitney must have been alerted by Bobby D'Amato, for he glowered at O'Malley as if they might leave him in Nicaragua to fend for himself. But it was quickly evident that the etiology of the White House chief of staff's distemper was ever more universal. It was predicated on an apprehension that something was in the works, and when, during the ceremony,

Ortega—a jogger—had with a certain evident grace gotten down on the ground and thrown his arms around the President's legs, Whitney was seen to throw his hands over his face.

So as the plane lifted off in the splattering rain, the order to proceed having been given by the Sandinista air-traffic controllers even if wind shears were coming, perhaps especially if wind shears were coming, O'Malley had sat ghostlike, until he'd convinced himself that Bill Tiswell and Whitney, and certainly the press pool, weren't paying the slightest bit of attention to him. They had bigger fish to fry. The press had to worry about how they could make an entire flight across the Caribbean and north up to Washington without breaking into giggles; the senior staff had to actively consider whether suicide was an on-board option. The absence of a tradition of hara-kiri was regretted. O'Malley's problems, even if they loomed on the radar screen, were inconsequential for now. There were others who shared his misery, and this was a respite. It wouldn't last long.

T here was this one WAC staring at her a little too longingly for comfort, the smoldering glance of an inmate in a female prison movie. Kit Bowles shifted uncomfortably in what passed for a terminal at Andrews, and terminal was the word, given how long it seemed she'd been waiting to surprise O'Malley as he got off the plane. She pulled down her skirt, looked around at the wives, husbands, the Air Force personnel and White House motor pool drivers who joined her in this vigil, and tried not to notice the Air Force sergeant who, her cap cocked to one side, had eyes that burned like a ranch hand's after a cattle drive.

Outside on the tarmac, the blinking red lights of the waiting helicopters gave the operation a faint military pulse. By the time Air Force One had landed and taxied toward the terminal, Kit and her compatriots were on their feet, noses pressed against the glass to watch the President transfer from Air Force jet to Marine helicopter.

They never even saw him. Somehow the plane landed and in a matter of a few smooth moments, the blades of Marine One began to slice the sky. With visible resistance against the gravity of the humid air, it lifted off into the night, its nose down as it was pointed in the direction of D.C.

The weary were welcomed back by Air Force aides, and they filed through the doorway, blinking, grumpy and thoroughly road-weary, into the fluorescent light of the lobby. Kit stood to one side, a little breathless with the thought of seeing O'Malley, with the expectation that her surprise would make him happy. She recognized some of the aides as they entered.

There was Lemlow Motrin, whose unflattering mug shot she'd seen in the *Post* when he'd been excoriated for wanting to declare war on the Senderos, and the black fellow in the double-breasted suit who looked as if he'd just escaped from the Island of Lost Souls was probably Willy Barnes. Evans and Novak had only that morning opined that Barnes was the designated scapegoat for all that had gone wrong on this trip, from the riot in New Orleans to the hug from Fidel Castro. By the same tortured logic with which they placed the blame on him, they exempted him somehow from Ortega's indicting suppliance. This was, the columnists had written, a glaring breakdown in the U.S. intelligence capabilities.

She looked out onto the floodlit tarmac as a cluster of reporters made their way toward her. She knew they were reporters because they were carrying laptops and laughing uproariously. Something was funny, and though she couldn't know what it was, she felt herself being drawn into their mirth. She was looking forward to seeing O'Malley, to springing her surprise. But where was he?

She began to get scared when it seemed the trickle of people walking down the steps onto the tarmac was slowing, but then she saw him, standing on the top of the staircase for a moment before he struggled with his bags and the same computer she'd seen him carrying across Seventeenth Street only three days before. Only three days, sure, but it was three days that would forever change her relationship with her boss. Kit felt an obligation to tell O'Malley just what kind of nonsense— an independent counsel—her boss had suggested. She needed to tell him what had gotten into Partridge before Tom found out from someone else.

And then she saw two men go out from where they'd stood in front of her outside on the tarmac, and her first thought was that they were the Air Force equivalents of redcaps, that they were simply there to help O'Malley with his bags. The surprise evident on O'Malley's face from thirty yards away banished that notion. She immediately tensed as she saw Tom resist walking with them. And then she witnessed him handing over everything, his computer, his Gurkha bag, the canvas hanging bag, and he fell into step with them. They were not heading to this entrance to the terminal. There was something wrong. She turned around to see if anyone else was left waiting along with her, but the only person she could see was the female sergeant she wanted to avoid.

As O'Malley was escorted through an entrance into a separate part of the terminal, Kit could see her reflection in the window. She looked scared.

She was so frightened, she waited for him there, occasionally getting up to see if there was a sign of him. She couldn't think where else to go.

After a long while, a door with its tide of light spreading across the floor was the first sign of life other than the janitor's banging that she had heard for hours. And there was O'Malley, kneeling next to her, kissing her cheek, her eyes, the end of her nose. "Thomas . . ."

"I didn't know you were waiting for me until just a minute ago."

"What's going on?" He looked tired, drawn, though it could have been worse, she supposed. In her mind, in the hours she'd been waiting, he had been not only drawn, she'd seen him all but quartered.

"Let's put it this way. If they'd wanted to search me any more thoroughly, they would have needed dental floss."

"Oh, sweetie, what have you done?"

"Let's get out of here."

And so she pulled his hanging bag over her shoulder as if it were a bag of tricks and they were out through the glass doors and into the surprisingly cool air. The suburban evening was surging with the summer cacophony of insects that had newly emerged. There were wisps of mist that lingered on the lawn toward the Quonset huts, and those cars that were parked there had visible puddles connected into a mosaic of dots on their hoods. It wasn't until they were through the gate and on the highway that O'Malley seemed ready to talk. "What is it, Tom?"

"You're not going to like it."

"Try me," she said.

He stared straight ahead. "Okay. It has to do with David Nicole."

The day following the return from South America was a Friday, which was not without its own consequence. Friday is the day in Washington when several of the talk shows that air over the weekend are taped for broadcast. If there is any such thing as conventional wisdom, it congeals on Fridays, gets shellacked over the weekend, and is displayed in the sculpture gardens of the newsmagazines on Monday.

All morning long, participants on the various shows called news sources, friends, in some cases other journalists, to make sure their take on the week's activities was correct. There was a contradictory premium on both originality and conformity, with a plus or minus factor for deviation, the outside edge of which could be disastrous. The ideal result of these phone calls—some called it reporting—was to make the stars of the shows look provocative, not pigheaded. The goal was to have quotable insights, the formulation of conventional wisdom with a memorable edge, and there was a corresponding terror of making a statement so deviationist, so easily, provably wrong that it would reduce the participant to that special hell for pundits: party patter dismissal.

Knowing what they were up against, with four or five shows taping this morning, and with the preparation for the Sunday shows proceeding apace by anti–public-relations experts at the networks, the White House got into high gear. They not only prepared talking points listing the President's accomplishments in South America, they began to orchestrate who among their legions would be dispatched to appear as guests on "Face the Nation," "Meet the Press," and Brinkley. There was a nasty buzz out there, or so was the consensus of the morning senior staff meeting, and they had to kill it, or at least reverse its spin.

By the time Thomas O'Malley showed up for work after what seemed like an eternity away, the White House had begun negotiations over who would appear on the networks that weekend. The talking points were being faxed by Willy Barnes's political shop to allies in the political community at large. The object was to have as many neutral consultants, operatives, and pollsters as possible spouting the White House line. It was their only hope of altering the physics of the existing spin.

The White House's only chance at portraying the President's trip in a favorable light was to get cracking, which meant that everyone, from the politicos to the press aides to the speechwriters, was to follow up with a consistent, compelling line. By the time O'Malley kissed Katherine, gave Colin and Will hearty handshakes, and in a brotherly fashion mock-punched Buffy on the shoulder, the countervailing arguments of the press were already blitzing those lines the White House had on sentry. No sooner had the press office put up a wall at the morning briefing by saying the President had achieved his aims on the trip—a new chapter in American-Chilean relations, a renewed dialogue with Third World countries on the vast debt that stands between Us and Them, an era of good feelings inaugurated in Managua—than tanks were rolling over them. O'Malley hadn't even nervously settled into his desk when the morning briefing McCurry was conducting sounded as if it was getting out of hand.

The questions ranged from whether there was going to be a shake-up in the State Department to whether the President was going to have to take to the airwaves to explain his fumbling performance on the world stage. O'Malley had barely unloaded his briefcase and begun to check on his computer for any messages he'd missed in the four days he'd been out of the office when Katherine was standing in his doorway.

"I felt so badly for you."

"Why?" A flash of paranoia settled over him. But then Katherine was in the office and walking over to the fireplace to flick the ash off the end of her cigarette.

"It just sounds like a terrible trip. I don't think any of us regretted not being on it. Colin and I were trying to figure out how it could have been worse, and the only thing we could come up with is if the President fell off the stage in the middle of that inaugural or something."

"Or if he and Castro rolled off it together." She didn't know anything, she was just schmoozing.

"The wingers are really going nuts. I can't wait to see what they do to us on the talk shows. And I've the feeling this is going to be one of those Saturdays where poor McCurry has to wheedle with *Time* to get a peek at the cover."

"I forgot they had to do that sometimes."

"You're okay?" she asked abruptly, stubbing out the cigarette in an ashtray on the prim table in front of the fireplace. She had to bend over to do it, and her full head of hair swept down over her long torso. He had the feeling she was like a parent checking in after final exams, just making certain everything was all right, with no clear reason to think he'd flunked miserably.

"I'm okay. Thanks for asking. You wouldn't have believed the event in the Superdome. T. John Thibodaux's amazing."

"I was beginning to think the networks were going to make it into a miniseries, they aired it so often. It was like watching a train wreck."

"That's the trip I was on." Without even adding his own problems into the equation, it had been an ordeal.

"The word just came down that the President's going to address all the Schedule C's this afternoon at Constitution Hall to give them a little briefing on the trip."

Great, O'Malley thought. They were in such bad shape they had to organize the President's own spin in front of his political appointees—people whose jobs directly depended on his largesse, and hence, the one group of trusties who could be guaranteed to hoot like sports fans at his every utterance.

"Who has to write it?" he asked.

"That's what I wanted to ask you. Can you and Colin give it a quick whirl? I'm sorry to hit you up so soon after you get back."

"No problem," he said. He knew the speech was necessary if they were to have some positive message going out over the airwaves this weekend. This was an instance where the presidency was, if not a bully pulpit, at least the highest ground for staging a defense against the media's ongoing assault.

O'Malley smiled at Katherine. She thought it was because he wanted to pitch in. How could he explain to her that he was eager to help to take his mind not off the disaster that had already occurred but the one he knew was looming?

o matter what chits he called in, Nicole couldn't lay his hands on seventy-five thousand dollars without placing major portions of his life up for sale. He either had to get John Santangelo to give him more time, not bloody likely, or else offer him the deed to Globe.

Tina was distraught, and he worried about her. She had sat in front of her mirror for hours, brushing her hair. Last night, even their dog knew something was up and circled his tail for minutes at a time before deciding where to lie down. Nicole moved around the restaurant this morning as if he were already dead, which he might be after his deadline Sunday. Dead was just among the bad things he might be when John arrived forty-eight hours hence and he gave him the bad news. Meanwhile, the waiters were staying out of his way.

He'd been able to put off the moment of truth for seventy-two hours, having persuaded John the day before that not only was he dealing with someone who was honorable, he was dealing with someone who was smart. "I've never doubted that for a minute, David. That's why I couldn't figure your taking a chance on this guy."

"Good point," Nicole had said yesterday, trying to shoo John out the door. John hadn't taken the hint. Then again, he also hadn't sat there and told Nicole how they'd take him out into the Chesapeake and feed him to the crabs, so he probably shouldn't complain. All told, he'd been a rather a good Mafioso about the whole thing. So far. It was a given that if Nicole didn't come through John would have him killed or worse, with regret only over not being able to get morning cappuccinos at Globe whenever he was in town.

Now Nicole went through the motions of his own morning ritual, surveying the waiters cleaning the dining-room tables with rags and club soda, listening to the din of the deliverymen off-loading provisions. There was a copy of the *Post* on a barstool and he leafed through it to see if there was any mention of what had happened in Venezuela.

The only thing he found out was that the presidential party was back and that the trip was being met with something on the shy side of universal kudos. It would soon be time to restrike his acquaintanceship with his old friend Tom O'Malley. If Nicole owed Santangelo and his partners only his whole goddamn life, just everything he'd worked for since his arrest ten years ago, what did Tom owe him?

It was a heck of a question. He was, however, so conflicted, his mind working—or rather, failing to work—like a machine that's slipped a cog, he hadn't even begun to formulate his plans for handling O'Malley. The one thing he knew was that he couldn't just pick up the phone and call him at the White House. If the operation had been broken up at O'Malley's behest, he might be trying to trap him. And if it were simply O'Malley's screwup, a not unlikely possibility, then surely they were on to him? In that case, O'Malley would be hot, and he'd have to approach him very carefully. But approach him he had to. O'Malley owed him, big-time, and Globe hung in the balance. Nicole's world hung in the balance. It was time to go over the plan with Tina, to urge her to snap out of it and turn her considerable insight to the problem at hand.

He reached over the bar and took the phone out from the shelf underneath the cash register. The phone at his nearby condo rang once, twice, three times. No answer. No problem. He'd call her later. But where could she be?

J ake Ingram had no wife, no children, one nephew, and a best friend, his brother-in-law. He had a house on Tracy Place, a beach house he didn't use, and a company car and driver that picked him up every morning and took him to his office at Twentieth and Pennsylvania. He had enough stocks and bonds, limited partnerships and real-estate deals that he didn't really have to work so hard at lawyering. And right now he had a headache and a plan as to how to get his sister and his brother-in-law, if not back together, then at least to stop their warfare.

It was Friday and quitting time. He paused to make certain his desk was organized before leaving for the weekend. He had two hours before he was due at Robert O'Malley's house, and whereas often over the years he'd gone there on Friday nights to drink prodigious amounts of just about anything offered to him, so on this night his best friend had asked him over to discuss the divorce papers his wife had filed against him. Resolved: this wasn't unusual. They'd spent hours on the phone or in Jake's office talking about the divorce. Which was silly, in a way. Bob O'Malley acted as if this were something that had come out of the blue, like a meteorite shower. However, Jake believed that the divorce was preventable, something from which Barbara could still be averted.

The key was his nephew, Thomas. And now Tom was back from the thoroughly embarrassing trip the President had gone on. And for some reason it was Tom who'd requested he be there at his father's tonight. Which was all right with Jake. If his plan was to work, he'd need Tom's participation. Especially tonight. For Jake had a surprise in mind.

t first, when Nicole arrived home in the afternoon, nothing seemed awry. It took a few minutes for him to guess why Bowser was so agitated. Tina wasn't just out shopping. Tina had left him.

She was very subtle about the whole thing, as if she thought she needed some kind of head start. She'd taken only those catalogue-bought Le Sportsac bags that were hidden in the bottom of one of their closets, and the blue jeans, t-shirts, and sweaters she had taken could easily have just been in the hamper. She'd skimmed non-essential possessions right from the top; leaving behind entire UPS delivery trucks' worth of stuff they'd accumulated in the two years they'd been together. But for the agitation of the dog, he might have had no clue for hours that she was gone.

He went prowling through the house to inventory her take. Among the valuables gone was her jewelry, which was fine. Either he'd given the things to her outright or she'd accumulated them from her share of the profits from Globe and their other business ventures. He couldn't begrudge her those.

What wasn't so fine was that she'd taken the bag of gold coins he kept in the false bottom of the bedroom bureau. He calculated how much that set him back in his goal to be clear with John Santangelo.

She'd walked off with precisely half their stash of drugs, almost two ounces of cocaine they kept for themselves, and a color wheel of pills— reds, greens, yellows—they kept for whatever ailed them, which usually was boredom.

With one exception, the credit cards she'd taken were her own. It was, however, more than a little alarming that she had taken the corporate American Express card, the one in Globe's name. She could go a long way on it, and he hadn't the slightest idea where. He'd never considered it. Okay, they had a joke: He would say, "Tina, if I lost all my money, would you still love me?" And she'd answer, "David, not only would I love you, but I'd miss you, too." But that was just showing off for company, a shtick everyone enjoyed. Now, standing in their bedroom trying to figure where next to look for what she'd walked off with, he heard that line over and over again, followed by a stale sitcom laugh track, and he felt rather sick to his stomach.

Truth is, she could probably buy one of those islands in the South Pacific and put it on the charge and unless he canceled it, the person who'd probably end up having to pay for it would be John Santangelo. That would be a terrific fake-out, the guy takes the restaurant and ends up having to pick up the tab for some island named Rikki Tikki Tavi just out of fallout range from the Bikinis.

Goddamn O'Malley.

ubject came out his front door at precisely 7:12 P.M. and stepped into the waiting Saab, New York plates. Female Caucasian, a looker, accelerated like the proverbial bat out of hell up to the top of California Street, quick right and a left around the 7-Eleven, and then swung toward Connecticut with barely a glance at the traffic either coming up Columbia Road from Dupont Circle or down from Adams Morgan.

Harlan Bryce would have been right on their tail but for the speed with which the female Caucasian drove and for the fact that some a-hole in a little Alfa pulled out with no warning and cut him off. Jesus, if you were going to follow someone, he thought to himself, do it in a regulation FBI clunker like the one he was in, a Plymouth at least four years old with enough dents to fit right in in this neighborhood. Whoever the asshole was who cut him off, who was obviously following the subject as he drove down Florida Avenue and cut over on Q, he wasn't particularly subtle. Harlan felt embarrassed for him, he was so bad. But who was he?

They were across the Buffalo Bridge in a flash, that little bastard O'Malley, the chick who was driving him, and whoever it was who was a sore thumb in third gear, whoever it was who was screwing up the tail so badly. They shot past the stop sign and Twenty-ninth Street, and if the light weren't quite red when the Saab turned left on Thirtieth, it was a pretty dark shade of orange. Any fool could have told you that in Georgetown on a Friday night, you didn't have to run red lights to follow a subject: they'd be stuck in the back streets like every other tourist and hipster coming to eat, drink, and be whatever it was that people, unlike Harlan, were on Friday nights. But the guy in the Alfa went through the light right after them, which caused a blurred honk and squealed stop from some guy in a Mercedes whose equilibrium just went the same way as his blood pressure.

Harlan calmly waited for the light, turned left down the hill, and watched the little convoy, Saab, candy apple–red Alfa—oh, that was subtle—and the upset Mercedes as they lurched through the stop signs, seriatim. As they crossed P, he turned left on it, shot back to Twenty-ninth, took a quick right, and sped down through one stop sign to N. Right again, and bingo! There was the Saab coming toward him, looking for a parking space. He watched the woman drive by a fire hydrant and without a second thought, back into the space in front of it. These people had no respect for the law, he said to himself as he prolonged his wait at the stop sign on the corner of Thirtieth and N. He had only to adjust the rearview an inch to see O'Malley—first time he'd seen the little bastard in the flesh—and the looker go through a gate and knock on the door of one of the street's stateliest homes.

Probably the drop, or would-be drop if the deal hadn't gone screwy in Venezuela. But Harlan was on the case, exercising his rights at following the guy he'd been assigned to weeks ago. The FBI had wanted a whole team on his tail, but this was one instance when Harlan could read the rule book to them. Until there was actual evidence that a suspect had broken the law, the Special Agent conducting the background check had rights of first refusal on the assignment. He smiled to himself. If it turned out he'd been right about the little bastard . . .

He and the Alfa passed each other three times around the block before either found a parking space. By the time Harlan lurched into an illegal slot by a stop sign, he and the guy in the sports car were familiar competitors.

it wanted to know what he thought things would be like tonight. They were standing by the door and hadn't yet knocked.

"Can you imagine 'Father Knows Best' with David Niven, looped on martinis, playing the title role?"

"I can try." She was a sport.

"It'll be something like that." He paused for a moment. "That, and an episode of 'The Honeymooners,' maybe. He might threaten to send me to the moon."

A shrug. But this was supposed to be serious.

"I know, I know, I'd deserve it."

Kit gave him a wan smile and squeezed his hand before he knocked on the door, thus setting off the dogs, who functioned as a doorbell for his old man.

His father had barely waved them in before it was clear the place was under assault. The dogs bounced around and off each other like the Clash in concert. The table in the foyer was stacked with unloaded bags from the grocery store, and he could see through the butler's pantry and into the kitchen where there were garbage bags waiting to be taken out.

"Hi, Dad, where's Carmela?"

"Welcome," he said, offering his bristled cheek for his son to kiss. "Kit, my dear, how are you?" he asked, holding up her hand for a kiss, which was about as suave a move as a guy with bloodshot eyes could muster. Kit took it in stride.

O'Malley turned to her. "Did I say 'Father Knows Best'? I must have meant 'The Addams Family.' "

It was pretty bad, the place obviously not having been cleaned since Carmela was last here, whenever that was. Zippy on hind paws toppled a paper sack of opened cans, spilling them across the linoleum. "Where is she, Dad?"

"Come in, come in, can I get you something to drink?"

"White wine?"

"Fine, my dear. And you, Thomas? A glass of warm milk?"

"Beer, Dad, what's going on?" He followed his old man into the kitchen, where they found stacked plates in the sink, boxes of Rice Krispies left out, a carton of ice cream that was soggy with its contents melted. There were murder scenes less splattered than the counter. Kit was torn between the urge to get out of there and the urge to clean up.

His father had the refrigerator door opened and was pulling out a bottle of Pinot Grigio he bought by the vineyard. "Carmela's in Houston with her sister until your Uncle Jake can figure out how we fight your mother's claims of my adultery."

"Poor Dad," O'Malley said quite genuinely.

"She's been driven off!" he said dramatically, as if he were talking about a stolen golf cart that had been over there not five minutes ago.

"Oh," O'Malley piped in sympathetically while his father looked at them.

"I could have made charges against your mother, you know. If only she'd even liked sex." His father looked up as if he'd just had an epiphany.

O'Malley looked straight ahead. This was a terrible thing to hear. "Shh, Dad, let's go sit in the den." He took the bottle of wine from him and after rummaging in one of the cupboards for a clean glass, he poured and handed it to Kit, who appeared to be standing on one toe. He hadn't expected things would be so quickly painful, nor that his problems would seem relatively trivial.

He grabbed himself a Bud while his father poured himself a large dollop of scotch over some hastily clutched ice from the freezer and then the three of them shuffled up the staircase, balancing their drinks as the dogs slipped through their legs and galloped ahead, expecting them to play.

At least the den was immaculate. Wherever his father was spending his time drinking and moping, it wasn't here. The vivid island scene was strangely calming even as it exhilarated, and O'Malley wondered if the mere fact of the Gauguin's presence suggested that some normalcy was to be found here, that dishevelment had reached its limits in the face of beauty. His father collapsed in one of the homey armchairs, and his descent with a drink in his hand suggested contradictory practice and grace.

Kit perched on the edge of an ottoman with O'Malley behind her, her perfect posture the result of either politeness or discomfort. "It's a truly beautiful painting, Mr. O'Malley."

"Ah, that. I'm not certain it's worth all this," he said with a wave of his hand they interpreted as a reference to his troubles and not their physical surroundings.

"You going to tell us, Dad? Because there's something I need to talk with you about, and Uncle Jake, if he's coming."

"He's coming," he said as if it were part of the natural order. Peggy and Danny sat beside him like bookends, panting sentries. "What's your trouble?" his father asked as if it would take a very great deal to impress him.

"I think I'm about to be arrested for conspiring to smuggle drugs on Air Force One."

"Thomas, you're not still doing that dope, are you?"

"No, Dad."

"I was certain you were off the stuff."

"I am, Dad."

"Because it's terrible for you," he said, taking a rather dramatic gulp of scotch.

"I know, Dad," he said with a little exasperation. "So's spending the next twenty-five years of my life in jail."

The doorbell rang, the dogs lurched. "I'll get it," Kit gamely volunteered, and O'Malley wondered if she'd use the excuse to flee. He wouldn't have blamed her.

"That'll be Jake," his father said. Kit was silent as she descended the carpeted staircase, but one of the dogs—probably Zippy—was so enthusiastic about greeting the guest, he could be heard to tumble down and bounce, hard, off the wooden door.

"Hello," they could hear Kit say warmly.

And then the hair on the back of his neck rose and his father all but dropped his drink as they heard O'Malley's mother ask, "Who are you?" The dogs began to whimper.

H e'd never tailed anyone before, but he couldn't believe it was so easy. Or so thrilling in its own way. David Nicole sat parked with his little sports car straddled across the driveway of a red-brick mansion, his view of Robert O'Malley's house nearly perfect. In spite of being in a convertible, he had the top up, for discretion's sake, and sat smoking cigarettes, one after another.

He couldn't shake the feeling that there was someone else following O'Malley as well, and he didn't allow himself the weakness of believing that perhaps his intuition was paranoia. It wasn't likely that the person being followed was himself, that John was having him followed. Yet. Surely they had that minimum level of trust.

It was a warm evening balanced on the cusp of summer. The kids marched two by two past him into Georgetown's main drag. He didn't know how long he'd be sitting there, didn't really know what he was doing there, other than staying out of his apartment and away from Globe. His apartment was awfully empty, just him and the dog. And Globe? Well, it was going to be more than a little painful to have to hand the deed over to John Santangelo. Globe was something into which he'd put his heart and soul, it was his creation every bit as much as a painting is the artist's, and it was going to take some adjustment to accept the notion of losing it just because O'Malley had fucked up.

Staying away from his home and his business notwithstanding, he wasn't entirely certain why he was sitting on N Street in a cramped convertible waiting for Tom O'Malley. He needed to talk to him, but not with Kit around. Scaring O'Malley would be easy; threatening Kit would be something else. He didn't suppose he could easily get away with that. Kit was neither afraid of him nor particularly pliable, while O'Malley, unquestionably, was both.

He sat there chain-smoking Camel Lights, getting depressed. He had none of his usual sense of being in control of his destiny. When Tina had left today, she'd walked off with much more than jewelry and gold coins, some drugs, and, he finally discovered, that $25,000 C.D. on which he'd been counting. She'd walked off with his sense of comfort and order, his dreams of making a stand in his hometown. She'd deserted him to this mess he found himself in, and it was a little embarrassing and tacky, to be sitting there staking out a house that he'd used as a kind of clubhouse as a teenager.

Back then, after O'Malley's mother had moved to New York and it was just Tom and the old man, they'd thrown parties here whenever Mr. O'Malley was off subverting democracy around the globe, which investigators had subsequently exposed as a fairly rhythmic occurrence. The house on N Street, mere yards from downtown Georgetown, was legendary among the boys at St. Albans, not just because it was beautiful, with a goddamn Gauguin in the den—they barely took notice of either of those things—but because here the motto was Anything Goes, a powerful inducement to visitation for boys and girls at age seventeen. They had entire teen movies' worth of adventures, and he couldn't quantify the number of times they'd left O'Malley to clean up the mess.

But clean up others' messes he most certainly had. It was on O'Malley's C.V., it was his karma. His attributes were out of some warped Boy Scout manual, and he and David were best friends because added to loyalty and truthfulness and all that rot was a firmly mischievous delight in thwarting authority. And O'Malley was now working for the White House, a betrayal Nicole hadn't been able to resist jeopardizing. Just to see if he was dealing with the old O'Malley or some new version.

And if O'Malley hadn't wanted to get involved in the scheme, he could have just said no. But if he'd thought he was going to have the last laugh, then surely he'd forgotten the real Nicole.

Nicole flipped a cigarette into the middle of the street and a moment later the tire of a moving taxi stubbed it out. Amazing. Perfect timing. But then, surprisingly, the cab screeched to a halt and emerging was O'Malley's Uncle Jake, who'd represented Tom when they'd gotten busted at Amherst. And far more surprisingly, so was O'Malley's mother.

She stepped out of the taxi and sniffed, doing a full 360 as if to see if there were paparazzi about. Wow. Barbara O'Malley. He hadn't seen her since they were in college, crashing at her apartment in New York when they came down for weekends to score and go to CBGB. She hadn't changed a bit. She was still overdressed, haughty, and pretty well preserved.

He slithered down in his seat and watched them go through the little black gate and walk up to the door. Maybe he'd have to check this out.

I f his mother hadn't given them assignments and herself taken over the cleaning of the kitchen, they might never have dealt with O'Malley's problems in a rational manner. The sight of his father cowed by being exposed in such squalor was as painful as the later vision of Uncle Jake was comic.

O'Malley's uncle stood, an apron around his ample girth, a drink on the countertop nearby, scrubbing pots and pans. O'Malley had the suspicion that his father's Guatemalan girlfriend couldn't be that happy a little homemaker if the place was this much of a mess in the short time she'd been gone.

Uncle Jake whistled while he worked, and when it was done, the five slumped around the table in the breakfast nook. By this time his parents were on speaking terms, his mother even drinking a Manhattan made by his father to her nostalgic specifications.

"I suppose you need a woman's touch around this place," she said generously. It was quite a concession.

"Of course I do," his father answered forthrightly.

"It's still adultery." She was yielding no quarter.

"Barb, what do you expect of him? After fifteen years?" Jake was hunched over the edge of the table, overwhelming it, breathing heavily with his brow still moist from his exertions. His tie was pulled down in a renunciation of formality that O'Malley, for one, never thought he'd see. He'd seen Jake at poolside barbecues refusing to relinquish his jacket. But there were barriers dropping left and right here.

"It's nineteen years, Jake," his father said without looking up. He stared morosely at the melting cubes in his glass. It was amazing the way he'd hopped to when his estranged wife cracked the whip. She'd refused to stay until the place was cleaned up, and within a few minutes had assigned Kit and O'Malley to various tasks. It hadn't taken long for Jake and Bob O'Malley to join in, and with so much bumping of each other in the narrow kitchen and pantry, with the exertion they shared, what tension as had been there upon Barbara O'Malley's sudden appearance disappeared along with the kitchen's visible grime.

"I expect him not to sell my Gauguin to finance some right-wing army in Guatemala, and bringing a divorce action against him was one way I could think of to ensure that didn't happen."

"Aw, for Chrissakes, Barbara, I'm not going to sell the goddamn painting. I don't know where you got that from."

"Actually, I think she got it from me," Jake allowed.

"I did, you're right."

"How?"

"Remember the time you asked me what I thought it was worth? You wanted an appraiser?"

"That was for insurance. That was for a new policy."

"I must have thought you were thinking of selling it." Jake looked about as sheepish as an immense man breathing heavily over his drink could do.

"Judas Priest. And you told Barbara." His father looked at his friend with incredulity at this betrayal.

"I don't remember doing so."

"You did," his mother said precisely.

Jake shrugged.

"You're some lawyer."

"This isn't the normal client-lawyer-adversary relationship, Bob."

"Excuse me," O'Malley broke in. All four adults looked at him. Kit was sitting at the edge of the table nearest the door to the backyard, stroking Peggy's head as the old dog panted, happy from all the commotion in the house. Kit seemed less than thrilled by the kitchen conversation.

"Now that you've figured Dad isn't going to sell the painting, which I'm going to assume, Ma, means you're going to call off the divorce, which in turn means, Dad, you get to have Carmela come back and clean the place, so we don't have to; meaning, Uncle Jake, you did good tonight; now that we have this little happy ending, can I bring something up?" He was a little out of breath.

"Oh, yes," his father said sarcastically. "My son, the French Connection." He didn't seem exactly bored by it, but it was clear his father's ability to be shocked by O'Malley's actions had been diminished by the years.

"What?" His mother's shoulders went rigid, and she leaned over the table toward him. Kit continued to stroke the dog, and O'Malley didn't know where to begin.

"I'm not sure where to start."

"The beginning?" Kit suggested quietly. This was the way he'd told it to her the night before as they drove back into the city from Andrews. He knew the way to spin the story, at least he'd discovered what worked with her. That Kit hadn't dropped him off out near the Beltway and told him to walk back into the city meant his explanation had a certain utilitarian purpose. Like any veteran of massive trouble who was articulate enough to talk his way around it, he could illuminate the path into the thicket he found himself in, and do so in a manner that made it seem almost logical that he'd lost his way. He knew he'd look foolish, cowardly, that he deserved to be treated as if he were the world's greatest fool, but these were his parents. Maybe that's the difference between adolescent and adult trouble. By the time you're an adult, you become convinced that surely this is one group likely to be on your side. At least O'Malley thought so.

"Do you remember David Nicole?"

"That horrid charmer. The one who had your girlfriend killed," she said in recollection.

"Your drug-dealing roommate from Amherst."

"I guess you would remember him, Uncle Jake." Jake would take this harder than his parents.

"David's in Washington. He runs this restaurant cum nightclub in Adams Morgan with his girlfriend. I hadn't had any contact with him whatever in six, seven years, when Kit and I ran into him at Primi Piatti." And so on. O'Malley told them everything that happened. Under the circumstances, he renounced an important part of his worldview. He denied nothing. He admitted everything. It was a very big step.

Harlan could hardly believe what a fool the guy in the sports car was. It was as if the bastard just couldn't sit still. First the guy parked across someone's driveway, not exactly the place to be if you were trying to avoid scrutiny. Then the mystery man got out, stretched, threw his cigarette into the bushes, and stood at the entrance to the narrow alley between the house O'Malley had gone into—the house where the fat man and the stuck-up broad in the lizard pumps had only recently entered—and the neighbor's house whose driveway the bastard blocked. Although it was getting dark, anyone looking out his window would see a most suspicious character look like he was casing the joint. Not smart. He could bring the cops down on both of them.

The fellow looked around once, twice, as if determining whether someone was watching him, and obviously convincing himself the answer was no, he proceeded to walk into the space between the two houses.

Harlan spoke into his microcassette recorder: "Eight-fifteen. Sports car guy acting stupid." He could fill in the blanks later.

It was when O'Malley got to the part about being in Willy Barnes's suite and reading the fax of *The Washington Times* piece that Kit exhibited some agitation. "Oh, Thomas," she said.

"What?" He was a little aggravated that she was interrupting his story. His parents had stopped squabbling long enough to listen. In fact, they seemed thoroughly spellbound.

"David didn't plant the story the second time."

"Huh?"

"The story in the Moonie *Times* wasn't planted by Nicole. I'm certain it was Mike Humperdink or Jerry Jetta, those sleazy consultants to Partridge. Remember I was telling you about them?"

"Partridge?" his father harrumphed.

"Do you believe it?" Kit asked sarcastically. Her days in Partridge's office were numbered. "These guys were boasting in advance that they'd gotten the White House, but good. This was supposed to make the environment better for Tony to come out blasting the administration, which is exactly what he did. Not that he was supposed to as far as I was concerned."

If a comet had plunged through the ceiling and clunked him on the head, it's doubtful O'Malley would have been any more thunderstruck. "You don't mean . . ."

"That David wasn't responsible for the second leak? Yeah, sweetie." She said this as if she were announcing the incorporeality of the Easter Bunny. His mother, sitting across the table, hadn't been nearly so tactful.

"You're kidding. I just assumed it was him."

"You're a bloody goddamn fool, Tom."

"Thanks, Mom, I never would have figured that out."

"I just can't believe you'd be so stupid. Jeopardizing your job at the White House."

"I thought you hated my job at the White House."

"I do. That doesn't mean you should smuggle narcotics just because I think the President you work for is a fool. I'd sooner you work for a Democratic president than tend bar or defend Dow Chemicals, or whatever it was you were doing at that law firm."

"Wow, Mom, that means a lot to me." He beamed. But he was quickly brought back to earth when he saw the look on Jake's face.

"You are up Shit Creek without so much as a swizzle stick, so don't go getting slaphappy, partner." Jake sighed and slumped back in his chair, almost upending it.

"How bad is it, Jake?" His father deferred to Jake in the manner of a patient braced for the professional verdict.

"Tom here conspired to import narcotics. It's an open-and-shut case. I have an associate who specializes in these things I'd like to check in with before I commit myself, but right now it looks pretty dismal if they can make their case. A White House aide smuggling drugs. Child of privilege, lawyer with no ignorance of the law." He shook his head. "I'm on his side, by the way."

"There were mitigating circumstances, Uncle Jake."

They looked at him as if this was going to be good.

"I was being blackmailed."

"Not good enough for a jury," his uncle said dismissively.

"It doesn't count at all?" Kit asked. She'd persuaded herself there was some legal basis for the only defense of O'Malley she could make in her own mind.

"It might count in the sentencing. It will take a lawyer more skillful than I to make it count with a jury." He said it as if a lawyer more skillful than he would be awfully hard to locate.

O'Malley buried his head in his hands. His mother barked, "Thomas," as if he had his elbows on the table during a dinner party. He snapped to.

"Darling, we'll do whatever it takes to get you out of trouble. Won't we, gentlemen?" She looked at her brother and her husband.

"Don't you have some other legal work you're in the midst of?" It was pretty clear his father was referring to the divorce. Jake was looking quizzical, like a show dog given a conflicting order by a new trainer.

This is when the dogs started howling, as if there was something or someone trying to get into the house.

H arlan left moments after the ambulance did, but not without recording some notes. The street was transformed from a cozy Georgetown block to the kind of brightly lit crime scene one saw ever more often in D.C.: police lights spinning, the small crowd of gawkers pressed as close as they could to see who was the victim. Thank heaven, even the crusty FBI agent was able to mutter, not into his recorder but at least to himself, it looked like the old lady was going to be okay.

It was only moments after the hotshot with the sports car had disappeared down the alley that Harlan heard the baying dogs. After that what happened was a little unclear.

He was prepared to report, if necessary to testify, that what happened was the fellow who had been following O'Malley and the girl was chased from behind the house by three snarling dogs. Just as he was about to hop into his Alfa and take off, this little old lady pulling a grocery cart down the street was damn near run over by the mutts.

She went down, hard, and it wasn't until the ambulance came and she got in it under her own steam that either O'Malley, the lady in the high heels, the girl who'd driven him, or the two older men seemed to breathe any easier.

Harlan noticed that the fellow who'd been following O'Malley, and who'd been caught by him in the moment he took to see if the old lady was alive, seemed to exchange words with him. He wondered what was said, but if he knew the criminal type, and surely he did, it must have been the arrangement of some kind of rendezvous.

Bronstein wondered why it was that all the stories that had the potential to land them on the front page meant they had to work Saturdays, but then, he really didn't mind.

Partridge's staffer was a pawn, he had to admit, in their exposing the hypocrisy of politicians. Her only sin, other than having gone out with some fellow who decade-old court records showed was a pretty serious collegiate coke dealer, was that her politician boss had decided to get into the middle of the controversy over the White House and drugs. He was trying to take advantage of a situation in which he was vulnerable, and they couldn't let him get away with that. Simple symmetry, simple fairness dictated to Bronstein that she needed to be exposed, not so much because of anything she'd done, but because of the hypocrisy of her employer. Even if this would disrupt her life, these were tough times and extraordinary measures were called for.

He worried that his editors would be fascinated to find out about Partridge's aide, but not enough to do a story on her. A common complaint he heard from colleagues, especially ones who worked for newsweeklies, was that their editors all seemed to think of gossip as private erotica that just maybe they'd share with readers. That wasn't the case so much at the *Post*, but the editors there certainly did look over their shoulders to see what other news organizations had the same stories they had. Often, if they were of a personal nature, if they were about, say, a politician's sex life, the *Post* wouldn't even run it, they just liked having it. They'd giggle over the rumors that circulated among their competitors about what it was the *Post* was going to print.

He worried that this story about Partridge's aide would follow the same pattern: it would provide editorial kicks but not get printed. What he needed was Cale to arrive and persuade the weekend editors to let the story run, and especially, to let it run on the front page. But Cale was tardy, which was typical.

There was nothing to do, now that he'd written the piece, but wait for Cale and read the paper. He noted with some humor the item that had Eunice Heseltine, the aging widow of the legendary Stewart Heseltine, being taken to the hospital after having been run over by her neighbor's dogs in Georgetown. Then he stopped himself. For shame. It was terrible to take pleasure in someone's misfortune.

H ow do you feel?" she asked. She was sitting on the edge of the bed with only a pair of panties on, her back curved ever so slightly as she slumped there clutching a steaming cup of coffee in her hands. He'd slept so soundly as not to have heard her knocking around the small kitchen, and O'Malley instinctively rubbed her arm, the only way he could thank her for her thoughtfulness until he had the power of speech.

"Did last night really happen?" he finally asked.

"According to the *Post* it did."

He took the coffee out of her hand and put it on the bedside table. He drew her toward him and held her tightly, perhaps to convince himself that she was there, that he hadn't yet been hauled off to jail. He rocked her in his arms, a degree to the east, a degree to the west, the billowing of her canopy rustling above his head as the fan on the bureau swept this way and that in the rhythmic arcs of a foghorn searchlight. "Have I told you I'm so sorry?"

"Shhh. Too many times. I'm willing to believe you can't help the fact that you're an idiot. I've met your parents." He reminded himself that this was no non sequitur. "When did you agree to meet him?"

"Four o'clock at the Lincoln Memorial."

"It certainly should be crowded enough." Her face was just inches from his and he remembered the amount of time he'd spent longing for her, even when she was David's girlfriend, even though he'd been in love with Tawnee.

"Sure, it will just be David and me and the twenty-five Secret Service agents they've probably detailed to us." He would miss her from jail, or whatever exile into which, once disgraced in Washington, it was expected he would disappear. He had that thought without any actual notion that things would get to that. He knew he was in trouble, bad enough trouble to have reversed a lifetime's automatic deception and brought those people who could help him in on the truth. But the step from vague threat to actually hanging from the rope, or however it was they dealt with people who had done what he had, was too big to make. There still was the notion that he could talk himself out of this mess, and a countervailing notion that this time he'd pushed things too far. His heart sank. He deserved whatever happened to him.

The thing that bothered him most of all was that he didn't have a plan. When you were in this deep, simply being honest only took you so far.

I t was at the end of his breakfast speech before the Crook County Rotary Club that Senator Partridge got word that *The Washington Post* was trying to reach him. He was standing near the doorway shaking the hands of the white-hatted Marlboro men and their Airstream trailer–like wives. He was trying to make small talk, when his aide self-importantly elbowed his way next to him and in a voice just a shade too loud informed him of the phone call.

"Can't you tell them I'm with these nice people and that I'll have to just get back to them?"

"But, sir, this is *The Washington Post* calling for you," the young man said. He whispered the name of the paper with awe. And thus ensued a little tug of war, with the aide trying to impress upon the ranchers how important the Senator was, and the Senator trying to impress upon them how equally important he thought *they* were. The result was he stood there until the last had complained about the price of wheat and gotten into their pickups to shoot off in the direction of Mount Rushmore, while the aide stood there dying over his boss's breach of the most basic political rule, in this case the one that says you drop whatever you're doing anytime there's the remotest chance you can get a line in the paper. And this was no ordinary paper.

The aide, who'd just spent two days trying to coax a television station all the way from Rapid City to cover this event, couldn't understand what Senator Partridge was doing, dawdling with a bunch of ranchers and their wives when he could be talking to a reporter who had tracked him down here all the way from Washington. There was nothing in the world the aide wanted nearly so much as a chance to go to Washington and be on the Senator's staff.

"Hello," Partridge finally said when he took the phone from the manager of the Best Western where the Rotary breakfast was always held.

"Senator Partridge?"

"That's me, sorry to keep you waiting."

"That's all right, sir. My name is Steve Bronstein, with the *Post?*" He said it like it was a question. "I'd like to ask you a couple of questions about an employee of yours. About Kit Bowles?"

Partridge instinctively gravitated toward the chair while the manager of the motel stood in the doorway, a self-satisfied look on his face as if he thought history was being made, in his very office. Only four clerks and a solitary guest, a traveling grain-feed salesman from Cedar Rapids who was a regular, crowded in behind the manager. "Go on," said the Senator.

"Well, first of all, does she work for you?"

She did. And he couldn't begin to imagine what this was all about.

f all the things O'Malley had to worry about, only the most immediate was keeping the upper hand when Nicole arrived. In spite of coming clean with the people he needed to back him up, the thought of going to the authorities and telling all never once crossed his mind. That was something to be done only under the most extreme circumstances, extreme being defined as the warden walking purposefully over to the switch after O'Malley was already strapped in.

He turned from where he sat at the top of the steps and looked at the giant marble Lincoln. The Great Emancipator had assumed the position; he could easily have been sitting in a nineteenth-century electric chair, though far more stoically than O'Malley ever would have managed judging from the way he felt now. He was nervous just with Nicole. They had a couple of things to settle.

He knew now that Nicole hadn't been the one who planted that story in *The Washington Times*, knew that it was a political dirty trick. Yet he believed that upon Nicole's arrival he ought to paint a word portrait of what it had been like for him when, hours from receiving the goods, he'd seen the story that had been faxed through the White House Communications Agency, a story that made him think Nicole had gone talking to the press again. After all, telling him the truth, that he'd decided not to do it, wouldn't compute in Nicole's mind. He knew it. So he decided that bringing up in an aggressive manner that he had thought Nicole was toying with him again might be what he needed to get Nicole under control, which was something to be accomplished at all costs. The truth—that he'd come to his senses—was just not good enough in this case. This was an extreme case. A new twist on the credo, admit nothing, deny everything.

A plan began to formulate, and just in time, for it was then that he saw him, wandering alongside the Reflecting Pool just like some tourist from the heartland.

The steps swept down in cascades from the delightfully modest classical architecture of the monument. We have, as a nation, this habit of not letting our presidents build monuments to themselves, but instead, only to their predecessors, which makes for a compelling modesty of scale. Nonetheless, millions of our compatriots make the once-in-a-lifetime pilgrimage to Washington, to these shrines to our civilian deities, and most do so in the summer, when the average humidity rests at about ninety-nine percent.

That Nicole wasn't just an American come to bask in the glow of this most sacred of our monuments could be discerned by the absence of Day-Glo shorts, ratty tank top, and white socks. No, David could be seen purposefully approaching as bicyclists and joggers shot by leaving vapor trails of perspiration, as fathers pushed baby carriages and children ran to the concrete water's edge on stiff little legs. Nicole in mirrored-glasses cool, with a light spring jacket and no doubt the preppiest polo shirt in his collection, trod toward O'Malley's perch. O'Malley prepared for his arrival the same way as the captain of a small vessel who sees the skull and crossbones waving above the ship about to overtake him. It begins with a vast intake of air.

Nicole spied him and came up the steps two at a time, as if he were trying to conquer gravity. He loomed, blotting out the Capitol at the other end of the Mall. He did not seem light of heart. "Maybe you should give me one reason why you shouldn't meet a fate like Lincoln's."

"I didn't free the slaves?"

Nicole sat down, a little awkwardly, as if he were being pinched by his underwear. He wouldn't look at him, he just stared off through his shades at the bright spring day on the nation's front lawn. O'Malley automatically began trying to figure which of the innocents poking around the Reflecting Pool were law-enforcement officials. "This is your worst fuck-up by far, my friend."

"Oh, there's no question about that, David. I've been saying that to myself for days."

"Why wouldn't you do what you agreed to?" He turned and looked at him, an almost pleading look, as close to being human as David could be when he wanted something.

He shrugged.

"If you were going to go down and just screw things up, you could have saved both of us a lot of problems. You could have just said you didn't want to do it."

O'Malley laughed. "That's really easy for you to say now that you're not blackmailing me. You seem to forget how you put this thing into play."

"You didn't have to do it."

Oh? Hearing him, it was clear that Nicole really believed that. Should he tell him then that was what he'd decided for himself? No, too complicated. He'd have to continue playing the role.

"David, this is so like you to conveniently forget the levers you pulled. You knew I was vulnerable because of my position, and you took full advantage of it. You knew exactly what you were doing. This wasn't a simple request, pal, you didn't say, Please, Tom, for old time's sake, as long as you're going to South America, would you mind bringing me back twenty keys of coke and a colorful sombrero? No. You black-mailed me! And like most acts of manipulation you engage in, you did it efficiently and well. I repeat: it was blackmail!"

He said that a little too loudly, as a tyke pulling his father up the steps to see the immense sitting statue looked at them suspiciously, then automatically moved closer to his father's leg.

He lowered his voice. "And what I can't figure, David, is why, when I was down there already, when I was already going through with it, you planted that story with the Moonie *Times*. What could you possibly have had to gain?" He wasn't much of an actor but he decided to give it a shot.

"I don't know what you're talking about," Nicole said flatly, though there was just an afterimage of uncertainty.

"Look, you can save your innocent act for the authorities, but you forget I've watched you hone your lies. Let me draw you a little picture of what happened down there. I'm sitting in one of the staff suites in Caracas when they faxed the piece on who the White House drug dealer was." There wasn't a flicker discernible through the mirrored glasses. "The piece said they'd narrowed it down to someone who worked in the speechwriting shop. Don't look so fucking innocent, David." His imaginary coaches were standing behind him, a cross between Vince "Best Offense" Lombardi and Lee Strasberg. As he said it, it was easy for him to imagine that it was true, that it was in fact Nicole who'd planted the story, precisely as he'd thought when he was in South America. He could easily be convinced it was Nicole's cruel behavioral modification technique that had the unintended consequence of forcing O'Malley to his senses. Right now, he couldn't even begin to remember Kit had told him it was those sleazy Republican consultants who'd done it, who'd attempted to do him in.

"You got the wrong guy. I didn't do it. There'd be no percentage in my doing so."

"Well, if you didn't do it, who did?"

"Beats me." He shrugged. Then, "So that's why you fucked up?" It seemed to make things clearer, though not necessarily better.

"It's why I didn't follow through on this lunacy. And if you didn't do it, then I'm not certain who I should thank for helping me come to my senses."

Nicole frowned and his face instantly became cold. "Thomas, Thomas, Thomas. You don't get it, do you?"

O'Malley shook his head.

Nicole leaned forward like he wanted to confide in him. For a moment, O'Malley thought it was a friendly gesture, meant to invoke the closeness they once upon a time had felt. "Why don't," Nicole said softly, "you look down inside my jacket." O'Malley knew in his mind what he was seeing, before his eyes actually made out the black spine of a pistol butt, the little knob that held the clip in place, the small bud of a hammer.

"That's a gun, David," he said like any rube from Middle America out there, climbing around the Memorial. It would be a peculiarly American way of settling things.

"That's what it is."

O'Malley didn't know what else to do, so he started laughing.

"Is there something funny about the gun I'm going shoot you with?" The look on Nicole's face could have done the job, if it came to that. "I'm the first to admire gallows humor, but you know, I could as easily shoot you here as anyplace. Of course, if I shot you here, I wouldn't have the pleasure of taking Kit down with you."

The smile left O'Malley's face. He was glad he wasn't standing, for his head began to go light. His reaction was a physical uncoupling of his grip on things. He felt his confidence leave him like a train that's just dropped off its boxcar.

It was the first time someone had ever threatened to shoot him, so he was a little uncertain how he was supposed to behave. "I'm not certain I know what you're going to shoot us for?" He held his palms up, questioning. He instantly thought of wrestling him down the steps and smashing his head against the marble, but it was a tricky proposition and the moment passed.

"I need the money I'm out from your having screwed up down there. If I need to spell this out, there are some people who were mightily inconvenienced by you. They need money, they want it from me, and I want it from you, *comprende?* You're going to get it for me. Or else you're just going to get it."

"I am, huh. I'm not even certain I'm going to get another paycheck. But just for the sake of argument, how much money am I supposed to get?"

"One hundred thousand dollars." He only owed Santangelo seventy-five, but the other twenty-five was for his troubles.

O'Malley giggled, in spite of himself.

"You don't seem to think I'm serious about this," Nicole said, once more. "And I guess I'm not about shooting Kit. But I am about shooting you. I find it offensive that you're not quaking in your Reeboks." It was more of a plea than a threat.

"Thanks for agreeing to spare your former girlfriend. Not all your girlfriends have been so lucky. But you're wrong about my not taking you seriously. I think you're serious enough to be carrying a pistol around in public, like some homeboy. But even if I had that kind of money, and I don't, you brought this on yourself. And I don't owe you anything, David." The thought flickered that if that had been his hard and fast attitude a week ago, they wouldn't be sitting here. He stood up, as if the matter were closed.

"Then I'll just have to send around the people with the truncheons and the brass knuckles."

"Oh, no, no, no, no, no, if they were after me, you wouldn't be threatening me with a gun. You're the one who's in trouble, not me. I'm in enough trouble, but not with the gentlemen who've driven you to this."

He stood there with the Washington Monument poking up directly behind his head, the Reflecting Pool framing him, his heart beating. He would have been more nervous if the entire Memorial and Mall weren't overrun with tourists and Park Police on their little motorcycles. David wasn't going to shoot him here, unless he truly was demented. And if that was the case, he was doomed anyway.

"You come within a hundred yards of me or Kit, David, and I swear to God, I'm on the phone with the Secret Service in two seconds and telling them everything. I'm sweating out whether I go to jail just for what they know already. But I'll be happy to make sure you go with me. It'll be fun to see you in the same prison I'm in. It'll be just like Amherst, won't it?"

He walked down the steps, his back arched.

I t was with a sense of his mortality so profound as to prompt consideration of his final meal that O'Malley agreed to meet Kit for dinner at a restaurant on U Street that served home cooking at outrageous prices. He intended to settle his bill with a credit card, so if Nicole were to follow through on his threat, it would be up to the executors of the Thomas O'Malley estate to pay for the damn meal. All the while he dressed, he comforted himself with the notion that there might be such a thing as a free meal. He visualized a Bergman film in which Death reached for the check.

That isn't funny, he said to himself. But it was best, right about now, that he keep himself amused.

"I have problems, too," was how Kit had put it when they spoke briefly at six o'clock. He didn't know what that could be all about. So as not to alarm her, he'd been rather nonchalant about the confrontation with Nicole that afternoon. He'd allowed as how things hadn't gone well, but hadn't filled her in on the details. He wasn't certain he would ever fill her in on all the details. The important thing was to figure out how to protect her.

They sipped beer that had been brewed next to a refinery in Biloxi, and ate collard greens and chitlins, and meat loaf and gravy the way Mom would have made it if Mom ever cooked. It was a relief, in a way, not to have some waiter prance out and describe the healthful lifestyle of every once-living organism that appeared on the menu: no recitation of how the chickens jogged on the free range, no invocation of a secondary menu of the organic worms the trout had been fed. If this was a last supper—and the thought bore in unmercifully that any meal he ate now had that potential—it was delightfully unhealthy. If it wasn't his last supper, it would hasten it, even if it didn't quite arrive for another forty years.

"So tell me what happened." She'd already given him the highlights of her conversation with *The Washington Post* reporter, whom she feared she'd handled poorly. She thought it unladylike to have told him to fold it five ways and stick it where the sun don't shine.

"Partridge fired me." She said it as stoically as one could under circumstances that included gravy on the chin.

"That little weenie."

"You know, he's absolutely screwed himself. Here he's worried that he's going to be accused of having done drugs when he was in college, and by leading the charge against the White House so he could get a little face time on the nets, all he's done is open himself up for attack. Of course, I guess it doesn't help that I'm the proximate cause of his worries."

"Sweetie, you're incidental in this. No offense. If it weren't you, it would be something else. That's the only symmetry in this whole disgusting mess. It's not in anyone's interest, certainly not in any baby boomer's interest, to start leading charges against people who've used drugs years ago. Unless they were on a desert island from about 1965 to 1980. I'm really sorry you were fired . . ."

"Don't be. I was going to quit."

"But things were bound to unravel sooner or later, now that I'm hot."

"You're about to get hotter. They've discovered I'm connected to Nicole. Just wait till they've discovered I'm connected to you."

"Who was the reporter you spoke with?"

"This sort of nice guy. He seemed apologetic that he even had to bring this stuff up. Steve Bernstein?"

"Bronstein. He's the little bastard that broke my drunk-driving story. Oh great. Oh, this is just great."

"So that's who he is. I was trying to place the name. I thought I'd met him at a party or something. But listen, tell me, what happened with Nicole?"

"He wants me to pay him one hundred thousand dollars."

She started to laugh.

"That's what I did, too."

"How did he take it?"

"About the way you'd expect."

hen Mike Humperdink read the piece in the *Post*, he almost lost his appetite. Almost.

His oatmeal cooled, the bacon congealed, the eggs went rubbery and hard. But sitting in the breakfast nook of his large house in Cleveland Park—a house that, other than the cleaning woman and repairmen who came to fix things, no one but he had entered since he bought it—he was transfixed by the coverage of Kit Bowles's past.

So, she'd been the moll of a college drug kingpin. Sitting in the opulent brick home he'd bought off the proceeds from his side business of cashing in on HUD grants, he thought her association with criminals despicable. So that explains it, he said to himself looking up at the chandelier above the table—a chandelier no one ever would swing from at a party, because it was doubtful Mike ever could get enough people to actually attend a party at his house. That's why she was so opposed to their strategy. She had something to hide! He could kick himself for not having done opposition research on her. Partridge would have proved malleable far sooner but for Kit's meddling with that stupid cholesterol agenda.

Of course, Partridge could have handled it a little better when the reporter asked him if Kit worked for him. He shouldn't have answered yes, only to add, "But she doesn't anymore," when the reporter told him about her background. That looked too defensive.

He knew how Washington worked; that episode would be what would spring from the lips of the elites when they discussed this at their fancy parties. "Do you believe how Partridge handled this?" they would ask one another. "Ho ho ho."

They would have to coach him, he and his partner, on the proper way to handle the press. Now that Kit was no longer on his staff, if in fact Partridge had fired her, there would be no one pushing their dinghy away each time they paddled alongside the Senator from Wyoming. Tony Partridge. Wyoming's Finest. Nah, not even the cattle would buy that one. They'd have to come up with a different slogan for his election.

He returned his attention to breakfast and was so intent upon it that when the phone rang, he almost didn't answer. It was the Senator himself. "Tony, how are you?" he asked enthusiastically. He had learned always to answer the phone with good cheer.

"Not too good, Mike. Our little strategy—I should say, your little strategy—sure has backfired."

"It's not that bad. So Kit Bowles had to go, that's no problem."

"That's not the problem. I have the *Casper Star-Tribune* asking me to list every contact I've ever had with any illegal substance. I think they're going to lynch me if it turns out I even know how to spell the word 'marijuana.'"

"No problem, Tony. You just tell 'em you experimented with pot once or twice, like so many members of your generation."

"There's a little problem with that. That's what I've been trying to tell you. My experimentation was more like the Manhattan Project. You're the one who got me into this. What do I do?"

"Uhhhh."

"Yeah, that's what I said. You're supposed to be the expert. What's the answer?"

It was a very good question. If he hadn't lost his appetite earlier, he sure had now.

teve Bronstein sat with Mandy Drabb at an outside table at the Childe Harold, feeling like a new man. Last night when he'd gone to take her home, he'd stood on the steps to her building, dawdling as he kissed her, waiting for her to say something like, "Why don't you come upstairs and have a nightcap." Instead, she'd surprised him by saying, "Why don't you come upstairs and kiss my nipples." She'd giggled. "Why don't you come upstairs and come, upstairs." He'd groaned.

Now they sat eating brunch and Mandy was reading the front-page story that, he'd told her three times, he couldn't have written without her. He'd been thanking her profusely for the tip almost every conscious hour on the hour, ever since the piece had been accepted by the editors and budgeted for the front page.

Ultimately, Cale had been the decisive element in getting their editors to see the necessity of their doing the piece. He'd persuaded them there was a certain rough justice to their doing to Partridge what Partridge was willing to do to whoever it was in the White House who was the object of all these rumors. Steve sat there while Mandy read, certain that when she finished, she would swoon even more lovingly than she had the night before. It would only be a matter of minutes before she insisted they pay the check and head to her nearby apartment on S Street for what she would euphemistically refer to as a nap.

"This is so unfair," she declared loudly when she was done.

"Wha . . ."

"Ooh, how could you?" Her pretty face was twisted in an expression of disgust.

"I don't under—"

"You mean, this whole time you were only interested in me to find out what you could about Kit Bowles? We were in the same dorm together, for godssakes, and all you were after was for me to betray her?"

"Wait a minute," he began. Two days earlier she'd been so catty it was a wonder she didn't lick her own fur. Anything he'd wanted to know about Kit Bowles's college history, she'd been more than happy to tell him. At one point she'd even called up various of her friends to compare notes. Now she seemed to be complaining about . . . He wasn't certain. "What are you complaining about?"

"This is so unfair," she hissed. She seemed on the verge of making a scene. "You're bringing disgrace upon Smith College!"

"I've hardly brought disgrace upon Smith College, Mandy. I've just reported much of what you told me about the behavior of one of Senator Tony Partridge's key aides. It's a legitimate news story, given the context of his accusations against the White House." He didn't know exactly what was going on, but he began to suspect that this sudden reticence about hurting a fellow Smith alumna was for show; that whatever was going on had more to do with Mandy and Kit than it did with Mandy and Steve.

"Oh, poor Kit. This is terrible. This is going to make things miserable for her. Partridge all but fired her."

"I think he did fire her. At least that's the way I interpreted what he said." He was in shock, completely dumbfounded at this change in her attitude.

"This is going to completely screw things up for her. Oh, and it's going to make life miserable for her cute boyfriend at the White House . . ."

"Her what?" He leaned over.

"Her boyfriend. This is going to be terrible for him, too."

"What boyfriend at the White House?"

"Tom O'Malley. He was David Nicole's best friend. I think they were roommates. He works at the White House now. He and Kit are dating."

He loved her euphemisms. Dating. He loved her prissy, preppy style. He loved her. O'Malley. And Kit Bowles. That's it! O'Malley was the White House drug dealer after all!

He leaned over the table to kiss her. "Don't touch me!" she squealed, pulling him toward her. "You're a terrible person."

"It was my editors, Mandy," he said, kissing her. "They made me, Mandy." All the while he was trying to figure how he could get to a phone to call McTeague.

O'Malley stared out over Rock Creek Park while Kit lingered noisily in the shower. What was in the *Post* was more than merely disturbing. As bad as he felt for Kit, the worst, most dangerous part was the naming of Nicole. He didn't like the notion of Nicole feeling any more cornered than he was already. But rather than being on pins and needles, O'Malley found himself becoming somewhat numb in advance, numb to this drama of discovery through newspapers, investigations, and trials to come. The piece on Kit's connection to Nicole was a sign that things had gotten out of hand. It was less real to him than the cars gliding over the distant Taft Bridge, the tiny specks of joggers down below them on the paths.

They'd taken a quick spin of the television dial and everywhere found hilarity. The President's trip to South America was a kind of nitrous oxide fog upon the talk shows, and normally sober guests with all the levity of hanging judges were nearly sliding off their chairs. He could stand it for only a minute; it added too much to his sense of unreality.

What was about to unfold, he knew, was very real indeed. And he'd brought it upon himself.

He didn't know what he was going to do. He didn't know what was going to happen. But standing there looking out the window, feeling like a fool, he was determined about one thing. He was going to fight when the moment came to do so.

ohn Santangelo hadn't come alone, and the thugs who arrived with him weren't nearly the snappy dressers he was. The Salami Brothers, as they were referred to on the streets of Baltimore, would never have been allowed in Globe at night. That they arrived with John at the appointed time was an unpleasant surprise. That they now held Nicole down on the pool table while John stood swinging a cue like he was Casey in the on-deck circle was enough to make him nearly wet his pants. He thought he was going to die.

He regretted and did not regret that the gun was back in the rolltop desk. Pulling the gun on O'Malley was one thing. Pulling the gun on people who knew what to do when a gun was pulled on them was another thing altogether.

"This isn't a joke, you know, David." Whoosh! He took a cut through thin air with the pool cue. "Frank Robinson," he declared.

Nicole struggled as the Salami Brothers held him down. They had fat, ugly faces, and breath like month-old clam chowder. "I know, I know, I know, John, I told you, for Chrissakes, I know."

Whoosh! "Cal Ripken, Junior." Santangelo was standing there in his usual black getup, this time with a Springsteen-like silver bola around his neck. He was a big guy who could take quite a cut at the ball in his imaginary Memorial Stadium. Whoosh! "Boog hits it outta the park!" said Joey Salaminticcolo, the dumber of the Salami Brothers, in an attempt at currying favor with his boss. As he said this, he kept Nicole pinned to the felt.

"You said you'd have it by Sunday. It's Sunday, David, and the only thing you have is your name in the paper, identified as a drug dealer. That really isn't helpful. In particular, that sucks. Whattayouthink? I don't have to answer to anybody?"

The pool cue came down on the table so hard even the Salami Brothers winced. Craaack!

"Jesus, John, I swear to fucking God, I'll get you more than the money I owe you. I'll give you something worth millions."

John Santangelo was over at the rack, choosing his next cue to break the way a caddy carefully chooses an iron. There were splintered pool cues all over the room. He turned back toward the table. The Salami Brothers were looking as quizzical as could be, like this was going to be good. They'd been in a lot of places with John Santangelo, trying to persuade someone to come up with the money he was owed, but they'd never been in a place like this, replete with zebra rugs and the other hip accoutrements collected around the world by Nicole—and Tina.

Santangelo walked over to the pool table. "Okay, David, what's the scam this time?" He began to crouch in the batter's stance, and just to taunt him, he slowly swung the cue just to show that a centimeter's difference was a broken jaw.

"How would you like a Gauguin? It's a real Gauguin, John. I can get it for you, quickly."

"Oh, yeah? And where you going to get your hands on a Gauguin? Whattayougonnado? Hold up the National Gallery?"

"O'Malley's got one. At least his father does." The Salami Brothers kept Nicole pinned down, but they looked up at Santangelo to get a sense of how rough he wanted them to be. That Santangelo placed the butt end of the pool cue on the floor like a shepherd's staff was a sign that they shouldn't hurt Nicole too much.

"And how are you going to get it from him?"

"I'm going to persuade him that he wants to give it to me."

"Oh, for crying out fuckin' loud, here we go again. And just how are you going to do that?"

"Just leave that up to me, John. Just give me another twenty-four, forty-eight hours."

"You've had three days."

"Please, man, I swear. This time I'll come through."

"Because if you don't, David, we're going to torch the place."

"Globe?"

"You betcha. Faster payback than actually taking it over. What do you have it insured for?" He was standing right over Nicole now, looking around the room as if to see if there was something salvageable before they spilled gasoline on the floor and dropped the match.

Supine, Nicole wasn't even bothering to struggle anymore. He had the real sense the offer of the Gauguin had appealed either to John's aesthetics or to his sense of greed. It hardly mattered which.

"I don't know what the place is insured for. Please, don't do anything rash, John. I'll get you the painting. It's worth millions. You'll be the only guy on your block with his very own Gauguin."

"Jesus, I'm a sucker. Let him go," Santangelo instructed the Salami Brothers.

"Let him go?" asked a dumbstruck Joey Salaminticcolo.

"You heard me."

"You won't be sorry about this, John."

"I'm sorry I ever met you, David."

"Hey, boss," said Giulio Salaminticcolo, who was actually the brighter of the Salami Brothers. "What's a Go Gan?"

John Santangelo rolled his eyes before leading them out the door. Nicole lay back on the pool table, just breathing. Simple pleasures were the best, he reminded himself.

 ecause Kit wanted to avoid her father's phone call, and O'Malley wished not to have to talk with anyone, they piled into her car and spent the afternoon in Annapolis, eating oysters and drinking beer. After reading the article on the front page of the paper, it seemed like the only thing to do.

O'Malley missed the several attempts by the White House Signal operator to track him down. He also missed an enraged Nicole. And, as it turned out, he wasn't there for the phone call from his Uncle Jake, who'd been deputized by his parents to deliver the message that should anything break he was to make certain he said nothing to anyone without Jake being there. He was not to talk to the press, he was not to talk to any law-enforcement officials, he was not to talk to anyone without Jake.

As they stayed away until it was quite late, and upon returning merely sneaked into his apartment to get clothes for the following day, there were perhaps two dozen calls O'Malley missed. Several were from Steve Bronstein, whose partner, Cale McTeague, ceased staking out O'Malley's front door mere moments before Kit pulled up in front of it. And most important, perhaps, he missed the calls from Allison Hardy of the *Los Angeles Times,* who did not have very good news for him.

When they arrived at Kit's apartment, the first thing she did was unplug the phone. His body wrapped around her, he slept very well. He would need it.

 he look on the uniformed agent's face when he held his pass up should have given things away. O'Malley normally went in the Seventeenth Street basement entrance because it was the only place that Secret Service agents sat next to the magnetometers and waved staffers by. The main entrance, or the entrance at the Southwest gate, were inevitably manned by grumpy assholes. It was the basement entrance you went to before your wake-up cup of java. Today, however, and he wondered why, the agent allowed him to walk by, yet glared at him as if he'd like to take him out in front of the West Wing and tear his lungs out.

He wandered down the hallway, his shoes echoing against the black checkerboard tiles of the first floor of the Executive Office Building, heading past the numerous doorways with their rather quaint titles painted above them, the deceptively permanent-seeming names in the little slots on the doors themselves. It was only then that he began to get the feeling something had changed.

When one secretary heading to the Political Affairs office with a tray filled with Danish and orange juice caught sight of him, her teeth were bared for a scream that didn't come. She froze, panic in her eyes, and the only thing he could think to do as he walked past was either stick the Danish in her open mouth or ignore her.

A door opened in the Office of Public Liaison, and some smug young special assistant jauntily strode out into the hallway only to take one glance at O'Malley, reverse himself, and slam the door shut.

He entered the brightly lit outer office to the speechwriting shop and found Buffy saying over and over, "You'll have to call the press office," all the while she held tightly on to the phone and squeezed her already-narrow eyes even closer together. O'Malley whistled the refrain from

"Take This Job and Shove It," as he took off his poplin jacket and hung it on the rack.

That's when Buffy looked up from where she'd slammed the phone down and, midway through taking a breath of relief, jumped when she saw O'Malley. "Tom!" she shrieked, then smiled and patted down the papers on her desktop as if nothing were wrong.

"Do I still work here?" O'Malley was compelled to ask. He still had the illusion he was being charming when he asked it.

"Of course!" she said in high-pitched voice, not very reassuringly.

A door was flung open, and there was Will, good, kind Will, possessed of Christian virtue. "Will, hey," O'Malley said with a grin. The door slammed.

It was worse than he thought. Buffy was handing him a copy of *The Washington Post*, but very carefully, the way a lion tamer delivers the slabs of meat. "You haven't seen this?"

"No, Buff, I usually like to ease into the day with a polite reading of the papers . . ."

And then he saw his picture, a ghastly picture he'd been trying to get them to take down off the wall of the speechwriting office for months, a joke photo of him with his jaw slack, looking particularly dumb. He whirled. It wasn't on the wall. He looked down. There it was! On the front page of the *Post*. Someone who was not his friend had taken it down off the wall and given it to them.

He slumped in the nearest chair like any guest or job seeker and read the headline: "WHITE HOUSE AIDE TIED TO CONVICTED NARCOTICS DISTRIBUTOR." He glanced from that to the picture of him taken one night when they'd stayed up until 1:00 A.M. getting a speech just right. In this context he looked crazed with drugs, looked like he'd been at the receiving end of a crack pipe for about thirty-six hours straight. The photo had been taken with some cheap instant camera Will had in his desk drawer, and they'd taunted O'Malley about how dopey he looked in it. Now, hundreds of thousands of residents of the greater Washington metropolitan area were being reintroduced to O'Malley, and this is how he looked.

He skimmed as quickly as he could. White House speechwriter. Roommate at Amherst to convicted cocaine dealer, David Nicole, reported yesterday to have ties to fired Senate aide Kit Bowles. Kit now came in for a double drubbing, due to her relationship with both Nicole and O'Malley. She sounded more like Anita Pallenberg than Lou Andreas-Salome. He was denounced by a couple of senators, Partridge not among them, and a pair of anonymous White House aides. There was always a pair of anonymous White House aides when a reporter needed them. They wandered around the grounds together, like asses walking up the gangplank to Noah's Ark.

They mentioned his drunk-driving conviction. They clued in the readers to his right-wing spook stock, and seemed to make much of his having gone to St. Albans, as if that had anything to do with anything. They quoted a rather surprised-sounding Amherst College official who said, yes, O'Malley and Nicole were roommates together, but there was never any direct evidence that O'Malley was as involved in the drug trade as his expelled rommmate. The word "as" was left to dangle there, and as it was not a direct quote, there could be multiple meanings given over to it. The spokesman made it very clear that he found it distasteful to have to bring any of this up so many years after the fact. "Hear hear," he said to himself as he read it. It was the first time since Nicole was busted that he found himself agreeing with an Amherst official.

"Thomas," said Katherine Tierney with some surprise. "Jesus, you came in."

He stood up when she entered from the hallway. She appeared to be in something of a rush, or else it was just panic. "I guess I've got to learn to read the paper with my morning Wheaties, huh, Katherine."

"Good Lord, you hadn't seen it?"

"Nope."

"Nor the local news last night?"

Tight grin, shake of head.

"Harold Whitney was convinced you'd hightailed it. When we couldn't reach you . . ."

"You've spoken to old Hal?"

"Tom, there's a meeting of the National Security Council going on over this. I'm supposed to write a statement for the President, just in case." She was a possessed woman, nearly crazed in demeanor. Christ, he hated the notion of having let her down. He cringed, thinking she was going to hit him, and Katherine was big enough to pack a punch. "They're scrambling over at the press office to try and figure what to say at the morning briefing."

"Okay, so they've identified me as the snipe and the snipe hunt's over. It isn't exactly a national security issue."

"I take it you haven't seen the *Los Angeles Times*."

"My subscription must have lapsed while I was in Venezuela."

"Your subscription, or your judgment?"

His face got hot. How did she know? And actually, it was his judgment that came back to him in Venezuela.

"What's going on, Katherine?"

"Oh, Tom, how could you get yourself into this mess? It's so stupid."

"Do you mean, how could I have presumed I could work at the White House when over a decade ago a roommate of mine was involved in dealing drugs?"

"No, sweetie, how could you have gone to South America on a State visit and gotten involved in an attempt to smuggle back two and a half million dollars' worth of cocaine?"

"Oh, that." He held his ground. He didn't know what to say. He was beyond trying to pretend this hadn't happened, but he was going to hold his ground. "What?"

Buffy looked like she was ready for Madame Tussaud's. Her eyes were the size of spoons with at least four layers of shellac on them. She managed to pull the copy of the *Los Angeles Times* off the side table next to her computer and hand it to him. He didn't want to look.

At least there wasn't a photograph. But in a story—this one completely unrelated to the one in the *Post*—he caught his name within two seconds of skimming. He sat back down.

"STATE DEPARTMENT SUSPECTS SECURITY BREACH," was the innocuous enough headline. "Medellín Connection Cited in Caracas Drug Deal," was the less benign subhead. Within two paragraphs he found his name being cited on background as the suspected mule of a package with a street value, the source claimed, of two and a half million bucks. He knew how the DEA did the math on these things: they multiplied the weight of the coke by the price of each little chunk of crack that could be manufactured from it and then added a couple of zeros at the end. By so doing, they'd just converted him from a relatively small-time amateur to Scarface. All he could do was groan and sit down.

The story went on to outline in fine detail how, while the President was at a State dinner, several of his staff members were enjoying themselves inside the Caracas Hilton. While the streets were choked with protesters, someone managed to make it into the hotel to drop off a package of cocaine destined for a White House aide. It was clearly to have been handed off to a White House staffer because the person was confronted by a Secret Service agent on the twenty-third floor, where only White House aides were booked. Sources were saying that the room the courier went to was that of White House speechwriter Thomas O'Malley, and that a variety of agencies were investigating.

"I should have given Allison the copy of the speech when she wanted it," he said to himself.

Buffy was kind enough to get him his Uncle Jake's office number. They hid him in his office and refused to tell the numerous reporters who called in for him that he was even back from the trip to South America. There was a certain loopy justice to that. He might as well have vanished in the wilds of the Southern Hemisphere. It was a lot more romantic than what he feared was going to happen.

Max Pearlman, suspecting he might be there, barged into his office with the news that all had not gone well at the morning briefing. O'Malley didn't have the heart to tell him he already knew that from the speaker system that hooked up the offices in the Old Exec with the White House briefing room.

"Say it ain't so, Tom, buddy. I'm counting on you." He was genuinely worried, it showed on his face.

"On advice of my attorney, et cetera and so forth," O'Malley said from where he was slumped on the couch, an eye on CNN. He made the motion of the priest blessing the sacrament.

Max sat down on one of the chairs. "I hope they didn't see me coming over here."

"For your sake, I do too."

"Do you think people noticed we spent time together on the trip?"

"Hey, Max, if you came over here to see if I'll keep you out of trouble, the answer is maybe. If you came to tell me you'll help me get out of this bind, the answer to the first question has just been changed to yes."

Max seemed embarrassed. "Actually, I came over to see if you're okay."

"I don't know what the answer is to that one. I've been told, and CNN confirms, that Harold Whitney wants me in his office in twenty minutes."

"Lucky you. The word is that Whitney's going to fire you outright as a way of protecting the President."

"Where did you hear that?"

"From reporters, of course. You know how the system works, the press office always finds out what's going on in the White House from what reporters tell us. We're at their mercy. But you know that. McCurry did a nice job trying to throw things back in reporters' faces, didn't he?"

The White House press secretary had gamely responded to the L.A. *Times* piece that said sixteen kilos of cocaine were found after a chase within the Caracas Hilton by asserting that, since there were as many reporters staying in the hotel as there were White House aides, there was as much of a chance that the drugs were for the news media as for any of President Hardison's staffers.

"That oughta hold them till noon," O'Malley said.

"CNN's going with the noon briefing live, you know."

"You don't say."

"It's pretty bad, Tom. I was offered a hundred bucks for a photo of you. If they could get a duplicate of your White House pass, they say it's worth five hundred."

"If you want me to give you my pass for a half hour, Max, just say so."

"C'mon, Tom, I'm your friend."

"I know, I know, forgive me." He shook his head. He didn't want to get into a fight with Max. Max was probably one of about three White House staffers who were on his side, the other two being Katherine and one of the waiters in the mess.

"I don't know what's going to happen, Max, but if I need to, can I call you at the press office?"

"Sure, but you'll have to use a code name. How about Johnny Rotten?"

"Too subtle."

"Sid Vicious?"

"He's dead."

And so forth and so on through Rat Scabies, Stiv Bator, Tyrone Slothrop, and Crocus Behemoth, Axel Wintergrin, Dee Dee Ramone, Papa Cueball, and Buck Mulligan. Max was a true friend. When he left to go back to the zoo for what was shaping up as a first-rate feeding frenzy in the press corps, they had a code name, Lester Bangs, but O'Malley was no closer to having formulated a plan.

he White House lawn was a factory for news reports this day. Full-fledged producers had been sent over by their bureaus to do nothing but keep tripods company as the correspondents worked to break more of the story. Unfortunately for them, at this stage that meant mainly waiting for McCurry or other White House officials to show up and brief them. There was limited information to be had and the press apparatus at the White House and the Justice Department did not yet seem keen on making it available.

They would have to tread carefully on this one, the media would, sizing it up as they went along, determining whether this was merely a crisis for the new President—it was clearly at least that—or whether it warranted a full-scale, no-holds-barred assault on his authority. The very second it appeared to follow the Machiavellian precept of not merely wounding the king, but going all the way and killing him, they would be off and running. They would bay like a hungry kennel's worth of beagles, chasing the fox over the countryside. No matter how mangy it was, or how quickly it was run down, they would shake its carcass this way and that, until every tick and clump of hair was analyzed, every possible conclusion drawn. O'Malley, of course, was the fox.

But this first day of the story demanded caution. They were wary of seeming overly eager to go after the new President who, though off to a shaky start, still had numbers of honeymoon proportions. Until the pack received the validating word that this was an approved, official frenzy—they would have to wait and see the size of the headlines on the front pages of *The New York Times* and *The Washington Post*, which were at this stage the only papers whose authority truly mattered—they would simply cover it revelation by revelation, choking down their excitement about the story that just came out of nowhere, like a gift. Breaths held, they would see where it went. Already, however, there was every likelihood that it would dominate every talk show, give inspiration to every tired columnist, and force a televised explanation from the big guy himself: the President.

For it had all the ingredients: intrigue in a foreign land, the chance for new revelations, and presidential hypocrisy. As Hardison had made intolerance of drug abuse a moral issue, and pledged, both during the campaign and after it, to do more than his predecessors had to end its grip on the nation's vitals, the fact that one of his wordsmiths was a major-league narcotics importer was just too juicy for words. Though words, millions of them, would follow.

The L.A. *Times* was being accorded by their rivals the grudging respect they were due for breaking the story; *The Washington Post's* simultaneous revelation of O'Malley's past was treated as an interlocking piece to the puzzle, one more entry in the dossier that was being assembled. Not without the help of White House aides, a picture was emerging of O'Malley. He was being painted as the relatively quiet son of a notorious spook and a socialite underwriter of radical chic, a lawyer who clearly had been close to the President during his time on the road as a candidate, though the official White House spinmeisters were quick to add, not since then. Photo agencies were poring over stock footage of the President emerging from charter jets during the campaign with O'Malley at his side, the object being to locate the photo that showed them simultaneously smiling: the "happier times" photo.

The next level of reportage, the one that separated the big boys from the pikers, was the investigation of David Nicole, now identified as the last angle, which, along with Kit and O'Malley, made for a classic tabloid triangle. Court documents were being requested by both the *Los Angeles* and *New York Times*, and as a segment of the drama went back to Massachusetts, *The Boston Globe* was all over this aspect of the story like a cheap suit. For their travails, McTeague and Bronstein were given the go-ahead to track down Nicole, though they knew that their shot at the big time had been harmed by the L.A. *Times* having the dramatic revelation that escalated this from a story about White House personnel to a drama with the sweep of history. But they knew the drill. Follow the money. Keep digging. It was about time to show up on Mr. Nicole's doorstep while he was doing his laundry, cooking himself dinner, and settle in to ask him a few questions, politely.

A rumor swept the White House that the L.A. *Times* had a second scoop on the way, but the word from the press galleries in the Capitol was that all the *Times* was breaking was what the congressional leadership had been told at their briefing by Harold Whitney himself, and anyone could get that.

"What matters now," Dirk Sandstorm of CNN told their viewers live, "isn't so much further revelations. Sources tell CNN they don't expect any more until the FBI, DEA, and other relevant agencies have had a chance to investigate further. This seems to be a case of a young White

House aide who, already in trouble for his personal life, used his diplomatic immunity to engage in drug smuggling. What matters now is how this is handled by the White House, and especially, whether the White House is forthcoming or takes on the appearance of covering things up. CNN has learned that Thomas O'Malley, the White House speechwriter with a long history of being connected to narcotics traffickers, will be fired, that is, he will be fired shortly by Chief of Staff Harold Whitney. What the White House does from there—and when and by whom charges are brought —is the important question, in this, the first serious crisis of President William Hardison's administration."

And so it was that O'Malley learned he'd already been fired before Bill Tiswell came over to escort him—hustle him—from the Old Exec across West Executive Drive to the White House. Luckily for him, the media were being kept busy by their second briefing of the day. There would be no footage broadcast either that night or with numbing, tape-loop consistency by CNN, of Tom O'Malley, head held high, an evident spring to his step, crossing from the EOB for what could well have been his final trip to the White House as an employee of the President.

Washington surely was the only city where winos watched C-SPAN, or at least those winos did who were deliberative enough to plunk themselves down on a barstool in a joint that had a satellite dish. Harlan Bryce had come for a quick morning snort to the Parliamentarian, an establishment with the pretense of being something other than a hangout for drunks for whom happy hour began at 10:00 A.M., and ended up staying when the sergeant at arms, as the bartender was called, got bored with the floor debate and turned the channel to CNN.

The moment Harlan saw what the all-news channel was carrying, he ordered a round for the house. One guy, his head down on the table before him, came to as if smelling salts were being waved before his nose and signaled thanks to Harlan. The bar's only other customer took the shot placed before him without a flicker of recognition and continued talking to himself about legendary practitioners of obscure House rules.

Harlan hadn't heard about the *Los Angeles Times* article, so he was puzzled by the references to it he heard now on TV, but he sure had seen the *Post*. He was convinced he knew who some of the players from Friday night were now. That guy in the Alfa was probably David Nicole. The looker was quite likely this Kit Bowles character. He wasn't certain, but it was possible that the stuck-up broad was O'Malley's mother. Who the fat guy was was a mystery, though it suddenly came to him that the guy with gray hair and pink face was O'Malley's old man. He'd heard agents talking about Robert O'Malley with awe. How a real American had gotten such a hosebag for a son was beyond Harlan's ken.

But this new information connecting O'Malley to what happened in Venezuela was an out-and-out triumph for Harlan. His jaw about fell when he heard the first few questions about it asked at the live White House briefing.

The White House press briefing was a hoot; the spokesman up behind the podium was doing a pretty good job, Harlan had to admit, giving very little ground while asserting that the administration was doing everything it could to get to the bottom of this controversy, which the spokesman refused to characterize as anything more than a minor matter involving only the suspected speechwriter. Even when he said that, the spokesman refused to admit that they were certain the speechwriter had actually been involved in a plan to bring drugs in on Air Force One.

The moment that made Harlan order the snort that gave him a bit more of a buzz than was good for him at this time of day was when McCurry asserted the FBI was working vigorously on the case. "Damn well told," Harlan said out loud, and the sergeant at arms shot him a look.

"Floor vote, floor vote," shouted the drunk who had been talking to himself. He clearly missed C-SPAN.

Harlan pulled out a wad of ones and threw them down on the bar. He wandered out into bright noon-hour sunlight and was forced to put on his regulation sunglasses, circa 1963, as he walked down Eleventh Street over on E toward the FBI building, filled with thoughts of triumph about his superior sleuthing having led him to O'Malley days before anyone else.

He would have to be careful about the preppies coming and wrestling this away from him now. They didn't like him, didn't like his old-fashioned style, his adherence to the rules set by Mr. Hoover. These preppies were contemptuous of Mr. Hoover, they probably cheered every time some pinko civil libertarian wrote a new book calling the late director a queer.

By the time he got to the FBI building, working half a pack of Dentine in his jaw, he was in a foul mood. He also was drained from the walk and needed to sit down at his desk with an open file and pretend to read. He'd caught the dope addict! He rallied and put on a happy face. He entered the hideous building with its squat honeycomb architecture and its revivifying air conditioning, and grudgingly flashed his badge to the guard at the metal detector. He was about to walk through when Rigby, Harlan's boss and one of the very few decent guys in the new FBI, sidled up next to him.

"Har?"

"Hey, Riggo, man, we got him! I was right about that little fucking rat fink, wasn't I?"

But Rigby seemed in no mood to celebrate. Standing right there in the wide first-floor lobby of the FBI, he confronted Harlan.

"You've been drinking, Harlan."

"Nah." He waved his hand as if it was nothing to be alarmed about.

"You're drunk, Har."

"I resemble, er, resent that."

"Badge and gun, Har, you know the rules about drinking on the job. We need to get you help, which we're going to do."

"No, Rigby, I caught the little bastard."

"Doesn't matter, Har, your gun and your badge. Please."

"No way," he said, suddenly sober. So, Rigby had joined the preppies. He was out to steal the case away from him.

Before the white-uniformed guard could be called, before Rigby could do anything, Harlan whirled and broke into a run. He was out the door before his supervisor could do anything other than yell, "Harlan! Don't do this!" Then he was on the sidewalk. He didn't stop until he reached the safety of the Parliamentarian. Inside, out of breath, he reclaimed his barstool. Panting, he recovered his equilibrium. Bastard had tried to ruin his day.

"What'll you have?" the bartender asked. "Motion to recommit?"

"Yeah." That sounded good. Motion to recommit.

They weren't in a joking mood when he got to the Chief of Staff's office. The scene resembled a corporate board meeting with O'Malley the recalcitrant book-keeper being called in to justify the deficit. He thought, walking through the door, how much pleasure Bill Tiswell must be taking delivering him up.

Sitting around the table were Harold Whitney; the White House Counsel, Rumson Dickering; his deputy, Rod Gardener; and Willy Barnes. Katherine sat there with a sad smile on her face, meant to reassure him, he knew, though it made her otherwise handsome face look like a soufflé that hadn't settled right. While she meant to tell him there was at least one ally in the room, the strain on her was enormous, that much was clear. "Come in, come in," said Whitney magnanimously, as if O'Malley were merely a late-arriving guest. His shoulders back—he was determined to take this like a man—he took the chair that was clearly meant for him and swiftly pulled himself to the table. Tiswell took a seat in the Hepplewhite behind Harold Whitney, near enough so he could whisper questions to him like a staff aide at a committee hearing. It was clear he could barely keep from showing his pleasure at O'Malley's predicament.

"How are you, Tom?"

"Oh, just great, thanks. A touch of allergies this time of year, but other than that, fit as an old bass fiddle. You?"

"Tom, you've caused the President an enormous amount of grief today," Whitney began slowly, and his gravity was something to behold. He swayed with pity for the President, the Chief Executive's pain was his own. But for one thing. He actually seemed to take pleasure in this. The way he cocked one white eyebrow and stared at him was to conjure the moral authority of the establishment in a single glance. He could easily imagine Whitney dropping the black ball into the sack at a meeting of the Membership Committee. "I've spoken with the President about this . . . matter, and he's given me the authority to discuss this with you before it's dealt with by the Bureau and the Secret Service, both of which, you should know, are investigating."

O'Malley nodded, and took a quick look around the group. Willy

Barnes, nearest to him on his left, was cool, without a flicker of recognition. Rumson Dickering was gazing down his long pink nose at the middle distance, his bow tie askew, while he thrummed the desk with bony fingers. His deputy, Rod Gardener, was staring at O'Malley with the smugness of the righteous witnessing the sinful man get his due. There was a trace of powdered sugar on his chin and on his blue pin-striped suit. Katherine was visibly suffering on account of him, and it was that which made him lose ground, as if he were to suddenly slip backward on the treadmill. He had to look away. And found Harold Whitney staring at him.

"I'm sure by now you've seen the papers."

He nodded.

"What do you think about what you've read, Tom?" Whitney was too calm.

"I'd like to discuss that with the President."

"Oh?" There went that eyebrow again. "And not with us?"

"Well, Mr. Whitney, with all due respect, I didn't bust my butt for a year for the pleasure of working for you. I did it for the President. I'll be happy to talk with him about this at length." He stopped talking, not wanting to state explicitly that it would take the old Nazi bare bulb and the shot of sodium pentothal before he'd confess to this group.

"I see." Harold Whitney seemed prepared for this contingency, though Katherine looked disappointed in him, as if O'Malley were confirming his guilt. Willy Barnes began to rub his forehead as if, with enough concentration, he could divine a way around this impasse.

"Well, you don't leave us much choice," Whitney said deliberately, with a glance over at Rumson Dickering, who nodded.

"This isn't the time to ask for a raise, huh?"

"No, Tom, it's not. The President has authorized me to tell you you're suspended, without pay, until further notice. You could have made this easier on yourself," he said with an inconclusive wave of his hand.

Suspended. Whitney had never looked more like the headmaster. But at least O'Malley hadn't lied. And he wasn't going to.

S omeone, and he would have liked to know who, must have tipped off reporters that he was departing the White House that very minute. They couldn't have been given very much warning. He barely had taken the time to pick up his satchel, remove a couple of personal effects from his desk, and manfully shake hands with the sobbing Buffy before he slipped down the stairs and was out on Seventeenth Street.

But then there they were coming around the corner from Pennsylvania Avenue, and he'd never seen such a thing. A herd of cameramen, jostling for space, glistening with sweat, elbowing their fellows, came thundering toward him with their sound men shaking it to bring up the rear. Within a matter of seconds he was surrounded. It took a minute of pandemonium in which he was no longer in control of his movements, no longer in control of anything, a prisoner of this sweating mob, a long chaotic minute before any of them had the presence of mind to ask him a question.

When the question came it was from a small woman who was squeezed in between two massive cameramen, her glasses knocked askew, her notebook in a hand held out like the last sign of someone about to go under for the third time. "Did you conspire to smuggle cocaine on Air Force One?" Having strained to get this question out, she disappeared as more cameramen piled on the rear and the ones up front now closed in to get his answer. He glanced up and the sky was dark with what looked like incoming missiles but in fact were only fuzzy boom mikes being lofted over the crowd.

"I am not going to answer any questions at this time. Really, I'd like to," he said with a pleasant, timid smile, clearing his throat as if for a speech, "but this isn't the time."

"Were you just fired?" Jack Carthage of NBC asked. How he'd suddenly been transported to the front was a mystery. O'Malley was drawn to him as the one person he knew in this gang of strangers, and even slightly flattered at his attention.

"Suspended, actually."

"Have you talked to the President about this?" Jack had now been handed a microphone and he had it right underneath O'Malley's chin, as if this were his one-on-one and the rest were interlopers who'd cut in on his interview.

"I'm not going to say any more. Please. I need to go."

But O'Malley wasn't going anywhere, not now, not when there were dozens of reporters who, having rushed from the pressroom, were trying to wade through the cameramen to get their own piece of him. There were still photographers lifting their cameras into the air and over the heads of the mob to take his picture, their auto-rewinds sounding like an infestation of strange cicadas. He was suddenly aware that he was no longer standing on the concrete sidewalk, he was being moved away from the White House by this mob of reporters and cameramen, being levitated without any control toward the street. He was sweating heavily. He looked into a bouquet of lenses.

Questions were being shouted to him and he began to panic. He took the cameras that were directly in front of him by their lenses and began to push them back. The cameramen stood their ground at first, but as his hand was covering their view and the cameras were being pushed into their eye sockets, they gradually relinquished their stance and began to move back, taking the crowd with them.

Once they'd moved back, he began to push the other cameras away from him, first to his left, next to his right, until he had a semicircle of at least two feet of space. "Look," he shouted, "I'll make a statement later. I want to tell my side of this. I really do! But I'm going to leave now! Okay?"

Fine with them. They'd just tag along.

The reporters and crews allowed him the space to begin to march up Seventeenth Street in the vast Third Empire penumbra of the Old Exec, the cameramen walking backward and occasionally breaking to turn around and rush up the street only to swivel and begin to film him again, the reporters falling into step with him to keep up their questions. "Who else is in on this? Did the President know? Why'd you do it?" He grimaced and ignored them. "How do you feel?"

"How do you expect?" he growled back.

The rat-faced guy who asked him that one was undaunted. "Would you characterize this as the worst day of your life?"

"Would you like a fat lip?"

They were at the corner of Seventeenth and Pennsylvania and as the circle of media moved into the avenue, cars swerved, honked, slowed down, and then there were police moving into the middle and, miraculously, giving him room. He stood for a moment trying to hail a taxi, but there was no way one was going to head toward 1600 Pennsylvania Avenue with this swirling mass blocking access. Rather than help him get away from this movable circus, the D.C. cops instead simply redirected traffic until they'd moved en masse across the street.

And so he began to walk, to stride as best he could, up Seventeenth Street, past the New Exec, past the entrance to the Metro on Eye Street, past Farragut Park. And the whole way, he was surrounded by camera and sound crews. They picked up pairs of the curious for a block or so, interested in seeing what was up. From the windows of Duke Zeibert's, the late lunch restaurant crowd looked down to see if Gorbachev, who had campaigned here once, had come back. Had he looked up, he would have seen the Mayor with a particularly plaintive, guilty look on his otherwise serene demeanor.

After a while the reporters dropped out. Not the camera crews. They marched together, O'Malley and them. He was merely the center of a storm that moved through Washington, past shoppers and people on their way back from lunch, up Connecticut Avenue and up the hill toward his home. He couldn't help it. He brought the invaders right up to his doorstep, and moments later, when he looked out the window, breathing heavily, his shirt torn and his tie in tatters, he found them bivouacked outside like an army getting set for winter. No matter what happened, until this thing was resolved, the media would be on his doorstep.

it answered on the first ring, a hysterical edge to her voice. "What's the matter?" he asked.

"Thank God it's you. I thought you were that FBI agent again."

"What FBI agent?"

"This guy was downstairs in the vestibule asking to come up. He said he had to 'debrief' me on you, only he was clearly drunk. He slurred his words and . . ."

"And what?"

"He asked me if I wanted to go to Vegas with him."

O'Malley looked up from where he sat by the window. Below him, the stakeout crew of fifteen or so representatives of the news media were eating lunch from the nearby deli. They looked like construction workers on break.

"I hope you said no to him."

"Don't worry, Tom!"

Easy for her to say.

rom Jake Ingram's contacts in the Justice Department, he learned they were some time away from being able to bring an indictment. Indict for what? Even though the person who'd leaked the news about the investigation to the L.A. *Times* had stated unequivocally that they knew the drugs found in the Caracas Hilton were meant for O'Malley, from a legal standpoint they knew no such thing. This whole mess could linger for weeks without resolution, and in the meantime O'Malley would be tried in the press. He hoped Tom would not talk to any reporters, that in fact he would stay as far away from them as possible.

The phone on his vast Biedermeier desk buzzed once, and Miss Kinchlow's voice could be heard over the intercom. "It's Mr. O'Malley."

"Senior or junior?"

"The previously indicted."

"Previously indicated?"

"You heard me."

It was his brother-in-law. "Hello, Bob. You calling to find out what I know?"

"No, I'm calling to tell you Tom's been suspended without pay, and that he has four film crews and a gaggle of ink-stained wretches camped out on his doorstep."

"He didn't say anything to them, did he?"

"He says not."

"Good, because the way they'll be able to put their case together is if he's stupid enough to talk to the media. An assistant A.G. who I once helped get a clerkship tells me the U.S. Attorney can't indict yet for lack of evidence."

"That's wonderful news."

"Unless Thomas is tried in the news media. If he is, and he doesn't handle himself, he could be worse off than with an indictment."

"Don't worry, Tom's too smart to make mistakes."

"Bob, I hate to poor-mouth my own nephew, but if he's capable of the whopper he's already committed, he's capable of another one at any moment. We're not talking about a percentage player here."

"No, don't worry, he told me he's not going to talk to the media."

"You know, I hope so. But if you'd asked, he probably wouldn't have told you he was going to get tagged with bringing in two and a half million dollars' worth of cocaine, either."

ightline' wants me?" O'Malley was asking Max Pearlman with amazement. He was flattered. Then he reminded himself of the circumstances.

"They're not certain if they're going to do a segment on it tonight because they've already set up a four-way debate between Henry Kissinger, Cardinal O'Connor, Lyndon LaRouche, and the Reverend Ian Paisley on the role of religion and the drug trade."

He waited a second for that to sink in.

"Anyway, my guest-grabber buddy just called me to get your phone number. I gave it to her, I hope you don't mind."

"I'm not certain," he mused. It had been a long afternoon, and he'd spent it pacing his small apartment, talking on the phone, and every few minutes looking out the window to see if the television guards had left yet. They hadn't.

At 2:00 P.M. he'd snuck down the stairwell and gently swung open the back door from the basement to the alley and found that two camera crews were leaning against the Dumpster, their equipment laid like weapons atop a station wagon that was parked illegally. They were just standing around, being paid union scale to hang out in a back alley in case O'Malley made a run for it. Footage of him hightailing it down a garbage-strewn back alley in Adams Morgan would be irresistible for network producers. He closed the door and climbed back upstairs, informing Kit by phone that he was a prisoner. It didn't make sense for him to come over to her place because it would simply bring the army to her doorstep. For her to come over here would just add another ring to the circus.

Now he sat at his table and heard Max's report on the activities of the day. "I don't know whose piece is going to be worse tonight, Wyatt Phillips or Jack Carthage, but both of their producers have been scurrying around like crazy. Someone in Whitney's office put out the word that you refused to answer any questions when they talked to you and that they suspended you without pay because of it."

"That part's mostly true."

"It doesn't look great, Tom."

"Go on."

"Everybody wants Whitney for the morning shows, but we're not going to do anything. Bad news is I think Senator Bligh is, and who knows what he's going to say. Oh, there was a wire story out of Denver that the *Casper Star-Tribune* says Tony Partridge was a major-league doper when he went to school in Colorado Springs, so there's a certain poetic justice at work."

"I have to admit that makes me feel a little better," he said, and it did. Anything they did to the twerp was much deserved.

"For now, you're very hot. You could go on with any of the anchors live tonight, if you wanted to."

"I don't, but thanks anyway! You have any suggestions how I could get these guys outside to leave?"

"No, I'd make good my escape if I were you."

"Can't. Can't get out of here. They've got the place surrounded." He knew he sounded vaguely like Mad Dog Coll.

"I'll keep you posted, then. What do you want me to tell ABC about 'Nightline' tomorrow night?"

"Tell them I'll consider it, but I doubt I'll do it. Advice of my attorney and all that."

With that he hung up the phone. There seemed no place he could go without an attendant media battalion. There was nothing further he could do. He was too nervous to read. He actually contemplated taking up the smoking of cigarettes, an activity he'd neglected for about fifteen years. Since there weren't any cigarettes in the house, the only way he could take them up would be to wander past that little entourage he'd collected outside his front stoop, and that was out of the question. He could see the caption to the *New York Post*'s front-page photo: "WH DRUG AIDE BUYS SMOKES." There wasn't any doubt in his mind that right now it would be a front-page photo. So he went and lay down on his bed, and within moments, he was in a sleep so deep it was as if he were drugged. This would forever complicate any theories he had about the relationship between a clear conscience and sleep.

K it received word about what happened to her former boss when she called in to the office to ask them to prepare her severance check. She bantered with Cindy, the receptionist, for a matter of moments before, surprisingly, Wilbur Todd got on the line.

"I owe you an apology."

"And three weeks' worth of pay, Wilbur."

"I'll see that you get it. Have you heard?" Wilbur sounded friendlier than he ever had when she'd been working there, than he had just this past Friday when she'd left work to meet O'Malley and go see his father. She'd thought O'Malley was the only one who could be in trouble by Monday. She'd no idea she'd be blindsided because of whom she'd gone out with in college, no idea that such a thing could end up on the front page of the paper.

"About which?" There was so much to have heard about.

"Tony was right. About the dangers of throwing accusations around."

"Don't I know it."

"No, I'm talking about Partridge. The *Casper Star-Tribune* went after him today, got him, too, with about eighteen anonymous sources steered their direction by the Governor, all of them claiming to have done drugs with our Senator."

"Jeez."

"What's this mescaline stuff?"

"It's a hallucinogen. You don't—"

"Yep, that too."

"Oh, boy."

"Feller was right when he told us to stay away from it. Now he's called Jetta and Humperdink out there to help him, though I told him I thought, under the circumstances and all, they'd be the last ones to give him advice."

"God, Wilbur."

"Well, he's a goner. We should have let him follow his instincts."

"Let Partridge be Partridge."

"He's a weird duck, but he could have turned into a right good senator. I am truly sorry about what happened to you. And I suppose, to your boyfriend. I didn't know."

"I appreciate it." She found herself, much to her surprise, actually liking him.

"These are crazy times, Kit."

He was right about that one.

t was still light out, but the afternoon was drawing to a close when he woke up with a momentary inability to locate himself or the circumstances he was in. First things first, he put the phone back on the hook. It rang immediately, and groggily he picked up the receiver. It was Hal, his court-ordered counselor.

"There you are. I've been trying to reach you all afternoon. I trust your trip to South America was a good one. Now that you're back, though, I'm going to have to report in to the court if you aren't at counseling tonight, Tom."

He didn't want to upset Hal, he was a nice guy, but the absurdity of his calling today, of all days, was just too much. Hal was probably the only person in D.C. who hadn't heard.

"Hey, quit laughing, Tom," Hal said, sounding a little hurt. "You don't seem to realize the trouble you could get in if you don't do as the court instructs. This could mean your driver's license for three more months!"

He couldn't even stop laughing long enough to apologize. Oh dear, he said to himself moments after Hal got off the phone and the tears that rolled down his cheek were a simple reminder of how dry his mouth was. Is this what it's like to lose it?

icole was enough of a professional to worry, first and foremost, about how the FBI agents ruined his restaurant's ambience. They clearly were FBI agents, no question about that. He knew it not so much because of their cheap suits, their undemonstrative demeanors, but because no one, unless they were ordered to stay there, would have uncomplainingly put up with what they were subjected to.

First, when Yolanda called upstairs and said there were some suspicious-looking characters waiting for a table, he asked her to describe them. If she described the Salami Brothers, he was going to pack the PPK and go down to ask politely what they wanted. He didn't think a shoot-out in his restaurant was John Santangelo's style, but you never knew. The description of the two understated, decidedly un-hip gentlemen for whom a variety of polyesters had died that they might wear the suits they had on could only mean Feds, though, and these were difficult to just throw out.

So he asked her to stall them at the bar, which she did, which she actually had to do, given how unusually crowded the place was for a Monday. She stalled them for an hour during which they drank tap water and showed no visible signs of pique. They just looked around as unthreateningly as could be, occasionally burdening the bartender with requests for refills. Eventually he let her seat them, at the worst table in the house, which he'd already cordoned off from the rest of the room with a hastily improvised line of tall plants. Cactuses were snatched from in front of ponytailed cognoscenti too hip even to acknowledge the ambience ripped from their midst, though everyone else in the room must have thought it a little curious that they made something on the order of the Bamboo Curtain surrounding the table behind which the Feds eventually were stashed.

There would be Feds, and almost as bad, reporters, all over the lot now. He'd seen the news and been amazed once again at just what O'Malley had wrought. His epic screwup shouldn't still shock him, but it did. What could he have been thinking of to involve that loser? He'd spun the dial and found O'Malley was the leadoff news story on all the networks. Amazing.

Dan Rather had been so serious Nicole thought a war had started or something. He was ready to look at the sky and see if the jets were flying. "Drug smuggling, drug dealing, on the mean streets of Washington. The address of the drug dealer that came to light today? Sixteen hundred Pennsylvania Avenue. The White House. Wyatt Phillips has the report."

And then there was footage of the briefing room at the White House with a little photo of the headlines from the *Los Angeles Times* and *The Washington Post* and the press secretary was intoning how seriously the President took these charges. It seemed every federal agency short of the TVA was investigating. He about fell out of his chair when he heard the correspondent describe the conspiracy. "Federal authorities confirmed on background they were investigating the charges first raised in the *Los Angeles Times* that White House speechwriter Thomas O'Malley entered into a conspiracy with a convicted cocaine trafficker to import narcotics from Venezuela during the President's trip there last week. Analysts said today, as if the President didn't have enough problems stemming from his performance in South America, now he has to contend with his being used by his own staff to bring in the very drugs he promised to stamp out. Wyatt Phillips, CBS News, the White House."

"Uh, Wyatt," Rather cut in. "President Hardison isn't the first president to declare a war on drugs. But he is the first one to have a drug dealer identified in the White House. How could this have happened?"

"Well, Dan, that's the question. There are already those saying that the President's lax management style, his absence of a vision, is what's really to blame here. That, and his refusal to spend more money on drug education and treatment programs. Dan?"

"Wyatt Phillips. Now," said Rather, "the Hardison Administration struggles to contend with the political fallout from the news of the speechwriter who wrote his own ticket on the Cocaine Express. We start with Rita Braver." The network immediately cut to their Justice Department correspondent, and from there to congressional reaction. Nicole sat dumbfounded. No one had told him about the *Los Angeles Times*. Certainly not John Santangelo, who had called to remonstrate and otherwise press the advantage that came from *The Washington Post* article this morning, the second front-page article in two days in which

Nicole had figured. One of the *Post* reporters who wrote that story had called today, but he'd instructed the bartender to tell him he wasn't expected in. There's been a run of them, reporters both large and small, calling a little later in the afternoon, but he hadn't spoken to any of them. He'd assumed all the attention stemmed from the two pieces in the *Post*. He didn't know there was more.

He sent Luis for the L.A. *Times*. He rummaged in the rolltop and finding what he was looking for, chopped a rock he'd been saving for good times and snorted it. For clarity. With the lift came a fresh surge of anxiety, however. "Hold my calls," he instructed the staff downstairs over the intercom. More chopping, another fat line, and he began to feel a little better. And then he knew what he had to do, first and foremost.

His reaction was confirmed when he watched Brokaw zero in on the same theme as CBS. "President Hardison came to office with a promise to wipe out the scourge of drugs," the anchor said. "Turns out someone who wrote that very speech for him wasn't taking him very seriously. NBC's Jack Carthage reports."

Carthage ran through what was largely the same drill as his CBS competitor, only when his piece was over, he engaged in some obviously prearranged cross-talk with his anchor. "Jack," Brokaw wanted to know, "why hasn't there been an arrest in this case yet?"

"Tom, because while White House sources insist they know who was responsible for the drugs that were found, they say the Justice Department doesn't yet have sufficient evidence to act. It may be days before they're able to convince a federal grand jury to do so."

With that Brokaw gave America a shake of the head that let the nation know, from sea to shining sea, that he, too, couldn't figure it, and from there went to Andrea Mitchell's rather testy piece on congressional reaction.

Nicole turned off the television and sat there, his armpits damp. That's about when the buzzer had sounded and Yolanda had told him about the suspicious characters. The Feds. He knew Feds. They'd almost sent him to a federal prison. Would have if he hadn't been able to convince a judge that sending him to a federal penitentiary was a terrible waste.

This was very bad. He wasn't a politician, but he had the sense that times had changed rather dramatically since he'd been able to talk his way out of a jail cell. He sensed that if O'Malley was going down, he was going down too. And it was a question of whether the Feds got to him before Santangelo's buddies did. He wished Tina, that ungrateful bitch, were here with him. She'd know what to do. That she'd known what to do was proved by her absence. He hadn't meant to break into the rock, but this was an emergency and he set to chopping. By then, he didn't need Tina to tell him what to do. He had it all planned. That goddamn O'Malley.

'Malley cradled the phone and rocked on the bed. "I wish I could see you."

"So do I!"

"But we can't."

"Right."

"Maybe I'll call you before I go to bed."

"That would be nice."

And then they whispered their statements of devotion as if they were evening prayers, and then he was alone in his cruddy little apartment listening to a slightly rowdy, beer-drinking group of cameramen and producers outside who rapidly were becoming part of the neighborhood, adding to its economy, subtracting from its ecosystem. He would have called the police on them, if the circumstances were a little different, if there was any chance they would have come.

The phone began ringing and he did his level best to ignore it, having worked out a code with his father and with Kit, with Max and with Uncle Jake, who were the only people he was even remotely interested in talking to. He was to answer the phone only if it rang once, stopped, and then rang again. This became a necessity on the order of life and death after the evening news programs had started yet a new round of reporters calling him here—he was listed, which meant defenseless—and he grew tired of saying, "I'm not talking, fuck off," before hanging up. He could still barely believe it, but Allison Hardy of the L.A. *Times* had called as if there were nothing out of the ordinary going on, as if she just wanted to flirt. He found her chutzpah gold-medal material, but he didn't reward her with an interview.

So, feeling more than a little wired, but remembering he hadn't eaten lunch, he went rummaging in his freezer, which wasn't something he would have recommended to the faint of heart. He briefly considered calling for a pizza, but that would open too many possibilities, that would cause him to open his door, and he believed the two things that would get him through the night were his police lock, and his refusal to pick up the phone without the proper cryptographic stimuli.

It was when the frozen lasagna was being brought back to life and he sat numbly before the television set, his eyes open but not really following this sitcom about a guy from outer space living with a transvestite who's adopted a precocious eight-year-old, that suddenly there was a knock on the door. He froze, pinned to his position on his bed. Thankfully, there was an eye-hole in the door, and so he hopped adroitly on his sneakers across the three feet to the door and peered into the hallway. It was his father, standing there nervously, clutching a bag that could only contain a bottle of booze.

"Dad, what a surprise." He stood in the doorway looking at his father standing there in an oxford shirt and chinos like the happy suburbanite he might have been had Fate not slipped the old joker or two into his hand.

"Fair Kit told me you were blue. Are you going to invite me in?"

He closed the door behind him and bolted the police lock and waited for the ritual lines about the room not being big enough to swing a cat in and other such gems of prep-school visitation, only he'd gone to day school and the only time his father had visited him at Amherst was when he and Jake flew into Bradley Field in Hartford and drove up with Jake prepared to litigate, if that's what it took to get O'Malley his diploma. His father, who had never visited him here, wasted no time. He went to the tiny kitchen area, where he unwrapped the bottle of Johnny Walker Black and tried the right cabinet the first time out, pulling down two glasses.

"Wait, I'll have a beer, Dad," O'Malley said, embarrassed about his apartment.

His father shrugged, as if he would have expected no better. He turned, sniffed, and not without some pleasure. "What's that?"

"Frozen lasagna."

"My."

"What, are you hungry?"

His father smiled and looked boyish, toasting him with the glass of scotch he'd poured.

"I'll split it with you, then." He walked over and opened the oven door long enough to get blasted with heat that could have melted his forelock and catch a glimpse of the baking, vaguely orange mess in the tin, which was nearly done. "Please, sit," he said, motioning him to a chair at what passed as the dining-room table, an old wooden job rescued from one of the neighborhood's antique stores for an extortionate price. "I had the funniest call," he said, grabbing a beer from the refrigerator and coming over to where his father now sat, a little uneasily, on the edge of his chair.

"Hal, you remember Hal, called to tell me that if I didn't go to counseling tonight, I'd be in real trouble." They laughed, and O'Malley had to shake his head. "Reee-al trouble." He sat down next to his old man, his body turned sidesaddle in the chair.

"To Hal," his father said, taking a sip. This was not his first sip of the evening.

"I wonder if I could have sent you in my place," O'Malley said with more than a twinge of seriousness.

"You could have, but if I'd been caught forging your name to whatever slip that was you had to sign when I was there, you might really be in reee-al trouble."

The sound of his father's giggle was a reminder of a time when he'd thought him invulnerable, absolutely indestructible. His so obvious frailty, despite the booze gut that hung suspended over his belt, was less the result of O'Malley's growing up and thus diminishing the size differential between them, and more the result of a genuine pathology of destruction, egged along by the circumstances of his career setbacks, the changed rules and accusations that must have been far more bewildering to the old man than even they were to his son, and his ongoing jolts that were attendant to the melodrama of his marriage to O'Malley's mother. This was not to mention the steady erosion of every organ, especially the brain, that resulted from such rhythmic and successive washing down by the amber liquid his father sloshed unceremoniously in O'Malley's cheap glass. His father was a wreck, and it was glorious to see him.

"I really am in trouble," he said to the old man, as if it were the first time he realized it.

"Remind me never again to discount what you're saying when you tell me you've got problems."

"No," O'Malley said, his eyes on the middle distance, as if seeing his way clear to a better time. "If I get out of this . . ."

"You'll reform. Right. I've said it a hundred times. And you probably will. Every time I promised myself that if I could only get out of Mombasa, or the Intelligence Committee's latest obsession, I would retire to the life of an adjunct professorship at Georgetown, my life ordered, but for the coeds. And it never happens."

The yellow light from O'Malley's floor lamp made his father look old, and the shadows from the television set, the street light outside where the camera crews camped out, jumped on the wall behind his father in an almost eerie facsimile of what home life could be like.

"It's no problem for me to say I'm not going to do something like this again, because it's just unbelievable that I did it at all. I've spent so much of my life trying to slip and slide out of trouble, that when Nicole threatened to expose me, I signed on to something truly immoral, just as a way of getting out of it. I should have made a stand, right then, Dad. I'm so sorry I didn't. If I hadn't been arrested for drunk driving, the night before my very first day in the White House . . ."

"I'm sure you can pull yourself along the rope backwards and undo your actions step by step . . ."

"If only I could."

"But the fact remains, Thomas, that this isn't the end. The end is death, and it may be hard to persuade you, but it's far, far worse." His father, whose body clearly could not much longer sustain the pace of drinking it had had to put up with for the last forty years—you could see it in the colors: his skin, his eyes, how lifelessly gray his hair had become—clearly was on a subject which he had been thinking about of late. "I'm not going to tell you that you're going to look back on this and laugh, because I doubt you'll ever do that, but the fact remains that you'll survive this, having paid a hell of a price, and you'll go on. You will go on."

There was nothing he could say. He knew his father meant this, having lost more than his job at the CIA. He'd lost his justification for his actions, the approval of his country for a life spent engaged in ambiguity. And he'd done so under the white-light censure of network news and front-page pictures in the elite newspapers, something O'Malley knew was his fate over the next few days at the very least, because these things had a predictable progression to them, and he'd already begun to run the traps, whether he liked it or not. Whereas O'Malley would be exposed for being, at best, a fool, his father had been exposed in a way that provoked arguments about different definitions of patriotism. He had his defenders and his detractors, he was seen by some as an archetypal villain of American imperialism and by others as a hero of John Wayne vintage. It was difficult for O'Malley either to find anything heroic in what he himself had done—quite the opposite—or to imagine there was anyone who would defend him.

"Jake tells me he's now convinced the government might not be able to indict unless they're able to find someone in Venezuela who would testify to having engaged in a conspiracy with you."

"Yeah, he told me that too. It's good news, of course, but whether or not I'm arrested, I'm just hanging out there. My little shadows are drinking beer outside." Just then, the group of reporters and camera crews could be heard singing camp songs in boozy harmony.

"You just have to make certain you don't give them anything to make it easy on them."

"But I can't stand the idea that I'm fired from my job and just waiting for them to put a case together."

His father arched an eyebrow at that. "Which would you prefer, hanging out here, walking the streets as a free man, albeit with a cloud over you, or hanging out in a prison cell for twenty or so years?"

"That's a no-brainer."

"There you go, then. It scares me to look at you and think you might go all confessional on us out of a misplaced urge for resolution. Trust me, it's better to have to explain why you won't tell them what you did than have to explain what you actually did."

Admit nothing, deny everything. He'd thought he'd gotten the ethos from his peers through osmosis; in reality, it had been his father's guiding principle of deception, and he wondered if this was universal, or something peculiar to the particular line he came out of, the culture of boarding schools begetting, in his father's case, Skull and Bones, the OSS, the CIA; the sense of secretiveness that came from a notion of privilege, that there were things they could get away with, even if they weren't for everyone, even if they would flunk some Kantian test of universality.

To an extent, when he'd used drugs, that's the way he'd thought. Even long ago, even when he'd aided and abetted Nicole in his trade, he'd been convinced that drugs were bad for most of the people who tapped on their door at 2:00 A.M., people who nonetheless were never turned away. But drugs were bad for society at large, you know, for morons, they weren't bad for him, and for his crowd. Tawnee's slow burial under a mound of cocaine, her disappearance at David Nicole's hand, had removed that snotty conceit, for if someone as elect as she was could be dragged under, then none of them were safe and their notion of protectedness was a typically solipsistic delusion of America's educated class in the Pepsi Generation.

"I don't feel the need for confession, Dad, but I want this behind me."

"Tom, trust me. You have to suppress your urge to hasten that along," he said, getting up to pour himself another scotch. He stood with his back to the room and peered for a moment into the oven. "Your confessional urge, on the one hand, proves you're your mother's son. If she could still purchase indulgences, she'd put them on her charge card. On the other hand, that's so goddamned typical of your generation. Having demanded pleasure, now you want to rush the absolution, too. You think purgatory's the thirty-second version of a sixty-second hell." His father stood unsteadily. There was no one else, in O'Malley's lonely life, who so looked as if he belonged there, or who gave him such pleasure with just the single, exceptionally rare instance of undivided attention.

McTeague and Bronstein were walking down the creepy back alley behind Globe when, utterly to their surprise, they saw David Nicole slip out the back door and hop into an Italian convertible. All they'd been doing was parking illegally on their way to drop in on him and then suddenly they were rushing back to the car and racing through Adams Morgan alleys, playing cops and robbers.

"He's getting away," said Cale as the little sports car zipped around a parked U-Haul on Eighteenth Street. When they finally got by it, Bronstein spotted Nicole on R Street waiting for a light. They pulled up two cars behind him and stayed on his tail as he crossed Connecticut Avenue and turned left on Florida at the light by Restaurant Nora, where Steve was thinking of taking Mandy for dinner and trying to coax her back into his arms.

They followed him through the sharp turn from Florida to Q, and bumped over the Dumbarton Bridge with Cale yelling. They had trouble keeping up as he suddenly turned down on Twenty-ninth, past townhouses and mansions, and over onto N. When he turned up Thirtieth and pulled over to back into a tiny parking space, the nose of the Toyota almost crunched the Alfa's tail. Fortunately, Nicole seemed to pay no attention to them other than to wave them around on the narrow street. They shot up the hill as if headed to Dumbarton Oaks, but when Steve saw in his rearview that Nicole was walking around the corner back onto N Street, they quickly pulled over and were out the door.

They had taken a leap from ordinary Metro staff reporting to the cloak and dagger of the big time. They weren't on National yet, but this sure was fun. Bronstein was almost giddy as they hopped down the street and then paused behind a tree, like bird dogs on point. McTeague turned to Bronstein. "Are you absolutely sure that guy's David Nicole?"

"Absolutely sure?"

"Yeah."

"No, I'm not absolutely sure. I think it is. He looks like the guy in those yearbook pictures from Amherst and St. Albans."

McTeague just shook his head. They went in search of him anyway.

ventually, when they'd polished off the baked lasagna, O'Malley lay on his bed with his back against the wall as the old man leaned back in his chair. His father's eyes were scorched, but they kept their sparkle, and he kept talking. Thought of chastising him for continuing to sip poison was the last thing on O'Malley's mind. They were coconspirators in an evening's revelation, even if one of them was like a tired old tugboat in whose boiler room the pipes and fittings could come apart in the next big storm. The pleasure of the evening was an incidental by-product of the trouble he was in.

"Are you really helping out Guatemalan guerrillas?"

"No, I thought I told you your mother got that garbled. I was just offering a little advice, is all, on contract, to some of my old colleagues. A banking network I set up twenty years ago to get money into the anti-communist parties throughout the region was, we found out, being used now to get money out. I was asked to help shut it down."

"You still do stuff like that?"

"No, not really, I'm too controversial for them to use. But I still have some institutional memory that they occasionally find the need to tap. And I still comply with my country's requests, even though there wasn't a soul, anywhere in the intelligence community, who came to my defense when it counted. I suspect you're about to discover who your friends are, too."

"I don't have any expectations about people coming to my defense. The only thing that bothers me is not being able to tell my side directly to Bill Hardison. You'd think after the amount of time I spent with him during the campaign, I'd at least get a chance to tell him my side. We were friends."

His father snorted at that, his entire body moving. "First of all," he said with a smile, "there are probably fifteen people determined that under no circumstances should the President have any contact with you. Your friendship with him is going to be discounted to the point where any photos they have of you together are going to mysteriously disappear from the White House photo library. I know how it's done. You've just become the Washington equivalent of a non-person, and there's no way you'll ever have contact with the President again. If this works true to form, the only way you'll ever see the Oval Office again is if you wait in line with the rest of the tourists. You don't exist. I've seen how it works."

"I just thought maybe I'd have a chance to apologize. I thought I'd get to tell him my side of things. I owe him that. He owes me that."

"Wrong." His father reached for the bottle, which he'd taken over to the table. "Maybe you'll have a chance to tell your side in court, if it comes to that, and if Jake decides it's in your interest to take the stand. The very best you can hope for short of that is that someone can get the President's attention and tell him the truth without the entire White House guard shooting them on sight. Not that the President should be all that goddamned comforted by the truth in this one, Tom." His father poured himself another shot. He was putting quite a dent in the bottle. "Tom?"

But O'Malley was staring. An idea had begun to germinate.

I t was when they saw the person they were almost certain was David Nicole casing the brick house on N Street that McTeague sent Bronstein to go fetch his car. This allowed them to wait in it, instead of having to hide behind trees and front stoops, looking as suspicious as Nicole did.

Nicole had walked by the building before pivoting and retracing his steps to its entrance, and they had immediately sat down on the front stoop of a lovely townhouse as if they were out to watch the midnight parade. Though Nicole craned his neck to see if anyone was watching, the street was quiet and he didn't spot them. He walked to the darkened front window of the house and pressed his face to the glass. The two reporters peered over the railing that bisected the stoop, only to have Nicole look over his shoulder once again to make certain there wasn't anyone watching. They ducked. He walked down the alleyway beside the house and it was then that McTeague sent Bronstein for the car.

Steve parked in front of a hydrant and McTeague ran across the street on tiptoes to jump inside. They slunk as far down in their seats as possible without saying a word. They could see down the alleyway Nicole had entered, but it was dark, and there was no sign of him, though the sound of dogs barking indoors someplace indicated he was probably close to the house. What the hell? They stayed glued to their seats, just watching as cars went by every few moments, barely stopping at the corner before heading up toward Dumbarton Oaks, or across on N. Even on a Monday, it would be crowded at this time of night with students, young congressional aides, and the class of lobbyists and lawyers who extended their working hours to include expense-account entertaining.

"You think he's trying to break in?"

"Sounds like the dogs think so."

"This is the oddest thing I have ever as a reporter had to do, Steve. I gotta tell you."

The lights of a car stopping somewhere behind them shone on the dashboard, and then there was Nicole walking nonchalantly out of the alley and directly to his car. The dogs continued to howl. It sounded like it was coming from inside of the house. If he'd been successful in breaking in, he had nothing visible to show for it. They watched him stride to the end of the block and look around before stepping around the corner. Though they couldn't see it, they heard the little sports car engine start up.

Bronstein was just turning the key when a figure leaned from the sidewalk onto the car, his hands on the roof, his breath a distillery. "What are you guys, FBI? You're pretty fucking obvious."

"Hey, man, we're not doing anything. Excuse me." He sat up straight and turned the key, but then the older guy, in spite of his obviously unstable condition, leaned in and turned the car off. "Hey!"

"What are you then, reporters?" By this time Nicole was getting away. They could hear his car change gears in the distance, its high-revving r.p.m.'s louder even than the barking dogs. The older man had his face right up to Bronstein's. The reporter thought he might get drunk from the fumes.

"Okay, we're with the *Post*. Who the hell are you?" It was McTeague, leaning toward the open window.

"I'm Robert O'Malley." Of course it was. "I've been standing here watching you watch my house." He now straightened up and swayed slightly, as if he might fall flat on his back. He had to hang on to the car and McTeague opened the door and stepped into the street, just in case the man toppled over. It would be a nasty fall onto the sidewalk. He could hit his head on the steps of the townhouse stoop.

"We've been watching someone try to break into your house, I think," McTeague said from across the car roof. "Why would someone do that?"

"Why would you watch my house?"

"We were following someone, the person who was trying to break in."

Bronstein was amazed that McTeague was telling Robert O'Malley this much. He opened the car door and got out, standing uneasily on the sidewalk next to the older gentleman whose son today had become the most talked-about person in the country.

"And who might that be, the person you were following?"

"David Nicole," McTeague said, and Bronstein's jaw about dropped off.

"He was trying to break in?" Old man O'Malley looked shocked.

"Yeah, you know why?"

"Haven't the slightest," he said, but it was hard to tell if he was acting. "Now if you don't mind, I appreciate your augmenting my guard dogs, but it's late and I'll thank you to be getting off my block."

"Can we ask you a few questions?" So this was why McTeague was playing it straight with the old man. "You know, for guarding your house and all." Cale gave him his biggest smile.

"Let me ask you one," O'Malley said, looking from McTeague to Bronstein and back again.

"Shoot."

"Why are you after my son?"

"We're not," said Bronstein suddenly, which strictly speaking was true. They'd been assigned to follow Nicole, not Tom O'Malley, who, last they heard, was holed up inside his apartment in Adams Morgan with a dozen or so members of the media, including a *Post* reporter and photographer, maintaining a stakeout vigil.

"No, we are," McTeague corrected him. "And I'll tell you why. He's a story." He said it so matter-of-factly it seemed to take the ex-gunrunner and arranger of coups d'état by surprise.

"Jesus, I thought I was in a sleazy business. I'm going to bed, gentlemen. Sorry about that interview." And with that, he walked in a vaguely straight line across the street, fishing the keys out of his khakis.

"What was that all about?" Bronstein asked his partner.

But McTeague wasn't listening. Instead, he leaned against the car and cradled his chin on one hand, his elbow resting on the roof. "Why was Nicole trying to break into the old man's house?"

"I don't know, Calc. Couldn't tell you."

"There's a story here. We gotta stay on this thing." While he marveled aloud, Bronstein got back into his car. It was late and they'd lost the person they'd been sent to interview. He deemed it a wasted evening, and he was mad that they weren't on the main story which had been taken over by Big Feet who covered the White House. But Cale was enthralled the way he got when they were on the verge of a big one. He was lost in his own world the whole way home. He barely said good night when Bronstein dropped him off, and walked to his building as if he were adding up numbers in his head.

'Malley, fleet of foot since high-school track, was out the back entrance and running down the alleyway before the camera crews even moved. He'd barely run in the last two weeks, what with the trip to South America and the troubles he returned to. It felt good to be out there jogging, to break free and head down the early morning streets of the nation's capital, heading for the Mall.

He was down Seventeenth Street at about an eight-minute clip before the first van of reporters caught up with him, and even as he crossed over on R Street, which was one-way, so they couldn't follow him, he got a sense of how angry they were, and how determined. They caught up with him as he approached the White House, cutting across Lafayette Park. Only, rather than go around the park, as he thought they would, as common sense and traffic laws dictated, this van with a crew in the back and the pencil press up front vaulted over the curb, ripping up the grass, and nearly toppling a number of homeless ladies and gentlemen who were sitting having a morning eye-opener. Only by running around the hedges and a statue could O'Malley keep from being run over by this rogue crew determined to track him down, and for what? Some video of his huffing and puffing on a morning jog.

By now he was suffering from oxygen deficiency, suffering from not having kept in shape, but adrenaline suffused the link between his legs and his brain. It kept him running.

He cut down East Executive Drive between the Treasury Building and the White House, certain they wouldn't fuck with the Secret Service and the surface-to-air missiles reputed to be on the roof. He hadn't accounted for the motorbike with the sound man driving and the cameraman strapped to him backward now buzz sawing toward him and past him, the agents—never had he so welcomed the sight of the Secret Service—on the phone as he sprinted past the social entrance. And then he was out through the Southeast gate and timing his dash through the traffic on E Street that cut along the Ellipse.

The motorcycle was stopped by the police cars that pulled up with full sirens blaring and lights flashing, uniformed agents jumping out with guns drawn. Hooray for them, he thought, and ran across the lawn of the Ellipse, the South Lawn of the White House to his back. He stopped when he got to Constitution Avenue, which was moving with brisk morning traffic as the sun rose over the Capitol to his left and touched the tip of the Washington Monument that loomed in front of him.

He caught the rhythm of the traffic and picked his moment to dash to the other side, to the Mall itself, and it was only after he was running up the hill to the Washington Monument that the van he'd been eluding since Seventeenth and R came growling up on the path beside him, this time along with a little Subaru that had a cameraman holding his weapon through the open window.

O'Malley veered from the paved sidewalk and onto the nation's front lawn, no longer shocked or amazed when they followed, though he was gratified to find that by now a whole crew of Park Police cars, at least five of them, were racing along the parallel path to intersect in front of the van and the crazed driver of the Subaru.

The media gave it a shot at following him in spite of the Park Police. Then, the cop cars cut across the lawn in great, muddy tracks, earth laid out by Frederick Law Olmsted, earth that had survived years of democratic trampling, flying in great wedges behind them. The media chasing their victim down in the shadow of the nation's monuments were forced to stop as O'Malley kept jogging. He was free to continue running—the police didn't try to stop him, they were on his side in this instance—and in considerable pain from his exertions, he ran around the Lincoln Memorial and past the Bureau of Engraving, where the smell of freshly printed money was strong. Jet fuel from National Airport across the river was heavy on the air as he rounded the Jefferson Memorial and headed home.

It was when he got to the top of the hill back at California Street that he found a fresh supply of reporters and cameramen waiting for him, reserves called in to save the day. There was twice the crowd as had been there yesterday, as had camped out there all night. And there were more where these came from. Only this time, there was no pretense of goodwill. They were really pissed off. O'Malley did the only thing he could think of under these circumstances. He walked up and said hello.

it sipped coffee and read the morning paper as sunlight graced the National Cathedral across Rock Creek Park. Yellow sparks flashed on the windows of ambassadorial residences she had long divided into a paltry smattering of democracies, the more prevalent totalitarian regimes, and the omnipresent authoritarian Third World outfits whose embassy staffs were diplomat-protected highway menaces.

Commuters driving into town from Maryland, rich folks living in the visible spires and colonnades of Massachusetts Heights, even the spies and apparatchiks in their listening posts atop the Soviet compound on Mount Alto: all knew by now what was happening to Tom O'Malley, as well as the comic sidebar of the fate that was befalling Senator Tony Partridge way out West. It was in the *Post*, read all about it!

Bad as O'Malley's day had been—and the picture of him nervously perspiring under the full glare of media scrutiny was the rectangular picture above the fold—the *Post's* story on the junior senator from the great state of Wyoming was a true hoot. Funnier to Kit by far than the stab the *Post* had taken on describing the relationship of Tom and David and Kit and Tom.

The *Post's* T. R. Reid had filed a piece on Partridge's day as he'd tried to go from a Lions Club breakfast in Cheyenne to the Spring Cattle Congress in Buffalo without answering questions about the story in the *Casper Star-Tribune*. Apparently, his home state's paper quoted numerous sources saying they'd done everything with him from Panama

Red to synthetic mesc. Finally, outside Gert's Donut Shop on the main drag of Big Horn, on a dusty afternoon with the sun high in the sky, the Senator had whirled and drawn, holding an impromptu news conference in which he declared it was true he'd smoked pot recreationally a few times while an undergraduate, and perhaps a handful of times as a law-school student, but never since he'd passed the Wyoming bar, and never had he taken that mescaline stuff. "Isn't mescaline that stuff you drink in Tijuana?" he'd innocently asked the crowd of reporters.

But by the time they got to Cody, the posse of press had nailed him. That line about not having toked since he had "passed the Wyoming bar" turned out to be less of a remembrance of things past than at first met the eye, in that the Senator had subsequently been forced to admit he hadn't passed the bar the first two times, and that there had been almost two years of remedial law courses before he finally did so. Near as Wyoming reporters could place it, this meant their Senator had last smoked reefer about four years ago. According to the *Post*'s bemused correspondent, this had set off an argument among Wyoming political analysts about just when the cutoff point for previous private behavior haunting public officials ought to be. Good question, Kit thought.

The piece ended on a fascinating note. It seemed that coming back from Cody to Casper in a rented car, two of the Senator's outside political consultants, Jerry Jetta and Mike Humperdink, had been pulled over by the Wyoming state police and arrested for possession of a gram of cocaine. They'd hollered about it being a setup by the Governor, who'd remained at least publicly silent about Partridge's woes all day long, but the fact remained that they were sitting in a local jail, bail having been denied.

If the trade-off was Jetta and Humperdink sitting in a Rocky Mountain penitentiary on trumped-up charges for every day O'Malley lingered in Media Hell, it still wasn't worth it. And what O'Malley had gotten from the major papers this morning could only be called the full treatment.

The New York Times had two stories on the front page and nearly an entire inside page devoted to the scandal, which some were calling "Cokegate." Both R. W. Apple, Jr., and J. D. Catlin were given full analytical rein, the former to show what this episode meant in the context of recent presidential history. He gave a snappy little rundown of those presidents wounded by the peccadilloes of their aides. Apple somehow was able to spin Sherman Adams's vicuña coat, the Teapot Dome scandal, and more petty crimes such as Richard Allen's acceptance of a watch from a Japanese journalist into a tale of the epoch, in which the personal behavior of aides was viewed as an extension of the pres-

own morality. On background, one U.S. Senator lashed out
ly at the new breed of political operatives, who he claimed always
eir own agendas, and wouldn't pick up his dry cleaning to boot.
verall theme seemed to be that aides were younger and more
uppity these days than ever they were before. They demanded the full
philandering and shakedown rights as had previously only been reserved
for the principals, which pissed off the principals no end. Somehow it
all got blamed on Richard Nixon. That this held the potential to be
more than a minor nuisance to a new president who had begun his
administration with his full share was evidenced by at least two paragraphs of blind quotes from Democrats and Republicans alike in which
the lessons of Watergate were once again stated, as if Hardison didn't
know them.

J. D. Catlin, who apparently was younger than R. W. Apple, wrote
about the countercultural elements to the story. There seemed to be a
great many political professionals—these self-same aides whose prolif-
eration and generational allegiance were so roundly decried by the
nameless senator in Apple's piece—made very nervous by the implications of O'Malley's fall from grace. "No one knows where this will
lead," said one nervous "key aide to the Republican leadership" whose
hands could be seen being wrung even through the newspaper print,
even through blind quotations. The source proceeded to spell out the
hazards, on background, of course, of having been born in the baby
boom era: Vietnam, AIDS, and now this, this witch hunt, this phar-
macological McCarthyism. A collective, nervous guilty conscience was
very much in evidence.

A rumor said to be sweeping Capitol Hill was that the Central Intelligence Agency had developed a drug test that went back a dozen
years or more and could name precise dates and dosages of everything
from pep pills to ice. But as usual, it was left to William Orloff of the
right-of-center American Enterprise Institute to perfectly sum up the
zeitgeist as it had existed the day before.

"This is all an extension," Orloff was quoted, "of media scrutiny
going beyond politicians themselves and intruding in the lives of their
assistants. It's a recognition of the importance of staff in the expanded
Welfare State." There was more analysis before Orloff got off the regulation post-modern Washington quote, which meant, of course, there
had to be a reference to Watergate. "The New Class," said Orloff,
"doesn't like it when they're held to the same standard they've held our
leaders to ever since Watergate. What you have here is nervousness that

people's behavior throughout the sixties and seventies is going to come back to haunt them, now that we peer backwards at those days in an age of crack, crime, and corruption."

If Washington worked the way it usually did, thought Kit, he'd be repeating that particular sound bite to television correspondents throughout the day. Orloff was probably choosing his most mediagenic tie to wear as she sat there, drinking coffee and leafing through the morning papers.

The *Post* played things straight, more news than the *Times*, but less analysis. Aside from their advantage in being able to write about O'Malley and Nicole as a local story, they had the faster-reacting op-ed stable. From the news pages she learned that O'Malley had been suspected by White House Counsel Rumson Dickering's office ever since the first item about someone in the White House with a drug-dealing past had surfaced in *Newsweek*. His file had been sent, along with a dozen or so others, to the FBI. As if to vouchsafe their own process, the White House sources told Ann Devroy that the background check on O'Malley had not yet been completed, and that the Bureau's investigator was taking his time because he had been planning all along to go excavating deep into O'Malley's past. If the investigator was the person trying to persuade Kit to let him into her apartment yesterday, the only thing he was digging deeply into were martinis. But to read it the way the White House was spinning it, the FBI had long ago assigned Eliot Ness to the case.

It was difficult to read the piece filed by McTeague and Bronstein, which should have appeared in the Style section rather than on the front page. They'd managed to find teachers at St. Albans whose memories were phenomenal: detailed remembrances of legendary parties, rumors of drug use by both O'Malley and Nicole. The story of Nicole's persuading the son of the Pakistani ambassador to import hashish—and his subsequent expulsion—was merely dropped in the story for the readers to connect to the present-day scandal. That Nicole had manipulated the young Pakistani to use his diplomatic immunity to smuggle drugs into America was something Kit had long forgotten; that it hinted at his future modus operandi made her slap the heel of her hand to her forehead. The pictures they ran from their yearbook made her crumble with nostalgia. They both looked so young, and innocent, fair-haired children from good families, which is how she'd found them when all three met, at a meat market–mixer their first few weeks at Amherst and Smith.

The only columnist who'd lucked into being able to write about the piece on its first day was Richard Cohen, who marveled amusedly over how many congressional staffers must be hoping their bodies would shed traces of their latest pot party in preparation for the inevitable universal drug-testing this saga would inspire. He turned seriously to address how odd it was that Washington was living through a crack scourge that made *The Panic in Needle Park* seem like a walk in the woods, and yet the focus of the new administration was on catching middle-class baby boomers who occasionally partied on weekends. He seemed to find it shabby that O'Malley has been summarily dismissed—he was wrong on that count, but close enough—without charges even having been filed. He supposed the President, the great liberal hope of the previous year's primaries, might have a thing or two to explain when he addressed the annual gathering of the American Civil Liberties Union two days hence.

The *Post* editorially suggested that the President get to the bottom of this very serious predicament with the same openness with which he'd conducted his presidential campaign. They seemed hair-triggered to detect a cover-up.

She read the papers as the sun rose above her building and Rock Creek Park began to swelter through a perfect Washingtonian preview of the summer that was on its way, commuting north. It was lucky for O'Malley, if luck was the word, that this all was occurring with Congress still in session, for Kit had been in D.C. long enough to know that timing was everything, and a scandal that burbled up in August invariably was fatal. The difference between a scandal in May and a scandal in August was the difference between deer hunting—solitary gunmen waiting for a buck to wander by—and a driven bird shoot, where hunters walk through a field with beaters churning up winged creatures for slaughter. If O'Malley was fast and artful enough, there still was a chance he'd survive.

"uess what," O'Malley said when he called. "I've gone and made friends with the media!" He sounded boyish, like he'd just tamed the school-yard bully. Kit immediately feared the worst.

"What do you mean, you've 'gone and made friends with the media'?"

"You wouldn't have believed the scene this morning. I nearly got run over by the bastards when I went jogging. But when I came back I asked them if maybe we couldn't be civilized about this, and they agreed."

She wondered how O'Malley could have reached the age he was at and still need a baby-sitter. "What exactly did they agree to?" She didn't have the heart to ask him if he'd read the papers, if he'd seen the chorus of the dink congressmen from hayseed districts calling for him to be strung up in McPherson Square.

He caught her tone. "You don't have to worry about me, Kit, I can take care of myself."

"Oh?"

"They agreed to our having a conjugal visit this afternoon."

J ust in case, David Nicole had a bag packed and stored in the trunk of his car. He had six thousand dollars cash and a Rand McNally road map on which he'd marked routes to Toronto, Key West, and Provincetown, Massachusetts. He lost control and began to sob when he hung up the phone with a kennel to which he had lied that when he would drop off Bowser it would be a temporary boarding.

Last night had been a failure, and this morning's press coverage a horrifying assault. If they could write these things about him without his cooperation, it became more important than ever that he not talk to any of those nosy bastards showing up at Globe with their smirks and their questions. He called Yolanda to tell her she was going to have to hold down the fort, and was gratified by her ability to grasp what was needed without any guidance. "I'll just tell reporters to fuck off then." Yes, well, he told her. There was that. Reporters and law-enforcement officials.

The clock was ticking.

Someone had tried to jimmy the back door, he saw that in the clear light of day, and if those reporters had been telling the truth, Robert O'Malley knew who it was. He sat in his kitchen with the dogs around his feet, drinking strong black coffee that altered his condition to the extent that rather than feeling sick, hungover, old, and asleep, he was reluctantly awake.

He contemplated telling Tom that David Nicole had tried to break in, but he didn't want to alarm him unduly. It must be bad enough for him right now. He remembered what it was like not to be able to get into his car and drive to the Safeway without being surrounded by television cameras. In his moment of scrutiny, he'd been caught in such banal activities as wiping the snow off his windshield, carrying in groceries. The networks seemed to delight in airing snapshots of him engaged in precisely those moments of normalcy in which a barrage of cameras with their bright lights and clumsy moving human tripods made the greatest interruption. There was no reasoning with them; to give them the slightest tidbit of an answer to their questions only made them hungrier. A smile was an appetizer, a wave a first course. It was a terrible thing to have to go through, a media stakeout. He was glad that Tom had the good sense to keep his distance from them.

Okay, fellas," he said around noon, dressed in a suit and ready to go see his lawyer. "I'm going to Two Thousand K Street, and I'll be there probably for a couple hours. And then after that," he said, arching his eyebrows knowingly, "I get to go visit my girlfriend, right?"

"Sure thing, Tom," said the producer from ABC. O'Malley couldn't remember his last name, but the tall guy with the blonde hair named Ken seemed to be the leader or the friendliest of the lot. It was he who had negotiated their arrangement: they wouldn't bore in and ask O'Malley questions—he'd made it clear he wouldn't answer any—but at the same time, O'Malley wouldn't try to give them the slip.

There were thirty of them out there today, cameramen in blue jeans and sneakers with their slightly more scruffy sound men, and a passel of suit-and-tied print brethren, their skirt-and-jacketed coequals, and today, for the first time, a few foreigners come to cover the story that had the G-7 nations groaning over the prospect of another American president brought low by scandal, the American disease.

There was even a reporter or two there to file stories on the reporters. One way to calibrate the extent of the scandal was to measure how many reporters were assigned to cover it, like tilting a mirror against a mirror and watching hallways of reflection stretch to infinity.

Though O'Malley had announced where he was going, perhaps it was the innate suspicion of their species, or else their need for footage, but when he marched out and stood on the corner of California and Eighteenth trying to flag down a taxi, they moved in chaotic sway, a rustling, competitive herd.

He clearly wasn't going to catch a taxi this way. "Ken," he said to the producer as the semicircle of camera crews were an eight-eyed monster keeping him from the sidewalk. "Can't you guys back off now and let me catch a cab? Do I have to go through this every time?"

"No, Tom," he said holding up his finger in the not-to-worry position. "Fellas, let him get a cab, okay?" But though the ABC crew listened to their producer, it was no good. The rest simply stood their ground. One taxi after another rattled by, the drivers rubbernecking, their heads shaking as they drove by. There was no way they were going near this guy who was the center of a media storm. He was clearly radioactive.

And so it was that yet again, Tom O'Malley marched through the streets of Washington with a sweating entourage, huffing and puffing as they jostled for advantage without regard to traffic, pedestrians, telephone poles, streetlamps, decorum, each other, or O'Malley's right to privacy. That was something he'd lost, something he'd booted, the moment he'd mixed the ingredients of the White House and cocaine. Like a high-school chemistry experiment gone awry, this one was blowing up in his face. It would take days of intensive care before he would know if he was going to be permanently disfigured.

T he second day of Cokegate was no easier on the White House then the first. Not to lose the least opportunity at getting face time on the nets, a group of the usual Republican suspects were pressing what advantage they had in their newfound majority status in the House of Representatives by calling for congressional investigations. Whether or not hearings broke out pell-mell in whatever subcommittee fiefdom had an arguably peripheral jurisdiction, or instead were coordinated on the Senate side as a full-scale assault on the White House, depended on the mercurial Democratic Majority Leader, Senator Nelson Bligh.

Even though he'd been at his state-of-the-art elliptical best on the "Today" show, the White House believed it was just a matter of time before he announced, in the interest of clearing the air, that they ought to have some hearings, perhaps before a select committee with consolidated authority.

Such a creation held the potential to turn obscure solons into media figures, and the selection of the membership conveyed upon the leadership of the House and Senate the power of a fairy godmother handpicking the latest Cinderella. It put Bligh in rather a good mood, and he wished to prolong it, which meant the White House had a little time to come up with a strategy.

There were those who argued that the President ought to address the nation and put this behind him, and others who argued that that would guarantee the whole matter would be dropped at his doorstep. Better to, if not ignore it—because it was impossible to ignore something that threatened to lead the networks a second consecutive day—at least minimize the perception of their own responsibility. To that end, there were numerous White House spin doctors ministering to the press corps with the prescription that became known as the Lone Smuggler theory.

They argued there were no signs whatsoever that O'Malley had engaged in any kind of conspiracy within, that whatever he was trying to pull off was a matter between him and his outside connections, be they mob or whoever. The fact that he'd once been in Medellín was repeated by everyone at the White House despite the fact that their critics were already saying this proved that O'Malley should never even have been allowed to meet Bill Hardison, never mind rise to his position as campaign speechwriter and White House official.

Anyone who tried to bring up the CIA, Lemlow Motrin, aid to the Peruvian freedom fighters, or anything that remotely enlarged the circle of conspirators within the White House was just plain wrong, argued the President's men. It was barking up the wrong tree. That dog don't hunt. It wouldn't fly. And so forth and so on.

Reporters who had talked to one staff member could finish the sentences of their fellows comparing notes on what the others had said. The White House public-relations counterassault was an impressive indication of their cohesion as a unit in this, the first flat-out defining event of the new administration. Everybody said so, and some of the reporters bought it.

There was the messy problem of not having enough evidence to be able to bring an indictment, but in this case caution ruled, and the Attorney General himself was said to have counseled patience. The positive side of this was it showed the White House wasn't spooked. The negative side of this, of course, was that their not being able to bring charges made them look a little foolish.

So vigorous was the jockeying in simultaneous concern and nonchalance, that there was no one on the White House staff assigned to working the press corps who conveyed the impression that they were trying to cover anything up. Quite the contrary; it was clear that the nanosecond they could nail him, the administration was going to tack O'Malley's sorry pelt to the West Wing gate, a trophy it was determined to deliver up itself. They would not be content to have the extermination handled by either the media or the typically nosy and meddling Congress.

Everything was being done on background, and very little, other than the usual briefing, lent itself to visuals, so the networks were left with long-range footage of advisers going to and from the Oval Office via the Rose Garden. There was the footage of O'Malley jogging on the Mall, but as five members of the media had been ticketed for the lengths they went to to get it, there was some question as to whether it would find its way onto the air.

The White House would guarantee more coverage of this than they wanted if the President did anything at all, including answer questions shouted to him. As luck would have it, upon the President's return from South America, there were no plans to have him leave Washington, and whatever photo ops might otherwise have appeared without warning on the President's schedule were quietly canceled. The only event coming up was an in-towner before the ACLU.

The networks collected footage of congressmen putting in their practiced one-liners and bite-sized soundings, as well as the roundup of pundits, as always the most ubiquitous being William Orloff at AEI, who had promptly canceled his daily appointments and waited, like a deb before the ball, for the calls to come in. This was the kind of circumstance pundits and politicians live for. This would have been worth canceling a vacation.

T hey stood outside the apartment building. O'Malley wished he had a chair with which to tame them, or at least keep them at bay. "Now, look," he said with some exasperation. "You said I could."

"We said you could come visit your girlfriend. We didn't say we weren't going to tag along." It was that guy from ABC, Ken Rudin.

"Come on! No fair! I gave you my word, I'm not going to give you the slip."

They'd filmed him going into his Uncle Jake's office, which he didn't mind, but he thought he had an understanding with them about this. But they showed no mercy. He let the doorman open the great glass doors for him with an impassive look on his face, as if notorious types passed this way all the time. His cheeks were burning as he waited for the elevator. In the mirrors that lined the wall, he could see the lenses of the cameramen pressed against the door. His optimism of the morning was being shattered. He suspected that there were FBI agents among them. Jake had told him that the pressure on the White House to do something was so great, even if they had to trump up charges to get him arrested, they'd do so. And, lest he think that was all, for some time he'd had the nagging thought that Nicole was lurking out there somewhere. Surely he wasn't less desperate now than he had been on Saturday. The elevator doors parted. He turned in the glaring light and saw the entrance to Kit's building as the doors closed. It was clear the media weren't going anywhere. Neither was he.

His dog clearly was in distress, needing to be walked, but too polite to do anything drastic, like tip over the table where Nicole sat chopping lines of coke that he snorted with a continual violation of the restraints he'd declared only moments before. I won't snort this line until seven o'clock, he'd said, bending over the chopping block. He was using the table itself—what use was there in protecting it with a mirror if he was going to have to abandon the place anyway? And then seven o'clock's line was sludge in his nasal cavities, which he was watering down with drips of water off the end of his fingers which he dipped in a glass and then held up over nostrils he exposed by tipping his head back, smoothing the way for seven-thirty's line to be scarfed up an hour early, with eight o'clock's line fast behind it. He was getting in trouble, and he didn't much care.

When the phone rang it shattered his peace far more than the sad eyes of Bowser, whimpering near the door. Sweat streamed down his face and his head throbbed, and the sound of the phone made him consider possibilities including cops in the vestibule announcing the place was surrounded. He contemplated not answering, but there was always the chance it was O'Malley.

"Hello."

"Well, well, well, playing hooky at home, I see."

"Hi, John."

"Been looking for you, David. They told me at Globe you were out, and would you believe it? I began to suspect maybe you were skipping out on me."

"I wouldn't do that," he said, crashing on the coke now, a plunge from rarefied air so swift as to produce flames from the friction. He needed desperately to get off the phone and get back to that table. Only through snorting a massive line, right now, would he recover his equilibrium. If he didn't, the reality of the shit he was mired in would overwhelm him. "You know I wouldn't do that, John."

"I know that I trusted you, I relied on you, I barely gave it a second thought. And now you just continue to make a fool of me. I had to cover for you, do you know that? I had to dig up the money I owed because of you, dig it out of my own pocket because it was too embarrassing to have this thing lingering on. I'll be there in forty-five minutes, and I would definitely suggest you be there. You wouldn't actually have the money you owe me, would you?"

"Not exactly, but—"

"I didn't think so. Don't go anywhere."

With that he hung up and Nicole was left in his darkened apartment. The first line returned some clarity. Another had him optimistic again, though it now seemed like he was stuffing his nose, his gurgling bloodstream, even his psyche, stuffing it with much more than it could handle.

He looked at the dog, who returned his gaze piteously, and thinking he might actually take him out, began to thwap, thwap, thwap the carpet with his tail. "Okay, Bowser. We're going to go." He collected his keys, his wallet, and a 35-millimeter film canister three-quarters filled with blow, fetched his pocket mirror and the tubed dollar bill with its edge of crusted coke and a stain of blood from where it had been poked up his nose all afternoon. He looked briefly at himself in the mirror. What a ghastly sight. It was time to find O'Malley. He was halfway out the door before he remembered his unlined jacket with the sleeves rolled up, and of course, the pistol it was to cover.

T he jets were already in their evening landing pattern, cutting in cool arcs across the sky as it quickened with color. O'Malley and Kit lay upon her bed with the sheets drawn back, contemplating getting up. The sky had just the beginning of a Creamsicle tinge to it, muted orange mixed with white clouds, and they stroked each other without talking, until Kit turned and said, "Why don't you just say that you engaged in the whole thing as a sting to nail David? I've been meaning to ask you."

"First of all, I doubt they'd buy it. Why would I do that without telling anybody about it?"

"You could say you told me. I'd back you up." She looked so sincere in her willingness to commit perjury that his heart sank.

"No, you can't do that. And anyway, I can't do that because it isn't the truth. We've been through this."

"I know," she said quietly. "It was a thought."

"Then it's settled? You'll drive home tonight?"

"I'll wait until it's late. I'm not exactly looking forward to seeing my father. You know what he said when I told him?"

"No, but I bet it was a typically Republican outrage."

"He said, 'Do you know how this looks? This could ruin my chances for a Cabinet position.' I said, 'I'm sorry my being fired on the front page of *The Washington Post* affects your career plans so dramatically.' I was really pissed off. But I do need to get out of here."

"Don't we all."

"I'm deserting you."

"Don't be ridiculous,' he said, getting up and wandering over to where his clothes were spread on the chair. She pulled the sheet along with her and followed him to the pile of clothes, her arms crisscrossing her breasts with the sheet a thin cape, her hands balled in a fist and touching her shoulders. He wrapped his arms around her and clutched her in the hollow of his body. Sending her away was precisely the right thing to do. Then how come it made that armor with which he'd protected himself suddenly seem as thin as the sheet that covered her? He'd meant to reassure her by holding her in his arms, yet now the only thing that kept him standing was her steady weight, the strength of her even stance, the warm resting place of her shoulders where his head was allowed to collapse.

I t was a good thing they'd worked out a code name, or so Max told him when he got home and checked in with his friend in the press office. "They're on to me, I'm certain," his friend whispered into the phone.

"How's that?"

"I just got a phone call from Bill Tiswell. He said, 'When you talk to your buddy, the dope dealer, tell him we've got the goods on him.' "

"What could he have meant by that?"

"I don't know, and pardon me if I'm a little more concerned about how it is he knows we're speaking than I am about the psychological warfare he's trying to engage in."

"That's easy. My phone's probably tapped."

"Oh, great, Tom. I mean, Lester," he said, referring to their code name. "I gotta go. NBC's about to come on and I need to see what they do to you, I mean, us. Jack Carthage was walking around all smug like he was going to scoop Wyatt Phillips."

O'Malley had missed CBS, not bothering to watch as he and Kit had taken their leave. "What did Rather do to me?"

"Not much more than yesterday. More congressional reaction. Asshole Republicans calling for hearings. William Orloff saying we had forty-eight hours to do something about you. But no hard news."

"I should thank my lucky stars."

"I saw you jogging. How'd they get that footage?"

"It's a long story."

" 'Nightline' is still after you. They're doing a show on you tonight. I know they've been trying to reach you."

"I think that's one invitation I ought to turn down."

"Me too. Look, I gotta go. I'll call you if anything comes up, okay?"

"Sure," he said, hanging up. He wandered over to the television to see what Jack Carthage could possibly do to him that hadn't been done already.

BC News had learned, rather NBC News had been leaked, that the White House was getting it together in their drive to prosecute Tom O'Malley.

"Phone records now show that prior to the trip to South America, Thomas O'Malley, the White House speechwriter suspected of trying to import two and a half million dollars' worth of cocaine on Air Force One, made several calls from the White House to a restaurant run by a convicted drug trafficker. The calls went to this man, David Nicole, who authorities believe was the mastermind of the conspiracy. White House sources tell NBC News it is now just a matter of time before evidence can be turned over to a grand jury that will be sufficient to bring the first indictment in what is becoming known as the Cokegate scandal. Congressional leaders believe it may occur just in time to stave off yet more damage to the Hardison Administration. This is Jack Carthage . . ."

O'Malley turned off the television. Either they were genuinely getting ready to indict, or the White House was trying to bluff its way through this next news cycle with the sensation being created that they were on top of matters. But if it were just a bluff, they would have spun that tale to everyone, and not just NBC. So the likelihood was that they did feel they had something in the phone calls between him and Nicole. Which meant Nicole was going to be feeling serious pressure from the licit side of the equation as well, not only from the people he owed money to.

Last night, when his father had been over, he'd had a thought of one possible strategy for dealing with the mess he was in. But then he'd rejected it as too great a risk. Not now . . . He could always take "Nightline" up on their offer and try to tell his side of the story, unedited and unfiltered. Jake would be dead set against it, and there was good reason. But the possibility of using the media, instead of simply being their victim, had its up side. It began to appeal to him. He paced around the room. Was it worth the gamble? Sometimes you take the one shot you have to get that last plane out of Beirut.

I t didn't take long to figure out where Nicole lived, and it should have been obvious that if he still was in town after the piece they'd written about him, or after the way NBC flashed his mug up on the screen, they weren't going to find him at his restaurant. They'd tried that, and nearly broken their toes tripping over all the FBI agents in the bar there.

"Jesus, I thought this place was supposed to be some kind of hip hangout," Bronstein said as they left Globe.

"It was," said Cale, for whom the phrase "hipper than thou" could have been the distinction between himself and his partner, and he said it as if there were no way Bronstein could have been expected to have ever been to Globe before. "It was last week. I guess those gumshoes must be driving the crowd away."

Having found out from the Alcoholic Beverage Control Board that the permittee was one Tina Mellen of 1868 Wyoming Avenue, they headed there in Bronstein's car, and prepared for their vigil by getting cups of takeout coffee from a local carryout, just like they were in an episode of "Adam-12" or something.

And it couldn't have been more than a half hour before they saw a Mercedes-Benz station wagon with Maryland plates pull up and park in front of the building in a space that almost miraculously had just been vacated. A tall guy in a sweatshirt with the sleeves cut off stepped out of the back door and laced his fingers together as he shot both arms straight into the air in an almost feline stretch. Then he twisted his neck as if putting it back on its proper hinge and stepped lightly to the car's front door. He looked around twice before he smoothly put his fingers underneath the handle and gave it a yank. And almost pulled himself crashing onto the roof. The door was locked.

The fellow with the head of slicked-back hair who was sitting in the passenger seat unlocked the door and without any help from the muscleman opened it slowly. He looked contemptuously at the schmuck who'd failed to get the door opened, and stood in the street, brushing imaginary crumbs off his black oversized suit. He was almost as large as his muscleman friend, only he carried it differently, as a statement of fact, not as a billboard.

Bronstein and McTeague sat silently in Bronstein's car, the coffee steaming on the dashboard, fogging up the windshield as they watched the oversized guys now joined by a third, the driver. They skipped up the steps to Nicole's building.

"That guy look familiar to you?" McTeague asked.

"Which one? The two torpedoes look like twins." It was true; the driver appeared to be a merely better-dressed version of the gent in the sweatshirt.

"The guy in the black sack. He reminds me of someone I ought to remember."

"I can't help you on this one." They could see just the back of the better-dressed goon standing on the landing at the top step of the apartment building. The group appeared to be waiting to be admitted, but it didn't seem like they'd said the magic words.

Then the three were halfway down the steps, the black suit apparently fuming, talking rapidly at the two others. Sweatshirt reacted by squinting his eyes and rubbing his right fist in his left palm, as if savoring the pummeling it would give whoever it was that had just caused them displeasure by not letting them in.

"Did this asshole pop right out of a comic book, or what?" Steve asked his partner.

"John Santangelo," Cale said excitedly, twisting in his seat toward him.

"Say what?"

"John Santangelo. The mobster who was supplying the Mayor with his coke! Oh-my-God."

"Wait, we wrote that the Mayor was dealing with Jamaicans."

"He was, until they broke his ribs. The word a few weeks back was he was going out of town to deal directly with this mobster from Baltimore. John Santangelo. I pulled his photo from the morgue, but then there was all that talk about an indictment coming down, and that became the better story than trying to track down these rumors about a white guy dealing coke to the Mayor. I dropped it, partly because you got so excited about this White House thing. But, uh, Santangelo was busted for running a call-girl outfit or something a few years ago. That's him. And he's waiting for Nicole. Ready to roll?"

"Whoa!" Bronstein held up all ten fingers on both hands. But McTeague had the door open and was walking the twenty feet up to the guy whose goons turned toward him as if they were soccer fullbacks and Cale was dribbling the ball too close to the net.

"Uh, Mr. Santangelo, how ya doin' tonight? I'm Cale McTeague from *The Washington Post*. I wonder if I could ask you a few questions."

"Shit," said Bronstein, and he was out the door, following his partner to their near-certain deaths.

But Santangelo just said, "I got nothing to say to you," and with that, he stepped lively toward the car and quickly got in. The torpedoes followed, though not without Sweatshirt shooting them a look that suggested he would love to meet up with them, say, behind Hammerjack's bar in Bal'more, where he'd crunch them like so many cans of Lite beer.

The Mercedes took off, and Bronstein stood there on the sidewalk, wondering why it was he put himself in these situations. Cale was going to get them killed someday.

But Cale was triumphant. This was great, his grin seemed to say. "We're on to something, Stevie. This could be the big time. Whoo!"

It would have been churlish not to slap his high five.

I t had taken a long moment of gathering clues before she remembered she was parked over on Kalorama Road beside the Chinese Embassy. She sure hoped her car still was there, since she'd left it parked in a diplomatic zone two nights before when she and O'Malley had arrived back late from Annapolis. That trip seemed as if it had happened in a different lifetime. It seemed as if it had happened to two other people.

She carried her first load, a hanging bag and an old cheap canvas sack, and she had to wait for the traffic coming off the Taft Bridge to settle down before she picked her way across Connecticut Avenue. There were a number of austere Chinese couples walking in silence, aloof in the apparent relief of people whose greatest pleasure in a foreign land seemed to be the lack of population density. She walked right in front of their stolid apartment complex where uniformed Secret Service agents sat on the edge of their motorcycles, clearly suppressing the urge to whistle wolfishly, and when she got around the corner, she found her car safe and sound, if littered with pink notes of endearment from the D.C. meter maids.

It took a minute for the Saab to rumble to life, but eventually it found its voice and sat there panting as she organized the tapes she'd brought along for the four-hour trip to Manhattan. To home. To a place removed from the bullshit raining down here, though of course, being at her parents' house on Sixty-ninth and Park came with its own complete collection of loopy dramas, trick-mirror realities, and the refracted atmosphere of a different world: Planet Bowles.

She turned around in the driveway of the old French Embassy, which looked more like a country chateau than anything you ought to see in a neighborhood as civilized as Kalorama, and then came roaring up the street to the stop light. She was waiting for it to turn green when, looking at her building which leaned over the precipice above Rock Creek Park, she instantly became aware of trouble. It was Bowser, Nicole's old Doberman, peeing on what daffodils had not already died. And if Bowser was there, Nicole could not be far behind.

A car behind her honked, the light was green. She panicked and gunned it across the street on Kalorama instead of turning left toward her building. What could David be doing there?

It took a series of left turns before she worked her way through the back streets of that border area between Adams Morgan and Kalorama, and as she shot up on her building's side she was instantly glad she hadn't parked in front and popped out to fetch her luggage. For standing there arguing with Sheiku, the Ghanian doorman, was Nicole whose agitation was evident from thirty feet away.

Which under any circumstances would strike her as very odd, given that Nicole's entire demeanor was cool to the point of calculation. She'd never seen him lose it, except, of course, when he had a headful of blow. And if Nicole had a headful of blow, she wasn't sticking around to see what he wanted.

She drove up to the corner and never even bothered to stop at the sign. She just hung another left and drove to the 7-Eleven on Columbia Road to use the phone. She didn't really need her luggage, she decided in an epiphany of almost Buddhist clarity, the realization upon her that on the scales that mattered, her clothing was less important than escape. It was 275 miles to Manhattan. It seemed almost anticlimactic that the only thing that stood between here and there was a handful of toll booths and an empty tank of gas.

The loss he felt at Kit's departure was nothing compared to his feeling of relief that she'd made it safely out of town. That was a close call.

Her description of Nicole in a desperado's dance was a compelling argument for doing what he was leaning toward doing anyway. Television wasn't catharsis, it was a strategic retreat. It was as if he could hear the helicopters landing on the roof, and it was merely a question of whether he could grasp the bottom rung of the rope ladder.

Then again, spilling one's guts out on national TV had become as time-honored an American tradition for dealing with a problem as a shoot-out was in frontier days. The prospect remained that a shoot-out at noon was no less common in a world where drug transactions happened all the time. The prospect remained that telling all on national TV and still settling things with gunfire were by no means mutually exclusive. The evening held the possibility that one might lead to the other. Wrestling with the possibilities ate up a considerable amount of time.

It was when he'd showered and was walking around the apartment in a clean shirt and tie that he saw Ted Koppel's discontented chipmunk countenance soundlessly gracing his television set.

The anchor was giving the fifteen-second commercial tease before the resumption of prime-time broadcasting, and while O'Malley wasn't quick enough to catch all of it, he did turn up the sound in time to hear Koppel say in that voice he'd purchased from Ethel Merman's estate, ". . . examine how the Hardison Administration could be wrecked by a conspiracy to smuggle drugs." And that was it.

He looked at his watch and panicked. He wasn't going to make it. And if he did, Uncle Jake was going to kill him. Surely Jake was right that the Justice Department wasn't going to be able to make a case against him, that admitting anything at all was the stupidest thing imaginable. He was compounding the stupidity of having agreed to Nicole's demands by now going out there and admitting everything. And he would admit everything. There was no point doing this and not telling the whole story.

He froze two feet from the front door, his suit jacket just a knot away from being a straitjacket, as he hadn't yet pulled it up onto his shoulders. He reviewed what he was doing this for, and quickly cut to what was important: he thought he had a case to make, and he saw this as the only way to make it. He wouldn't be able to put his own spin on things so long as the news media were being manipulated by others, meaning some people at the White House and their allies. And he suddenly realized how important this was to him—it was the only possible way he could get his explanation across to the President.

He didn't know what he expected, not forgiveness, surely, and a pardon only came into play when they had you strung up on the wall by the rusty links of manacles.

He supposed he wanted to look the nation in its eye, its TV eye. He had a notion, part calculation, part naïveté, that he could get it to crinkle in understanding of the conditions that had led him to do what he did. He was haunted by the hollow thought that the case he had to make wasn't much more complicated than that the devil made him do it.

At first they didn't notice him, his media entourage. They were lined up on the California Street sidewalk in lawn chairs. Ken Rudin, who really should have been home by now—he'd been on the case for what seemed like forever—was regaling them with the story about the stakeout of a prominent former presidential candidate whom they'd caught sneaking out of his hotel room in the middle of the night in search of a fresh batch of condoms.

"I'll do it," O'Malley said from halfway across the street, and Rudin practically jumped. The others snapped to and began to jump for their cameras. He had taken them by surprise.

"What, you're deciding *now?*" Rudin put his cigarette in his mouth and looked quickly at his watch and then at O'Malley. No one else knew what they were talking about, but several times over that afternoon, he'd sidled over to O'Malley and said, in the manner of someone selling dirty pictures in a public square, "Pssst. Wanna do 'Nightline'?" He'd made certain none of his competitors heard his offer.

"You think they'll still take me?" O'Malley asked it as if disappointment were his greatest worry.

"They'll take you. Lets' go," he said, patting him on the elbow. "My car's up here," he shouted over his shoulder, and O'Malley followed him, with the cameramen and their producers now shouting, "You bastard, Rudin." Then they too scrambled for their cars.

"Hey, where you going with him?" a small but bellicose producer asked.

" 'Nightline,' if we make it," Rudin shouted back.

And then they were in his compact car—it was a wreck inside—and revving up the hill in order to turn down toward the ABC studios on DeSalles Street right in the heart of downtown D.C.

"I think you'll just make it," Rudin said with some intensity, as O'Malley hung on. His driver did not take the turn onto Florida Avenue by the Washington Hilton with anything that approached grace.

"Can I ask you a question?" He was a broad-faced, good-looking guy with a slight Long Island accent and a devilish air.

"Shoot," said O'Malley, cleanly biting off a hangnail.

"Why'd you do it?"

"Tune in," said O'Malley, with a smirk. "I've always wanted to say that," he said as an aside.

They bumped along for moment, then were stuck at the light on the corner of Connecticut, with the all-night drugstore doing a steady business, the streets alive with couples walking arm in arm, utterly unaware that he was sitting there, America's most-wanted idiot, biting his nails in a Japanese car. "Let me ask you a question?"

"Go ahead." He turned toward his guest and then accelerated into an illegal left-hand turn that left a smear of honking horn from a horrified driver hanging in the evening air.

"Is this what you do? I mean, hang out all day long waiting for people to come out of buildings? It seems like kind of an odd business to be in." He didn't realize until he heard his own voice how lonely he was, Kit on the highway, his having been imprisoned by the media, only answering the phone according to a predetermined code.

"I specialize in death watches. I was the last thing seven candidates for president found perched on their doorsteps on the mornings they announced their withdrawal from the race. I do congressmen who have to get out of Dodge City one step before the Ethics Committee. I cover major government figures the day before they're sentenced."

"You do my father?"

"Robert O'Malley? No. I'm the guy, though, that when a candidate saw me greeting his plane at the airport after he lost the Minnesota caucus or the South Carolina primary, it was a signal from the networks it was time to go home."

"Subtle."

"I became know as the Angel of Death."

"I'm honored."

"But you still got some fight in you." They were stuck at the stop light on Dupont Circle, only a minute away from the studio. "This is smart, your doing 'Nightline' tonight."

"Oh?" This he had to hear.

"Sure. If you waited a few more days into the cycle and things headed south on you, you'd have been stuck doing 'Geraldo.' "

William Orloff didn't want to get up. "Hey, what is this?" he asked nastily as the technician came to unstrap him from where he sat. The makeup lady looked in with concern, annoyed at the prospect of undoing what she had just done to make Orloff's forehead quit shining like a freshly mopped kitchen. "I don't believe this," he said, refusing to get up. "I turned down 'GMA' tomorrow morning so I could do this."

O'Malley stood at the side of the small studio, waiting to get strapped in, and he had the momentary flash that there was something similar indeed about the technician putting the microphone on you and your sitting in the electric chair as they wire you to the hot seat.

A producer was squatting on his haunches whispering to Orloff, and the floor director stood nervously behind him waiting for the no-longer-wanted guest to leave. The analyst continued to sit and glare at O'Malley. "Look, I don't care if you got the bastard here, you asked me on the show. Put me on with him."

The producer was clearly a father used to being logical with children, for he continued to speak in a low voice while O'Malley, getting nervous more from the commotion in the studio than from the prospect of what he was about to do, stood politely waiting for his orders.

"Yes, Ted," the director suddenly said, standing up and holding the little white shovel that hung from his headset down beside his mouth. "Yes, like I said, Mr. O'Malley is in the studio. He's standing by. We'll do a sound check in just a minute."

"Okay," said Orloff, standing up and ripping the tiny microphone from where it was hooked on his blue striped tie. "I'm out of here, but you tell Ted how fucking pissed off I am. You tell him I'm going to do CBS 'Nightwatch' the next time they ask me. You got a phone so I can call 'GMA' and tell them I'll do it?" And then he was walking across the floor toward O'Malley, in front of whom he stopped as if to take the full measure of the man who had caused all this trouble. Rather than looking at him as a windfall for commentators, Orloff just sneered something about O'Malley breaking his leg.

As Orloff followed the producer off into the darkened half of the studio, O'Malley was smart enough to know he would need good luck, not on television tonight so much as beyond it, for however long this continued to percolate on the media's front burner. For he had just pissed off Washington's preeminent political diagnostician. It was likely Orloff would pronounce him as being, no matter what he did from now on, a very sick puppy indeed.

"Mr. O'Malley, would you mind coming over here?" the director asked politely seconds before bellowing to the cameraman and associated techies, "Two minutes to air!"

O'Malley was in the seat, the lights bright upon him, his blood rising. There was an unreality to this that made him, for the first time in his life, understand what people meant when they talked about out-of-body experiences. If he had been floating on the ceiling looking down he would have seen the nervous bustle of a crew preparing for airtime, and sitting in a chair with the spotlight upon him an almost serene fellow, convinced he had nothing to lose, repeating the mantra, "In the future, everyone will go on 'Nightline' for 1.5 minutes."

They were almost through the signature sound track with its portentous urgency before O'Malley realized this was real. He didn't even hear Koppel's introduction through his earpiece, as his blood began to race. He only came to as he heard his name mentioned, as in, "We'll talk to White House speechwriter Thomas O'Malley"—the red light on top of the camera suddenly came on—"in his first interview since the controversy broke in the pages of the *Los Angeles Times* on Monday."

They went to a couple of commercials, and then Koppel was back introducing a taped segment that recapped the news of the past two days. The news about the mess O'Malley was in. He had no idea whether or not he should smile when the camera came back on him. After accompanying the campaign entourage to a number of tapings and debates during the primaries, he'd been taken off that job after the general election when they had no longer needed him to coach the nominee on what to say extemporaneously. That was a contrivance for the platoon of consultants who moved in and commandeered the campaign. Locked up on the plane with a laptop and multiple speeches to write left him with very little recall about how Hardison had been coached to sit in moments like this. He decided to sit up in his chair as if it were a job interview, or an interview with the admissions officer to a school he wanted very much to get into. This was no time to slouch.

He saw where this was going. Although O'Malley caught only the audio, the taped piece had been prepared for a discussion with Orloff, and, he had found out only moments ago, with a pair of campaign consultants, one Republican, the other Democrat, who were supposed to give advice as to how the President should handle the mess he was in, the mess O'Malley had gotten him into. It appeared the discussion they'd planned on having would have focused on the legal and political elements at work here, and the nexus between the two. Now, with O'Malley the lone guest, anything was possible.

The piece over, its conclusion being that the nation was in the midst of some kind of crisis in which the President could either rise to the occasion or allow the very fabric of democracy to be rent anew, Koppel announced that they were going to another commercial and that they'd return with Thomas O'Malley. O'Malley didn't know what happened to the two campaign consultants, but he assumed they'd been hustled off the set along with Orloff. He hoped they had taken it better.

"Mr. O'Malley," said a voice in his earphone.

"Uh, roger." He'd seen all the Apollo missions, a long time ago.

"We're going to be coming back live in one minute thirty. You okay?"

"That's a ten-four." He was sort of getting into it.

And then it seemed about fifteen seconds later that the voice of Ted Koppel was in his ear saying, "We're back with Thomas O'Malley, the White House aide accused, not by the government but by the news media, of conspiring to smuggle into the country some thirty-five pounds of pure cocaine. Let me start by saying to you, Mr. O'Malley, welcome . . ."

"Thank you," he blurted a little nervously.

". . . and asking you, did you do it?"

"Yes."

Koppel seemed taken aback, or so it looked to viewers, among them O'Malley's Uncle Jake, who groaned and reached for the phone on his bedside table. O'Malley knew only that there was a pause before Koppel asked him the next question.

"You've just admitted to a very serious felony. I suppose the next obvious question is, why would someone working for the President of the United States do such a thing?" Koppel was the boss, Koppel had seen it all, but he was, after all, a creature of conditioning. It was odd to have a guest he expected to have to corner and poke with a stick come right out and dispose of the question of guilt or innocence in the first fifteen seconds of the discussion.

"Well, you see," O'Malley began, "I was, um, being blackmailed. It's not that I, you know, dreamed up this idea of smuggling in coke all by myself."

Phones were ringing throughout the nation's capital, reporters calling editors, editors calling reporters, Justice Department officials fumbling with their VCR's, senators sitting agape. In a bar near the Convention Center, a recently suspended FBI agent was practically fighting with the bartender to get him to turn up the sound.

"All right, Mr. O'Malley," Koppel said as deliberately and calmly as he could given the unexpected news that was being created on his show. "Why don't we start at the beginning." Although Koppel was in a studio just one floor away from where O'Malley was sitting, he could have been looking down on him from heaven above. O'Malley sat with an anxiously forthcoming look on his face, with an American openness to him, not so much confessional as matter-of-fact, and viewers watching the anchor saw him lean toward the large monitor on which his guest's face loomed. The anchor did not seem either hostile or skeptical, but instead had assumed the manner of a gentle hospital authority getting a patient to list the symptoms of a disease that defied medical science. "Why don't you tell us, if you would, who was blackmailing you, and why you succumbed to it."

"All right. Uh . . ." His eyes shot up as if he were having to rack his scattered thoughts into an ordered narrative. "When I was in college? I roomed with a guy who was arrested for dealing drugs, okay? I guess I should say, not just for selling, you know, nickels and dimes of pot . . ."

"This was at . . . Amherst College?" Koppel asked, looking at notes.

"Right. Um. And, you know, though I knew this was wrong, there was a different atmosphere back then about drugs, and on occasion, when people came to the room looking for David—my roommate's name was David Nicole—if he wasn't there, I would, um, fill the order for him."

"You sold drugs."

"Not my own. I was like a shopkeeper, I guess. But at any rate—and this was all a long time ago—but when I went to work at the White House . . . David, that is, David Nicole, who now lives in Washington, appeared and asked me to pick up a package for him when I was with, uh, the President on that, on that trip to South and Central America last week."

"And what did you say when Mr. Nicole asked you to smuggle drugs? I'm assuming the package was the cocaine."

"Well, it was, Ted. I told him no. I told him no, in no uncertain terms. I absolutely refused to do it."

"Then perhaps you'll tell us what happened. Why did you end up doing it?"

"Let me back up for a moment. Um, on inaugural night, the day before I was to go work at the White House, I was arrested for drunken driving, in the, uh, District of Columbia. And this, several weeks later, became a news story. I was told by Chief of Staff Whitney, Harold Whitney, that I would be fired if I caused the administration any more embarrassment."

"Well, Mr. O'Malley, attempting to smuggle sixteen kilos of cocaine onto Air Force One could be considered a further embarrassment to the administration . . ."

"Right you are, I'm kind of aware of that, Ted. But at the time, I was in trouble with the White House, and David Nicole told me that if I didn't do as he asked, he'd start leaking stories that I'd been involved in drug dealing, which, given the environment in Washington, where everyone's obsessed by scandal, was destined to start a, a . . ." He looked up as if trying to find the word.

"Witch hunt?" Koppel offered helpfully.

"That's it, a witch hunt. And it did. He somehow leaked to *Newsweek* that there was a, he didn't say who it was, but that there was a former drug dealer working at the White House . . ."

"And this was the story several weeks ago that started the investigation of White House personnel?"

"Right," O'Malley said, nodding.

"I'm going to hold you right there, and we're going to go to a commercial and be right back," Koppel said, looking directly into the camera.

And then they were off the air momentarily and O'Malley heard the voice of the producer in his earphone say, "Very good, nice television, Mr. O'Malley," as if all this were mere entertainment. O'Malley sat there, his heart racing, watching the director move around the set, occasionally talking into his mouthpiece, then shouting, "Ninety seconds." He paid no attention to the guest in his chair, and O'Malley thought he could have confessed to a previously undisclosed string of serial murders and neither the producer offstage nor the director here would have been judgmental about anything other than the way he presented his tale. The producer probably would have said, "Great television!" to Ted Bundy.

Throughout Washington, people were calling neighbors, friends, co-workers to make certain they tuned in. By now, Jake Ingram was downing a shot of straight scotch, having alerted Robert O'Malley to his son's public suicide. The night rewrite staff at *The Washington Post* was scrambling to take down what O'Malley said in order to break into late editions of the paper. The White House operators were patching calls through, setting up conferences, busy in a manner usually indicative of a national emergency. It was the call that came from the third floor, from the President to the Attorney General, that alerted them that the crisis was domestic, not international, which meant, given the news of the last few days, it had to do with Tom O'Malley. The White House operators had a better sense of the ebb and flow of a crisis than the National Security Council.

"Thirty seconds," shouted the director.

"Okay, here we go, Mr. O'Malley," came the voice of the producer through his earphone.

"We're back with Thomas O'Malley, the White House speechwriter who moments ago admitted he planned to use diplomatic immunity to bring several million dollars' worth of cocaine back from the President's trip to South America. Mr. O'Malley, you were saying a moment ago that you were blackmailed into committing a felony because David Nicole, your college roommate, planted a story that someone working at the White House had previously sold drugs. Why didn't you just go to the proper authorities and turn the fellow in?"

"I was trying to explain, Ted. I was in trouble already, because I, you know, drank a little too much celebrating the President's inaugural. It was a public embarrassment to the White House, and it was made clear to me that if I did anything else, I'd get fired, and I didn't want that to happen."

"So you committed a felony?" When Ted raised his eyebrows, it seemed an entire mammal was about to spring off his head.

"Well, actually, I never actually went through with it."

"We'll leave the question of your guilt to the Justice Department, then. The question I have is, why is it you succumbed to the attempt to blackmail you?"

"I guess I'm stupid," he said. "I've also asked myself that question, as you can imagine, about a hundred times. First, I was very scared I'd lose my job at the White House, and Nicole played on that fear. Second, the drunk-driving conviction and the search for the person in the White

House who once had dealt drugs made me panic. I was more than just momentarily light-headed, I was thoroughly thrown. And even though I knew all along it was wrong, it wasn't until I was in Venezuela and came to my senses and realized that I couldn't go through with it that I was able to pull out and stop myself. And by that time, I guess, I'd already gone too far." He stopped, and furrowed his brow.

"That's first and foremost. But you know, there's a point to be made here. I was vulnerable, granted, because I did break the law, what, twelve, thirteen years ago. But the bottom line is that in Washington today, I'm part of a generation that can be blackmailed for having done something that was a natural part of being an adolescent in the nineteen sixties and seventies . . ."

"I daresay selling drugs wasn't a 'natural part' of adolescence a decade ago," Koppel said like a stern father, the voice of American authority.

"Okay, but the point is, we're, all of us, my age or nearabouts my age, when we go into government, we're expected to either lie or at the very least, minimize our connection to even having done things like smoke pot, and that, in my opinion," he said, pointing to himself, "makes us either have to be hypocrites, holding our breaths that someone doesn't come out of the woodwork and destroy us with a simple accusation made to the people who do background checks, or in my case, the news media. Or else, if you tell the truth, you run the risk of being kept from getting a job in government."

"And what you're suggesting, if I hear you right, is that no activity you engaged in in the nineteen sixties or seventies ought to be held against you?"

"No, I'm not saying that . . ."

"Such as drug dealing, which was a felony then as now . . ."

"No, I'm not saying that. Although I do think there should be some kind of amnesty, some kind of statute of limitations about drug use when you're attempting, as an adult, to work in public service."

"Mr. O'Malley, let's get back to what you say happened. This David Nicole, who The Washington Post reported had been arrested, while you two were at Amherst, for selling large amounts of cocaine . . ."

"I was never involved in that. At the worst, I sold a few ounces of pot."

"Okay, we'll take you at your word. Is this David Nicole currently a drug dealer?"

"I don't know. I assume he has to be if he had the connections to set up what was supposed to have been a twenty-kilo package for me to pick up in South America. He runs a restaurant and nightclub here in

Washington. But I'm assuming he's still involved in the drug trade, I mean, if he was trying to get me to agree to smuggle in drugs."

"It sounds like he persuaded you to agree."

"Yes, but I didn't actually do it. I couldn't do it."

"I'm not a lawyer, but it certainly sounds to me like you engaged in a conspiracy to import drugs." Ted had regained his prosecutorial edge.

"I'm telling you, Ted, I did. But look. I didn't do it. I realized it was wrong. I did consider it, I admit. But only because I was stupid, and scared, and I was being blackmailed. I know I reacted precisely the wrong way. I'll always have to live with that. All I wanted to do was to work for this President."

"All right, we're going to break for another commercial here. I'm going to take this opportunity to say to our affiliates that it looks like we're going to go over our normal time tonight. We'll be right back with Thomas O'Malley."

The Associated Press was already sending out copy from just the confession O'Malley had made; Reuters was feeding to a European morning. Guest-grabbers for the morning shows were being roused at home, expected to completely change the lineups for shows that would begin in less than seven hours. While *The New York Times*'s National Edition was long since printed in each of their regional printing plants around the country, their late editions for New York City and environs were being reworked, with some reporters sitting around the television sets in the newsroom on West Forty-third, others working the phones to gather reactions. Driving across the Delaware Bridge, Kit Bowles was oblivious to anything other than the feeling of relief from having put multiple waterways between herself and the District of Columbia. She was blissfully unaware of the drama unfolding on television sets in the living rooms just behind her in Wilmington, or two dozen miles to her left in Philadelphia, or even in the yellow specks of light in the homes she could see in the New Jersey woods visible through the spires of the bridge.

It was when they came back that O'Malley and Ted Koppel talked about how it was that O'Malley had made such a mistake, putting the authority of a President he had only wanted to serve at risk. It was after fifteen more minutes of talk that, with more people watching the ending than had watched the beginning, refugees from Jay Leno's monologue who stumbled across this strange confession, people home from night shifts just tuning in, those who had been alerted to the news being made; it was only after some forty minutes of conversation between Ted

Koppel and Tom O'Malley that the normally fierce anchor said to him, "Mr. O'Malley, I wish you luck. You're going to need it." O'Malley smiled uncertainly into the camera. Whatever was going to happen next, at least he'd had his say. He felt unburdened. Only in the modern age would a Catholic think of network television as an adjunct to the confessional booth.

t was after Ken Rudin got him out of there, away from the studio with its backslapping functionaries, away from the reporters who had congregated on the sidewalk, that O'Malley headed home, his real home, not that hovel with a kitchenette he'd been living in since the Hardison campaign.

His father at once treated him as if this were nothing out of the ordinary, as well as a permanent return. He met him at the door and immediately concentrated on such amenities as towels, fresh sheets, and a glassful of whatever he desired, though he made it clear that he hoped this latter wasn't warm milk or "some other goddamn confection."

To be surrounded anew by the Orientalia his father had collected, from the mosaic pattern of the rugs on the floor to the jade Buddha atop the stairwell, was like lolling in the net that saved him after a particularly perilous high-wire act. Odor of dog, the musty breath of cedar, even the vague reek of his father's boozy fumes: it was home on the elemental level, the place where you crawl for your collapse.

"I thought your performance was quite good. At least I was persuaded."

"Persuaded of what, though?" O'Malley asked as they stood at the kitchen counter, his father pouring himself a fresh scotch, O'Malley digging in a box of Triscuits as he drank a beer.

"Leniency?" his father suggested, his eyebrows raised, his pink face on the verge of mirth.

"You mean you wouldn't call for my prosecution, I mean if you were an average American?"

His father bristled at the notion of having to try on such a role. "I'd probably call for your prosecution, but I'd temper it with the proviso that capital punishment was out."

His father was kinder than the reporters waiting for him outside ABC had been. When Rudin went to fetch his car, O'Malley had found himself surrounded for the first time by truly hostile Injuns, whooping and hollering and desirous of his scalp. They'd skipped to the bottom line, his confession.

"So you admit you tried to smuggle drugs?" asked one correspondent whose trench coat covered his pajama top, though it was a pleasant seventy degrees out. There was fierceness to his face and a dishevelment to his hair that suggested he'd been called in just moments too soon. O'Malley's hide was now the object of his disappointed hormones.

"I made a statement to Koppel—"

"How about to us grunts as well?" the guy had said, giving him no room.

"Okay. I admit that I was being blackmailed. I admit that I was stupid enough to allow myself to be threatened." He was really angry, and it showed.

"Tom, settle down. Don't mind him," said Jack Carthage, who had looked utterly unprepared to go on camera. He was unshaven, bleary-eyed, and he practically had on a nightcap and a bathrobe. "Just tell us this one thing. Is this going to be your defense? That you were being *forced* to pick up the cocaine?"

"If it comes to that, Jack, I'm going to tell the truth, just like I did tonight. I'm going to admit I was a gutless bastard with about as much sense as a scarecrow. But I also think I've got something to say about how easy it is to make people my age vulnerable, if, in fact, they engaged in what was common enough behavior at the time."

And then Ken Rudin beeped the car horn and O'Malley ducked underneath the cameras, and now he was home with his old man, who was not asking him hostile questions or even how long it was he planned to be home. The toughest question his father had for him was whether he wanted to sleep in the room in which he'd grown up or in the more comfortable guest room on the second floor. His old room it was.

Upon the old man's suggestion, O'Malley first went to call his mother, who was certain to still be awake at the Hay-Adams. She was in town for the ACLU convention, where she was fully prepared to catcall the President if the White House was still shunning the only thing she liked about them: her son. She'd called halfway through the show to tell her estranged husband that their only child was acquitting himself with dignity.

O'Malley headed for the stairwell. The dogs thumped their tails as if they had a new playmate.

L ong after the place had shut down, after Yolanda had called in from outside the door to tell him she was going, Nicole sat in his office at Globe. He'd watched "Nightline," having been tipped off midway through that O'Malley was on. Now he slumped in the easy chair by his rolltop desk, his gun on the table before him, the nearly empty canister of cocaine no longer bringing him pleasure.

In fact, quite the opposite. His head was throbbing, he still had the clarity of mind the coke brought in its better phases, only now it had jettisoned the euphoria like a rocket dropping off its booster stage, and still he was out there, heading into space, but with a vision of oblivion, not nirvana, as his immediate destiny.

He got up and turned off the brightest light, one of those modern stand-up jobs that Tina had ordered from the Lightolier catalogue, and then crossed the room to fetch a beer from the small fridge under the pool table. The place was a wreck, he knew that he stank, his dog was twitching in his tormented sleep, and he felt headachy and exhausted, as well as wide awake and alert on the level in which anything, a pin drop, a creak in the staircase, could provide his mood with a fresh excuse to plummet further, to drop as far below emotional sea level as earlier in the evening it had been elevated. The trouble now was, unless he could leaven it one way or another, he was headed to a kind of introspective hell that, rather than the flaming kind, was all dull aches, sleeplessness, and analysis of the errors he'd made, worse even than when he'd been arrested by Feds more than a decade ago.

He screwed off the top of the beer and sat back down in the couch, and by this time, he'd determined that the only way he could possibly relax was to turn off even the light above the rolltop desk. Serenity could only be reached in darkness.

Though it was hard to figure out how he could be serene when fucking O'Malley had just gone on national television and, he had to admit, been pretty goddamn good at wriggling out of the mess he was in. That was a new talent for old Thomas, for trying to talk your way out of trouble had always been Nicole's job when they were growing up.

The darkness of his office was soothing and though his palms were cold and clammy and his heart was still clanging like a burglar alarm, he directed himself into a groove of calm where he could live with himself for at least the next few minutes, if only he could sit still.

Often when he was alone and had snorted massive amounts of co-caine, the particular perch that he found himself sitting on hours later, outside of himself and peering in with the full scroll of his personal history able to be unwound and reexamined from the fresh viewpoint of changed consciousness, he would go through a recitation of the facts of his life and wonder just what it was that had gone wrong. But then, over the last year, he hadn't gotten so far out there on a vapor trail of blow, for Tina had held this impulse in check, just as she had controlled so many other of his tendencies, not the least of which was the sheer joy he got from the money he made, the excitement he felt from the danger of dealing first-rate drugs.

He shouldn't have dug so deeply into his stash tonight, not just because he didn't have all that much coke left, but because he would need to be fit in the days ahead. With Tom O'Malley puking his guts out for all the world to see, with John Santangelo pissed to the point of serious violence, he would have to negotiate between the Scylla of the Feds and the Charybdis of broken kneecaps. It depressed him to the point that for a second he thought he might like another little line, just a nightcap. That perked up his heartbeat. But when he realized there was no point to it, it was nearly three-thirty in the morning and he'd be up all night if he did any more, he was depressed anew.

And that's when, sitting there in the darkness, Bowser suddenly was on his feet and heading over to the door that went to the hallway leading to the dance-floor bar. The old Doberman was wagging his sawed-off tail and beginning to whimper in a fashion that usually preceded his beginning to howl at strangers.

In a flash, Nicole was over to the door with the gun, his heart chugging along from more than just the high-octane chemicals pulsing through it. He leaned toward the old dog. "What is it, Bow?"

The dog stamped his feet and let his entire back section shimmy and sway like he was a "Solid Gold" dancer. And that's when Nicole saw just the faint rivulet of light flow for a moment underneath the door. He grabbed the dog—he wouldn't bark if commanded not to—and hushed him, though the big old thing trembled like a racehorse in the gate.

Now Nicole could hear the person who was bumping around in the bar area, though only for a second or two. He flashed on who it might be, and there were no satisfactory answers. Yolanda had a set of keys, and so did Nguyen. Neither of them had a good reason to be there. No one had a good reason to be there.

Hushing Bowser, putting his arms around him and stroking his smooth coat with the heel of the automatic, he made to leave him in the office for a moment while he went out to see who was there. If it was one of the Salami Brothers, he was fully prepared to order him off the premises at gunpoint. If it was anyone else, he was fully prepared to shoot. He didn't have a permit for the gun, but he'd rather have to explain why he had one than have someone else explain on the local news how he died.

And then a thought crossed his mind, somewhere near the intersection where cocaine was being introduced to adrenaline and they were hitting it off like playground chums. He thought that the person out there, wherever he now was, might be an FBI agent, planting bugs, just searching the place, doing whatever it was G-men did in the post-Hoover era other than stand in cheap suits in bars, drinking ice water. It would be messy to shoot a federal agent. But no messier than being shot by a federal agent.

Slowly, shushing the dog he left behind, Nicole opened the door from his office, making certain that there was no sign of the flashlight or whatever it was that shone beneath his door a few moments before. His eyes were already adjusted to the darkness as he began to sidle down the corridor that ran behind the bar, the cases of booze stacked floor to ceiling along the narrow hall.

He stopped when he got to the bar's edge, the large room so quiet and dark. There was someone else in the building, he knew, sensing the person's almost palpable presence.

His elbow crooked with the gun at a forty-five-degree angle, Nicole tiptoed along the edge of the dance floor, around the end of the bar. Though his nose was nearly out of commission, he thought he could smell something that was out of place in a room that normally smelled of beer.

He realized he was standing in a puddle; the floor was wet with something. Only when he knelt down and put his finger in the wetness and held it to his battered nose, tasted it on his tongue, only then did he realize it was gasoline.

And then up the stairs in a vast combustion that sounded like the very molecules of air sizzling came a moving sheet of flames that was upon him in a half-second in which he jumped, possibly saved by that nexus of cocaine and adrenaline, out of its flow, away from a flaming wall. He leapt and rolled across the dance floor in front of the bar and was on his feet with the gun outstretched as he realized the flames were headed, by design, it was clear, down the hallway he'd just walked down, right into the office he'd just left. Right into the office where he'd just left Bowser, who now was barking piteously, mewling in a voice of pure canine terror.

He moved toward the sheet of flames for just a second, but by then it was so hot, had engulfed the bar, was finding purchase on the couches near the back of the room, that the only thing he could do was try to find his way out. The staircase was a solid, roaring flame. He started to choke and thus ran, almost automatically, toward the darkened plastic wall on whose map of South America came the reflection of the flames that chased after him. It took only a second to knock through it and get to the window behind it, behind which was the fire escape that D.C. fire inspectors had pronounced safe and sound. Coughing, almost choking, with tears running down his cheek, he made it to the fresh air that had never in the history of Adams Morgan smelled so sweet, and within seconds he'd dropped to the back alleyway behind Globe. He stood there for a moment and watched it all, depictions of the world, state-of-the-art sound system, even his faithful old dog, go up in smoke and flames that brought sirens from which he could only run.

It was unusual, in Curt Helden's experience, for two dozen reporters, many of them from out of state, to show up at a Chamber of Commerce breakfast at 7:00 A.M. on a Wednesday morning, but then, Tony Partridge was news. Surely half the crowd of one hundred businessmen in their best suits and cowboy hats had shown up here at the Casper Holiday Inn not because they expected to hear a stem-winder full of insights from a Washingtonian on such items as water rights, PIK payments, and high-yield super fertilizers set for approval by the Ag Department. Though the ranchers among them probably had their questions about that damfool cholesterol-labeling legislation Partridge had last week announced and promptly forgotten about, they were there mostly for one reason: to see if the idiot didn't step on his dick in public again, the way he had ever since this drug story broke a few days before.

Curt was pretty pleased with the role his newspaper had played in sparking a controversy that had brought Rocky Mountain bureau chiefs of the big Eastern papers up here all the way from Denver. For Senator Partridge was in a heap of trouble, especially now that the *Casper Star-Tribune* had a story on its front page that described a party five years ago at Jackson Hole. It seemed a number of attendees were willing to state for the record that they remembered the pretty boy leaning over a table with a straw in his nose scarfing up the mound of that cocaine stuff just as easy as you please. When you coupled that with the A.P. story about that White House aide who'd claimed last night on Koppel that he'd agreed under duress to mule drugs, you had a veritable phenomenon, a national scandal with a Wyomingite involved.

The one hundred or so good businessmen who ate their pancakes and eggs while they waited for the Senator to get up and speak, clearly expected Partridge to make some kind of reference to the scandal, and if he didn't, it was a certainty he'd get asked about it. It was a certainty that Curt himself, smoking a cigarette and leaning back in his chair at the press table, would stand up and put him on the spot.

So when Ike Outlaw, the flamboyant president of the Chamber stood up and twisted his flaming red mustache and announced they were pleased to have their guest with them today, people paid attention, even to the point of stopping the daubing of buttered toast in their egg yolks. Ike looked fiendishly into the crowd and said, "And so I introduce to you a man with a great deal of explaining to do, our Senator—for how long, no one knows—Tony Partridge!"

There was only polite applause, the dozens of Republican boosters noticeably confused about whether they should put any feeling into their greeting because he was a Republican, or whether they should stifle their response due to the precise nature of the accusations against him.

Across the back of the room, cameramen focused on the young Senator, who Curt thought looked more than a little bit too Washingtonian in his expensive blue suit. Partridge was clearly nervous as he surveyed his crowd. His eyes seemed to catch on the press table and he seemed to get spooked and depressed, all at once, as if he were saying to himself, So those bastards are back. Curt flicked his cigarette ash onto his half-eaten pancakes and took out his pad and tape recorder, his expectations of the sorry bastard making unprompted news very low indeed.

"I want to thank you all for coming this morning," the Senator began, without a grin, without the endearing joke, as serious as if he were giving the Gettysburg Address. "Some of you are old friends, some of you new friends, and some of you, namely that table of the press back there, aren't friends at all."

People began to laugh, as if to say, Here it is, here's the politician's dumb opening joke, but the Senator was serious. "Today, with sadness, I have an announcement to make. I am not now, nor will I be, a candidate for senator next year. I have made this determination based on the controversy I find myself in, with the knowledge that I have done nothing that millions of others have not also done, but with a full knowledge that what I have done is unacceptable for someone seeking the high office of the United States Senate."

Partridge kept on, reporters furiously scribbling down what he said, the tables of ranchers as shocked and silent as if they were watching a steer sing "Stormy Monday." But Curt just sat there as his cigarette burned down on his yellow-stained fingers, amazed at this turn of events, thinking that the Governor had done it. He'd spooked the bastard out of the race.

'Malley awoke with sunshine in his face. It streamed through the familiar window as an announcement of improved outlook. There was a sense of safety conveyed by the tonier surroundings of the tree-lined Georgetown street outside, the worn sheets and blanket that smelled of a home life that hadn't existed for him, really, since his parents' separation; and the smell of the coffee his father was making downstairs made his spirits soar. He had awakened in a good mood for the first time since David Nicole had reentered his life several weeks before—it seemed longer ago than that—when there had been a chill in the air.

His feet touched down on the creaky wooden floor and he padded to the bathroom in the hallway, a feeling of sureness about who he was and what he was doing on this planet suffusing his being in a manner it had not for a very long time. This felt like vacation more than exile, more than imprisonment. He went back into his room and found the dress shirt he'd worn on national television the night before, and putting it on as a kind of bathrobe, he made to go down for breakfast.

Sunlight poured in through the window in the upstairs den and he looked in as a corner of the Gauguin was touched by it, its shadow along the dark blue wall, the old coffee table and cracked leather couch engaging his senses with a solitary message: home.

When he got downstairs, his father and the dogs were gone, out for a walk, no doubt. The coffee machine was finishing its dripping and he went automatically to the cabinet where the coffee mugs were stacked, though none too neatly. Carmela was due back over the weekend.

His father had left the *Post* spread on the kitchen table, and there he was, a picture of him facing the camera, Koppel with his back to it, printed with the graininess that meant it had been taken right off the television. He desired coffee more than he desired news of his predicament, so he took the time to pour himself a cup, and then sat at the table where so many breakfasts had been served to him as he was growing up.

The *Post* clearly had been taken as much by surprise by his appearance on "Nightline" as had the people at ABC, for while they had a brief article about the "dramatic appearance," it was wedged in between other stories about the White House having leaked the telephone logs of his calls to Globe, with more background quotes about how the Justice Department was determined he be prosecuted to the fullest.

The important thing was that the story on his appearance announced he'd "changed the dynamic of his prosecution" by "confessing his guilt, while at the same time foreshadowing his defense." Somehow, the reporter had reached William Orloff at home, who'd allowed as how "the cocked-gun-to-my-head defense probably won't work in court." Oh, thought O'Malley, the guy's now become an expert on the judiciary as well. Maybe it had been a mistake to displace him; there was much damage Orloff could do as he established conventional wisdom quote by cookie-cutter unquote.

The sound of the dogs bumping into the door preceded the sound of his father's keys. And then they were in the front door in a tear, Zippy nosing against his bare feet, Peggy deliberately thwacking her tail against the refrigerator, Danny trotting toward him with his mouth open and his tongue working around his thin black gums, before he dipped his shoulders and yawned.

"Morning," his father said cheerfully. He was carrying a bag of pastries from the American Cafe, his walk surely comprising more exercise than the old man had gotten in months.

"Hi," O'Malley said, scratching Zippy's head.

"Sleep well?"

"Great. It looks beautiful out."

"Almost summer," his father said, putting the bag down on the counter and then taking a plate from the cabinet. "We've got visitors."

"Oh."

"Camera crews. I recognized a couple of them from when they were staking me out. I said hi to the bastards."

O'Malley blinked for a moment, taking in that the crews had staked him out here as well. It made sense they would know he was here.

"Did the phone wake you?"

"No, I didn't hear a thing, I don't think. Someone called?"

"It was Kit. She didn't want me to wake you, but she called here when she couldn't reach you at your home. Seems she was a little surprised this morning when she read the headline in the *New York Post*."

"Yeah?"

" 'MULE COKE OR FACE MUSIC, WH DRUG AIDE SEZ,' I believe was the front-page headline. Something like that. Danish?"

"Sure." Not even a headline like that could shatter the good mood O'Malley was in this morning. Never before had he understood the maxim that the truth shall set you free. Today it beamed at him as sunnily as the three dogs crowding the kitchen. His father put the pastry out as they discussed the Orioles. Snapshot of normalcy. It felt good.

it's father, oblivious in the morning to anything other than the sport of accumulating power, merely kissed her on the forehead before he pressed the elevator button in the vestibule of their co-op, preparing to descend into the pit of money-making, which is how he described the outside world. She wasn't quite so lucky when it came to her mother.

Babe Bowles, silver-haired but no less elegant than she had been as a deb, was on the whole a good friend to her only daughter, though when Kit caused the family to come under social scrutiny, as she had over the last few days, Babe wasn't shy about expressing her feelings. She was fully prepared to make her daughter pay for the right to retreat here in their fourteen-room Park Avenue spread with its studied re-creation of an English country home.

"I suppose you realize this finishes your chance to ever be anything in life," her mother pronounced over breakfast served in their paneled dining room by McDougal, the family's ancient Jamaican butler. "I mean anything that matters."

"Mother, if you don't mind, I have not had a very easy week." She stirred her coffee and went back to flipping the *Times*.

"I'm sorry for you, dear, but do you suppose this has been easy on us?" her mother asked. "I can't tell you how many reporters have called your father's office asking for him to comment."

"Look, Ma, it's not like I'm Patty Hearst or something. We went through all this years ago when David was arrested."

"I see your taste in men certainly has improved since then," her mother said sarcastically, holding up the *New York Post*, with its photo of O'Malley on "Nightline." While Kit hadn't seen his performance— she'd gotten home at half past one in the morning—she'd caught the snippet they showed on "Good Morning America," and CNN was showing an excerpt every fifteen minutes, or so it seemed.

Her shock at seeing Tom wrestle so sincerely with Koppel was second only to her surprise at the wire-service report from Wyoming that Senator Partridge had just announced he would not run for the seat he'd been appointed to. CNN's anchor had perkily intoned that this followed the disclosure that witnesses placed the U.S. Senator at a cocaine party some five years before. With O'Malley's performance and her former boss's destruction to take in, her tolerance for her mother's intolerance was limited.

She sat at the table eating the grapefruit and fresh muffin McDougal served, and wondered what possibly could be next for O'Malley, whom she missed with a vehemence equal only to her determination to get out of this house and away from her mother's concern with their social standing. Her mother chattered on, but Kit's eyes glazed over, locked on the Audubon print on the far wall, the flower arrangement in the center of the twelve-foot table. In Kit's mind, her mother's concerns were reduced to the level of ambient noise.

After breakfast, she took a bath. The door was closed to the sound of the maids vacuuming the miles of carpet, and Kit lay in the tub, talking on the telephone, laughing as O'Malley described the scene. "He named names, he laid it on the Governor's doorstep."

"You're kidding," she trilled.

"I kid you not. Reporters told Max that Partridge claimed those two consultants were set up by the Gov, and apparently he got all huffy about it. He said he was going to use what power he still had as a senator to get the bastard impeached, if it was the last thing he ever did, or something like that."

"Who would have thought he'd have taken it to this level?" she asked, lazily soaping herself as the water cooled and she leaned against the inlaid Mexican tiles at the back of the tub in this bathroom half the size of her Washington apartment. The price of having to deal with her parents was worth it, if contact was limited to mealtimes.

"You know, I'm glad Partridge has some fight in him. The funniest thing he's gotten into the middle of is the story I heard that when what's his name, Mike Humperdink, got to make his call from jail, the person he called was Rod Gardener at the White House. Max told me the Governor of Wyoming is out there trying to get reporters to look into whether Humperdink and Jetta got their drugs from the Deputy White House Counsel. Gardener's denying it, but it sure is fun. By the way, that *New York Post* headline's hilarious."

"I'm glad you take it that way. I wish I'd seen you on 'Nightline.' "

"Max said reporters think I did okay. They're pestering McCurry this morning, apparently, asking him what the President's going to do. This in turn is causing an internal problem for them because the President's supposed to speak to the ACLU at the Marriott tonight, and they don't know what to say about me."

She reached with her foot to turn on more hot water. "I don't get it."

"After last night, according to Max, the ACLU folks are saying my case raises all sorts of questions about what's fair in terms of looking into people's past lives before they're allowed to work in government."

"Is anybody listening to them?"

"The White House press corps is, but mostly because Hardison's gotta talk to them tonight. A happy coincidence." He sounded pleased.

"That's great, considering the lengths he had to go to during the campaign to distance himself from those pointy heads."

"Kit, no one who's on my side can be characterized as a 'pointy head.' "

Kit turned the tap further so more hot water came out. "I wish you'd escaped with me. I have this bad feeling about you being in the same town with Nicole. The *Times* story on him this morning was pretty tough."

"I haven't seen the *Times* yet, but I'll have plenty of time to luxuriate in the papers when this thing burns out. Considering it's going to be years before I get another job! I don't know whether resolution means setting a court date, or precisely not setting a court date, though that would be nice. This is such a terrible town," he said, apropos of nothing.

"But I'm safe here for the time being. There are a bunch of reporters outside, but I'm okay otherwise."

"What about Nicole?"

"Haven't heard a work on that front. If he's looking for me, he'll find me here. Dad says he was here the other night, but we don't know what he was up to. I suspect he's got troubles enough with the law right about now."

"You're okay, though?" she asked.

Because in his father's house he was able to chalk up the jam he was in as a human mistake, as something he could cope with, it was easy for him to tell her he was fine.

There was one thing he knew. If to be stupid is to be human, he didn't have a touch of immortality to him.

Harlan stood on the sidewalk and gawked like all the others. The building was still smoking, its insides charred and gutted. There still were firemen crawling through the wreckage, sifting this way and that, and from what he could glean from the way the inspectors huddled, they must suspect this was a torch job.

The place was practically overrun by D.C. police, squabbling with the firemen, not to mention the agents, most of them unfamiliar to him but nonetheless easily identifiable. They stood at the periphery of the crowd, trying to make sense of why the building had burned down, and how it fit into the saga of David Nicole and Thomas O'Malley.

Harlan was beat, he was angry and hungover. It sickened him that he wasn't at work, that this wasn't his case, given that his instincts had been correct all along. The race was on to nail these bastards, though clearly, someone other than the authorities appeared to be trying to nail Nicole as well.

I t was the phone that would not stop ringing that finally roused him from the sleep that is not sleep, that shallow, suffocating exhaustion which follows overindulgence in the Bolivian stimulant. Nicole woke up instantly panic-stricken.

"David, we find you home. At last. Don't worry, I'm not downstairs." It was Santangelo, sounding simultaneously kindly and threatening. "Have you seen what happened to your nightclub?" John asked incredulously, as if it were a shock to him too.

"I was there," he said in a voice that was parched as a yucca plant. He tried to sniff, but his nostrils were like a foundation after the cement has hardened.

"No!" said John. "You were there? Then maybe you can tell me. What was it? Spontaneous combustion? Lightning? A gas leak? Don't tell me arson, because that might be discovered and then the insurance company wouldn't pay out, and you'd still owe me seventy-five K, and then what would you do?"

"I'm going to get you the painting, John. I told you that."

"There are about a dozen things you've told me that haven't come through for me, sweetheart. Not least of which is that painting, whose existence I'll believe when I see it auctioned off at Sotheby's, or Hank's Frame Barn in Baltimore. But your ideas don't catch fire. There's no spark to your imagination. I mean, are you prepared to go down in flames over the failure of your plan?"

"Very funny." Nicole was lying flat on his back staring at the ceiling, almost ready to hang up the phone.

"I'm, how you say? Deadly serious about this. You don't seem to take me very seriously, however. I thought batting practice would have changed that."

Nicole hung up on him. Which was a stupid thing to do, he realized. But it wasn't like it was going to make Santangelo madder than he already was.

He lay there with his head throbbing as the phone rang and rang and rang.

is father had a gadget that let him know the phone was safe. So he spent some time calling up his chums. Based on the updates O'Malley was getting from Max every few hours, the dynamic among the media appeared to have shifted, and in his favor. Senator Bligh, whose antennae were sharp, was suddenly asking whether or not the White House had attempted to spirit the correct information out of O'Malley, instead of just threatening him with prosecution. Perhaps, suggested Bligh, the White House should be dangling immunity from prosecution in 'order to get the bastard to implicate whoever else was involved, and there were others involved, the Senator just knew it. "That fool could fuck up a two-car funeral," the Majority Leader announced to the press that gathered in his Capitol office. "Obviously, someone else was the brains of the operation."

Reporters converged on Willy Barnes, as the Assistant to the President for Political Affairs came out of a private briefing at the downtown Marriott with a number of the Hollywood stars who had come to town for the ACLU convention. He was forced to admit the White House was doing polling to see how the nation was reacting to the Cokegate scandal. Under duress—they weren't going to let him get into his White House car unless he coughed up some kind of answer—he admitted there were early indications that, among baby boomers at least, there was some support for the arguments O'Malley had made last night on "Nightline." Mostly, it appeared, there was admiration for O'Malley taking it like a man. The public, Barnes confided, trusted O'Malley after his "Nightline" confession.

CNN reported that the dapper political director had admitted that the President was under conflicting pressures, with some of his advisers saying the White House should throw the book at the speechwriter and others saying they should show lenience. Now that commentators were hyping up the baby boomer angle, there were those arguing that the President could go a long way toward solidifying his support with the majority of voters between twenty-five and forty-five if he were to show some understanding of the peculiar pressures felt by those who came of age in the sixties and seventies.

All this, said Max, was reflective of an easing of hostility toward O'Malley in the official White House line. "I'm not saying you're off the hook, man, but I do know we're supposed to at least pretend we were moved by what you had to say last night. Oh, and don't worry, buddy, I don't have to pretend."

hough it clearly was one of the most beautiful days of the year, Nicole took the time to put the top up on his Alfa before speeding away from his neighborhood just as quickly as he could. This wasn't the day to be seen driving around the District with the top down. He was all the way out in some suburban mall at a fairly dingy Denny's, drinking mid-afternoon coffee and poking listlessly at a garden salad while he leafed through *The New York Times*. The article on him was riddled with inaccuracies.

It wasn't because of that article, though it was because of the *Times*, that he made the decision not to cut and run. There was another article, on page B4, that got his attention, this one about the police informant rubbed out by the Mob six years after he'd squealed. Nicole had to consider what Santangelo's chums had wrought.

They'd already burned down his nightclub, killed his dog, and frightened his girlfriend into running off to some Pacific isle. While the FBI was hot on his trail, not to mention the media, it was the Mob, Santangelo's loose alliance of business partners, that put the fear of God into him; a reckoning God who knew how to settle scores.

Of all the things that had happened, the one that haunted him was the notion that, wherever he went, John Santangelo would follow him. He already had a West Coast drug dealer with a reason to tear him limb from limb, and the attention he was getting now must have caught the attention of even that bozo. Santangelo and the people he hung out with were not the kind to let something drop. They were not the kind to just let something go. They were more like the Mounties than the FBI were: unlike the Feds, the Mob always got its man.

He sat there in the tacky suburban surroundings smoking cigarettes and drinking cup after cup of bad coffee the waitresses kept serving him without being bidden. In this way he wasted nearly two hours, until finally it was time to get back into the Alfa and head back to D.C., his plan for at last getting the painting that would buy him his freedom formulating in his weary mind. In his latest plan, he would surprise O'Malley's father, shoot the dogs as just recompense for the way Bowser had been killed by John Santangelo, and waltz off with the Gauguin strapped to the top of his Alfa. He hoped it didn't rain. It was a simple plan, but he had simple needs. He had to get his hands on a million-dollar painting and then get out of town.

He was driving past the Pentagon, his mind wandering to questions of the firepower it would take to get into old man O'Malley's house, when WHFS broke mid-song with an update on the Cokegate scandal.

"This just in, and it's a doozy," said the nerd who played such great afternoon music. "Mutual News is reporting—get this—the President put out word that Thomas O'Malley—he's the guy who confessed last night he was trying to smuggle kilos of coke in on Air Force One—is back in the White House's good graces. Do not adjust your set, do not turn the dial. You heard it right, and you heard it here first. The White House is bringing Thomas O'Malley back to work until he goes to trial for conspiracy to distribute narcotics. Hmmm. Wonder what the President was smoking when he made that decision. We'll be back with a full report later, but now here's the Rolling Stones with 'Sister Morphine.'"

Nicole did not drive off the road, though drivers in the cars behind him would be forgiven for thinking that's what he was doing. It took moments for him to bring the car under control. He was going to have to go get that painting before there were any more surprises.

I t seemed he answered every one of Jake's questions with either a "Yessir" or a "Nossir," as if he were either a grunt freshly arrived at boot camp or a character in a Ray Davies song. It was guilt that had made him do it, not that he felt he'd done anything wrong by going on "Nightline," but he should have asked Jake's permission before actually going and, as Jake said to him in no uncertain terms, jeopardizing his defense of him.

"You have probably screwed things up about as completely as could be, you realize that?"

"Yessir."

"Did you think before you went on 'Nightline,' or were you as much on automatic pilot as you were when you conspired to distribute Class-A narcotics from Venezuela?"

"Nossir."

"Nossir what?"

"Nossir, I didn't think, sir."

"For crying out loud, Tom, don't patronize me. I'm just telling you you may have bollixed the whole goddamn thing up. You don't leave me very many options. 'Not guilty because I was being blackmailed' isn't much of a plea, unless the law's changed since I last was in court, which it hasn't, by the way, since I was in court on Friday."

"Yessir."

He was sitting at the desk in his father's den, his father was napping, the dogs all asleep on the floor. It was an interesting series of calls he was on, first having been told by Ken Rudin that Globe had been burned down and that the fire department clearly had determined it was arson— set by whom, they either didn't know or weren't saying. He'd been told by Max that McCurry had been among the officials called in to a meeting in the Cabinet Room, and Anna Bennett, the President's pollster, had been called in along with officials from the Democratic National Committee. Also, according to Max, McCurry—who knew he was in contact with O'Malley—asked if Max knew where O'Malley was right now. Why he wanted to know where he could be reached, Max couldn't say, but since McCurry was his boss, he'd told him. The important thing was, something was up.

Right, thought O'Malley. First and foremost, Jake's dander. "Do you realize that until last night there was better than a sixty-to-forty chance we could have prevented there even being an indictment?"

"Yessir."

Suddenly there was a third person on the line. "Operator," said a singsong voice, identifying herself. "There's an emergency phone call from the White House for Mr. Thomas O'Malley."

"That's me, operator."

"Please clear the line."

"Yes ma'am. Uncle Jake?"

"I'll talk to you later."

Within a minute of his hanging up the phone it rang again, and

O'Malley picked it up with trepidation. He didn't know who it was for sure, but he had an idea.

"This is the White House operator for Mr. O'Malley."

"This is he."

"Hold please."

And then ninety seconds later it was the President on the line, and the first thing he asked was if O'Malley was ready to come back to work. Being used to saying "Yessir," he didn't waste any words. He was barely shocked by the offer, for this was the fantasy he'd played in his mind for the last few days, whether he knew it or not.

When he tried to tell the President how much he regretted the difficulties he'd caused him, how disappointed he was in himself, and how much he appreciated this chance to come back inside the White House gates, the President hurriedly told him they'd have plenty of time to talk about it.

Then he asked O'Malley if he wanted to come back right away, meaning that in about two hours a White House car would pick him up for the ACLU affair at which the President would announce O'Malley's reprieve. It didn't seem like he had much choice. O'Malley heard himself saying, "Yessir."

There was just one thing, he said to the President. He would like his father to be able to come along, too. He wanted the old man to have just this taste of rehabilitation.

"Done," said the President.

"Yessir," said O'Malley, and then he was whooping down the hallway to wake up the old man.

 had to tell them," Rudin was saying at the door. He was trying to be nice, but clearly his job was at stake. "They'd have killed me at work if I hadn't told them you were back in good graces. Okay, okay, they blackmailed me into doing it," he said with a smile. "Because of something I once did in college. Yeah, that's the ticket. Thanks for telling me first, by the way."

Behind him, with faces set in about as friendly a manner as inmates about to be served baked beans for the third night in a row, was a motley crew of some fifty members of the media, including at least a dozen cameras.

O'Malley stared at his would-be interrogators. "I'll be right there," he said with resignation.

"What's going on?" his father asked, as he came down the stairs. The dogs were clearly riled up and ready to roll. They ran against the door and bounced off it with loud thuds, knocked into the table in the center of the entranceway, ran up the stairs and right back down again as if chasing a backflipping muskrat.

"My media chums have found out about the invitation to come back to the White House."

O'Malley went into the small guest bathroom off the hall to the kitchen and emerged a moment later with his tie on and his hair combed. "You almost ready for your big evening?" he asked his father.

"I will be shortly," he announced.

And then O'Malley went out the front door, careful to keep the dogs inside. The press was clearly more respectful today now that the White House had confirmed they were going to allow O'Malley to come back to work until such time as the Justice Department brought charges, *if* they brought charges.

He walked down the steps and along the hedges on each side of the four-foot-wide brick path that led to the street. There were so many people crushing around the house that the police had had to put saw-horses up on each end of the block to keep cars from turning onto it.

"How does it feel to have the President call you and tell you all is forgiven?" asked a reporter in the front of the crowd.

"Well, he didn't, but it feels pretty good," O'Malley answered sincerely, somewhat joyously. Thus began the half-hour news conference that just a brief time later would show up on the evening news. If O'Malley had been able to look at the periphery of the crowd, he might have noticed David Nicole, hanging back, careful to stay hidden, looking awful, watching as his friend shucked and jived before the cameras.

He had the television set in the living room tuned to CBS while over the phone Kit told him what ABC was doing to him. "Jennings just said, 'Not precisely pardoned, but aboot to go as the President's guest to a gala celebrating civil liberties.' "

"He said, 'A boot'?"

"That's the way it sounded," Kit breathed over the phone, excited for him, wishing she were there.

Just then Dan Rather was saying, "A presidential 'What, me worry?' in the current White House cocaine scandal. President Hardison called suspected drug smuggler Thomas O'Malley this afternoon saying, 'All's not forgiven, but let's have dinner anyway.' Wyatt Phillips has the story."

"The phone call came at four-thirty this afternoon, and a relieved Tom O'Malley heard the good news." O'Malley suddenly saw himself on the screen, standing right in front of the window that now was behind him, and he heard himself say, "The President came on the line and just asked me if I wanted to go back to work."

"And how did you feel?" someone asked.

"How do you think? It was a real rush."

I didn't actually say that, did I? O'Malley asked himself.

"Oh, Tom," groaned Kit over the phone.

"What?"

"You didn't actually say that the President's call was a rush, did you?"

"They have that on ABC?"

"Yep."

"CBS, too. Guess I should have used different language, huh?"

"Kind of," she said, without wishing to push it, as if this wasn't the time to lecture him.

His father came into the room with a drink in his hand, his hair slicked glamorously, his best Savile Row suit on. He looked like an elegant playboy on his way to the gaming tables. He stood for a second and watched the news. Senator Chester Berretta, the Republican Leader, looked like he was about to explode with all the things he wanted to say about the President's lack of judgment in bringing O'Malley back to the White House until he was prosecuted on drug charges. "That little smuggler should be in a jail cell, not the Oval Office. If the Constitution had a clause that said you could impeach a president for stupidity, Hardison'd be gone by Friday."

"I guess your vote of confidence from the President isn't getting universal raves," his father said dryly as O'Malley watched CBS and listened to Kit's play-by-play of ABC.

The doorbell rang and his father said, "I'll get it," and turned and walked back into the foyer while the dogs barked and rushed from where they were to converge once more on the door. They never seemed to tire of this ritual.

"It's the White House car, Tom. You ready?" his father called.

"Kit, I gotta go. Wish me luck, and I'll call you later," he said, and hanging up the phone, set off with his father.

ameras crowded around the black town car that came to old man O'Malley's to pick the two of them up. Nicole sat on the hood of his car, almost a block away, disgusted. When the car pulled down the block to make the turn down to M Street, a police officer moving the sawhorses out of the way, Nicole casually walked over to a tree and stood behind it. He did so just in case O'Malley was taking a nostalgic glance at the old neighborhood on his way to meet with the President.

The good news for Nicole was the way the media broke and rushed to their cars to follow the White House town car with the father- and son-team in the back, thus giving him a convoy to tag along with. The bad news, however, was that several reporters continued to stand guard outside the O'Malley home, staking it out for the return trip. It didn't make sense to try breaking in for the painting with numerous camera crews there to film him fighting with the mutts. If he was going to get in and out with the painting tonight, he would need a passport. Either O'Malley or his old man was going to be the passport.

He threw the cigarette he was smoking into the bushes and got in the Alfa. He hoped there was parking, wherever they were headed.

Even some of the other regulars here at the Parliamentarian felt the same way Harlan Bryce did, and though he didn't often get in conversations with them—these guys were drunks, lushes, you didn't want to talk to them—he found himself drawn into the denunciations of what it was they'd seen on television: the triumphant little dope addict standing pleased as could be, announcing that he was going back to the White House tomorrow, and that he'd been invited to a party for—and this made sense—the ACLU tonight. The ACLU. While Harlan would soon be out on the street, looking for work as an investigator, and knowing he would probably end up as a director of corporate security someplace, that spoiled little fuck-up was going to be feted at the White House mess. Washington was certainly no place to look for justice.

So he sat at the table near the door, occasionally looking out on Eleventh Street, occasionally looking up at the television above the bar, which had a bunch of legislative pointy heads discussing the implications of the President's seeming pardon of the little jerk. Some fat senator was getting worked into a lather about how terrible a precedent the President had set, while some slick young cowboy, an unctuous Democrat congressman from a safe seat in the Northwest, talked about "the quality of mercy," or some such hogwash. Harlan growled to himself, ordered another Stoly, and then put his feet up on the chair across from him, just watching the cars roll by out the window of the bar.

It was when the car pulled up underneath the awning and the tall doorman in the pith helmet and regimental uniform leaned over to open the door that O'Malley realized his change of status. Rather than the media that surrounded them appearing to be adversaries who needed footage for "Meet the Press," they were more like groupies filming a lead-in for "Entertainment

Tonight." They urged him to smile, they racked him in a pose with his old man, they held the door open and rushed to get in front of them so they could film from underneath as the O'Malleys descended the steps into the basement floor where the ACLU dinner was to be held.

Women in elegant party dresses, men in dark suits, a few in tuxedos, stared at O'Malley as if he were a film star. They waved and gawked and it was rather unsettling. The many tiers of the Marriott lobby were like D. W. Griffith's version of Babylon, with fountains and a variegated landscape on which choruses chanting Mesopotamian pop songs would not have seemed out of place. They strode down the steps without anyone leading, other than the cameramen who nearly crashed over the railings as they stumbled backward. They could have been heading to precisely the wrong event, to an event for the CPA's of America, not the ACLU ball, not an event with the President of the United States standing up to give the keynote address, O'Malley serving as his prop.

But no, there were Secret Service agents everywhere, which made it a pretty good bet that they were headed in the right direction. They continued to walk down the steps and could see that at the foot of the stairs there was a crowd milling around outside the magnetometers, women proffering their handbags to the agents, and the circular, hand-held metal detectors that were rubbed all over those people who flunked the metal test screeched above the din of voices, the thump of the tumbling cameramen.

"You okay?" he asked his father.

"Marvelous." And it was true, the old man clearly was enjoying himself, was clearly thrilled to have been invited along at the President's request. O'Malley would never tell him that it was he who requested the President invite him.

They were coming down the final steps when O'Malley saw Max Pearlman, who looked like he'd had a long day, waiting with a big grin on his face. "Yo, man of the hour," Max heralded him.

They hugged at the bottom of the steps while still photographers surrounded them and the flashes went off. Then Katherine Tierney was upon him and clutching him to her ample breast. "Oh, Tom, it's great to see you," she said, grabbing him by his arms and pushing him back from her so she could take in his whole being, and then yanking him back to her. She crushed him with a bear hug that had him gasping for breath. "Goddamn, it's great to see you."

"Katherine, Max, this is my dad."

"Oooh," said Katherine, charmed. "So you're the right-wing ter-rorist."

"In a former life," his father said, mock-bowing. He was on his best behavior, but he clearly wanted a drink. He was looking around the room to see if any waiters were walking by with silver trays topped by champagne flutes.

"I just met your wife," Katherine said to the old man.

"Yes, she's here, isn't she?" He said it with a marked absence of hostility.

"She's inside."

"You want a drink, Dad? We can go in in a second."

"Let me grab you for a minute first, and tell you what the drill is," Max said to him seriously.

Katherine, who was at least a foot taller than Max, took Mr. O'Malley's arm and linked it in hers. "We'll go in together. Tom, see you in there. You're going to love the speech the President makes. We updated it when he made the decision to let you back. Will and Colin had a hand in it, but if you like it, I wrote it. If you hate it, I'll blame them."

"Thanks, Katherine," he said sincerely. And then she was taking his father through the ring of media that surrounded them and O'Malley was left outside the magnetometers with Max.

"So tell me what I'm supposed to do," he said.

"Okay, here's what's going to happen," Max said, fishing in his pocket for the line-by-line schedule that made O'Malley almost weep with pleasant recognition.

The traffic around the Marriott was just about impossible to get through, which in itself was a sign the President was around there someplace. The ACLU had made it as easy as possible for the President to come to their event, or conversely, as difficult as possible for him to avoid it, in that they were having their gala less than three blocks from the White House. Police had entire blocks closed until the presidential convoy—ambulance, travel press and all—made it into the underground entrance by which the President could get to the ballroom with barely a moment's exposure to a crowd.

Knowing now where they were headed and fearing he'd be stuck in traffic forever, Nicole spun the little Alfa around on Fourteenth Street and headed back up to New York Avenue, on which he turned east. He headed all the way over to Eleventh Street before he bothered turning down, and when he saw a fire hydrant in front of Modern Wigs and Beauty Aides, he backed the little car into the space. He locked up and then stood in the street staring at his reflection in the glass of the store, the Afro wigs looking about as sorry as he did. He'd never make it past the Secret Service looking like this.

So he buttoned his top button, straightened his jacket, and neatened his hair, hoping that if worse came to worse, at least he'd look like a hotel guest, a German tourist or Southern salesman who happened to be staying overnight without having had a clue that the President of the United States would turn up there. After a minute, he passed his own muster, and looking down toward Pennsylvania Avenue and then up toward New York, he decided to walk up F Street. It was about a three-minute walk to the National Press Building, which was the back entrance to the Marriott.

He walked briskly past Hecht's department store, past the entrance to the Metro Center, and paused for a moment to light a cigarette in the reflection of Olsson's Books and Records. *If I were to see me in the crowd, would I think that person was carrying a gun?* He smiled to himself in the window. A salesclerk inside was looking at him like he was crazy and Nicole frowned. He took a deep drag from the cigarette he'd just lit and flicked it against the picture window before turning back toward his destination.

When he got to the corner of Thirteenth Street and came to the doors of the National Press Building, he straightened out his jacket so that the automatic he had stuffed into his pants was as unobtrusive as possible. Breathing deeply, he went over in his mind what he was going to do, deciding between Option A and Option B.

Option A was to go to one of the people at Call Waiting—there always was a Call Waiting at events like this—and tell whoever was sitting there that he had desperate need to talk to Mr. Robert O'Malley, that he was a reporter for . . . *Time* magazine. That should work, he thought, trying to imagine which was the publication that the old spook must have most often worked with over the years. *Time* would do it.

Then he would wait for him at some distance from the entrance to the event, and when old man O'Malley came out, he'd flash the gun discreetly and get him to come with him back to the car, and eventually, back to the house. Reporters or no reporters, they'd go inside and . . .
He preferred not to cut to that part, for one reason because he wasn't

certain what he'd do there, though he hadn't the slightest doubt that he would do whatever was necessary, whatever it took to get that painting outside and strapped onto his car. He always had bungee cords and string in the Alfa's little trunk, and it would be easy to get the painting out of there.

Option B wasn't so easy. He stood there outside the entrance. It took a minute for him to admit that he didn't know what Option B was.

T here were people O'Malley had never met who came up to him as if they were old friends, admirers, people who said they'd been in his corner all along. "Hey, Tom," guys said confidently; women winked.

"How're you doing?" he asked back, and then turned each time to Max and rolled his eyes, as if to acknowledge his strange turn of fortune.

"Okay. You want to go in?" Max was asking.

It was a strange combination of people: Hollywood starlets, Washington power brokers, and bearded civil libertarians who appeared to believe their first right was the freedom from bathing.

"Sure. It's nice of the President to get my dad and me a seat at a table up front."

"He's a great American," said his diminutive friend. "Let's go in."

"Give me just a minute. I'm going to hit the head."

"Okay, I'll meet you inside. Don't get waylaid by any admirers."

"Don't worry about me."

N icole was washing his face, trying to cool down after breaking into a sweat as he descended the staircase, trying not to attract attention. He had the lyrics, but not the music, for as smoothly as he walked, as deliberately as he moved downstairs, it was when he passed the first Secret Service agent talking into his cuff link that he realized how serious what he was doing was, and began to perspire so much he thought he was going to drench through his jacket.

When he got to the bottom of the stairs, he gravitated almost automatically toward the men's room, whose entrance was against the wall a mere thirty feet away from the metal detectors. Whoever designed this place, he thought, put the john right where it ought to be, for he hardly had to think, his feet brought him right to it.

He let the water run until it was lukewarm, and then he leaned over the sink, careful not to let his gun clink against the porcelain as the door swung open and someone walked in. He washed his face with the fancy liquid soap the hotel provided even for those who walked in off the street, even people like him, and when he rinsed the third time, he reached somewhat blindly for the paper towel in the dispenser to his left. He was wiping off his face and scowling at himself in the mirror, hoping that he'd now stop perspiring like the Washington Redskins at halftime, when he saw someone standing at the urinal across the bathroom: a familiar back. He was the only other person in the room.

"Nah," he said to himself, "it couldn't be." He continued to play with the towel, and then crumpled it, threw it in the metal wall-basket, and in one movement was over against O'Malley, pushing him against the urinal, placing the gun against his back.

"Don't fucking move, Tom. I have no qualms about shooting you. None whatsoever."

O'Malley, the porcelain urinal jammed around the bottom of his rib cage, was pressed with his face against the wall tiles, the damp metal levers pressed against his shirt and tie. He could only think to say, "Easy, easy, easy, all right, all right." He wasn't going anywhere, he wasn't going to do anything.

"You feel the pistol."

"Yeah."

"All right, I'm going to lean back. You just stay as you are, right?"

"Yeah."

And then Nicole eased back and stood a foot behind him. "Turn around, slowly," he commanded O'Malley. O'Malley slowly balanced himself back on his heels and began to fumble with the front of his pants. "Do as I fucking say, Tom!"

"You mind if I zip my pants!" He went ahead and did it, which made Nicole feel more than a little foolish. He didn't say anything, and O'Malley turned around, his shirt and tie wet from the humidity of the fixture, his dark pants stained almost imperceptibly from where he'd pissed on himself when Nicole pushed him.

Nicole fixed the pistol on him as if he were going to shoot right then, but O'Malley suddenly turned and flushed the urinal anyway. "Sorry," he said when he turned back, and Nicole felt all the more foolish. Jesus, what am I doing here? he asked himself.

"Now that you've seen the gun, Tom, I'm going to make it disappear, okay?" And with that, he put the gun inside his jacket pocket. "We're going to go walk up the stairs quietly and quickly, like we have some business to attend to, which we do, by the by."

"Where we going?" O'Malley looked utterly resigned. There was an almost contemptuous passivity to him, Nicole thought. Who could blame anyone for taking advantage of such a dweeb?

"You'll know when you get there. Now come on," he said with his hand in his jacket pocket suddenly poking the gun like a pointer toward the door. "Move."

And O'Malley did. He walked to the door of the bathroom and pulled it open, just as a fellow burst through. "Excuse me," the guy said, heading right for the urinals.

But Nicole was right behind O'Malley, whispering, "Remember, I don't mind shooting you," as they walked out into the foyer once again.

The crowd was backing up at the magnetometers, uniformed Secret Service agents poking through the ladies' handbags as O'Malley headed right for the the staircase, Nicole right behind him. They headed up the stairs as if they were friends with some secret destination, which in some ways was true. O'Malley's eyes desperately sought out an agent he could signal through a facial contortion Nicole could not see, but there's never an agent when you need one, unless you're a member of the First Family.

They were almost all the way up to the top of the stairs, the sound of the crowd below rising behind him, when the lights were dimmed for a second to signal it was time to head into the ballroom for dinner, and O'Malley used the distraction to burst forward in a run.

"I wouldn't!" Nicole shouted, just loudly enough for O'Malley to freeze, for heads to turn, but unfortunately, not for an agent to hear them. They were too high up now, in the upstairs lobby of the hotel itself. In a second, Nicole had caught up to him, and was standing right behind him, not even having to show off the gun in his pocket.

"That was really dumb," he said. "Turn left toward the Press Building."

They walked down the corridor by the jewelry store and began to leave the hotel behind. In a moment, they were in the mall that made up the bottom three floors of the National Press Building, crowded with shoppers who were there for the grazing stands and the Benetton, the Sharper Image and the Banana Republic. In a matter of seconds, they'd crossed the threshold from hotel to mall, and moments later, were out through the entrance in front of which Nicole had stood only a short while before, desperately trying to figure out what Option B was. There was no way of knowing Option B would comprise O'Malley all but dropping from the sky, no way of guessing it would be so easy to get him out of there. Was God looking out for David, for the first time in his life?

C-SPAN was broadcasting live from the event, and the President could now be seen entering the elegant ballroom, "Hail to the Chief" being played by the Marine Corps Band. The C-SPAN announcer was whispering like a broadcaster at a golf tournament, letting the home audience in on the fact that the ACLU had volunteered to let the Marine Corps Band play, though they'd let it be known it was their *choice* to let the band play the theme that traditionally preceded a presidential entrance. They didn't believe it was the government's right to order them to precede a presidential entrance with any particular song, but they actually liked this one. Either that or they were smart enough not to insult the President just before he spoke.

"If we wanted to," the ACLU spokesman was telling the C-SPAN announcer, "we could have had him walk in to the theme from the 'Tonight' show."

"Oh, that's good," whispered the nerd from C-SPAN.

"Oh, shut up," said Harlan, turning his back once again from the television and staring out into the street.

icole pushed O'Malley along. The street was almost deserted.

The President entered the ball-room and Robert O'Malley craned his neck to see where his son was. He couldn't find him, but he did catch the eye of his wife, three or four tables away. He found himself winking. Where's Tom? he asked through body language, familiar cues.

Out on the street, he had a little more latitude, marginally more space to move in, but O'Malley had the very real sense it would be easier, not harder, for Nicole to shoot him here. They walked past the entrance to the Metro on F and a homeless person shook a cup at them. Cars drove by on Twelfth Street. There were few enough people here that Nicole could easily shoot him and run, if that's what she desired.

"What are you doing this for?" he asked as they crossed the street. He asked it with equal parts resignation and exasperation.

"We're going to go to your house, Tom, just like we used to do."

"What for?" he said, turning to Nicole as they continued to walk across on F, his captor a little behind him, the gun a little more obviously poking against his pocket.

"Art appreciation," Nicole said enigmatically.

"No," O'Malley said, stopping on the sidewalk. They were standing in front of a gaudy stereo store out of which loud rap music came booming.

"C'mon, keep moving." Nicole nearly had to shout to be heard.

"You're not thinking of taking the painting." O'Malley looked at him with almost open wonder. Some rapmaster was shouting at them from huge speakers.

"Move it."

He had the gun out in plain view, though there was no one on the street to see it. O'Malley began to walk backward until he was able to turn around again, walking just ahead of Nicole as they came around the corner onto Eleventh Street.

Nicole spotted his car down the block by the wig store, a few yards down from the grungy bar. He pointed O'Malley in the direction of his car, and they headed toward it. They could both see some guy stand up and walk out into the entrance of the boozers' hangout, staring at them as they walked near it, staring as if he recognized them, but couldn't believe he was seeing them. They paid him no mind, Nicole with the gun visible even as the evening darkened and the empty streets fell into dusk. A kid in a car with an obnoxiously loud sound system boomed by toward Pennsylvania, a trio of cabs passed toward New York Avenue.

Harlan Bryce stood there, ten feet away, more than a little unsteadily, his eyes squinting at the two of them. He looked bewildered that these people were standing here and that there was a gun being held in the open just three blocks away from the FBI building. "What do you think you're doing?" he asked incredulously. "You're that little shit, Thomas O'Malley. You're under arrest, mister!" he shouted, holding up his badge.

Nicole whirled on him and O'Malley froze. But the suspended FBI agent just reached into his jacket and without fooling around, pulled out his service revolver and shot Nicole in the chest before Nicole even had a chance to fire his gun. Nicole crumpled, his gun clattering on the sidewalk, and in a matter of seconds, or so it seemed, there was blood spilling out of the corner of his mouth as he lay there, his head tilted toward the dirty concrete.

O'Malley looked with horror at the drunk who had shot his gun just once. He got down on his knees to see to Nicole. The blood began to seep around his chest, and his shirt went brown. O'Malley looked up with panic in his eyes, then back down at his former friend, who clearly was dead. The sleazy old goat who'd pulled the trigger stood there looking quite horrified, like he was going to be ill, like he hoped O'Malley would take care of him when the nausea set in.

O'Malley just knelt there by his former high-school chum, looking up questioningly at the bum who had shot him, waiting for the police or the media to arrive, whichever came first.

They didn't have long to wait. Someone from the bar had called 911. But as was not unusual these days, the media beat the authorities there by a mile.

T he President came to the part where O'Malley was going to be mentioned, but O'Malley wasn't there. When he heard his son's name, his father was, first and foremost, embarrassed. It was only when he stopped blushing, standing there with the crowd applauding the empty seat next to him, that he wondered where it was his son could be.

Two tables away, his wife was applauding, and basking in her table's admiration such that she didn't even notice Tom wasn't there.

In New York, in her room, Kit was watching C-SPAN, straining to catch a glimpse of O'Malley. She knew how badly he wanted this official forgiveness.

On the streets of Washington, O'Malley was being questioned by an earnest police officer, to whom he was respectful. To whom he made no wisecracks. He didn't want to be brought in right now, not for questioning or anything else. There were people waiting for him, someone in New York he wanted to talk to. There was a life to get on with.